THE ART OF *Appreciation*

AUTUMN MARKUS

OMNIFIC PUBLISHING
LOS ANGELES

Omnific Publishing
1901 Avenue of the Stars, 2nd floor
Los Angeles, CA 90067
www.omnificpublishing.com

First Omnific eBook edition, December 2013
First Omnific trade paperback edition, December 2013

The characters and events in this book are fictitious.
Any similarity to real persons, living or dead,
is coincidental and not intended by the author.

Library of Congress Cataloguing-in-Publication Data

Markus, Autumn.
   The Art of Appreciation / Autumn Markus – 1st ed.
   ISBN: 978-1-623420-64-2
   1. Love — Fiction. 2. Long-Distance Romance — Fiction.
   3. Beach — Fiction. 4. Summer — Fiction. I. Title

10 9 8 7 6 5 4 3 2 1

Cover Design by Micha Stone and Amy Brokaw
Interior Book Design by Coreen Montagna

Printed in the United States of America

To my HLM, Sandy. You know why.
And to M. Always.

Chapter One

"Sarah Martin, please." Abby tapped a pencil on her desk. "Yes, I can hold." Cheesy elevator music assaulted her ear, and she winced. "C'mon, c'mon." She slipped off her pump and rubbed the ball of her foot. Wedging the phone between her tilted head and shoulder, she dug around her cluttered desk with her other hand, searching for her little yellow heaven. Her eager intern rushed over to help, but she pointed toward the door, waving him away. After an unconvincing protest, he grabbed his satchel and hurried out.

Abby rooted around her top drawer, humming along with the music. She grinned when she finally spotted the tennis ball. A grant proposal spilled to the floor, but she disregarded it in favor of bouncing the ball once and then rolling it around with her cramping arch.

A soft moan of pleasure slipped from her lips, and she heard Sarah's snort of laughter. "I can hang on until you're finished, if you like. That sounds just sinful."

"Yeah, yeah…funny." Abby grabbed her bottle of hand cream and squeezed some into her hand. "Listen, I'm calling to cancel our dinner tonight. I decided to take a sabbatical after all, and I'm going to Maine for the summer. I leave tonight."

"Whoa, there, Bessie. Back it up. Why the hell would you go there as opposed to somewhere interesting?"

Abby sighed. "Because I can't afford anywhere interesting. It's either my family's cabin in Maine or my parents' house." She shuddered at the thought of a whole summer with her mother. "Or I could crawl into my bed and not leave the house until September. You'll find me half-eaten by a German Shepherd next fall."

"Ooh…badly misquoted *Bridget Jones* reference. That's never good." Sarah considered for a minute. "Might you be acting a bit of the drama queen, bubala? Have you even talked to your boss yet?"

"I might be," Abby acknowledged reluctantly. "And no."

"Meet me at the restaurant for dinner, babes. Maine can wait until morning, right? What you need is a good daiquiri and a little time for reflection before you throw your summer away. I'm hanging up now, so you'd better be there."

The line went dead as Abby lowered the handset.

"What I need is a new life." She slipped her shoe back on before she stood. Checking that her hair was still caught up in a clip at the back of her neck, Abby painted on a smile and headed out of the office.

One night. Then she was out of Boston for the summer.

Four hours and a few drinks later, both shoes were off and Abby's feet were propped on the seat next to Sarah. Thank God for dark booths and friendly restaurants. The waiter flashed a wink as he picked up her empty glass and deposited another whiskey sour.

Sarah examined the dark hair that tumbled over his forehead and slapped the bottoms of Abby's feet. "See? Men find you attractive."

Abby snorted and downed half her drink at a gulp. "Yeah, men who are angling for a big tip." She focused on the waiter's tight backside and broad shoulders as he walked away. "Which, who am I kidding, he's gonna get just for being pretty." The women snickered and finished their drinks. "Besides, he's practically a baby."

Craning her neck for a better view, Sarah whistled beneath her breath as he bent to retrieve a dropped spoon. "Doesn't look much like a baby from where I'm sitting." She pointed at Abby. "You're only thirty-seven, and he has to be at least twenty-one to be serving drinks, which means—"

"Which means that I was playing tonsil hockey with my first boyfriend when Mr. Sexy Waiter Guy was in diapers. No. Thanks." Abby flipped an ice cube into her mouth and crunched it as Sarah laughed. "I'm tragically old. And uninteresting. Ask Eric."

Sarah rubbed her hands together. "Now we're getting into it. What exactly did he say?"

Abby closed her eyes. "I don't want to talk about it."

"Bullshit. You want to tell Auntie Sarah everything, remember? There's no way mousy little Eric told you that you're tragically old. Christ, he's pushing forty himself. It couldn't have been that bad."

Abby took a deep breath and let it out in a rush. "Sare, the most boring man on the Eastern Seaboard said, 'It's not you; it's me,' to me." She stared at her friend.

Sarah gasped and gestured for the cute waiter to bring more drinks. "It's that bad." She clasped Abby's hand. "I'm sorry he broke your heart."

Abby rolled her eyes. "Right. Like Eric would be capable of that."

Sarah tried a shocked face and failed, giving up with a laugh. She dropped her friend's hand and lounged in the booth. "I just thought since you've been seeing each other for a couple of years…"

"Please. Eric's a nice guy, but…" Abby smiled at the waiter as he deposited their glasses. He grinned back before he walked away.

"'Nice'? You spent two years on 'nice'?" Sarah raised an eyebrow, and Abby shrugged. "I'm guessing in bed…?"

"Acceptable."

"Ouch. 'Nice' and 'acceptable.' How about 'clean'?" Sarah snickered into her drink.

Abby moaned and covered her eyes. "Oh, fuck it. He was a date on major holidays and for the company picnic. Satisfied?" Sarah cackled. "My point is, I should have been the one to end it, right? I managed to bore the most boring man on earth. I never thought he was The One, but…where is that guy, and why haven't I tracked him down and bagged him?"

"Ab, you know there's only one perfect Man." After years of parochial school training, their signs of the cross were automatic and simultaneous. "I don't think He's taking girlfriend requests. And besides, are we talking about a man or a wildebeest?"

"Is there a difference? They're both rare and elusive."

Sarah snorted laughter. "About the boring thing, though—"

"And—" Abby held up one finger to halt Sarah's protest "—and Gretchen landed me with another of her earnest-and-eagers last week. I swear she's trying to get me to quit. How can I babysit another intern? Clint is enough of a time-suck for three people."

They both contemplated Abby's office mate, an effete young man, prone to long lunches, effusive praise, and backstabbing dagger-wielding. "Have you told Gretchen this?"

Abby downed the rest of her drink. "Sure. And she hinted that I was just too old to appreciate my good fortune in having such an attentive intern—another pair of eyes 'to be sure our displays are fresh!'" She deflated from her righteous indignation. "Hell, maybe she's right. Maybe it's all too much for me." She laid her head on the table. "I suck. I'm old and boring and I suck. So now you see why I have to go to Maine."

Sarah gestured for the waiter to bring them two more drinks. As soon as they were deposited, she tapped on Abby's head until she raised it. "Aside from the tremendous implied insult to Maine-ish people, I don't get the connection. Here's my plan: Come to California with me instead."

Abby blew a raspberry and mimed pulling out empty pockets. Sarah slapped a hand down on the table. "I'm totally serious. My Aunt Filiz lives in Santa Cruz, and I just happen to know she's going to some artist commune thingy in Taos for the summer. I can use a break, too. David owes me some time off, so I'll tell him I'm using it this summer. I don't see why this can't work out."

Abby eyes filled with alco-tears. "You'd do that for me?" she squeaked, reaching for Sarah's hand and smacking her glass in the process.

"Abso-freaking-lutely, sister. I only have one rule: no boring, sucky Abby allowed. We're going to do new things and meet new people and do new people and eat different foods, and…where was I going with that? Oh yeah. *Change.* Our mantra is change. Deal?"

Sarah stuck her hand out, and Abby tried to grab one of them, managing to grasp the tips of Sarah's fingers. She shook them.

"Change. Yeah. Now get me to the bathroom before the cute waiter is disgusted."

Abby raised her head from the couch cushion reluctantly, moving only because she had to or else the shrilling of her phone from across the room would make her head explode. The riot of color and texture in her small living room usually cheered her up; today, it just made her eyes hurt.

She stumbled across the room and grabbed her phone just as her foot slipped on the cool linoleum. She looked down in horror, catching from the corner of her eye the sinuous slide of a cat in trouble.

"Damn you, Salvador Dali," she growled, pulling off her stockings and tossing them at the waste can. She forgot the phone in her hand until she heard a low chuckle amidst a rumble of office chatter.

"I can't imagine a man that's been dead for years is giving you that much grief, so am I safe in assuming your pet left you a little abstract art?"

Abby grabbed a handful of paper towels, smiling as she recognized David's voice. "Dali was a surrealist, you Philistine. And, yes, the damned cat is still litter box challenged." She wiped up the mess and bundled the whole thing into a plastic bag before tossing it to join her stockings. "I'll bet I know why you're calling this early."

"I'll bet you do." The volume of the babble in the background diminished, and she knew he'd closed his office door. "So. I hear you're kidnapping my employee for the summer."

Abby nearly laughed at the studied casual tone of his question. After over a decade of friendship, she could read his anxiety just as well as if he'd been wringing his hands before her.

"Maybe." She snagged a bottle of hand sanitizer off the counter, flopped on a stool, and coated her foot in the cold goo. "It was mostly bar chatter. I'm not even sure if I can get away right now. Gretchen—"

"Mrs. Dahl is a cave troll. I know this," he said impatiently. "Sarah made it very clear that you both have to get away. From everything."

Abby let his significant pause hang in the air as she decided how to proceed. She'd been doing this dance of don't ask/don't tell since nearly the first meeting she'd arranged between David Strain and Sarah Martin. David's interest had been immediate…and there it rested, apparently unrequited.

Once again, when faced with either confronting his unspoken interest in her friend or letting it go, Abby backed down. "I'm sure she didn't mean you, David. You're the best boss, friend…whatever. Sarah should be thanking the gods your photographer didn't show up at that gallery opening and that you've taken her along as you've moved up."

He chuckled, and she could almost see the way his wild red curls, now closely cropped as befitted an editor at the *Boston Post*, had bobbed the first day she'd introduced her job-seeking friend to the young reporter. His eyes hadn't left Sarah all day. "I wouldn't say that, Ab. Sarah is an incredible wom—photographer. She's made it on her own."

The noise level behind him rose, and Abby heard his secretary. David was suddenly brisk and businesslike. "Right. So I can count on having Sarah back by the first of September. Excellent." His voice lowered. "Be careful, and take care of each other. Call if you need anything." He hung up.

Abby tossed the phone on the counter and slouched back to the couch. As soon as she lay down, Salvador Dali slithered onto her chest like the smoke his coat resembled. His eyes closed to slits, and he began to purr. She considered shoving him to the floor, but the confident way he snuggled down softened her ire.

"Stupid cat." She began stroking the soft fur. "What the hell will I do in California if Gretchen doesn't find a reason to make me skip my sabbatical again this year?" A vision of herself, gray, wrinkled, and chained to her desk rose in her mind's eye. Still puttering with other people's art. Still ignoring the pictures that floated in her own mind. Still alone, if you didn't count Salvador Dali IV. Even life with Eric sounded good right about then. She winced at her unfairness to a nice man, and then gasped as the cat dug his claw into her chest in protest at being disturbed.

"Behave!" Her resolve strengthened. If that was to be her fate, she deserved one last summer of irresponsibility, damn it. But how best to approach the Dragon Lady? Carefully, and with all of her ducks in a row. Particularly the two ducks that were in her especial care; Clint would revel in the chance to prove he could do her job, and New Boy, whose name she had yet to learn, would be okay…

Plans skittered through her head as she considered whether it might be just barely possible to arrange her work so the interns could handle upcoming shows without her, yet still not have a chance to steal away her contacts. She scratched Dali's ears and smiled at her vague daydreams about sunny beaches and tanned, young skin.

Which reminded her of the lonely wrinkles that lay ahead of her.

"Forget California," she sighed, fingers tightening in Dali's fur. "How long do you think it will be before Clint manufactures some crisis that requires me to miss my first day off in a month, Sal?"

As if on cue, the phone rang.

"I hate you, Sarah," Abby said for the hundredth time in four days.

It had taken her a week to convince Gretchen that she was serious about the sabbatical she'd been putting off for at least five years. To show that it would work, she had to delegate responsibilities to her interns and other curators of the museum, firm up dates for upcoming shows, and reassure regular contributors that their treasures would be properly cared for in her absence. All had to be done by her personally to keep Clint's mitts off her contact list.

Despite all of her preparations, she still tried to back out a day before she and Sarah were scheduled to leave. The calculation in Clint's eyes when he considered their boss, Gretchen, and the gleeful way he took over as many of Abby's responsibilities as he was allowed made her nervous. It had taken Sarah's appearance at the museum with a car full of luggage and eyes snapping with irritation to get Abby to slam her desk drawers shut, lock them against Clint's prying fingers, and walk out the door. To ease Abby's mind about leaving, Sarah had taken them out for a drink or eight.

Abby had been amazed to wake in the car the next morning, her head pounding. She couldn't remember the exact point at which they'd stopped at her house to gather clothes into the two suitcases that were jammed haphazardly in the back of the car, but there they rested. The tiny Hyundai buzzed down the freeway, Boston having been left in their rearview mirror long before she'd awakened. Apart from a quick call to ask "Grandma" and "Grandpa" to pick up Salvador Dali, she'd spent most of the last four days in quiet recovery.

"No you don't. You love me," Sarah replied, unruffled. She checked the mirror and sped up to just under light speed. "Let me know if you see a cop."

Abby squeezed her eyes closed. "Like I'll be looking out the window any time soon."

Sarah had the grace to look abashed. "Yeah. Sorry about that." She pushed her sunglasses up on her head to hold her dark hair back. "I could have sworn I read that ginger pills help nausea. The shoes weren't expensive, right?"

Abby raised her own sunglasses to glare at her friend.

"Anyway," Sarah continued, "you'll be thanking me by this time next week, when you're lying back in the arms of some twentysomething hottie, watching the sun set over the water…" She sighed, as if lost in her fantasy. Her own escape from the office had been blessedly smooth, the way eased by her considerate boss. Abby wondered how long David could take it before he called her for reassurance that Sarah was okay.

"Riiight. Keep dreaming. I have no desire to make a fool of myself as a public cougar. Bi-coastal humiliation is too much even for me." Abby's phone beeped in Gretchen's tone for the third time that day, and she flashed a look at Sarah. With a grim expression, her friend mimed tossing the phone out the window, so Abby hit "ignore."

"Impossible. We can't be public cougars, because we're not cougars at all. You have to be over forty to be a cougar. We're more like… pumas. We're older and more experienced, but still hawt, baby."

"Oh God," Abby moaned, covering her head with her arms.

"Anyway, we're here."

The car rolled to a stop in the driveway of a weather-beaten cottage. Gathering their bags, Abby and Sarah walked up two steps, and Sarah opened the door to the screened, wraparound porch. The door promptly ripped free of its top hinge and dangled like a loose tooth.

"Maybe we should be paying your aunt for this summer," Abby said doubtfully, already dreading what might await them inside.

Sarah snickered and walked onto the tidy porch after propping the screen door closed. Faded wicker rockers flanked the front door and hanging plants abounded. "Not freaking likely. My aunt's loaded. It takes a lot of money to live this crappily." She shoved the key in the lock and wiggled it. "Buying here, one of these houses just off the beach? It's like buying on Martha's Vineyard, but it might even be more expensive, foot for foot." She struggled for another minute, cursing, and shouted in victory when the key finally turned.

Abby breathed a sigh of relief when she could get around her tall friend to see the room. This was more like it. Sarah was right—the room was the model of beach luxury and comfort. The stress of her job and the long road trip fell away as she sank into an overstuffed chair. "Mine."

Sarah laughed, tossing her stuff to the floor and flopping into the mate of Abby's chair. "All Ralph Lauren and Laura Ashley, of course. Aunt Filiz only takes her Bohemian lifestyle so far." She propped her lean legs on a cushy ottoman that contrasted with her chair. "Bedrooms are upstairs; a full bath with clawfoot tub, I might add, is up there, too."

She checked her watch and jumped up. "I almost forgot the best part. C'mon." She dragged Abby from her tiny slice of heaven and led her toward the back door, stopping only to grab the last two beers from the lightly stocked fridge. "Have to remedy that," Sarah muttered before shoving Abby out the door and handing her a bottle.

Just a few hundred yards from the back stoop, the wide expanse of the Pacific rolled gently up and down the sand. Gulls cried overhead, and Abby could hear children's laughter in the distance. "Wow." She sat on the top step and took a long pull on her beer.

"No kidding." Sarah flopped down beside her and shaded her eyes. "And here comes the best part."

Abby shaded her own eyes, searching for whatever held Sarah's interest. A tiny blob in the water grew larger, coming toward the beach at an alarming rate; it gradually became a figure of a man on a surfboard. Another board appeared behind him. The surfers rode the wave as far as it would take them before they waded onto the shore, laughing and talking. The shorter of the two, a burly blond, glanced up the beach at the women and smiled, exposing a deep dimple in his right cheek. Sarah leaned back on her hands with a happy sigh. "They always come in somewhere along this piece of beach. Something to do with the currents. Swells. Waves. Whatever. This time of day is great for voyeurism."

The blond looked up the beach, laughing. Sarah's voice had obviously carried.

The buddy finished peeling his wetsuit down to his waist before turning. Abby froze in the motion of raising her bottle again, slowly lowering it to her side as she took in the view of neoprene clinging to tightly muscled legs and slim hips. The dangling top half of the wetsuit emphasized the tight V of the surfer's abdomen. Her eyes traveled upward to his tanned chest and broad shoulders, one of which shifted and bulged as he raked a hand through wet hair.

It was hard to tell from a distance what color his eyes were, but she clearly saw them crinkle at the edges when he smiled. With his board under one arm, he swept his other out in front of him in a "ta-da" gesture.

"Shit," Abby groaned, forgetting that her voice would carry until both guys laughed. Sarah joined in.

Dropping her bottle to the sand, Abby stumbled up the stairs and through the door. Re-entering the living room, she flopped into the chair she'd claimed.

Sarah careened into her own chair, still laughing. "I think you just made a friend, Abby. You should have seen your face when he caught you perving. Not like it was difficult, because your tongue was practically hanging out."

"Shut up. I hate you, Sarah. What if I see him again?"

"Say, 'Nice abs?'"

"I take back my 'I hate you' and raise it to a 'fuck you.'"

Sarah came over to sit on the arm of Abby's chair and punched her on the shoulder. "Hey, it's California during tourist season, baby. Santa Cruz is packed with newbies like us. You'll probably never see him again."

"And if I do?"

"Fake a seizure?"

"I hate you, Sarah."

Sarah kissed Abby on the head and tugged her hair. "Ooh. Twice in less than an hour. I might start to believe you if you say it again." She stood up and pushed Abby toward the stairs. "Go take a nap, and I'll call you when dinner's ready. You need to recover after all that hotness. Or something." Sarah wiggled her eyebrows suggestively and then screeched as she dashed for the kitchen.

Chapter Two

"And lean forward…forward…let your body hang. Relax every muscle. Pretend you have no bones from the waist up…now swing from side to side…you're an anemone in the crystal clear azure sea, waaaaving your fronds…"

Abby stifled a giggle. A week of idleness followed by a depressingly tight pair of shorts had led to the realization that all of the walking she did to, from, and at her job was more than nice — it was necessary to offset her love of good food. Yoga class twice a week and daily walks on the beach for the last two weeks had been the trick to getting back to her normal size. She appreciated the relaxed and stretched feeling she got from the yoga workout, but the hippy-dippy drone of the instructor, Tiffany, often made her grimace.

"Don't be afraid to laugh, my friends," Tiffany advised, as if she'd read Abby's mind. "Laughter helps our minds and souls rise. It forms us into clouds of happiness, waiting to rain down showers of joy…"

The woman to Abby's left snorted. "Make up your damn mind. Am I an anemone or a cloud?" the ash blonde murmured as she stood and smiled down at Abby. "Either way, I'm tired of standing with my ass in the air." She smoothed loose hairs back into her sleek ponytail and straightened the hem of her shirt.

Other members of the class followed suit, smiling. Tiffany turned her waving anemone dance into a slow roll upright. "Thank you, Claire, for the reminder. No one should feel obligated to remain in poses that make them uncomfortable. Do what you can comfortably do. Age or physical limitations should not hamper your yoga experience." She looked at her phone as it rested on the beach towel next to her. "That's enough for today class. See you two days from now, bright and early."

Abby was shaking the sand out of her mat when Tiffany approached the woman beside her.

"That wasn't very nice, Tiff." The woman pouted.

"Neither was distracting my class, Mrs. Eastman." Tiffany draped her towel over her shoulder and laughed. "I was just about to finish up anyway. You have to be patient; you know that. I'll see you in a couple of days." She waved and headed down the beach, ponytail swaying against her tanned back.

"I don't have time to be patient." Claire shoved her mat into a bag while Abby's gaze drifted toward the sea. "Waiting for the surfers to come in?"

"Wrong time of day," Abby answered absently, and then colored. She'd outed herself as a voyeur.

Claire laughed. "Don't be embarrassed. I've lived here for twenty years, and I'm still looking. Just for information, of course, but this is the best time to catch the morning crew."

Abby smiled, shoving her own mat into its bag. "Good to know. No, I was just…looking." Her eyes traveled back to the surf as she considered and rejected paint colors. "It's like something out of a painting."

"Ah. Yes. Maybe a Monet?" Claire's indulgent smile turned curious when Abby rejected her suggestion.

"No, not really. Too fussy. I was thinking Diebenkorn. He was an American painter—"

"Bay Area Figuratives. Yes, I know. I was lucky enough to have taken a class from him at UCLA." Claire stuck out her hand. "I'm curious now. Are you an art scholar? I'm Claire Eastman, by the way."

Abby shook her hand. "Abby Reynolds. Yes, of a sort. I curate for a museum in Boston."

Claire's smile widened. "I own a gallery in town, Abby-from-Boston. Small world, isn't it?" She pulled a pair of sunglasses from her bag and slipped them over her eyes. "If you're interested in local art, I have some marvelous pieces." Her voice lowered conspiratorially, "Some absolute garbage, too, to be honest. My husband means well when he brings these things home to me, but…such is life. If you do come by when Charles is around, be a dear and humor him. He does try so hard." She laughed and then waved as she headed for the car park.

Abby trudged up the beach. She'd barely taken a dozen steps before her cell phone intoned the doleful song that indicated a call from the museum. She stopped to dig it out of her mat bag, glancing around as she did so. A week of Sarah's nagging and threats to smash the phone every time Abby took a call from Clint or Gretchen had her behaving like a teenager with a secret boyfriend, and it had to stop. Besides, Sarah wasn't anywhere near.

She straightened up and put the phone to her ear. "Abby, I am just in a pickle." Clint's apparent concern was belied by his cat-that-ate-the-canary tone. "Silly me, I've completely misplaced the Baxter file, and Gretch is determined that we need to call them to firm things up for the fall display of their terra-cottas. Be a love and tell me where the extra key to your desk is. Or should I have janitorial force it?"

Abby paled. It had taken years of work to amass the goodwill of the donors on her list of potentials and "call-me's." Her ability to bring loans into the museum had been a part of her getting a job in a very competitive field, and she be damned if she'd let someone else trade on that. "That won't be necessary, Clint. I have the Baxters' number right here, and I'd be glad to give them a call." She stopped and dug around in the bag for pencil and paper and made a note to contact them. She'd also contact the office secretary, Sylvia, to be sure that Clint wasn't calling to cover for a dirty deed he'd already done.

"Oh, then I guess you've got it in hand." Clint sounded discouraged. "Are you sure you want to work on your vacay, Abby? Because I've so got this."

I'll bet you do, you little bastard. "Nope, it's fine, Clint. I'll call Gretchen and tell her she may contact me herself if she has any other concerns." She smiled at his indrawn breath. *Gretchen wanted you to call, my ass.*

She returned to the house and made her phone calls. Just as she was finishing up with Sylvia, the screen door slapped into place. Not up for another lecture about the meaning of vacation, Abby rushed out a response to the secretary and hung up.

Sarah stopped in the doorway to slip off her bike shoes. Their hard soles clonked together as she dropped them in the basket beside the mat. "Nice save. It's sort of cute how you think you can fool me." She nodded toward the phone. "How's Sylvia?"

Abby's shoulders dropped. "Fine. This time—"

"Nope." Sarah held up a hand, palm out. "No excuses, Ab. I've tried to get through to you, and I'm done. Maybe change isn't in your vocab." She yanked open the refrigerator door and reviewed the scanty contents.

Abby's temper rose. "Or maybe I can't afford to risk my job. There aren't a lot out there for curators, and especially not a lot that will let me eat regularly and live indoors. I don't have an excellent boss like yours, Sarah. Just yesterday he said that—" She stopped, cursing herself for mentioning David's call.

Sarah's head jerked up. "David called *you?* I mean, *yesterday?* What did he want?"

"To see how we're doing, I suppose." Abby rose and drew a glass of water, debating what else to say. David had sounded worried and tired and lonely…none of which Sarah would admit to caring about. "He's stressed over some big hubbub going on in editorials—I know, when isn't there—and he watched something on TV about jellyfish pods. Wanted to make sure we knew they were dangerous and how to spot them."

"David." Sarah shook her head and resumed her search of the fridge. "I was wondering if he—they—needed me back at work." Her tone was wistful. "Good thing that wasn't it, because I intend to enjoy every minute of this vacation." She tore into her apple, swallowed hard, and then wiped juice off of her chin. "Let's go out tonight, Ab. We've been here two weeks and haven't spent a single night on the town."

Grateful that Sarah's usual "work vs. life" lecture had been diverted, Abby agreed. Maybe it would be fun to discover the wonders of the Santa Cruz beach boardwalk.

That optimism was difficult to remember a few hours later when she was nursing her fourth drink and nodding along with the music of an enthusiastic, if barely talented, local band. Somehow, she and Sarah had ended up at an after-hours party on the patio of a small beachside hotel. She had just located Sarah on the impromptu dance floor and was wondering which of the three men dancing nearby was her partner when she felt a tap on her hand. It was with effort that she returned her attention to the man in the chair next to hers. She vaguely remembered that he was a sales rep for some drug firm, but couldn't have recalled his name even if she'd been facing a firing squad.

"This band is great, isn't it?" he shouted, tapping his toes opposite the beat.

To avoid conversation, Abby pointed to her ears, indicating a deafness she feared was coming. Unfortunately, he took that as an invitation to move his chair closer to hers.

"Of course, this isn't what I usually listen to," he bellowed. "I used to like ska before it got popular, but now I'm really into jazz. That and Christian pop. Ever since I found Jesus…"

I didn't know He was lost. Abby grinned and let the drug rep's voice flatten to a "wah-wah-wah" in her ears. She caught sight of Sarah again and sent her an eyeball plea for help. Sarah missed it during a dramatic spin between two partners.

In desperation, Abby launched into a joke about an apple, a banana, and a penis—it had brought down the house when she was in junior high. Hipster drug-guy stopped in mid-rhapsody about his mega-church and stared at her like she'd sprouted a third ear in the middle of her forehead.

A splutter of laughter alerted Abby to someone passing behind her chair. She was mortified to recognize the taller surfer from her first day on the beach. He turned to look back at her and gave her a thumbs-up with the hand he wasn't using to balance a pony keg on his shoulder. She smiled back, wishing that the light from the outdoor fireplace was a little brighter so she could make out whether his eyes were blue or gray, and whether the definition she thought she saw in his forearms was real or a trick of light and shadow. At any rate, he definitely looked enough younger than her that he would fit Sarah's admonition that she find a "boy toy" for the night.

She turned to apologize to her seat mate and found he'd taken his chance to escape. Too bad Surfer Dude had also disappeared when she looked for him a second later.

"Story of my life," Abby said. She shouldered her way to the makeshift bar and picked up another beer. Then she settled down to wait for the Sarah-gizer Bunny to run out of energy.

Waking in dim morning light, Abby checked the bedside clock. Despite it being only four hours since she'd dropped into bed, years of early rising had made it impossible for her to sleep late. Rising and stretching, she grabbed a robe and headed for the bathroom. A delicate snore from behind Sarah's door indicated her friend was alive. After a quick shower, Abby held her wrists under the cool running water and studied her features in the mirror. She focused on the fine lines that were growing more prominent around her eyes, no matter which miracle cream Sarah pushed on her, and thanked God that otherwise her skin was still smooth. Bar interest the night before indicated the yoga and walking she was doing in Santa Cruz were enough to keep her in fighting trim, though many more nights like the previous would require something more drastic, like a gym.

She frowned, idly contemplating whether there was a public gym nearby and wondering what the man on the beach did besides surf to stay in such great shape. Wondering what color his eyes really were. Wondering what those sinewy arms would feel like under her hands…Her stomach rumbled.

Laughing at herself, she crept to the kitchen to start a pot of coffee and scrounge something for breakfast. "We really need to shop," she said, digging through the cupboard until she found a possibility. As she settled onto the back stoop with her makeshift breakfast and watched the morning gradually brighten, she felt hopeful for the summer for the first time.

"Yello." Sarah's voice made Abby jump and spill coffee on her hand. She cursed, and a couple of people running on the beach turned to look. One waved, and Sarah laughed. "I do believe that was your friend, Abby. He's gonna think you have Tourette's."

"You don't know the half of it."

"Ooh, did I miss something?" Sarah asked, eyes bright with interest.

"Never mind. I'll never see him again, huh?"

Sarah shrugged. "I said probably never. *Probably.* Big difference." She nudged Abby's shoulder with her knee. "Ready for a day of fun and relaxation?" She sat down and snatched a cracker from Abby's plate. "Based on what you told me about last night's penis joke fiasco, we're clearly not getting maximum fun value this vacation." Ignoring Abby's sideways glance, she munched thoughtfully. "Before I came downstairs, I took the liberty of researching what we can do in this burg that might be new and different."

Abby groaned. "I thought that's what last night was about. My head can't take much more of that. I haven't been a college kid for a long time."

Sarah blew a raspberry. "What was new about that? Aside from the surfer sandwich with me as the filling, it was a normal Saturday night for me. I've decided that we're going biking today."

Abby stared. "Biking? Sarah, I haven't been on a bike since I was twelve." Still, it was change…Abby's heart fluttered in mixed anticipation and reluctance.

"All the more reason to go." Sarah was determined. "Change, remember? Difference. You don't bike in Boston, so you're biking here. End of story."

"Can't I just crash? I'm going to yoga tomorrow."

"Yoga." Sarah's derision was clear. "Nothing you didn't do back home. Nope. We have plans."

"No fair. You bike all of the time. Why don't you have to do something different?"

"No fair? What are you, eight?" Sarah grabbed another cracker before continuing. "Besides, I am courting change. I'm meeting new people of the male species every day, and I'm bugging you about something that's bugged me for years: your stick-in-the-muddiness. Change!" She rose and tugged Abby to her feet before steering them both toward the stairs despite Abby's grumbling.

Watching for Sarah's reaction, Abby protested all through dressing and renting a bike and buying a helmet and joining the group that would be touring downtown Santa Cruz and the boardwalk. She protested when she got on the bike and continued to protest in hissing whispers as the guide explained the intricacies of riding in a pace line. Sarah ignored her, choosing instead to smile gently at the people around them, who listened in amusement.

The guide finished his explanations and started to buckle his helmet. Abby looked at hers doubtfully. "We're not going fast, right? So why do I need this?"

"It's the law, Ab." Sarah buckled on her own helmet before grabbing Abby's out of her hands and smashing it down on her head. "Lift your chin, or I'm gonna take off skin," she ordered. Abby complied. She'd agreed to this, right? If change required a stupid hat, a grown woman should accept that.

"I bet I look like a dork," she muttered, trying to shift the helmet and finding it unmovable.

"Whatever. Get on the damned bike."

Abby grinned. Though it had been fun to exasperate Sarah, she was actually looking forward to the ride.

The group set out at a slow pace, allowing the assembled riders to adjust to riding in a pace line. After a few minutes, the leader increased the speed and called out points of interest. Abby started to enjoy herself, looking around at people as she passed them and smiling at little kids who stopped to stare.

Big mistake.

As the pace line slowed to round a curve near the boardwalk, she didn't slow down quite enough, and her front wheel grazed Sarah's back tire. Instantly, Abby flew off her bike. Her shoulder hit the pavement a moment before her head slammed down, and she was grateful for the protection of the denim shirt she wore over her tank. Her hip wasn't so lucky. She gasped when the friction of sliding against the road pulled her waistband down and skin met asphalt.

When her violent movement stopped, Abby lay on the pavement, blinking up at the sky and wondering if she was okay. She gingerly moved all of her limbs, finding them hurty but functional, and tried to sit up as a crowd gathered.

Gentle hands held her down. A horribly familiar face floated into her field of vision, and she closed her eyes. "Nice to see you again, too." Deft fingers moved under her chin, unbuckling her helmet. She opened one eye and saw the sharp angle of Surfer Dude's jaw as he stared off into space, his long fingers gently probing her neck and as much of the back of her head as he could reach without removing her helmet. "Do you feel like you're bleeding?" He searched her face. His eyes were a color that could easily morph into blue or gray, and the lines around them were deeper than Abby had expected — maybe he wasn't in his early twenties after all.

"Just my hip."

His hand hesitated over the tail of her shirt. "May I?"

Abby nodded, and he lifted the cloth gently, drawing air between his teeth in a hiss. "Wicked road rash. That's gonna hurt for a while. I hope you have some low-cut pants."

"I'll bet you say that to all the girls," Abby cracked, chuckling as he reddened. As he moved to grab her hand, she avoided his grasp and removed her helmet.

"Hey! You shouldn't do that. You could have a head injury."

The bike guide crouched next to Hottie McHotHot. "Thanks, Matt. I just called the EMTs. Is she okay? Whoa!" He took Abby's helmet without waiting for an answer and stared at the cracked, flat spot on the right side. He held it up so the group could see. "This is why we wear helmets, people. This crack would be in the pretty lady's head if she hadn't been wearing one."

There was a collective "Aahh" as the crowd leaned closer to look at the smashed helmet. Abby raised her hands to cover her face, but strong hands captured her wrists. "Let me look at your eyes, pretty lady." Calm blue-gray met startled brown in careful calculation as he instructed Abby how to move her eyes.

Uncomfortable under his scrutiny, Abby followed his directions. "I'm not as bad as you probably think I am. I don't have a mental condition or anything."

He laughed. "I'm not thinking anything, I promise."

Well, that's discouraging.

After a minute, he smiled and kissed the back of her hand. "You're gonna be all right, pretty lady. Take care." He rose to his feet and talked to the guide for a minute before he waved and moved off down the boardwalk, navy tee clinging to his back in the heat and outlining the lean muscles that disappeared into his shorts.

Sarah crouched next to Abby, and they watched him walk away, hitching his board shorts a little higher. He looked back, saw them watching him, and grinned, shaking his ass before slipping on a pair of Ray-Bans and disappearing into the crowd.

Sarah kissed Abby's cheek. "I think he likes you, Ab. Change is good, right?"

Abby looked up at her and grinned.

"Oh hell yes."

Chapter Three

The pavement seemed harder than normal when Matt set off on his run the next afternoon. He greeted familiar faces with a smile and a wave, pacing himself so he could make the whole circuit before pooping out. As the sun baked the back of his neck, he cursed himself for putting this off until afternoon, but that had been the best he could do after falling into bed sometime south of five that morning. God forbid he forgo killing himself in the heat altogether — the days of eating and drinking anything he wanted and trusting the universe to keep him fit had been over for several years now; he had to make a conscious effort to work real exercise into most days. Luckily, his job was physical enough that even on the days that he couldn't run, he was exhausted and considered himself exercised in a half-assed way.

Reaching the halfway point, he hesitated before deviating from his normal pattern for the second time that week and leaving the road to run on the beach. The sand was softer than the road, right? He laughed at himself. The first time he'd used that excuse, he'd justified it by saying he was taking the opportunity to work a little harder by running on sand — he was almost convinced by his own bullshit, too, until he realized that he was scanning the back porches of the houses and trying to place which one he'd surfed up to and first seen the pretty lady.

It had been pure chance that he'd decided to get some fresh air and walk downtown to grab a sandwich the day before, and mere luck that he'd happened to look in the right direction to see the tail end of the bike touring group turf it. Boom. Pretty lady again.

Maybe it was her quick wit that drew him back to the beach, or maybe it was the interest he'd glimpsed in her eyes that had him running behind her house. Either way, he snickered at his junior high disappointment when no one was outside. He checked his watch, then veered back toward his home and a shower.

The door slammed shut behind him, and Matt heard something clatter on the kitchen counter. An accusing face peeked around the refrigerator door. "You scared the crap out of me. I didn't know you were up yet."

"Hey, Chris." Matt stripped off his sweaty shirt and tossed it in the direction of the laundry room before opening the refrigerator again and grabbing a drink. He dropped the empty OJ carton in the garbage can and leaned against the counter, looking at the frying bacon and eggs with interest and taking in the stocky shape of his cousin only incidentally. "I thought you were living with Jessica."

Chris shook his hair back from his face and grimaced. He gave the eggs a final stir before shutting off the flame. "So did I. Unfortunately, she forgot to tell the last guy that he didn't live there anymore, so when he got back from San Fran…" He shrugged. "Not cool. I left them screaming at each other and used your spare key to get in here. Slept on the couch. I figured I owed you for the crash, so I'm making breakfast." He scratched his bearded chin.

Matt slapped at his cousin's hand. "Not over the eggs. Neither beard hair or chin-druff is acceptable in my food."

Chris chuckled and grabbed plates from the cupboard, splitting the eggs and bacon onto two plates and handing one to Matt. They ate in companionable silence, silverware enthusiastically scraping dishes. As they finished, Chris took Matt's plate and loaded all the dishes into a waiting sink of sudsy water.

Matt hooked a cup out of the cupboard, poured himself some coffee, and watched as Chris cleaned up the breakfast mess. He was a quiet mystery, a slightly-younger cousin whom Matt had known only vaguely before he'd showed up on his porch a year before, fresh out of the Army and ready to lose to the forgetful Pacific his memories of service. He'd stayed with Matt only briefly, until he found a job as a fry cook in one of the local restaurants and moved into a small, dingy apartment with several other employees. Since then, he had drifted from job to job and house to house, occasionally squatting at Matt's place for a night or two before the next thing came along. Matt had heard rumors he was doing a fortune-telling schtick at the boardwalk again; that was usually a money-maker.

"You can always use the spare room," Matt said.

Chris gave him a sly grin. "Wouldn't want to disturb any freaky bedroom goings-on by wandering around your house like a ghost, cuz."

Matt snorted and pushed away from the counter to rinse his cup. "No worries on that account. I never sully my morning peace by risking a scene. No sleepovers here, I promise." He raised his arms and grabbed the upper frame of the doorway that led to the hall. "If I'd known you were here, I'd have made you run with me."

Chris raised his T-shirt, running a hand over washboard abs. "I think I'm good." He slapped Matt's stomach with the back of his hand. "Not bad for an old guy." He hustled down the hall as Matt swiped at him.

"I'm only five years older than you, idiot," Matt yelled. Chris snorted laughter before the sound of the TV drowned him out.

Though conscious of the time crunch he'd put himself under by changing his running route, Matt shaved carefully after his shower. The meeting he had that day had the potential to generate a commission that would set him up for the rest of the year and allow him to concentrate on the projects that mattered to him — sculptures that would end up in galleries or private collections rather than decorating someone's poolside, which is what this lot was intended for.

He paused while brushing his teeth and took a good look at himself for the first time in a while. No double chin, absence of man-boobs, stomach still flat, and hips lean. Of course, there was the matter of another gray hair nestled in the center of his chest. He frowned and yanked it out viciously, hissing air between his teeth at the sharp pain, and took stock again. Not bad for a guy less than two years from decrepitude at forty. *Give Chris a few years of eating round the clock the way he does, and he'll kill to look this good,* Matt reassured himself.

Today, though, he planned to put Chris's six-pack to use.

Dressing quickly, he shouted for Chris and went hunting for his dress shoes. He found them in the laundry room behind a pile of wetsuits and towels and hoped they hadn't been ruined by saltwater.

A low whistle behind Matt motivated him to turn around. Chris lounged in the doorway, bowl and spoon in hand, grinning. "Niiice. What happened to the whole I'm-an-artist-and-I-don't-give-a-shit vibe? Isn't that what the horny housewives want to see?"

Matt finished shoving his shoes on his feet. Pushing past Chris, he picked up the tie he'd dropped on the kitchen table and slung it around his neck. "Maybe so, but this horny housewife is bringing happy hubby along, and he's not likely to hand a big, fat check to a guy who looks like he'll smoke most of it away before her statues are half-finished." He smoothed his shirtfront and paused for a minute. "How do I look?"

"Creamtastic, cuz. You always were the shit. Is that what you dragged me away from Rachael Ray for?"

"Nope. I want your body."

Chris's eyebrows went up.

"Since you're here, I can take a few sample pictures to show the buyers instead of just describing the poses." The idea took off in his mind. "Hey—call Zoe. See if she can come right over. I need to find my suit jacket." Matt tossed his phone to Chris.

He snagged the jacket out of the spare room and threw it over a chair in his studio and began snapping photos. By the time he heard Zoe's sharp rap on the outside door, Chris's solo pictures were almost finished. He shouted for his next model to come in and nodded toward a chair in the corner. "Just leave your stuff over there and strip to the waist. Torso shots only today. If we hurry, I'll have time to print these out."

Zoe's whiskey-rich laughter filled the room as she dropped her shirt on a chair. "You say the sweetest things, Matt," she purred. Stepping close to Chris, she stood with hands on her hips, highlighting the twin curves of breast and hip. "How do you want me, boss?"

Matt shook his head. Zoe Mendez had been angling for a hookup since the first time Matt called her to model a couple of years earlier, and he was probably crazy not to take her up on it. She was pretty in an over-lush kind of way, but the almost fifteen-year age difference made him a little queasy. He wasn't quite ready to join Hef in his bunny hunts.

He took a few shots of Chris and Zoe twined together before he released Chris to the tender mercies of the Food Network and finished up with Zoe's solo shots. "Turn to your left, please," he directed. He looked at the screen and then up at her. "Okay…hold still." He pushed the button and waited to be sure the image was good. Beautiful. "One more and we're finished here. Can you shift…?" Matt pointed to her tangle of hair, and she lifted the mass and settled it over the opposite shoulder. "Great." Once Matt knew the shot was right, he shut the equipment down and started printing. "You can put your shirt back on. We're finished."

"Really? Are you sure?"

Matt felt the soft press of Zoe's breasts against his back. Her arms slid around his body, hands teasing the buttons on his shirt.

Matt couldn't help smiling. She never gave up. "Anything else would be a really bad business decision on my part."

"Come on. It's not like it's unheard of." One hand had managed to undo a button, and Zoe's fingers tugged gently at the hair on his belly. "Come out with me tonight. Have some fun." There was a smile in her voice. "You know you want to."

Matt sighed. He did want to. "Fine. When and where?"

"I thought you'd say that, so I already have a place in mind," she said matter-of-factly. She slipped her shirt over her head and named a popular club downtown. She shrugged on her leather jacket and picked up her helmet as Matt put on his own charcoal gray jacket. Zoe ran her hand across his shoulders, smoothing the fabric before trailing her fingers down his back with a wicked grin. "Don't change. This is hot."

Already mentally kicking himself for his weakness in saying yes, Matt thought rapidly. "How about after my meeting? Meet me here about four?" He hoped for a quick drink and an early departure for an imaginary dinner date.

"Make it five," Zoe dictated, patting his ass. "We'll have dinner and hit a couple of clubs. It'll be fun." She was out the door before Matt could say anything. He heard the roar of her Harley.

"Finally decided to throw the girl a bone, man?" Chris's voice, coming from behind him, was amused.

Matt kept searching his desk for a folder. "I'll keep my bone to myself, thanks. Not even close to being interested."

Chris laughed. "Pin-ups aren't really my style, either. Too much maintenance." He took a bite of the tortilla in his hand. "Still, you could have fooled me. You sounded pretty into the idea."

"Moment of weakness. Dinner is all I'm sharing with the luscious Zoe." Matt shuffled through the shots as they printed, a handy excuse for not looking his cousin in the eye. Chris made a noncommittal grunt and drifted back into the living room.

Gathering up the best of the shots, Matt slipped them into a folder before heading for the gallery.

Claire Eastman met him inside the door of her gallery and gave him a hug before looping her hand through his arm and leading him toward the executive conference room. She'd schmoozed deep-pocket patrons and made or broken more than a couple of careers there.

"Impeccable timing," she said, smiling up at Matt. "I've already given them the rundown on how fabulous you are and shown them the pieces we have of yours. Not that they'd know real art if it crawled up and bit them on the asses." Matt laughed. "Jessica Rabbit wants your typical Greek gods and goddesses—but nothing that anyone else has, of course—and the geezer just wants to get laid one more time before his old ticker pops. Charm her and sell him, and you've got it made."

They stopped at the head of a short hallway that led to the conference room, and Matt took a deep breath. "Claire, I can't thank you enough for putting me on to this."

She squeezed his arm. "Believe me, it's my pleasure. Now these people will finally have something of value in their collection, because Lord knows I've foisted off enough of Charles's unfortunate choices on the husband as fine art." They both chuckled at the thought. Claire examined Matt critically, adjusting his tie and sweeping her hand through his hair. "Good choice, by the way. Methuselah in there controls the checkbook, and he'd no more hand over a check for a quarter mil to Surferboy than he would give up his own probably non-functional left nut."

Matt eyed her skeptically. "A quarter mil for pool statues?"

Claire grinned and led him to the door, whispering, "If I don't get you at least that much, I've totally lost my touch."

She smoothed her chignon and swept the door open with a bright smile, then introduced Matt to his potential patrons. The wife was a barely-out-of-her-teens, surgically-enhanced wonder that made Zoe look flat-chested, and her husband looked like he could have babysat Moses. Matt launched into his spiel, handing around the pictures he'd taken and discussing possible poses. He directed the bulk of the information at the husband and ignored the obvious flirtation of the wife. Once the fossil determined that Matt was only going to be polite to the girl, no matter how often she pressed her boobs on him, he relaxed and became all business about costs and materials. Teen Bride pouted as her husband studied the same picture of Zoe for several minutes, then declared Chris "too short" and Zoe "obviously fake." Matt covered a laugh with a cough when Claire stomped his toes under the table, then he offered to find different models. Geezer allowed that he didn't care one way or another about the male, but he insisted on the woman in the picture.

Gathering up his test shots as the couple argued, Matt left Claire to work out the details. Chuckling at the sweet victory it was going to be to tell Chris his perfect pecs weren't good enough and thinking about the short list of potentials he could on call to fill the position, Matt made his way through the gallery on his way out. A victory drink was definitely in order before he had to meet Zoe. He was looking down at the folder in his hand, loosening his tie and already calculating what materials he needed to get started, when a sound drew his attention.

Just when he thought his day couldn't get any better, there was Pretty Lady, studying Matt's favorite piece with a soft smile. She ran her fingertips along a small detail before stroking the larger curve with her whole hand, chewing her lower lip as she circled the statue and studied it from every angle. Matt eyed the curve of her cheekbone in profile as it arched into the flat plane of her cheek and wished for his camera.

On impulse, he walked up behind her and murmured, "I know the artist. I can work you a deal on that one."

Pretty Lady gasped and stumbled forward, nearly toppling into the sculpture, and Matt grabbed her waist, pulling her back against him to save a year's hard work from crashing to the ground. A soft whisper-scent of sunshine and skin tickled his nose, so much nicer than Zoe's cloud of Juicy perfume. Soft hands covered his as the woman twisted from his grip, taking a step forward and two to the side. She turned, wearing a crooked smile, and hitched her beach bag higher on her shoulder. "If I didn't know better, I'd say you were stalking me, Surfer Dude." She looked Matt up and down, coloring. "Sorry, I guess I shouldn't make assumptions."

Matt leaned against one of his bigger pieces and unbuttoned the top two buttons of his shirt. "Meeting a friend. Believe me, I'd rather be dressed like me today."

Pretty grinned. "I guess you would." Matt found himself fascinated by the bathing suit top strings that lay taut over the hollows of her collarbones.

She noticed him looking and raised an eyebrow. It was Matt's turn to flush. "So how's the…?" He pointed to her head, and she groaned.

"Mild concussion. I spent the night in the hospital, throwing up." She grimaced. "You probably could have done without that factoid, right?"

Matt shrugged. "Dealt with the possibility and reality of a concussion every time I've gotten on a board since I was ten. Surfers learn to check each other out after wipeouts, generally—can't call the ambulance every time. You wouldn't believe the gnarly injuries I've seen over the years." He shifted to rest his arm against the sculpture.

She looked around before leaning forward to whisper conspiratorially, "I don't think we're supposed to touch the statues."

Matt laughed and nodded toward her hand, which was smoothing over a large curve of his abstract. "Hello, pot, meet kettle."

She snatched her hand away from the statue and held both of them behind her back while a guilty smile washed over her face. "I can't help myself. I know it's bad for the medium, but I'm a sensory person. I feel like I can't really appreciate a sculpture unless I can touch it." She raised a finger to stroke the marble in front of her. "This is lovely," she said softly.

"Sculpture is meant to be touched, no matter what anyone tells you." Matt watched her hand, seeing in the bone and sinew along the back, the strength beneath the softness. "It's a great compliment to an artist if their work can draw a reaction like yours." He straightened when she smiled. "Have a drink with me, pretty lady? I've had a great day, and I'd love to celebrate. Maybe you'll even tell me your name?"

Her smile dimmed when arms wrapped around Matt's waist.

"Hey, sexy," Zoe whispered. She kissed him on the chin. "I couldn't wait. Thought I'd find you here."

Pretty eyed Zoe's barely-there dress and carefully crafted bed-head, and her lips twisted sardonically. She slid her sunglasses off the top of her head and over her eyes. "Maybe some other time, Peter Pan," she answered, waving as she walked out into the late afternoon light.

"Who was that?" Zoe asked.

Matt watched Pretty cross the street. "Tourist. She cracked her head the other day when I was walking by, and I was asking how she was."

"Oh. Cute for being middle-aged." Zoe straightened the front of her dress and adjusted herself so that even more boobage spilled out of the deep V-neck.

"Ouch."

Zoe smiled. "It's different for guys, Matt. You're still at the hottie end of the scale and can't seriously be considered middle-aged for at least another ten years. Ready to go?"

"Sure." Matt smoothed his hand down Zoe's back and led her toward the door, slipping on his own sunglasses. Just as they reached the exit, he hesitated and pointed back toward the sculpture Pretty had admired.

"Zoe, what do you think of that?"

She glanced back and shrugged. "Nice. What's it worth?"

Matt realized that for all she'd enjoyed his sculpture, Pretty hadn't put that admiration in terms of money. Nice. Of course, now she thought Matt was a pervy old guy. He wrapped his arm around Zoe's willing body. Maybe he was being stupid to not just enjoy the woman beside him. He tried to pay attention as Zoe chattered about her plans for the evening.

Now he just had to live through them.

Chapter Four

"Abby, you sneaky bitch!" Sarah's voice preceded her as she struggled up the walk, arms loaded with shopping bags. She stopped, grinning, when Abby dropped her BlackBerry and grabbed the book beside her. "Gotcha, babe. Stop answering work calls, or I'll throw the CrackBerry into the big ol' blue." She dropped the bags she was carrying where she stood and ventured back to the car for a second batch of groceries.

Abby marked her page in the newest Nick Hornby novel with a ribbon, wishing for another hour of quiet. It would have been nice to read some of the book she'd been anticipating for months. She thought about telling Sarah about Clint's latest stab at undermining her, but discarded the idea. Sarah would just tell her to quit again, and that was a path Abby didn't care to revisit.

Rising from the wicker settee Sarah had wedged into a corner of the porch, Abby dropped the book on a cushion and eased the screen door open, hoping that the bottom hinge would hold out until either she or Sarah started feeling Mr. Fix-Ity. Groaning as she picked up the bags Sarah had been carrying, Abby shuffled toward the porch stairs. Sarah zipped past her with a similar load before Abby struggled into the kitchen.

"Holy God, woman! Do you have arms of steel or what?" Abby dropped the bags on the floor in front of the cabinets.

Sarah smiled and shoved some cans into the cupboard. "That's what my morning bike rides are doing for me. I keep telling you to get up, get moving, get—"

"A life?" Abby suggested, ducking as Sarah swatted at her. "Yoga every other afternoon is enough for me. This is my freaking vacay. There's no way I'm getting up at the butt-crack of dawn to haul my ass up and down the roads around here, even if it does mean getting to peek at the group leader's ass in bike shorts." Sarah colored. "Didn't know I knew that, huh? I'm not blind. What is he, about twelve?"

Sarah leaned against the counter. "Twenty-six, thank you very much. The face may look twelve, but the body…" She thumped her head against the refrigerator. "All for naught, I'm afraid. Some chick brought him a water bottle and a kiss on the cheek this morning, and she's as built as he is."

Abby started putting the contents of her bags into the cupboard. "So, basically, you've been killing yourself every morning for a gander at a nice ass, and you never even asked around if he was attached? Poor you." She envisioned Sarah's sweaty, red face when she got back from her rides and laughed.

"Yeah, yeah…laugh it up." Sarah tried to frown, but ended up chuckling herself. "We need to get out tonight and drown my sorrows. I'm a woman on the edge."

"Gonna ask bike guy? I mean, you get up early for him, the least he can do is stay up late with you." Abby tried to keep a straight face and failed utterly.

"Very funny," Sarah said with a sniff.

"Don't worry. He might not be serious with this girl, and I have faith that you'll bring the boy toy around by the end of summer."

Sarah shoved a six-pack of beer into the fridge before turning with a sly smile. "Oh, and speaking of nice asses, guess who I ran into in the grocery store."

"Hmm?" Abby said, trying to get another box onto the already overloaded shelf.

"The butt-shaking beauty? Gorgeous eyes? Wicked smile? Fingers that make me drool just to look at them? That voice I can feel in my hooha?" Sarah rattled off a list of attributes until Abby held up her hand, laughing too hard to speak.

"Okay, okay! You saw Matt. So what?"

"Oh, so now it's *Matt*." Sarah rolled her eyes. "Well, the reason you're a sneaky bitch, besides the work calls — we'll discuss them later — and thank you so much for asking, is because you didn't tell me you saw him at a gallery the other day. What's up with that?"

Abby shrugged. "Didn't seem worth mentioning. He shops in the junior section." She gave a rundown on the chance meeting with Surfer Dude.

Sarah frowned. "Well, shit. He didn't look the type. I'm damn sorry to hear that." She put the last of the cold items into the refrigerator. "He asked about you." Her slanted smile showed that she picked up on Abby's interest. "How's your head, how you're enjoying your vacation, if we're getting settled in, if we need anything — he didn't know what a loaded question he was asking there." Sarah chuckled. "Normal, everyday stuff. Not the type at all." She shook her head.

"What's 'the type'?"

"Oh, you know. So busy he doesn't have time to talk to a woman anyway, so who the hell cares if she's got a brain, or so insecure about getting older that he needs a sweet young thang to stroke his ego and make him think he stopped at thirty-hot."

Abby laughed. "That's what I called him — Peter Pan." She closed the final cupboard door and put the shopping bags in the broom closet. "Not worth worrying about, even if he did seem nice." A wistful note crept into her voice, and she braced herself for another attack, but Sarah was muttering to herself as she worked two beers out of the crowded fridge.

"I always think Peter Puny at those times, but that doesn't work out in this case. The wetsuit does not lie." Sarah slipped her sunglasses over her eyes before gesturing toward the back door. "Speaking of wetsuits," she said again, "shall we, m'dear? The eye-candy should be rolling in any minute now, and I've gotta find a new perversion to dwell upon."

They headed to their early evening hangout, plopping down on the beach chairs they'd established a few yards down the beach. Sarah adjusted the large umbrella, and they settled back to enjoy the passing entertainment of people walking by. Those who'd gotten used to seeing them every evening smiled and waved.

Sinking lower in her chair, Abby stretched her legs out of the shade and into the sunlight. "I don't ever want to leave this beach," she said, leaning her head back against the canvas. "I'm getting some color for the first time in my life." She held her leg up for Sarah's inspection, and Sarah obediently raised her glasses to look.

She patted Abby's arm and generously didn't mention her own long, deeply tanned limbs, courtesy of a Turkish grandmother. "From pasty to merely pale. Good job, girl. Maybe by the end of summer you'll be the color of light toast."

"Bitch," Abby accused without conviction.

Sarah sat up straighter and raised her glasses to squint at the water. "Here they come." She gave Abby a sideways glance and smirked. "Don't expect your man, unless he lives right on the beach and doesn't mind getting wetsuited up for a real short ride. Not much time left to surf."

"I don't have a man, but if you're talking about the butt shaker, who cares? He's a candyman."

Sarah started to giggle. "As in 'made of candy' or 'melts in your mouth'? 'Cause I'd gladly be the taste tester." She raised her bottle to take a sip of beer.

"As in 'wanna piece of candy, little girl'?" Abby did her best "old perv" voice, and Sarah spewed golden ale down her front.

"I can't believe you, woman," she sputtered out. "Now it looks like I've been in a wet T-shirt contest." She held her drenched shirt out from her body and flapped it around. "If there's anyone around here who likes teacup boobs, they're gonna get an eyeful. Or at least a pupil full." They both snorted laughter at the thought of that happening in the silicone capital of the world. Abby closed her eyes and took another swallow of beer, relishing the heat of the day and the cold drink sliding down her throat.

"What do you think he does, anyway? The Candyman?"

Abby shrugged. "Doc, maybe? Your bike god deferred to him when I turfed it. Now shut up and let me enjoy the sun."

"Showtime," Sarah murmured. After weeks of this, Abby knew Sarah would be leaning forward and shading her eyes until she thought the surfers could see her, then she'd sit back and coolly look around like she didn't even notice they were walking through the waves at the shoreline. "Aren't you going to watch?"

"Nope," Abby answered, not even opening her eyes. "You tell me if there's any good man meat to peep at." The sounds of the gulls wheeling overhead and the repetitive whisper of the water on the shore had nearly put her to sleep when Sarah whistled.

"I'll be damned if he didn't make it," Sarah said, poking Abby in the side with a wickedly sharp fingernail. "Open your freakin' eyes! Your man is on his way in. Skipped the wetsuit, though. I'll bet he didn't want to miss you."

"Oh, shut up," Abby groaned. Still, she raised her head and scanned the shoreline. The first surfer to hit the beach was Candyman's companion from the first day, the dimpled blond, who ended his ride at the shore. He waved at Sarah and Abby, grinning, and Sarah waved back. As the second rider came into shore, Blondie gestured for Sarah to come down toward the water, and she acquiesced. When she got there, Abby watched her talking animatedly to both him and a new guy with an oh-my-God body. He stared at Sarah in open admiration as he peeled the top half of his wetsuit to his waist and shook his short black hair to spray her with even more liquid. Sarah laughed; so did Abby, because Sarah's drying shirt was wet again, and the slight breeze off the water made it abundantly clear that she'd skipped the bra. Abby could tell the exact moment when that occurred to her friend: she went from hands clasped behind her back to arms crossed in front of her in an instant.

Abby was giggling so hard that she nearly missed the arrival of the third rider as he waded through the surf at the shoreline, carrying his board and pushing his hair back from his forehead. He stopped to talk to the others, and she heard his surprisingly young laughter, not at all the deep chuckle that she imagined rolling out of that chest. Matt set his board down on the sand and straddled it, crossing his arms and listening as the dark-haired man spoke. He laughed again, and Abby had to smile at the joy in the sound, even as she admired the long muscles of his back, wondering what he did to accomplish that perfect round symmetry in his thick shoulders and corded arms, more characteristic of a gymnast or swimmer than a gym rat. Matt's hands shifted to his hips, drawing her gaze to his clinging board shorts. Damn, something *could* outdo the wetsuit.

With her mind wandering dangerous and wonderful paths, her eyes drifted up again, watching the muscles in his back bunch and twist when he moved — wait. Moved?

Her horrified eyes shot up to meet Matt's. *You like?* he mouthed, looking at his own backside. He grinned and motioned for her to join them.

Abby see-sawed her hand in a "so-so" movement, laughing at his exaggeratedly hurt expression. She rose from her chair and waved as she headed toward the house. Looking back as she reached the door, she noticed that Matt had walked up the beach a few yards and was watching her. She felt a curl of tension — attraction coupled with anticipation — and had a sudden impulse to call him to her. He raked his hand through his hair, which was beginning to dry into wild waves and tiny curls around his neck. Dragging her mind firmly back to a reality that included his girlfriend, she forced a pleasant smile and waved again before closing the door. With a sense of regret, she walked into the living room and flopped on the couch.

Sarah sauntered in a couple minutes later, grinning. "The hell you don't have a man. I'd say he's yours for the taking." She lifted Abby's feet off the couch cushion before she sat down and rested them on her lap.

"I play nice, babes, you know that," Abby said. "I don't take the other kids' toys. Especially baby toys."

Sarah shook her head. "Geez, one little screw up with Mr. MarriedBob LiarPants, and you give up? That was two years ago, for God's sake. Give it a rest. Live…" She trailed off, and Abby could see the wheels in her friend's brain churning. "Oh my God. Now I get it. You wasted two years with the most boring man in recorded history because of *that?*" She snorted. "I've been caught by that particular lie so many times that I'd have to get me to a nunnery if I thought like you."

"It's not just that," Abby insisted. "It's the whole…*thing.*"

"What *thing* are we talking about, my love?" Sarah leaned her head onto the back of the couch and settled in.

"Dating. Lies. Half-truths. I'm sick of walking the tightrope of *I'm independent, but I need you. I'm smart enough to run a business, but you're the boss, dear.* Wives, ex-wives, kids, step-kids…" Abby sighed. "I want to admit my weight and my age and claim Salvador Dali without feeling like I'm apologizing for being a crazy cat lady." She sat up and pointed at Sarah. "I'm pretty happy right now, when all is said and done. I have a good job in a tough field, an apartment I love, friends…I'm done looking for what passes for love, especially on vacation. Is that so wrong?"

"You want to admit your weight?" Sarah whispered.

Abby groaned, flopped back on the couch, and covered her eyes with an arm. "I make my personal stand on relationships, and that's all you retained? Philistine."

Sarah laughed and slapped the bottoms of Abby's feet. "I'm joking, you fool. I guess I know what you mean. I've had those same thoughts and experiences, you know, but you don't see me giving up on finding *the one*."

"Unlike you, Sarah, I learn from my mistakes, and the two things I learned from LiarPants are, A —" Abby held up one finger "— I don't share. And B —" she held up another finger "— I don't take what isn't mine, no matter how pretty the package."

"And C," Sarah mocked, "you never know until you try. Even if Surfer Dude's arm candy did look like Slut Barbie."

Abby gave Sarah the slow blink. "If you're quite done analyzing me, here are my final words on the subject: I'm not interested in any man who's interested in that girl."

Sarah considered. "Movie mis-quote. Niiice." She shoved Abby's feet off of her lap and stood up, grabbing Abby's arm and dragging her to her feet. "A better mis-quote, and so apropos to this conversation: 'Younger men are less complicated.'" Abby chuckled reluctantly. "With that thought in mind, get sexy and let's go blow the stank off with a few dozen young men. No baggage, no big history." Sarah eyes went big and round as she backed up the stairs, towing Abby with her. "Just fun and lust. Change, right?"

Abby took a deep breath and let it out in a gust. "Right. Change."

Sarah shrieked and ran for the shower. "You'd better not wuss out on me, I swear to God."

Abby flapped her hand at her. "Go already, before I change my mind."

Two hours later, after a change of clothes and a meal grabbed at a small bistro on the boardwalk, they walked into The Catalyst, Santa Cruz's hotspot for food, drinks, and dancing. They were headed toward the bar when Sarah spotted some of the people from her bike group. "Grab us a spot, babe," she shouted over the crowd. "I'll be right back."

A gin and tonic later, she was still MIA. Abby ordered another cocktail from the harried barmaid. As bright and cheerful as the room was, it really wasn't her style. Clubs might have done it for her a decade and a half before, but now she appreciated a well-mixed drink, cozy atmosphere, and music over which she could hear herself think.

"Change is good…change is good," Abby muttered to herself, turning back toward the bar when she couldn't spot Sarah. She lifted her hair off her neck and looked down, fanning her nape with a cocktail napkin.

"That right there is beautiful." A gentle finger ran over the arch of her neck. "I wish I had my camera."

Her head jerked up, and she stepped closer to the bar before half-turning to see Matt, his eyes unfocussed and his face a mask of concentration. He shook his head after a second and smiled, looking at his still upraised hand before lowering it. "Sorry. Force of habit. I'm a sensory learner, too." His smile widened. "It's like I can't really 'see' unless I use my hands. Know anyone else like that, pretty lady?"

Taking a swallow of her drink, Abby grimaced at the burn in her throat. "I might. You know, I'm beginning to think you really are stalking me, surferboy." She narrowed her eyes. "Are you the one who told Sarah about this little slice of heaven?"

Matt chuckled and gestured at his clothes. "Do I look like I spend a lot of time here?"

Abby compared his navy tee and worn jeans to the bright vacation clothes on the majority of the people in the room. She shook her head. "Don't you own another shirt?" she joked.

He looked down at himself in surprise. "I *was* wearing this shirt the other day, wasn't I? Glad you noticed." Matt smiled. "I happen to like things that have stood the test of time. Take these jeans, for example." He slid onto the stool next to Abby and nodded toward its companion. She scooted up onto the seat, and he gestured at the barmaid for two more drinks. Looking down at the leg of his jeans, Abby tried to ignore the muscles underneath, instead concentrating on the denim, pale from many washings and with a sheen like velvet. She caught herself as she reached out to touch Matt's thigh, and he laughed, raising one leg toward her. "Go ahead. They really are that soft. I've had them since high school, which makes them older than some people in this bar." Abby shook her head and turned back toward her drink. Matt grabbed her hand gently. "C'mon. You know you want to," he teased as he drew Abby's fingers toward his leg. "You won't be able to sleep for wondering."

She relented, brushing just the tips of her fingers on the fabric right above his knee. "Soft," she murmured, looking up to find Matt watching her. He let go of her hand and lowered his leg.

"Why didn't you come down to the water today, pretty lady?" Matt asked. He watched Abby's hands as she fiddled with her drink stirrer.

"Because I don't poach," Abby said, looking back toward the dance area. "You seem to be attached at the moment, and I respect that." *Even if I can't respect your choice*, she added to herself.

Matt's warm hand, surprisingly rough and dry for that of a doctor, cupped Abby's cheek and turned her face toward his so he could catch her gaze. "I'm not attached," he whispered.

"Does she know that?" Abby whispered back, removing Matt's hand from her cheek. She put her own hand lightly on his jaw and turned his face toward the stairs, where the girl from the museum was waving her arms and trying to get his attention.

"Crap." Matt gave a half-hearted wave back before turning toward Abby. "I realize what this looks like, but I swear it's not what you're thinking. I came here with friends—*guy* friends—and we've been waiting for a pool table to open up there—which apparently it has. I don't know where Zoe came from."

"Okay." Abby shrugged. She slid off the stool and onto her feet, gulping the last of her drink and setting the empty glass on the bar. "None of my business anyway." She spotted Sarah at a corner table, huddled close to the dark-haired guy from earlier that evening. "The hottie is waving at you again. You don't want to miss your table." Abby said, looking at Matt and wishing he were different. "Thanks for the drink. I'll see you around."

As she brushed past him, Matt snagged her arm. "You will see me, Pretty," he said, rubbing his thumb on the crook of her elbow and smiling when she shivered. "Tell me your name?"

Abby reluctantly smiled back. "Pretty will do. Bye." She walked toward the bathrooms, hoping to snag Sarah along the way. No such luck. Sarah slid through the crowd and toward the dance floor, her surfer guy in tow. By the time Abby could get in and out of a stall and up to the sinks, she'd had time to make unflattering comparisons between Matt's Barbie and herself, and she was feeling pretty blue.

Stepping back to the bar after a fruitless search for her wayward friend, Abby ordered an Amstel. The thump of the bass and the constant clamor was giving her a headache, and she wondered how she was going to get home if she couldn't find Sarah.

"That must have been some nasty road rash when it was fresh," a voice drawled from beside her. She glanced down at her hip. The motion of leaning forward to take her bottle from the server had pulled her top up, exposing the scabby patch that was still too sensitive for tight clothes.

The man next to her chuckled and ended his frank appraisal when she yanked her shirt down. He raised his own bottle to his lips, shaking his head. "Don't worry about it. I've seen and had much worse than that." Raising one muscled arm, he pointed to the deep scar across his triceps. "Middle of a race, I was shoved off my bike. A chunk of steel that was embedded in the soft shoulder gave me this. After sixteen stitches—" he pointed to the outside of his left knee, which had its own shiny, hairless scar "—another race. Another wreck." He started to pull up his shirt, exposing a muscled stomach. "And there's this one on my chest—"

Abby grabbed his hand. "I believe you."

He dropped the hem of his shirt, grinning and rubbing the curly dark hair on the back of his head. "I was just kidding anyway. Wondering how far you'd let me go." He looked at Abby with a raised eyebrow and chuckled when she shook her head. "Although I did wreck on a motorcycle while wearing a T-shirt and no jacket once and ended up sanding off half my chest hair."

Abby had to laugh at his enthusiasm. "You sound pretty accident prone. Maybe you'd better stay off of all forms of two-wheeled transportation."

"Can't do it. It's my passion and my avocation."

"Bike wrecker?" Abby joked. He was a big guy, built broad and hard, but the open friendliness in his eyes and across his dark, handsome face made him non-threatening.

"Very funny. No, bike racer." He held up a hand, palm-out. "And, before you ask, not motorcycles. Bicycles. Do you ride often?"

"Not if I can help it. The one time I've been on a bike since I was twelve netted me this." Abby raised her top enough to wave at the mess on her hip. "So, no."

He nodded, smiling. "Fair enough. So, do you swim? Run? You're doing something to keep that shape."

"Ooh. Confident, aren't we?" Abby said archly, and he shrugged. "I walk an insane amount every day in my real life, though I've been doing a lot of lying around during this vacation. Weeks of vegetating so far—well, with a little bit of yoga."

"Not good. Not good at all." He shook his head sadly. "We'll have to get you back in the saddle or you'll start to lose muscle tone." He looked Abby up and down. "That would be a damned shame."

Cheeky bastard…but Abby sort of liked it. She slid onto the stool next to him and drained her bottle of beer before answering. "Thanks. You do realize that I'm old enough to be your…" She searched for the term she wanted.

"I'm twenty-five. How old are you?" he asked boldly, turning toward Abby. She couldn't help noticing the way his shirt stretched across his chest and shoulders, accentuating just a couple of his multiple assets.

"Thirty-seven."

"Then 'mother' wouldn't fit. I may be from West Virginia, but even my hillbilly mother wasn't pregnant at twelve." Abby laughed. "So, are we finished with that crap? Age isn't an issue. Are we in agreement?"

Abby blew out a gust of air, enjoying the man's candor and really enjoying looking at him. "Um…this might be a weird question, but… aren't you a big guy for bike racing? I thought they were little 'uns."

He laughed loudly, drawing friendly looks and smiles from the other patrons. "Bikes, not horses. Racers aren't jockeys. In answer to your question, though — yeah, I am bigger than US norm, though some Europeans are close. I'm agile, though, and powerful." He raised his bottle to his lips, smiling and looking at Abby out of the corner of his eye. "You ought to try me."

"Down, boy," she deadpanned, liking him more all the time. "Is there a big bike scene in Santa Cruz to bring you down from the hills, Billy?"

He shook his head at Abby's bad joke. "Yeah, there is, but I have to work, too. I'm modeling for an artist this summer. Well, hopefully. I meet with him tomorrow."

"Modeling?" Abby grinned. "How did you stumble into that line of work?"

He shrugged. "Gotta feed the obsession somehow. New frames for a guy my size don't come cheap." Abby nodded. "Besides, I've done worse gigs." He drained his bottle, winking at the barmaid and wiggling his bottle to indicate that he'd like another.

Abby watched the play of the muscles in his shoulders and back as he leaned forward to take the drink, and her interest was piqued. "Liiike…?"

"Liiike…department store Santa. That sucked."

Imagining him in a full beard and padded suit, Abby started laughing. After a minute he joined in, leaning forward to rest a hand on her knee. "Listen, I have an early morning, and I'm an upfront guy. Would you be interested in a drink at my place? The noise in here is getting to me. I live just around the corner, and I swear to God, I'm trustworthy." He placed his other hand over his heart. "And besides, my best friend-slash-manager will be there. Her name's Chelsie, and she can kick my ass. You wanna?"

Abby's mind flew back and forth between interest and caution. He seemed friendly enough, but he was miles from her usual type. *Suck it up, Abby. That's what this summer is all about—change.* "Sure. Why not?" Slipping off the stool, Abby linked her arm through his and slid her other hand over his bicep. "Hey, I guess I should ask you what your name is, right?"

He smiled down at her. "It's Jason. Jason Shaw. And you are?"

"Abby Reynolds." She caught sight of Sarah at a table not far from the door. Sarah gave her a double thumbs-up before re-engaging with her boy toy. Abby paused. She was about to walk out the door to an unknown destination with a really large guy who she barely knew. Change was good, but stupidity was not. "Listen, Jason, come meet my friend Sarah. I want to give her your address so she can pick me up in an hour or so."

"So that's how it's gonna be, huh? If I didn't have to be at Clarke's studio first thing in the morning I'd be turning on the charm right now."

Abby smiled at him. "It would probably work too, but, alas…" She shrugged, and Jason groaned before following her lead. She made the introductions and explained her plan, but a glance let her know that Sarah was probably already past the driving stage.

"I'm not drinking," Sarah's companion said, only briefly taking his eyes off of Sarah. "I'll come get you and drive you both home."

"How will you get home?" Abby asked.

He smiled at Sarah and skimmed his hand over her thigh. "We'll work that out later," he said. Sarah giggled.

Jason wrote his address on a cocktail napkin, and Abby shoved it into Sarah's hand. "Don't lose this, and don't forget. I'm counting on you." Sarah smiled and nodded, already disengaged from the conversation.

Jason walked toward the door. "And you thought I was forward. That guy doesn't have balls; he has boulders."

Abby laughed, looking back at Sarah's table. She caught a flash of sun-bleached hair as it moved through the crowd toward her. When Matt caught Abby's eye, he stopped where he was, taking in Jason's encircling arm before smiling crookedly, shrugging, and changing his vector to walk toward the bar. Abby followed him with her eyes, wishing for just a second that she was still sitting there.

"Ready?" Jason's voice tugged Abby back to the present.

She looked at him and smiled. "Yep."

The walk to Jason's home, part of a larger house that had been split into three tiny apartments, was as short as he had said, and he was soon opening the front door. It was small and shabbily furnished, but neat. A lanky blond woman looked up from the Xbox game she was playing, startled.

Jason laughed. "Gotcha! I knew you were practicing when I wasn't here." He gestured toward Abby before heading to the kitchenette. "Chelsie, Abby. Abby, Chelsie. Do we have any more beer?" He opened the refrigerator and peered around.

Chelsie smiled at Abby tentatively, turning her game off and gesturing at the other side of the loveseat. "Nice to meet you. Have a seat." Abby sat awkwardly, smiling back and nodding.

Jason cut the tension by handing each woman a beer and flopping on the floor by Abby's feet. "Chelsie is my manager and my best bud since…" He looked at her fondly. "Fifth? Sixth?"

"Fourth grade," Chelsie said, smiling at him and brushing a hand over his short hair. "You have the memory of dirt. I, on the other hand, remember everything."

"That's why you're my manager," Jason said cheerfully. He wrapped his large hand around her calf and grinning up at her. "Abby Reynolds is a very nice woman I met at The Catalyst tonight, Chelsie."

"I figured, bonehead." Chelsie made a goofy face before turning to Abby. "What brings you to Santa Cruz, Abby? I assume Jason told you why he's here, because he tells everyone." She stage whispered, "He got the big head from having his body chosen for those statues; don't let his false modesty fool you for a minute." They all laughed, and the ice was broken. The rest of the visit was easy as the three of them talked casually about lots of things, from the tiny city in which they currently resided to a mutual love of horror movies. As the hour before Sarah was expected drew to a close, Jason moved closer, sliding his hand up Abby's calf to stroke the back of her knee with a fingertip. She looked down into his inviting dark eyes.

"And that's my cue to leave," Chelsie said wryly, standing and patting Abby on the shoulder. "It was really nice to meet you, Abby. Come back again, okay?" Chelsie opened her mouth to say something to Jason before shaking her head. "Right. Night." She headed into the small bedroom and shut the door.

Jason eased up onto the loveseat in her place and trailed a finger down Abby's arm. "So. You wouldn't change your mind about leaving, would you?" he asked.

"You have to get up early," Abby reminded him, watching his hand as he trailed the back of his fingers up her arm and over the ball of her shoulder. She shivered as he brushed his lips over the same spot on her shoulder that he'd just touched.

"I'm young. I recover quickly." Jason's full lips pressed against Abby's jaw.

Abby's head spun at the possibilities that rested in that short statement. "Food for thought," she murmured, and she felt him smile against her skin. He drew back and took her hand.

"No pressure here. Let's just enjoy the few minutes we have left, okay? I like you, and I think you like me. Just fun." He leaned toward Abby, looking at her mouth.

Abby met him halfway. Jason's lips were firm on hers, his hands gentle as he ran them from her wrists to her shoulders before wrapping one arm around Abby and cradling her head with the other. Her hands rested on his waist before moving up his back, stroking the hard muscles under his shirt. A pleased sound rumbled in his throat, and he pulled her closer.

After a while, Jason drew back. "There, that wasn't so bad, was it?" he asked in an uneven voice.

"Not bad at all," Abby said breathlessly, watching the rapid flutter of the pulse at his neck. And it really had been…nice. Warm and slightly exciting and…nice. Abby grabbed Jason's arm and looked at his watch, cursing Sarah.

Jason smiled and straightened his shirt. "Well, it's been over an hour, and I haven't attacked you and left your body in a ditch yet.

Trust me to walk you back to the club?" He laughed when Abby threatened to hit him with her shoe, then he called out to tell Chelsie where he was going.

The walk back was quiet but not uncomfortable, and Jason soon wrapped Abby's hand in his. He began chuckling. "I wonder if your friend had fun with that skater kid."

"His name is Skater?" Abby asked. "And how is he any more of a kid than you are?"

"I can't remember his name, but I've heard about him. He's in some skater gang that terrorizes tourists. And he's a kid because he is. Seventeen, maybe eighteen. I've seen him skateboarding around town. Believe me, he looks younger with the beanie on his head and his ass hanging out of his pants."

Abby stopped dead. "What the hell was he doing in the club, then?"

He shrugged. "It was crowded. He probably slipped in with a group. I'm sure he would have been thrown out if he'd been noticed. He wanted to be there, so he didn't mess with trying to buy a drink is my guess. Problem?"

"Hell, yes, it's a problem." Abby yanked Jason toward the club. "He looked a lot older than that tonight and earlier today when Sarah first met him. I thought he was about your age. Sarah wouldn't be doing whatever she's doing if she knew that he wasn't. No way." Abby scanned the lot, which was still full, trying to remember where the car was parked. She spotted Sarah's Hyundai, windows heavily fogged, and dashed over. She yanked the passenger door open. Sarah blinked owlishly in the sudden light. Her hair was mussed and her shirt half-unbuttoned.

"Abby!" Sarah tried on a smile. "I didn't forget; I just got distracted." She grinned at her distraction, whose shirt was entirely missing.

Jason laughed loudly and opened the driver's door, gesturing for the kid to get out. "C'mon, Romeo. Haven't you learned yet that it's not nice to take advantage of sweet, drunken ladies? What's your name?"

"Tyler." He glared at Jason. "This is none of your business, you know. The lady wants me to go home with her."

Looking up from adjusting Sarah's shirt, Abby growled, "Not in this lifetime, Junior Mint. Jason, if he doesn't get out of this car under his own power I'd like you to help him."

"Yes, ma'am." Jason crossed his arms and looked down at the kid. "You heard the lady, Tyler. Move."

Reluctantly, Tyler slid from behind the wheel and plucked his shirt from the backseat. He pulled it over his torso. "Sarah, I'll call you tomorrow afternoon." He shuffled toward the back of the lot.

Abby buckled Sarah's seatbelt before walking around to the driver's side. With a light hand on her arm, Jason stopped her from sliding behind the wheel. "Well, that was an interesting way to end the evening," he said. Abby chuckled and nodded. "I really enjoyed meeting you tonight, and I want to see you again, if you'd like that, too."

She thought about the past couple of hours and smiled. "I'd like that." After exchanging phone numbers, Jason tipped Abby's face up for another pleasant kiss before he headed across the parking lot, waving as he went.

Sarah mumbled in her sleep and caught her breath. Abby got in and started the car. "Sarah, if you hurl before we get home, I swear to God I'll kill you."

Sarah looked up blearily. "I think I'm gonna wish I was dead anyway," she croaked, closing her eyes and holding very still.

Abby laughed. "Not before I get to tell you about your boy toy. Then you'll wish you were dead."

As she drove home, Abby took a mental tally of the night:

One sick friend.

One teenage lothario to poke sick friend about for the rest of her life.

Two beautiful men who had promised to see her again.

Not a bad night at all.

Chapter Five

Matt's lungs burned, and his legs ached. The drinks that had sounded like a good idea the night before were coming back to bite him in the ass. The Catalyst wasn't a place he went often, as he didn't usually care to listen to drunken girls ask each other stupid questions over music with bass beating loud enough to change heart rhythms, but Chris had felt like playing pool, and The Catalyst had a lot of tables. Seeing Pretty there had been a treat that he hadn't expected. For some reason, she'd gotten into his head, and being blown off by her had stung.

A screech of brakes brought him back to the present; he'd narrowly missed being run down by his elderly neighbor. After a flash of a smile and a wave, she barreled past him toward the beach, her VW Bug belching smoke.

"Head in the game, Clarke," he muttered, pushing himself harder. That lasted for about three minutes, then his mind was back in the bar the night before. He'd spotted Pretty again, near the door, talking to a tall guy. Matt had waved, surprised by the sheepish look on her face until he realized that her companion was younger than he'd at first appeared to be. Something about the guy seemed vaguely familiar, but he couldn't place him.

Smiling at the irony of Pretty's dirty little secret—and after calling *him* Peter Pan—he was starting to anticipate seeing her again. He hit the halfway mark in his run and felt his temples pound; maybe a glass of water and a couple ibuprofen would have been a better idea than running.

Matt hesitated at the edge of the road. He really shouldn't. He still had to get back and shower before the potential model showed up for his briefing. Matt regretted the motivation that had led him to suggest such a god-awfully early time.

He'd turned to retrace his steps when movement on the beach caught his eye. A smile curved his lips as he recognized a hank of hair and curve of hips. He pivoted to hit the beach running. It took longer to catch up than he expected; Pretty walked faster than he thought she would. She'd moved a few hundred yards farther down the beach before he caught up and murmured in her ear, "Hi there."

Pretty stopped dead and swung her fist sharply backward. Yelping, Matt was able to turn enough that she caught his quadriceps rather than his nuts, but it was close, and it was still enough, given the pain already his legs, to cause him to plop down on the sand.

Her angry face as she turned was almost as funny as the situation, and Matt lay back, laughing. "Well, that didn't work out the way I'd planned."

Crouching next to him, Pretty looked both irritated and apologetic. Her hand fluttered over the spot she'd thumped, clearly both desiring to soothe it and realizing that it would be inappropriate. "I'm sorry, Matt. But what the hell were you thinking?"

"Not about being attacked, that's for sure." He leaned up on his elbow and used the opposite hand to slide up the leg of his shorts so he could examine his injury. Yep, already bruising. Thank God she'd missed her original mark, because that woman hit hard. He caught her eyes as she shifted them away from his leg. "Help me up, Wonder Woman?" He smiled. "I think my run is over."

Pretty got to her feet in one fluid motion. She extended a hand and pulled him up. "It's your own stupid fault," she said cheerfully. "How was I supposed to know you weren't a masher?"

Matt chuckled. "Masher? Who says that? Grandmas?"

"I say it. I don't need your permission. And I suppose I could be mistaken for a grandma, compared to some…" She set off at a brisk walk. Matt enjoyed the view, loose pants rolled down at the waist in deference to her wound and a stretchy tank that didn't quite meet her waistband, leaving a strip of silky-looking flesh between top and bottom. His impulse to touch her came back in a rush. He was glad he'd had the sense the night before to sketch out the sculpture idea the graceful arc of her neck had given him.

He caught up to her. "Nope, definitely not grandma material. Trust me. Compared to anyone."

Pretty's eyes softened. "Thanks." They walked a few more steps. "So, how was your evening? Exciting?" Her lips twisted into a smirk, and she glanced at Matt from the corner of her eye.

"Drank too much and went home." He sent a silent thanks to the sea god that he'd resisted Zoe's offer to share his bed after she'd helped him stagger to his front door. One kiss was all they'd shared — surely Pretty couldn't fault him for that. Matt looked over at her, a grin playing around his lips. "I should ask you the same thing. Working out the kinks? Was he a little too energetic?"

The smile dropped from Pretty's face. "That's—" Her lips set in a firm line.

"Fair?" Matt suggested, and she snorted. "Why is it that I'm a dirty old man when you think I'm sleeping with Zo—which, as a matter of fact, I am not—but your rec time with the boy toy is off limits for discussion?"

"Jason is not my boy toy, and discussion of my 'rec time' is off limits no matter who you're asking about."

Matt winced. All he wanted to do was to tease her a little, and now he'd made her mad. He tried to think of something to say, but Pretty beat him to it.

She stopped and put her hand on his arm. "You're right about one thing, though. It's not fair for me to shit you about Biker Barbie when I was with Jason. I'm sorry."

"No problem." Matt shrugged. "Guys my age get used to that." They walked in silence for a while, and then Matt noticed that she was gently covering the scuff on her hip with one hand. "Hurting?"

Pretty grimaced. "A little." She stopped and pushed down the fabric that was brushing her road rash. "Does it look like it's healing all right to you?"

After a glance at her face to see if she was serious, Matt crouched in front of her and studied the injury, looking for signs of infection. Resting one hand lightly on the hip opposite the wound, to help with balance, he raised his other hand and looked up again for permission. Getting a nod, he pressed the periphery of the scabbed area gently, watching for any weeping. He couldn't resist letting the backs of his fingers trail over her unblemished skin as he lowered his hand. It was as soft as he'd suspected, and Matt stood back up so he wouldn't be tempted to stroke it again with the pads of his fingers. He cleared his throat and scratched the back of his neck before he answered, giving him a chance to swallow and lubricate his dry throat. "Looks okay to me. Normal for a nasty scrape. Have you seen a doctor?"

Pretty rolled her eyes. "That's where you come in, right?"

Matt stared at her. "I'm not getting you, Pretty," he said, starting to walk again.

"Hold up." Her voice was strident, and Matt turned to look at her. "You're Doctor…whatever-the-Hell-Your-Last Name-is, right?"

He started to laugh. "Nope. Not a doctor. I've just seen a lot of injuries over the years from surfing. Concussions, water inhalation…" He pulled up the back of his shirt and twisted around to look at the scar along his lower back. "I've even had a scrape like yours, but I guess you'd call it coral rash. I was surfing off Maui, and—"

"You ass!" Pretty burst out, and Matt looked around to see that her face was completely red.

He dropped his shirt and held up his hands. "Hey, I didn't say anything to make you think I was a doc. I'm past making up stories to impress a girl. I told you that Scotty had me check your head—"

"Because surfers know about head injuries." She snickered and shook her head. "No wonder you looked so startled when I asked you to look at my hip. I'm sorry."

"I'm not," Matt replied, and she smacked him on the arm.

"Well, then, Matt—that *is* your real name, isn't it?"

Matt grinned and nodded, and they started walking back toward her house.

"Well, then, Matt-who-isn't-a-doctor, what *do* you do besides walk around looking hot in board shorts?"

"Remind me to keep you around; you're good for my ego." Matt nudged her, and she laughed. "I'll tell you if you tell me your name."

"Pretty works," she teased. "Give me a hint."

"Mmm…I know a lot about anatomy. Professionally and personally." He traced the soft lines of her body with his eyes. "Yours is very nice, by the way."

They had reached the beach at the back of Pretty's house, so she stopped. "Talk about ego boosts. Thank you so much, sir." They stood looking at each other for a minute before she laid a hand on Matt's arm. "Hey, would you like to come in for coffee? Sarah is still in her alco-coma, but I promise that I don't bite. Much."

In extending his elbow to her, he caught sight of his watch.

He dropped his arm. "I forgot that I have a meeting this morning. I should be back in the studio, showered and dressed, in about five minutes, in fact. Can I have a raincheck?"

Her smile faded. "Sure. I'll see you around. I'm supposed to meet Jason for lunch anyway. I should get cleaned up." She smiled. "Thanks for checking out my hip, Not-a-Doctor."

"Anytime. I like your hips." Matt started backing away. "I intend on inviting myself over, you realize. The boy toy needs a little competition to keep him on his toes. Or maybe we can get rid of him altogether?"

"Maybe. He's awfully cute, though…" Pretty backed toward the stairs, shaking her head doubtfully. She smiled at Matt's mock-stricken face. "You're now officially late for your meeting."

He grinned at her, watching the ends of her hair flutter in the slight breeze off the water. "Worth it. He can wait."

"Well, my shower can't. I'll see you." She smiled again and gently closed the door, leaving Matt with an image of the graceful lines of her body exposed as she stepped under the water; he could almost feel the smooth curve of her thigh as the first drops beaded on her skin.

A flash of inspiration struck. Matt took off for his studio, favoring the leg she'd bruised until the stiffness wore off. Running up to his door, he peeked at his watch again and groaned. Fuck a duck. The model should be knocking, he still needed a shower, and he knew from experience that leaving an idea unsketched often led to it slipping away forever.

He caught a break with the flashing light on the answering machine. Jason Shaw had called to say that he was running late and would get there as soon as he could. Breathing a sigh of relief, Matt grabbed a pencil and the sketch he'd made the night before, adding legs, one lifted as if stepping, to the twisted torso. He refined her hand holding the hair on top of her bent head and adjusted a few lines, making sure the shape of her hips was correct in the three-quarter view he'd drawn. Having just studied the originals, Matt wanted the copy to be perfect.

A knock on the door startled him. He'd missed his chance at a shower again. "Come on in," he shouted before he corrected the arch of Pretty's neck.

"Girlfriend?" an interested bass voice asked from beside him. Matt looked up with a smile, and there was Pretty's boy toy. He straightened up and gave himself a mental shake. That's why he'd seemed familiar—from the photos that had accompanied his resume. Pictures could deceive, though, and didn't convey the subject's attitude, which is why Matt required an in-person interview before offering the job. Shuffling the paper off to the side, he smiled. Shaw obviously didn't know Pretty intimately enough to recognize the figure on the paper. "Nope. Another project." He stuck his hand out after wiping charcoal-smeared fingers on his shirt. "Matt Clarke."

Jason shook Matt's hand firmly. "Jason Shaw. I called to say I'd be late, but..."

"Sure, I got your message." Matt looked his prospective model over and was grudgingly appreciative. Jason had chosen dark twill slacks and a dark button-down shirt that had to have been tailored to fit his arms. He was obviously taking this interview seriously, which was a relief after working with Tyler Oda. Tyler had shown up in cutoffs and a muscle tee and had goofed around so much that Matt had been forced to fire him and work from old snaps of Chris. "I was running, as you can probably smell, and got held up anyway. Do you have a few minutes to kill? I can jump in and out of the shower real quick."

Jason nodded, and Matt left him examining the pictures he'd taken of Zoe and Chris. Ten minutes later, he was back and feeling more up to the interview. Jason was studying the body shots of Chris and Zoe closely. "What's wrong with using this guy?" he asked, waving a picture of Chris. "He's ripped as hell."

Chris's reaction when he was told that the client thought he was too small still made Matt laugh. "The buyer wanted someone bigger."

"My win. I'm kinda glad that Chelsie heard about this gig." He waved a shot of Zoe, looking at Matt with a raised eyebrow. "Is this who I'm posing with?"

"Eventually," Matt said. "I'll get individual shots of each of you first, and then we'll see about the couple sculptures. The client hasn't specified what she wants yet." A thought crossed his mind. "Will that be a problem, working with another model? I won't purposely ask you to do anything that's likely to become…embarrassing, but you will be spending time together stripped to the waist. Zoe has modeled for me several times and is used to it, but—"

Jason waved his hand. "Forget about it. I'll be fine. I'm a quick learner." He looked at the picture again. "She's my usual type, but lately I find myself preferring someone more like that sketch over there." He gestured toward the table behind Matt.

"Come on over and sit down." Matt went to the table and sat in front of a stack of folders, making sure his sketch was covered. He opened the folder that contained Jason's photos, headshots and full body, and the letter he'd gotten in response to his original inquiry. An artist friend had recommended Jason, based on seeing him at a race, and Matt had contacted Jason's manager for photos.

Tapping his pencil on the edge of the table, Matt wondered idly how serious things were between his model and Pretty. He stole another look at Jason. Damn, the guy was a big, good-looking bastard. Matt rubbed the back of his neck, the motion reminding him of Pretty's beautifully arched neck last night, how soft her skin felt and the texture of the tiny hairs at the base of her skull. His hands itched to start molding that image in clay, despite the time it would take away from his paying job.

He dragged his attention back to the task at hand. "Okay, this all looks fine, and I think you're a good fit physically. The last thing I want to go over is the time commitment involved." *Time speech #1*, Matt thought. "Out of respect for the real lives of my models, I try to keep regular hours, but there might be times it's not possible. And the hours themselves will change, since sometimes I'll need you in the studio physically, and other times I'll be working from photographs and won't need you at all for irregular stretches of time. That can be hard on personal relationships. And posing with Zoe…" He nodded toward a particularly provocative shot he'd taken. "Will that be an issue?"

Jason studied the picture. "Maybe?"

Matt smiled. An opening. "What's her name?"

"Abby." Jason scratched the back of his head and lowered his voice confidentially. "She's a bit older than I am, but whatever. And she did say she'd go out to lunch when I called this morning, so it must not bother her either. Can these things work out, do you think?"

"I'm the last person you should ask about that." *Don't count on it, kid,* Matt thought, leaning back in his chair and crossing his arms across his chest. "I'd have to be cruising nursing homes to have a real opinion on the topic."

"Right," Jason scoffed. "What are you, about thirty or so? Abby's not that much older than I am."

Matt rose from his chair and extended his hand. "You're hired, if only because you seriously misjudge my age."

Jason rose, too, and shook Matt's hand.

"Be here tomorrow for some photos, and we'll go from there. Don't have too much fun on your lunch date. I need you here and whole tomorrow."

"It's lunch, dude. Can't get up to much trouble there."

You'd be surprised what can happen at lunch, Matt thought, but he kept his mouth shut. No need to give Jason any ideas. After setting a time to meet the next day, Jason headed out.

Before the door was completely closed, Matt was on the phone to Claire. Looking at Jason had his brain working; ideas for poses that would be classical yet fresh were already forming. After going through the receptionist at the gallery, Matt heard Claire's greeting.

"So, do we have a deal with Bambi and the corpse?" he asked.

Claire laughed. "What happened to 'Hello, beautiful woman that I want to run away with'?"

"Self-preservation kicked in. Charles would beat me down, and I wouldn't want to mess up his pretty face." They both laughed and then got down to business. "Deal?"

"Of course, sweetness. I always come through for you." Claire named a figure for six sculptures that left Matt gasping.

"Holy shit. That'll set me up for a while." Matt thumped down on a chair. "I don't even know what to say."

"Don't thank me yet. There's a catch. They want to display at least three of the six at their annual shindig in mid-September."

"There's no way." His wonder deflated.

"Matt. Think rationally. They aren't looking for high art here, and you know Bambis are never big on originality. We're talking a few twists on run-of-the-mill Grecian-ish statues. And you only have to get half out to them in almost three months. You have until the end of the year with the rest." She paused. "What else were you going to do this summer?"

"Well, I wasn't planning on spending sixteen hour days in the studio, that's for damned sure." Matt rubbed his forehead with his fingertips. Six months of hell in exchange for at least three years of freedom to do whatever he wanted. Matt took a deep breath and let it gush out. "Okay. I'll try. I must be insane."

"Just very smart, lovey. These people may be idiots, but the geezer has influence with friends who *do* know something about real art *and* have money to burn. You've done well so far, but this is something else entirely." Matt agreed and sat silently for a moment.

Claire started again on a less serious note. "One night you're taking off is the twenty-fifth. Charles will be in town, and we're planning a party at the Poet that night to celebrate the birth of our favorite artist and meal ticket." Claire acted as if the commission Matt paid her for selling his sculptures kept them afloat, but Charles's status as trust fund baby made Matt's contribution to their budget superfluous. "Any prospects for a party companion?"

Matt thought about Pret — *Abby* — and smiled. "Maybe. I don't want to jinx anything, but…maybe."

"Wonderful! Make sure you bring her along so we can grill her unmercifully and embarrass you to death."

Getting three sculptures out quickly was no joke, however, and Matt ended up spending just about every waking minute in the studio, taking photographs of the models and then starting the process of sculpting the first figure in clay. The times he stole away to try to catch Abby at home, no one had been there. Claire was thrilled to hear he'd met her newest "find" — she'd shanghaied Abby into helping with the summer art studio she sponsored for local kids — and gave her blessing to his pursuit, but it went nowhere fast. He did have the joy of hearing all about how much fun Abby was having with Jason on her off hours, though, from the man himself. It chapped his ass that he could be losing his chance with her by default.

By the night of the party, he'd resigned himself to listening to Claire heckle him all night about his lack of a date. After a shower, he put on his favorite jeans and hesitated over a shirt, deciding on a chambray button-down instead of his usual T-shirt, in honor of the occasion. As he strapped on his watch, he reminded himself to not drink too much. Jason was in Indiana for a few days for a race, and that left him working alone with Zoe. He had to be on his toes for that, because if she wasn't bitchy she'd be flirty, and Matt didn't want to deal with either state while he had a hangover.

Running his hands through his hair a couple of times, he hollered for Chris. His cousin and his single duffle bag of clothes had taken up residence in the spare bedroom the day Matt made his sculpture sale. Matt didn't mind having him around; he was clean and quiet and someone to talk to at the end of the day.

Chris came out of his room, tugging on a T-shirt and slipping on his sandals. Loose cargo shorts hung easily on his hips, and Matt had a moment of regret that Bambi hadn't liked Chris's form, because it was a challenge and a pleasure to try to capture the lean muscle he carried.

"The Poet and the Patriot, right?" he asked, and Matt nodded. "Thank God. No pool, but no headache from screaming over music, either."

"There's darts, if Claire got there early enough to get a board. Good beer and good music, too."

"Oh joy. Drunken people throwing sharp objects," Chris joked, shaking his blond waves away from his face. "Charlie gonna be there?"

"Yep." Matt smiled crookedly, knowing why Chris asked. Charles Eastman's easygoing approach to spending money was legendary in Santa Cruz, and shopkeepers rubbed their hands gleefully when he was in town.

"Free drinks, then. Excellent." Chris slapped Matt on the shoulder and grinned. "Happy birthday, cuz."

The Poet was pleasantly busy for a Sunday night: full, but not the crowded mess it became on weekends when the university was in full swing. Claire greeted Matt with a kiss when he and Chris stepped into the darts room. Matt waved at several friends who lounged around the tables. Charles grinned broadly, shrugging before he rose to shake Matt's hand.

"How much did this private party room run you, Charlie?" Matt asked, shaking his head.

"Happy birthday, Matt," was his friend's only reply, given with an arched eyebrow as he swept his hair back from his forehead and sat down next to Claire. He pulled one of her legs across his lap and massaged her knee.

Drinks flowed freely as the party guests mingled and chatted, taking turns at the six dartboards and having a great time. Matt took a certain amount of ribbing about his advanced age, of course, but it was all in fun. He eventually had to make a bathroom run and was surprised at how crowded the front section of the bar had become in the hours since he and Chris had arrived. Envious glances at the roped-off dart room made him feel vaguely guilty as he stepped into the men's room…but not really. He could accept a birthday present with the best of anyone.

Stepping back into the short hallway outside the restrooms, Matt glanced at the back of the woman exiting the ladies room and smiled. He let the door close behind him and moved behind her until he could grasp her forearms from behind. "Hi there, Abby," he murmured in her ear. "Is it safe to let go of your arms yet? I might not be able to move fast enough this time."

Abby relaxed and twisted her torso to smile back at Matt. "Who told you my name? And if you'd stop sneaking up behind me, you wouldn't have to worry about the boys, you know."

"True." He ran his hands down her forearms until he had to reluctantly let go when she turned to face him. She leaned against the wall.

Matt studied her large, dark-lashed eyes and full lips, imprinting the soft oval of her face on his mind. He was anticipating forming it in the covered clay figure at the back of his studio. "You're a hard lady to get hold of, Miss Abby. Ask a guy for coffee, and then you're never home."

Abby looked uncomfortable. "Well, I saved some coffee for you for a while, but when I didn't hear from you, I started giving it to Jason." She bumped the heel of one shoe against the wall. "We've been seeing a lot of each other. When you let him out of your dungeon, that is."

Matt chuckled. "I'm found out too, I guess." He wiggled his fingers in the air. "I play with clay for a living. How do you like that?"

Abby's lips twisted into a smile. "That's strangely fitting. And it makes this even harder to say." She combed her fingers through the side of her hair. "Listen, Matt. I'll feel really stupid if I'm misreading things, but I think there's some interest here?" He nodded. "Um…I don't know if I'm saying this right. I don't see more than one person at a time. Maybe you do, but I don't. Too confusing."

"I don't either. There's nothing going on between me and Zoe other than her modeling for me every once in a while." Matt reached out and snagged one of her hands. "See just me."

Looking down at their joined hands, Abby shook her head before gently disengaging her fingers. "You are the devil. Way too tempting," she said softly, making him smile. "It's not fair to Jason. He's not even here to—I need to talk to—"

Matt pushed away from the wall and took her hand again. "Nothing has to be decided tonight. Let's just have fun. It's my birthday today, and I'd like you to come to my party. Beer, darts…" he coaxed, drawing her into the main room.

When she saw that they were headed toward the cordoned-off darts room, she laughed. "So you're the one causing all the congestion in here. You're not very popular tonight."

He shrugged. "Coming with me?"

Abby hung back, but Matt could see anticipation growing in her eyes. "I have Sarah with me. She only came here because she wanted a drink, and I refused to visit the meat market again."

"Bring her along. My friends are nice, and they don't bite. Much." Matt tugged Abby's hand gently, smiling at her. "I want you to. I promise, no cha-cha, cher," he drawled in his best Cajun accent.

Abby groaned and dropped her head back, laughing. "Accents! Now you do accents! Totally unfair." She shuffled nearer, so close that Matt caught a whiff of her perfume. For an instant, he toyed with the idea of drawing her that crucial inch toward him.

Instead, he started walking backward, still holding her hand and towing her along, toward the tables where the rest of his party sat. He let Abby catch up with him. When they were toe-to-toe, he brushed her hair back from her face. "I have no shame when it comes to using whatever I've got to get you to change your mind." Abby caught her breath as Matt's cheek brushed hers, and he smiled. "Let's find your friend."

Abby changed her grip, towing Matt toward a table where Sarah sat, looking bored. She was game to join the party, especially when she recognized some people from her bike group. Claire rose to pull Abby into a hug, and the women were off, discussing kids from the program and a planned show of their work.

Matt reclined in his chair, smiling. Living in the same town for years had its advantages, and having many friendships wasn't the least of them. His eye lingered on the honey head leaning close to the ash. Being a destination town had its advantages too.

When his foot was nudged under the table, he glanced over at Charles, who was grinning. "Birthday taken an upswing?"

"Perhaps." Matt grinned back.

"Has Cupid perhaps…?" Charles mimed shooting a bow.

Matt snorted. "Hardly." He finished his drink and wiped his mouth with a napkin. "What is it with you and C? Trying to get rid of your third wheel?"

Charles leaned back in his chair. "Just want you to have the tiniest bit of the bliss I feel every day. And we need a fourth for tennis."

"That's deep." Matt laughed and studied the Claire's profile. "You guys are practically twins. Creepy matchmaker twins. I want no part of you."

The women had returned, and Claire rested her head on Charles's shoulder. "What are you two whispering about over here?"

Matt had a moment's discomfort, unsure what Charles would say. He breathed a sigh of relief when Charles replied. "Darts, my love. Would you ladies care for a match?"

As the provider of the night's festivities, he and his group were cheerfully allowed the next available board. Matt was careful to keep things friendly and respect the boundaries Abby had set, though he probably stood closer than was strictly necessary when he thought he was showing her how to play darts. To his chagrin, the women promptly handed them their asses. When Matt lost his third straight game, Sarah laughed, relaxing against her night's chosen companion and tossing down her fourth or fifth Imperial pint.

At the end of the night, Abby latched Sarah's seatbelt like she would a child's. She closed the passenger door and whooshed out a breath. Catching Matt's eye, she giggled. "I promise she's not always like this. She's taking this vacation from responsibility to heart this summer." She came around the car. "You'd think she would have learned her lesson a couple of weeks ago."

"What, with Tyler?" Matt asked. He laughed at Abby's surprised expression. "Pretty much everyone around here knows about that one. He's not quite a gentleman yet, so she's damn lucky his eighteenth birthday was at the end of last month, so he's legal."

Abby's eyes twinkled. "Can't wait to tell her that. She was hoping that he'd keep his mouth shut, and really hoping Jason was wrong about his age." She laughed. "Gotta love what alcohol does to the dignity." She turned to open the driver's door, and Matt put a hand on her arm.

"Hey." He smoothed his palm over her elbow and onto her upper arm. "I behaved tonight, didn't I?"

Abby smiled and nodded.

Matt's mouth opened and closed, and then he laughed.

"What?"

He leaned an elbow on the roof of the car, bringing his body into close proximity to hers without actually touching her. "I was going to ask you for a birthday kiss, but I just realized how stupid that sounded." He chuckled again.

"Matt…" she said uncertainly, her eyes dropping to his mouth and raising back to his eyes just as quickly.

"Am I the only one feeling like I'm in high school?" he mocked himself. He slid his hand to her neck, using his thumb to stroke her jaw. "I'm not sure I would be able to keep my 'behaving' promise anyway."

Abby inhaled deeply, looking at his mouth again. "You're not the problem."

He smiled. "Good. That's how I want it to be. So good night." He couldn't resist running his fingers down Abby's neck and over her arms again, just to feel her pulse flying at her neck and wrists. After a final squeeze, he stepped back.

"I still think you should change your mind about Jason," Matt tossed over his shoulder as he walked back toward the pub.

"So do I," Matt heard her say softly, and then the car door closed.

Chapter Six

"Okay, Sarah. It's safe to get out."

"Are you sure?" Sarah's voice from inside the car was muffled.

Abby looked up and down the street. "Yep. No sign of the hilariously smitten child. Now get out of the car." She snickered as Sarah peeked out of her window before dashing for the front of the hardware store.

The cool of the store's interior was a blessed relief. Abby stopped inside the doorway to let her eyes adjust to the dimmer light.

"You know, if you'd wear your sunglasses, you wouldn't have to do that." Sarah sighed, waiting for her friend to be ready to continue.

"I left them at Jason's yesterday," Abby said. She looked over Sarah's shoulder to test her vision. A chuckle burst out of her mouth a second before a hand rested on Sarah's shoulder.

"Hey!" Tyler's voice was full of delight. Abby noticed the apron emblazoned with the store's logo over his T-shirt and skinny jeans and smirked. She started to slide away, but Sarah grabbed her forearm. Tyler grinned. "You found me."

"I wasn't looking for you, Tyler." Sarah plastered on a smile for the girl behind the counter. "I'm just here to get some things I need." She towed Abby toward an aisle that held paint and painting supplies.

"Yeah. Like me." Tyler followed them into the aisle. "You need something fixed? I'm your man. Just tell me what and where, and I'm there."

A small clump of employees peeping into the aisle dispersed under Sarah's glare. She ignored Tyler and continued into the next aisle, her face darkening when he followed. She stopped at a selection of screwdrivers.

"Something at your house need to be screwed?" Tyler asked. There was a burst of laughter from the next aisle. Abby bit her lip to keep from joining in but gave Tyler a thumbs-up before Sarah turned around, her face crimson.

"That's it." She dug her nails into Abby's arm and grabbed Tyler's shirt with the other hand. "Outside. Now."

Tyler covered Sarah's hand with his own. "Both of us?" He grinned in delight.

Sarah snatched her hand back as if it had been scalded. "Outside." She followed Tyler as he led the way toward the rear of the store and presumably a back door. Glances from the other employees and local patrons tracked their progress, and Abby waved at a few she had come to know. Sarah slapped her hand. "Don't make a scene."

"Oh, the scene has already been made. I'm just not sure why I have to be involved," Abby whispered. She waved at the man who walked his dog past the house every afternoon while she and Sarah watched the eye-candy roll in. Of course, Abby wasn't supposed to be looking for anyone in particular to wade to shore, and it was a good thing, because she hadn't seen him in days.

Sarah shook her arm, bringing Abby back to the present. "You're my witness, so no one thinks I'm attacking him in an alley. Or you'll be a witness to his murder. I haven't decided which yet."

Tyler led them into a storage area and held an outer door open so they could pass him before he followed. As the door closed, he leaned against the side of the building, crossing his arms over his muscular chest and placing one skater-shoed foot against the salt-faded paint. "Now that you've got me alone—almost." He raised an eyebrow at Abby. "What's up?"

Sarah closed her eyes. "Tyler—"

"Ty," he corrected.

"Tyler, this has got to stop. Stop looking for me. Stop talking to people about that night." Sarah blushed, a new thing for her. "It was a huge and terrible mistake."

He took her hand and raised it to kiss the back. "I don't regret a thing."

Sarah yanked her hand away. "Stop that. And of course you don't regret anything. You're a stud, and I'm Mrs. Robinson."

His forehead wrinkled. "Who? I thought you weren't married."

Abby snorted laughter, and Sarah raised a warning hand at her. "That's it exactly, Tyler. You have no idea what I'm talking about. I mean that I'm the one being laughed at for seducing a child."

Tyler rolled his eyes and raised a finger. "Okay, first…if anyone was seducing anyone, it was me." He grinned. "I'm good like that. And second, I'm not a child. I'm eighteen."

Sarah shuddered when Tyler confirmed his age. "Yeah, and I'm thirty-seven. More than twice your age, buddy."

He traced the curves of her breasts with his eyes. She grabbed his chin and forced his face upward.

"Eyes are up here, Ty. I'm old enough to be your…mother." She blurted the word out with a sour expression.

Tyler turned his head to kiss her palm. "See, I knew I was getting to you. You called me Ty." As she jumped back, he opened the door. "I have to get back to work, but I'll drop by later and fix whatever you need fixed. Just give me your address."

"No way, Junior."

As he stepped in out of the summer heat, he called, "By the way, you don't remind me of my mother at all." He swept his eyes over Sarah and whistled softly. "She's forty." The door closed with a pneumatic whoosh.

Sarah tugged Abby toward the car. "Don't say a fucking word." She glared at Abby as they exited the alley.

"Change," Abby managed to squeak out before collapsing against the car, laughing so hard that she couldn't get her door open.

"I hate you," Sarah whined before starting to chuckle.

The ride back to the cottage was punctuated with sniggers. After parking the car, Sarah glared at the front screen door, for which they'd forgotten to get the repair materials, and headed for the back of the house. Pointing to the beach chairs, she ordered Abby to sit, and then she went into the house through the back door and returned with a bottle of Cuervo Gold.

Sarah spun off the cap. She took a deep swallow, shuddering as it went down. "I need this. What a nightmare."

Taking the bottle from Sarah's hand, Abby sipped before taking the cap and screwing it on tightly. She placed the bottle next to her chair. "Isn't this what caused the problem in the first place?"

"Yes, Mom," Sarah droned. She laid her head against the back of her chair. "How could I have been so stupid?"

"Not stupid. I thought he was older, too, in the wetsuit and dressed for the club. It's only when you see him riding a longboard in a Children of Bodom T-shirt that you get the real picture." Abby snickered.

"Change sucks," Sarah moaned, flinging an arm across her eyes.

"Oh, I don't know about that," a deep voice said from behind the chairs. "I kind of like the changes this summer." Jason leaned over the back of her chair and aimed a kiss at her lips. Just before it landed, she turned her face toward Sarah so the kiss landed on her cheek. Sarah quirked an eyebrow, but Abby ignored her.

Jason dropped to the sand by Abby's chair and grabbed the bottle of tequila. He opened it and swallowed a few mouthfuls, then looked at the label and grimaced. "I thought you mature ladies appreciated the finer things in life."

Abby ran her fingers over his hair. "I'll have you know that Cuervo was the gold standard in our day, sonny," she creaked out.

"Yeah, well, now the minimum acceptable standard is Patron. Get with the times." He wrapped his large hand around Abby's calf and ran it up to stroke the back of her thigh, just above her knee. Abby sat up a little straighter, and he had to move his hand down. He looked up at her, and she leaned forward to massage his shoulders. He exhaled, dropping his head forward so she could reach more of his neck.

Sarah snorted. "It all tastes like ass to me, but it gets the job done. Now, hand it over."

Jason held the bottle out toward Sarah without looking at her. Abby watched her take a gulp and then reached for the bottle. Sarah reluctantly handed it over, and Abby sipped before capping it again and setting it down. She stroked Jason's head.

"Now, that feels good," he said. "I'm exhausted. Who knew standing in one position all day could be so tiring? All I want to do is take a shower and go to bed, and it's not even dinnertime. And I still need to get my ride in for today."

Abby's hands paused, and she frowned. "That doesn't seem right. Why didn't Matt just have you pose for one day and get everything he needs in pictures for this rough work stage? It's normal to save the longer, personal sessions for the detail work."

"Hell if I know. He's the boss, and I do like the pay. The bennies suck, though." Jason scowled. "I'm too tired to spend the kind of time I'd like to spend with you. Instead I have to spend time with the biggest airhead in California."

She chuckled and started playing with his hair again. "Your posing partner?"

"Partner, my ass. She's more interested in getting into Matt's pants than anything. She's constantly shoving her tits in any direction he happens to be facing, whether it's how he's posed us or not. He has to reposition us, and everything takes twice as long as it should. And when she talks…" He shuddered. "Nothing but innuendo, celebrity gossip, and idiocy. She *is* hot, but I don't know how he's stood using her as a model more than once." He took two more swigs from the bottle and capped it again. "Hot-but-stupid doesn't do anything for me."

Sarah snorted. "Why aren't there more like you? Hot-but-stupid seems to be a requirement for most men our age."

Jason grinned at her. "Tyler doesn't seem to mind your brains."

She tossed a handful of sand at him. "Shut up. I'm an idiot. But I think that problem might be solved. I had a talk with him, and I don't think we'll see him around here."

Abby chuckled. "Yeah, until his day off from the hardware store."

They laughed as Sarah deflated in her chair. Nudging Jason with her foot, Abby asked, "What do you know about fixing screen doors?"

"Not a damned thing." He kissed her knee. "Give me a bike, and we're in business, but home repairs are beyond me. Ever think of hiring a handyman? That's what I'd do." He turned to kneel on the sand next to her. "Speaking of days off and bikes…come for a ride with me tomorrow?"

She shifted in her chair, torn between expressing what she really thought and reluctance to dim the hope that showed in his eyes and his smile. "Well…I don't have a bike, and all of yours would be way too big for me."

"You can borrow mine." Sarah ignored her friend's death glare. "Abby is a bit timid on a bike. Can you handle that?"

"I can handle anything," Jason said. He rested his forehead on Abby's. "Please?"

She hesitated; the night before had been the first time they'd spent together since he'd returned from his race, though they'd been together often before he left. Nothing had changed—he was still smart and funny, irreverent, beautiful, and a nice kisser. Of course, thinking about kisses was just distracting her from deciding what to do, because Jason wasn't the one on her mind.

"I have to work with the kids in the morning. Color palettes," she hedged.

"I should do a training ride in the morning anyway—I suppose you'd like to skip that?" Abby nodded. "Then that's perfect!" Jason beamed.

Screw it. Change.

"Sure," Abby said, trying to be positive. "Anywhere in particular?"

Jason sat back on his heels and grinned. "Somewhere good for a picnic? Chelsie can help me get some things together tonight. She's good with stuff like that. How about you meet me at the studio a little after one? It's on my way back and in a good spot to head out from. It will give us a little longer if I don't have to ride through town and back out again."

Abby couldn't argue with his logic, but she felt a twist of anxiety at the thought of seeing Matt again. She had only seen him once since his birthday party the week before, when he ran past the house just as she was stepping in the back door after her walk. He'd smiled and waved but kept running up the beach. It wasn't until he turned a slight curve and disappeared that she realized she'd been watching him.

"Abby? What do you think?" Jason touched her arm, and she nodded. He tried to talk her into returning home with him and visiting with Chelsie until he was back from his ride, but she pled weariness and an obligation to cook dinner on "her night." Sarah shot her a quizzical look, but Abby ignored her again, walking Jason out to where his bike rested against the porch.

The screen door was hanging by a single hinge again. "I went to the front door first." Jason looked sheepish. "I'm glad to know it was already broken. I thought I did it. I would have told you anyway, I swear, and paid to have it fixed."

Abby snapped her fingers. "Damn. Missed our chance." Jason laughed and folded her into his arms, kissing her forehead before tilting her face up. Her hands rested on his hips, holding him away, and she felt no urge to slide them around his back even as she enjoyed the feeling of his mouth on hers.

A beep from the road caught her attention, and she looked up to see a familiar hand waving out the window of a faded Jeep, surfboard on top. She craned her head as it passed, catching a glimpse of Ray-Bans and a smile.

At that moment, a mid-sized Toyota pickup pulled smoothly to the curb. Chelsie dropped to the ground from the driver's seat, smiling at both Jason and Abby.

"I thought I might find you here," she said, crossing in front of the car and looping her arm through Jason's. "As your manager, I need to remind you that you have another race in a few days and you should be on a training ride right now." Chelsie studied his eyes, and Abby stepped aside with guilty relief. "As your friend, I have to advise you to get some sleep." She sighed. "After your ride. We need the sponsor money if you're going to keep doing this, so you need to place high."

"You worry too much, slave driver. Let me toss my bike in the back of the truck. I need to change into my gear." Jason lifted her off her feet.

Chelsie pushed at his chest. "Let me down, you ass," she grumbled, but he walked toward the truck.

Looking back over his shoulder, he flashed his dimples at Abby again. "Tomorrow, right? Don't forget."

Nodding, she pushed his bicycle to him so he could put it in the bed. "Sure you won't come over later?" he asked in a low voice, stroking the back of Abby's hand with his thumb.

She pecked his cheek. "Positive. You need your rest. I'll see you tomorrow."

With a deep sigh, Jason folded himself into the cab of the truck and shut the door, beeping as he drove away.

Maneuvering past the hanging door and trying to tug it back into place as she passed, Abby entered the house through the front door to find Sarah lounging in her chair and flipping through a magazine. She set it aside as Abby closed the door. Lacing her fingers over her chest, she stared. Abby shook her head and went into the kitchen for a bottle of water. Returning and dropping onto her chair, she spun the top off and took a swallow before looking at Sarah again. Sarah smiled thinly. "Spill," she demanded.

"What?" Abby asked, raising the bottle to her lips again and sipping.

"'Tired,' Abby? Really? I seem to remember that you didn't get up until noon today, and the most strenuous thing you did was get dragged around a hardware store for a few minutes."

"I was up late last night, finishing a book. And I hauled a bratty six-year-old to her mother's car."

Sarah blew a raspberry. "So what? You stay up all night reading or writing grants for your museum all the time and walk the hell out of me the next day. And how about that 'my night to cook'? When did we institute that little gem? I seem to remember that dinner lately has consisted of salad and whatever cold thing we could scrounge up because it's so freakin' hot outside."

Abby shrugged.

"Trouble in paradise? 'Cause otherwise I can see no reason that you wouldn't be hittin' that hard and often, woman. No commitments, no drama, no baggage, just twenty-four seven lovin'."

Abby rubbed her palms on her legs. "I don't know. I like Jason, and he's a great guy. Funny, smart, great kisser…but it's not there, you know? Is there something wrong with wanting…more?"

"If you can say he's a great kisser, he obviously doesn't repulse you. Or are we on that 'perfect man' thing again?" They crossed themselves without thinking. "Enjoy what you have today, because we're going home sooner than you think." She thought for a minute and then giggled. "This wouldn't have anything to do with the birthday boy, would it? He looks at you like you're a cupcake and he'd like to take a bite."

"Be serious," Abby said. "I haven't seen Matt since that night, except in passing. I barely know him. And remember, I don't want a man at all." She rose from her seat and headed for the kitchen. "Since I did say that I'd cook, how about some Ahi and rice with our salads?"

With the subject changed, Sarah set about deciding on a wine while Abby made dinner. They spent the evening settled into their outside chairs while they watched the sunset and discussed their jobs; Abby's behavior with Jason was forgotten.

Or so she thought — until they were heading up the stairs to bed. Sarah turned in her doorway and leveled a glance at her friend. "Abby, seriously…don't be hasty in writing Jason off. He's a nice guy, way good-looking, and he's into you. This is just a summer fling — it doesn't have to be a luuuuve connection."

Abby looked askance; casual hookups weren't exactly her personal style. But then again, "her style" had stuck her with Eric for two years.

Sarah seemed to read Abby's mind, and she grinned. "Change is good, baby."

"I thought you said 'change sucks'?"

"Change sucks for me. Because I'm an idiot. It works for you." Sarah looked Abby over in satisfaction. "I haven't seen you this relaxed in years. Must be all those strenuous workouts with the stud?" She looked at Abby hopefully.

"Good night," Abby said, waving in Sarah's disappointed face as she closed her door.

The next day was a comedy of errors. Abby woke up late after a restless night and ended up rushing to the park to help Claire. Responding to her distraction, the kids seemed more interested in eating the tempera paint than creating masterpieces, leading to a personal panic and a call to Poison Control. To top off the day, all the anxiety upset little Michael Jacobs, and he spewed electric blue paint down Abby's front. And she still had to face a damn bike ride with a damn guy she couldn't figure out how to shake.

Cursing art, Jason, and whatever insane urge she'd ever had to work with children, Abby stomped up the walk, recklessly tearing the front door off its tenuous grip of the top hinge. She woke Sarah from a catnap, ordering her to make coffee. After a shower, she shimmied into Sarah's spare pair of bike shorts and her own sports bra. Yanking a pink moisture-wicking T-shirt over her head, Abby smoothed it down and French-braided her hair so Sarah could adjust the fit of her helmet. All outfitted, Abby stood in front of the bathroom mirror and looked at herself, noticing that her eyes were wide and her cheeks flushed.

Sarah placed her folded hands on Abby's shoulder and rested her chin on them. "Someone is nervous already. I wonder who she's more excited to see." There was a glint of devilish humor in Sarah's eyes.

"Someone looks like an incredible dork with this thing on her head and is wondering whether she's fated to die from embarrassment or exhaustion first today." Abby shook off Sarah's hands and headed out the door. She set off across town at a leisurely pace, determined to arrive at the studio after Jason.

After almost spilling at a traffic light when she forgot how to get her foot off the pedal, two near sideswipes by gawking tourists in cars, and a chorus of wolf-whistles from Tyler and his boys as they whooshed past her on their long boards, hair flying back and beanies pulled low, Abby glided to a stop in front of a low bungalow on a corner lot. She checked the address that Jason had given her, but even without verification, she was certain this was the right place. Each house she'd passed had its own character, but this was an abode realized in its surroundings. The Craftsman-style cottage seemed to grow right from the earth; it and the plants growing in the yard and up the lattice at the sides of the deep porch complimented each other perfectly. Different shades of green and silvery plants were layered and drew the eye toward the faded, sea-green paint and soft redwood hues of the house itself. The look was pure art.

Jason had said that he'd meet her around the side, by the street entrance to Matt's studio, so Abby wheeled her bike in that direction, hoping he'd be waiting with a smile.

No luck, but she did hear loud music. Catching a snatch of a memorable bass line, Abby tried to identify the song. With a chuckle, she realized that she recognized it from either junior high or high school. Checking the door, she found it unlocked. She pulled it open just enough to slip through and found herself in a small foyer with a desk and a few chairs. Curious, she peeked through an inner doorway and into the studio itself.

Despite the popular conception of artists as crazy, messy people with a tendency to fly from one thing to another as inspiration struck, Abby had known enough artists to not be surprised by the clean, organized space. Tall cabinets lined two walls, and worktables were set in several spots. One corner held a host of screens and photographic lights and equipment, while another had a revolving table holding something, presumably a sculpture, covered by a cloth. Everything was lit by overhanging fixtures.

Abby's eye stopped on the figure in the center of the room.

Matt was a picture of concentration as he circled a nearly finished sculpture. Though the two-foot terra-cotta statue was set on a low, revolving table and a stool sat nearby, he moved around the piece himself. He held a carving tool in his hand, and he flipped it between his fingers absently as he studied his work, often referring to photographs tacked on a wheeled, chest-high corkboard. He squatted, well-muscled thighs and calves flexing as he balanced on the balls of his bare feet and shaved a tiny amount of clay from a couple of spots before referring to his pictures again. He stood and hooked the stool with his foot to pull it closer. Balancing on the edge of the seat, Matt made minute adjustments to the statue's shoulder, his own shoulder and arm muscles shifting and bunching under his worn T-shirt. Smoothing the spot he'd carved with delicate fingers, he stood again, wiping clay residue on the front of his shirt. He moved to his left, giving Abby a perfect view of his profile, and stood motion-less, only his eyes moving between his work and the pictures on the corkboard. With a satisfied chuckle, he dropped the carving tool on the table. He stripped off his shirt and wiped his fingers carefully on the cloth in his hand.

Abby had managed to stand quietly while he worked, unable to tear her eyes from the graceful movement of his body and hands. His hair was clay-flecked from his habit of pushing a hand through the strands as he considered his sculpture. The analytical side of her mind admired his careful work, his economical motions. A deeper, more instinctive side simply admired the man, from the tiny frown lines on his forehead as he concentrated down his body to his single article of clothing, a pair of faded cargo shorts that rode low on narrow hips.

She must have made some sound, though it was hard to believe he could hear anything over the pounding bass line, because his head turned toward her, and he studied her as well. He traced her shape from shoulders to feet, lingering at hip and breast and hands and throat, until his eyes met hers with an intensity that sent her pulse flying. Abby could sense how those hands would feel against her skin, and her breathing became shallow, sure in that instant that he was thinking the same thing.

Matt blinked, lashes brushing his cheeks for an instant before he smiled and sent whatever was going on between them underground. "Hey." Abby read his lips and pointed to her ears, shaking her head. Matt grinned. He crossed to a small desk and turned the volume down.

He walked back toward Abby, still holding his shirt. She forced herself to stop staring, remembering that she was there for Jason. Not willing to meet Matt's eyes quite yet, she nodded toward the stereo that sat on a low shelf beside his desk. "Smithereens, Matt? Really?"

He rested against his stool and motioned Abby closer. "It's my studio, my music, even if it does date me." The song playing changed to a grunge classic, and they both laughed. "At least Jason doesn't complain about this one," Matt said. "Apparently Soundgarden is still acceptable, though he calls it oldies." They both winced.

As the laugher died down, Abby found herself falling into Matt's eyes again. He stood up, startling her. "I could use water," he said, heading toward a small refrigerator near the desk. He looked back over his shoulder as he opened the door. "How about you?"

Though Abby's mouth was desert-dry, she shook her head, afraid that the slight tremor in her hands would be revealed by water sloshing around in a bottle. She turned to his sculpture. "Is this the finished piece?"

Matt laughed, stopping where he was standing in the rear of the studio and opening his bottle. "Hardly. The client wants poolside statues. That's just a mock-up."

"Damned detailed for a mock-up. What medium for the finished sculpture?"

He shrugged. "Bambi hasn't decided. I'm pushing for terra-cotta, like that one."

Abby raised an eyebrow. "Bambi?"

He grinned, and she looked at the statue again.

"Marble would be traditional for this style."

"True, but terra-cotta is easier and will stand up to the salt air around here better. Personally, I'd like to see it in granite, but I won't suggest that. Takes too long to work."

Abby had visions of Matt's upper body working as he wielded hammer and chisel on stone. "What's your time frame?"

"Three complete sculptures by mid-September."

She spun to look at him. "Are you crazy? No one does that. You'll kill yourself. No wonder you want the terra."

Matt smiled and took another sip. "Right. So, what do you think?"

Walking around the model, Abby studied it from every angle. From the corner of her eye, she could see Matt watching her. The motion of his throat as he swallowed was almost as distracting as his bare chest, but Abby dragged her mind out of the gutter and back to the statue in front of her. "You've captured Jason well, Matt. You're good."

"So I've heard. I'm working from photographs as well as live modeling," he said as Abby returned to the front of the statue. "The client hasn't decided if she wants full nudes or not, so I haven't had Jason or Zoe in nude poses yet. Some of that is guesswork."

Abby's gaze went immediately to the sculpture's groin, and Matt laughed. Raising his bottle to his lips, he said, "Maybe you can tell me how far off I am." He smiled slyly before drinking.

"Funny man. Fishing?"

"Maybe." He put his bottle down and leaned back on one hand, scratching the back of his neck with the other before gently placing it on the cloth-covered item beside him on the worktable. His fingers moved restlessly, shifting the cloth, and Abby could see what looked like the base of a roughed-in sculpture. Matt caught her gaze and edged the cover down again. He flushed and said, "Hell. Yeah, I'm fishing."

"You should know that a lady doesn't kiss and tell," Abby joked. She walked toward him.

Matt took her hand, drawing her forward until her legs were almost touching his knees. "I've seen the kissing," he said. "I'm wondering about what comes afterward." His eyes were intense as he traced the lines of her face.

She turned her face back toward the statue, pretending to study it as she denied a wild urge to smooth her hands over Matt's shoulders. "Hmm. Well, to the best of my incomplete knowledge, your sculpture seems to be correct," she said.

"Incomplete is good," Matt said, tugging Abby's arm so she looked at him once again. "So my guesswork…"

"Would be guesswork for me as well," Abby finished, flushing as the corner of his mouth lifted in a smile. She chuckled and stepped back, giving herself some much needed distance from his body. "Though I'm sure I'll have a better idea in a few minutes. Bike shorts don't leave much to the imagination." *And neither do wetsuits or wet board shorts,* her brain teased, flashing images of Matt walking out of the surf.

"No, they surely do not," Matt said softly. A gentle finger traced the curve of her Lycra-encased hip. His eyes met hers, and he dropped his hand, clearing his throat. "I take it you're having a day out with the man himself?"

"Yep. He asked me yesterday, and I didn't see any way out of it. I haven't seen much of him since he got back from Indiana, so…"

"Sorry about that. I'm probably wearing him out."

"On purpose?" Abby teased. Her heart stuttered when Matt cocked his head and answered.

"Maybe." He grinned at what Abby knew had to have been a stunned stupid look on her face, and then he asked about Sarah.

Abby answered him in a shaky voice that grew stronger as she explained the situation with Tyler. By the time Jason walked in, they were leaning next to each other against a low table, cracking up at Sarah's dilemma.

Jason's eyes went from one to the other, wary, though a smile crept across his face when Abby explained what she and Matt were laughing about.

Walking over to the table, Jason helped her to her feet and dipped his head to drop a firm kiss on her mouth. She glanced toward Matt and found him regarding her, a smile on his face though a muscle jumped at the side of his jaw. "Sorry I'm late," Jason said, wrapping his arm around Abby's waist. "I had a flat, and it took a while to fix it. Ready?"

She nodded, avoiding Matt's eyes, and headed for the door. After a second, she realized that Jason wasn't behind her, so she turned to see the men having a low-voiced conversation. Tension showed in the set of Jason's shoulders, but Matt was relaxed. He glanced at her and smiled. Jason turned his head and smiled too, though it was tight. He walked toward Abby, enveloping her hand in one of his as he pulled her sunglasses out of a pocket of his jersey and handed them to her.

"You left these at my apartment the other night," he said, louder than necessary. "You'll need them today." He stepped out of the studio and into the vestibule ahead of Abby; she turned to wave at Matt uncertainly. He offered a mock salute back.

Jason was quiet as they started their ride, but he gradually returned to his normal, voluble self, breaking a cardinal rule of biking by riding alongside Abby instead of in a pace line and pointing out interesting or unusual things along the way. His natural enthusiasm carried the conversation even when she was quiet. Chelsie's picnic, packed in panniers on Jason's bike, proved to be delicious, and they ate fruit, crackers, and salami in a small beach cove, washing it all down with a split of Gewürztraminer and bottles of water.

When the last dark chocolate was finished, Jason packed away the lunch remains, and they headed home, moving more slowly and talking less than on the trip out. At his apartment, he got off his bike and crossed to Abby as she straddled her own bike with feet on the ground. He unclipped her helmet with one hand, tossing it to the side as he cupped the back of her head in his other broad palm, pulling her face to his for a lingering kiss. He explored her mouth thoroughly and well, his hands roaming over her back and resting against her bum as he tried to get closer.

"Stay," he murmured. "I want you right now."

Abby rested her hands on his chest. "Chelsie—"

"—will understand and go to a movie," he finished. Abby felt him smile against her skin as he kissed her jaw. "It's how we work."

"Jason." Abby grasped his wrists and held his hands still. "It's not how *I* work. I don't catch quickies while the roommate is out." She smiled at him, trying to lighten the sudden tension. "Hazard of dating an older woman, I'm afraid. I outgrew relishing that kind of thing a while ago."

Jason chuckled. "Message received. Can we try this again when there's time to enjoy?"

Abby felt guilty; the possibility of an audience wasn't the only reason she was going home. "When do you leave again?"

"Day after tomorrow. New York, this time, I think. Chelsie keeps track of that stuff. Don't suppose you'd like to come?"

She shook her head. "Can't afford the trip, not on two days' notice. I have the tiny artist crew too." His face fell, and Abby rubbed his arm. "Tell you what. How about we have a victory party on the beach behind my house after you get back? Beer, food, music."

The smile returned to his eyes, and he swept Abby's helmet off the ground, put it back on her head, and buckled it before starting for his own bike.

"Hey, you don't have to do that," she said. "You've been on the damned thing all day. Give your seat a rest. I can make it home all right by myself."

"Are you sure?" he asked, relief evident.

"I was riding a bike before you were born, sonny," she joked. Jason chuckled and picked his bike up, resting the top bar on his shoulder. "It's not even dark."

"Call me when you get home, so I won't worry?" he asked, walking backward toward his door.

Grinning and nodding, Abby clicked one shoe into its pedal and started down the road with a wave before setting the other shoe in place. The ride home was relaxing, and she started to understand the high Sarah and Jason seemed to get from riding.

The sight of a faded Jeep at the curb in front of her house made her wobble and nearly tip over. Finally remembering how to get her foot off the pedal, she caught herself and extracted her other foot, pushing the bike up the driveway as she listened to the sound of a drill.

Matt put a final screw into the shiny new brass hinge of the front screen door and turned the drill off, smoothing his hand over the fresh redwood into which it was now firmly anchored.

"Hey, Handy Manny, what's up?" Abby called from the foot of the stairs. Matt smiled down at her, his eyes narrowing as the lines around them deepened.

"You said this needed fixed, and I had a free afternoon." Matt descended to stand in front of Abby. "Your wood was rotting, so I replaced the jamb and reattached the screen. No biggie." He'd put on a shirt since she'd seen him last, though it was only half-buttoned. The urge to straighten the placket and maybe brush his skin was strong.

Matt sat on the bottom step. "Have fun today?"

Unbuckling her helmet, Abby set it beside her as she sat next to Matt, their shoulders brushing. "The view was nice. I could do without the brain bucket and the funny shoes." She yanked them off and glared at them before dropping them beside the helmet.

Matt took one of her hands, sweeping his thumb back and forth across her knuckles. "I have an idea," he said. "I have to work with—what did you call her? Biker Barbie?" He snorted laughter, and Abby joined in. "I have to work with Zoe tomorrow, but how about you come surfing with me the next day? No helmets, no shoes…" Abby hesitated. "Come on, Pretty. You let Jason demonstrate his sport. Let me show you mine." They both laughed at Matt's unintended innuendo, and he squeezed her hand. "What do you say?"

Rising to her feet, she tugged Matt until he stood too. It was time to fish or cut bait, as her dad would have said.

"I say okay. What do you say to dinner?"

Matt grinned and followed her into the house.

Chapter Seven

Sliding into the driver's seat, Matt smiled again as a denser darkness appeared in the shadowed porch. Though the evening couldn't have been less like his normal routine, it had felt comfortable to spend time with Abby and Sarah. He waved, and Abby waved back. Driving away this time was far more satisfying than it had been a day before, when he'd almost hit a parked car while watching Jason pull Pretty into his arms. Who could blame Matt for tooting the Jeep's horn? Their PDA was a hazard to unsuspecting drivers.

He hurried into his house a few minutes later, eager to transfer his latest impressions of Abby to the raw clay that lay under a damp cloth in the studio. The sculpture's left arm, upraised to hold her mass of hair atop her head, was essentially finished, though Matt made a few refinements based on the way Abby had brushed her hair off her neck at dinner. Her right arm, reaching out before her, was just emerging from the clay. He used his mental picture of Abby's arm as she pulled the refrigerator door open as a guide, and soon lost himself in his work. He ended up dropping into bed just as the sun was rising, and he didn't move until Chris knocked on his door to let him know Zoe was in the studio and already stripped down.

Matt sat up, scratching his head with both hands and trying to remember if he'd covered the statue of Pretty before he'd left the studio. The momentary conviction that he hadn't drove him out of bed and into a pair of shorts and a T-shirt.

Zoe quirked an eyebrow and looked up as he rushed into the room. "Did you miss me that much?"

He ignored the question. After a check of the covered statue, Matt set up the screens he needed and got his camera in order. Zoe was her normal vapid self, and he found himself gritting his teeth as the day dragged on.

"All right…just a couple more shots. Don't move." He adjusted the lens.

Zoe deliberately took a deep breath, swelling her already impressive chest and putting the shot off again. Matt closed his eyes and counted to ten before dropping the camera to his side. Zoe laughed. "What? Everyone has to breathe."

"Zoe, do you want this job?"

Her eyes snapped with a burst of outrage. "No, Matt. I'm standing here bucky-assed naked and in a fucking awkward position because I don't want this job. Don't be an ass."

"Then don't move." He snapped a shot, admiring the flow of her hair toward the floor as she arched backward.

Zoe huffed, but she stayed as Matt had positioned her for once. "So, where's tall, dimpled, and studly today?" she asked. "This was a hell of a lot easier with him holding me up."

"Race. He'll be back in a couple of days." Matt adjusted the curve of her arm, and then took another picture. "If I can see you without Jason in the way, we can skip an extended session later." Pictures weren't his preferred method of dealing with detail in an almost finished human sculpture, but he'd had it with the both of them. Between Zoe's blatant flirting and Jason's…existing…Matt was on a knife's edge of tension most days.

Zoe eyed Matt and started to turn toward him. "Damn it, Zoe!" he snapped, pushing her none too gently into the right position.

A slow smile spread across her face, and he cursed under his breath, realizing that getting a rise out of him had been her goal. "What are you gonna do, Mattie? Fire me like you did Tyler?" Her brain seemed to shift into another gear. "And what is up with him and that old woman? He's following her around like a puppy."

Matt grunted noncommittally and moved in for the last shot, aiming at the sweep of her thigh as her foot rested on a chair. The finished statue would have her leg wrapped around Jason's thigh, but this was close enough. "What does Tyler see in her bony ass? Tiny tits would be a deal breaker for most guys I know." She ran her hands over her breasts fondly as Matt carried the camera to a table and started shutting off the lights. Zoe lowered her foot and closed the gap between them.

Matt ignored her, stepping to the side to shut off another light and then looking down at his notes to see for how many more days he would have to endure her. "Sarah is a nice woman," he said, grinning as he remembered how entertaining she had been at dinner the night before. Every story about Abby had been one more thing to add to his scanty store of information.

"Since when are you on a first name basis with the tourists?" When Matt didn't answer right away, Zoe finished buttoning her top and yanked on a pair of cut-offs. "I suppose you were playing patty-cake with her friend too, huh?" She snorted and took a brush out of her bag and attacked her hair. "At least she has some kind of a figure."

Thinking of Abby's shape took Matt's mind to the corner of the room where the clandestine statue stood. He'd given up even pretending to himself that it was merely an exercise to relax him from the stress of working faster on a sculpture than he had ever worked before. The Pretty sculpture was his favorite project in a very long time, and Matt couldn't imagine leaving it unfinished. He'd worked diligently to get the hair and arms correct, the hips were perfect, and he had the legs roughed in. He hoped the surfing lesson would fill in some blanks when it came to her upper body and thighs.

He forgot Zoe was still standing there until she tapped him on the chest. She stood with a hand on her hip, glaring. "What the hell's up with you, Matt? You're grinning like a goob, and you haven't heard a word I've been saying, have you?"

"Guilty as charged. I have a lot on my mind." He consulted his calendar. "I won't need you again for quite a while, I don't think. I'll call you."

"If I'm available," she said with a snort, stalking to the vestibule. The outer door slammed.

Chris peeked into the studio. "Did I hear Madam Tata's dulcet tones?"

"Yeah. Lord, I wish I hadn't used her for the test shots. The buyer's husband has become attached. Otherwise I'd find someone else tomorrow."

Chris looked around the studio. "Speaking of tomorrow, are you interested in running over to Monterey? I feel like a day off from the boardwalk."

"I'll bet." Matt grinned. "Exhausting work, guessing people's deepest secrets." He finished shutting down the equipment. He expected a joking comeback, and when it didn't come he glanced at Chris. He was gazing at the floor, a tiny frown between his eyebrows.

"What?" Matt asked.

Chris sank down on a kitchen chair. "There was this girl, you know? Yesterday?" Matt nodded. "She was the saddest person I've ever met. I almost didn't have to guess at anything, because her eyes told the whole story." Chris let out a huge breath of air and scratched at his head with both hands. "I have to admit, it threw me a little. This fortune-telling thing is usually just a laugh. People tell so much with their faces that I don't feel guilty for taking their money so they can hear it out loud, but I need a break. So, you up for it?"

Matt shook his head. "Sorry, I have plans. Teaching a nice lady how to surf."

Chris stretched out his legs and crossed his arms over his bare chest, leaning against the wall. "That nice lady wouldn't be named Abby, would she?" Matt nodded, and Chris laughed. "Teaching, my ass. Showing off is what you mean, cuz. Isn't she dating Jason The Tank?" Chris tsk-tsked. "Shame on you."

"Purely platonic," Matt said. "She's interested, and what kind of representative of our sport would I be if I didn't give her a chance to try it herself?"

"A living representative, 'cause Jason is going to pound you when he hears about this."

"Don't be ridiculous. It's surfing, not sex. Everyone will be fully clothed the entire time."

Chris stood up. "Riiight. If you call bathing suits or wetsuits fully clothed." He smirked. "Don't even try to tell me that you wouldn't hit that if you'd gotten there first, because I hate calling a family member a liar. I saw the way you guys were circling each other at your party. I'll find somewhere else to sleep tomorrow night."

"No need." Matt put his glass in the sink and opened the refrigerator, hoping something would jump out at him as a dinner choice. "Even if you were right, and I'm definitely not saying that you are,

I told you that I don't bring drama home. My Fortress of Solitude remains inviolate—that's a personal rule."

Chris shook his head in disbelief. "You're a stronger man than I am. I likes my comfort, and you never know what kind of crappy-ass bed you're gonna find in someone else's house. Plus, you have to get up and get dressed right when you're most comfortable. If you want them to leave your house, you just snore really loud and that usually does it. Or play sleep coma." He pointed out some fish on the bottom shelf.

When dinner was over, Chris slipped off to his room, leaving his cousin to stretch out on the couch with a beer. Though it was Matt's norm, the silence that night seemed oppressive. Grabbing the remote, he put on some music and leaned his head against the back of the couch. With his eyes closed, he replayed the moment when he'd cupped Abby's warm hip in his hand as he was leaving. He recalled the feeling of her fingers on his back when he'd pecked her cheek. Pleasantly occupied, he eventually dropped off, only blearily stagger-ing into his room when Chris shook him and told him to go to bed.

A tap at his bedroom door as the first rays of light peeked around his blinds interrupted the lingering sound of Dream Abby's tiny gasp when Dream Matt traced the lower curve of her breast with his thumb. Damn if that didn't make it difficult to contemplate leaving bed right then.

"You awake?" Chris asked as he poked his head in the door. "I checked Surfline, and you'll want to take Miss Abby out early this morning. The swells are supposed to get wicked this afternoon." He paused. "Where you taking her? Capitola or Cowell's?" Chris named two of the local beaches known for being beginner-friendly.

Matt rubbed his hand over his face, feeling the roughness of stubble and wondering if he should bother shaving. Wondering what Abby liked. "Cowell's, most likely. It's close, and it shouldn't be too bad on a weekday."

"And close enough to Steamer Lane that you can get in a good ride when she gets tired." Chris grinned.

"That, too," Matt admitted, swinging his legs over the side of the bed and snagging a pair of shorts with his big toe. Chris looked away as Matt stood and pulled them up, letting them hang loose on his hips.

"Underwear, man," he said as he looked back around. "You could at least wear underwear."

"Can't sleep in clothes," Matt answered, mentally running over what he had to get done before he picked up Abby. Deciding to forgo the razor, he changed into board shorts and a T-shirt. He crammed a wetsuit and towels into a bag before loading that and a couple of surfboards into his Jeep.

Chris toted a cooler down to the car, saying nothing even as he smiled at Matt's impatience to get going. "See you tomorrow!" he yelled as Matt drove off.

"Tonight!" Matt shouted back, waving.

Abby answered the door immediately, gesturing for Matt to come in. "Coffee?" she asked, and he nodded, following her into the kitchen. She poured another mug, offering cream and sugar, before settling against the counter. They sipped for a minute before he thought to ask about Sarah.

"Biking with another kiddie," Abby said. "Apparently she hasn't learned her lesson about younger men."

"I've heard they're pretty irresistible," Matt said, sipping his coffee and raising an eyebrow.

"I wouldn't say that." Abby yawned and shook her head. "Sorry. I was up late last night with Jason. He left this morning for New York." She dropped her eyes to her cup. "We had some things to talk about."

"Hmm." Matt said noncommittally.

"Listen…" Abby fiddled with her spoon. "What were you talking about with Jason the other day?" She looked at him intently.

Matt wondered if the truth was what she really wanted. "He wanted to know if I was planning on moving in on you."

"Are you?"

Matt brushed the side of her free hand, from palm to the tip of her pinky, with his finger. "Not while you're dating Jason. I don't poach either."

Abby nodded, but her small finger wrapped around Matt's, anchoring his hand with hers. "What if I wasn't seeing Jason?"

Smiling, Matt stepped forward until he could rest his free hand on the side of Abby's neck, where it curved into her shoulder. "That, Pretty…that would be a very different story." He ran his hand down her arm, squeezing her fingers before he stepped back. "Ready to go?"

"Uh…yeah," Abby answered, shaking her head and smiling.

"What?" Matt asked.

She grinned again. "Never mind." For a minute, he thought she had changed her mind about going along, but she nodded. "I don't have a wetsuit," she warned.

"Don't need one. A bathing suit is fine. I won't take you out to the really cold water, I promise."

"Baby-pool surfing," she joked, and Matt chuckled and nodded. Abby took a deep breath and let it out in a gust. "Sounds like fun. A nice change after the brain bucket and those damned lock-in shoes. Shall we?" She scooped up a bag that Matt hadn't noticed at first and headed out the door, waiting for his exit before she closed and locked it.

They were walking down the stairs at Cowell's beach within minutes, talking easily about their differing beach experiences on each coast. Matt was surprised to hear that she wasn't entirely unfamiliar with surfing, having seen it done during visits to her grandmother's house on the Washington coast. She had also done some research in the last day and asked a thousand questions about the differences between various beaches, shortboards and longboards, tides, and marine life. Matt finally covered her mouth, laughing, and asked if she ever wanted to try it.

Abby flushed. "Sorry. Endlessly curious here. Plus, I'm a little nervous."

"Don't be." He stripped off his shirt and started applying sunscreen to his shoulders, tossing Abby the bottle when he had a handful of lotion. "You're with a pro. I wouldn't hurt you."

Abby almost missed the bottle. "Thanks," she said, pulling her own T-shirt off and revealing a deep plum bikini top that accented the paleness of her skin. She rubbed lotion onto her arms and legs. Matt eyed the curve of breast that Dream Matt had traced with his thumb, wondering how it would feel when he was awake.

Abby tossed the bottle back to him. "Can you get my back?" she asked, turning and presenting it to him.

He studied the sweep of skin before him, entirely exposed aside from a narrow strip that was covered by the top's band. Hell, yes, he could. Squirting the lotion into his hand, Matt smoothed it over her shoulders, stroking downward to coat her shoulder blades, feathering the lotion onto her sides.

Abby arched forward, chuckling breathlessly. "Sorry. Cold," she murmured, drawing a breath as the tips of Matt's fingers brushed the outer curve of her breast.

Checking his own internal temperature, Matt acknowledged that "cold" was nowhere near accurate.

Resisting the impulse to let his fingers linger at the low waistband of her swimsuit bottom, he finished and stepped back. "Done."

"Thanks." Abby crouched and pulled a white, long-sleeved T-shirt out of her bag. She tugged it over her head, covering the body he had been trying to impress into his mind so he could take it home to his unfinished statue. "Extra protection. I hate burning, and I nearly always do," she confessed, tugging at the lower hem of her shirt.

"No problem." Matt looked out over the ocean, judging that the biggest morning swells should be about over. "Ready?" Abby nodded, and Matt went into teacher mode. Starting with the basics, she practiced stances with the board on the sand. Matt stood behind her, holding her hips and demonstrating how she should move. Eventually, she practiced on her own before moving to the water. Matt took his time, explaining things thoroughly. He both wanted her first surf to be a pleasant experience and wished for the day to last.

Her first ride on a small swell ended in a wipeout a few yards from the beach, but Abby came up laughing and shrieking in triumph. She immediately paddled back out to try again and again until she could ride her board almost to the beach before leaping into the water. Each time, Matt followed her back out, straddling his board as she mirrored that position while they waited for the next wave to come in. After several rides, they went out once again and sat quietly, watching the next wave build.

"How long have you been doing this, Matt?" Abby asked.

"Mmm…I think I was seven or eight the first time, so about thirty years." He winced theatrically, and she laughed, eyeing the water. She shifted to one knee, with a foot braced and hands gripping the sides of the board, measuring the ocean with her gaze.

Cutting her eyes toward Matt, one side of her mouth lifted in a smile. "You look pretty good for an older man. That year between us makes a huge difference, you know."

He grinned back, ready to stand on his board. "It's always about age with you. You're lucky I like slightly younger women." Abby laughed, and then the wave rushed in, and they got on top of it, riding it nearly to the beach before slipping off the boards and taking them to shore.

Matt headed toward the blanket that he'd anchored on the sand with the cooler and their bags. "Hungry?"

"Starving. Being in the water always does that to me," Abby said from behind him, and he nodded, opening the cooler and picking up two bottles of water before turning around.

Holy hell. Matt stood stunned, holding out the bottle. Abby walked closer, twisting her hair over her shoulder and wringing water out of it. Far from hiding her curves, the T-shirt that he'd resented now accentuated every one, clinging to her body as the deep plum top, showing through the translucent shirt, accentuated her chest.

Taking the bottle from Matt's hand, she gave him a curious look, and he dropped his eyes to the cooler, busying himself with unpacking it and willing his body to behave itself. "Chris put this together, so I don't know exactly what's in here. He has pretty good taste, so I'm sure it's okay." *Enough babbling*, he told himself.

Abby didn't seem to mind. She sat beside him and reached for some grapes as she gushed about her rides. Matt relaxed, laughing at her enthusiasm and answering another dozen questions as they snacked on fruit, cheese, and bread. Opening a thermos she'd retrieved from the bottom of the cooler, Abby took a deep swallow and started coughing. "Wasn't expecting sangria," she gasped out, laughing as Matt cursed Chris for not warning him. Sharing the rest of the wine, they rested on the blanket, talking about different styles of sculpture and the funny "buys" Charles had made over the years.

Matt eventually looked out at the ocean with a calculating eye, glad for once that the gnarly swells Surfline had predicted hadn't come in. Still, it was getting late, and the tide would be rolling in soon.

"One last ride? The waves will be too big for junior riders soon," he said with a smile.

"It's been a long time since I was a junior anything, thank you very much," Abby retorted, leaping to her feet and extending her hand. Matt grasped it and pulled himself up, holding on longer than necessary as he examined the incoming surf.

"Wanna try a bigger wave?" he asked.

Abby grinned. "Hell, yes." She moved to grab her board.

Matt tugged her upright. "We're gonna do this one together." He let go of her hand to hoist his longboard onto his shoulder.

"You can do that?"

"It's how my dad taught me." He took her hand. "Trust me?"

Abby nodded, searching Matt's eyes before she started for the water, towing him in her wake. After wading out as far as they could, he helped her onto the board and pushed it out to a distance that would be challenging yet safe before shimmying up behind her and waiting for the wave. He caressed her shape with his eyes, lingering on her vulnerable nape and the soft swells of her hips, looking up only when she gasped. Flicking his eyes to the water, Matt watched a silvery-gray pair of dolphins arc out of the water well in front of them.

"Beautiful, aren't they? You should see the gray whales out further, over at Steamer Lane. They'll swim around your legs and it's just…" He trailed off, at a loss for words.

"Can we?" Abby whispered, and Matt laughed.

"Not this time. That's advanced." The swell started to grow, and he turned into it. "Get ready to stand up. Count of three, okay? I'm going to hold on to you, just like when we were practicing, so don't be startled. Move with me, or we're going under."

Abby got ready to stand. Matt watched the oncoming water, deciding the right moment for a slow countdown. At one, they rose in tandem, riding the crest of the wave. Gripping her hips, Matt both steadied Abby and used subtle pressure to indicate which way she should shift her weight. They moved like one body as the board rushed toward the shore. Her delighted laughter floated back, and Matt smiled, dodging errant strands of hair that whipped toward his face from the loose braid she'd twisted. A few dozen feet from the shore, Abby looked back at him, eyes sparkling, and that was all it took for them to overbalance. Luckily, the wave had diminished enough that rather than being sucked under, Matt merely plunged below the surface. His heart stuttered in his chest when he didn't spot Pretty as soon as he rose. He ducked under the water, looking around frantically before spotting a pair of white legs scissoring near him. He rose to the surface with a splash.

Abby grinned and hung on to his board. "Worried, Matt?" she teased.

He smiled back, leaning his arms across from her. "I love this board, and I'd hate to lose it."

She laughed, sleeking hair back from her forehead with one hand. Without thinking, Matt reached across the board and smoothed the hair above her ear, letting his palm drift down until he cupped her cheek. The laughter in Abby's eyes became tempered by something warmer. Matt brushed his thumb over her lips before leaning forward and kissing her forehead. "I was worried about you," he said against her skin before drawing back. "I shouldn't have been, though. You're a natural."

She studied his face before she nodded and let go of the board. She swam toward the shore. He watched her for a minute before paddling after her.

By the time he got back to their spot, Abby lay on the blanket, one knee up and one arm flung over her eyes while the other rested beside her. Tendrils of hair had escaped from her braid and were curling around her face as they dried, creating a frame. Her lips curled into a smile, and it took a mighty effort to sit next to her, hands linked loosely as his arms wrapped around his upraised knees.

"That was damned incredible," Abby said.

"Glad you liked it." Easing onto his back, he mirrored her position, though he turned his head toward Abby so he could still see her through one squinted eye. Despite the summer day and the radiant heat from the sand beneath them, Matt could identify the unique body heat of Abby's hand as it rested a hairsbreadth from his on the blanket. "So…how did you come to be a museum curator?"

Abby laughed. "Started as a painter, but I found out that I wasn't as good as I'd hoped. Switched to art history." She glanced over at Matt. "Don't get the 'I'm sorry' face. I'm fine with it. We have a joke in the community, in fact: 'Those who can't do, teach. Those who can't teach, curate.' I like my job." Her hand twitched and came into full contact with Matt's. Abby looped her wrist over his, lacing their fingers together.

Matt was going to have to reconsider his statement to Jason. He'd meant it at the time, but…damn.

"What did you have to talk about with Jason that kept you up so late?" he asked, closing his eyes and absorbing the warmth of the sun and the heat of her hand in his.

"Us. Jason and me."

"Did you come to any resolution?"

"I suppose so. For me, anyway." Her hand tightened around Matt's, and she shifted closer to him. "Jason's a good guy, Matt, he really is…but…" She sighed. "It's just not there for me."

"But it is for him?" He peeked at her through one eye.

She shrugged. "He thinks so. He asked me to wait to make any decisions until he gets back from New York. I agreed." Abby's lips twisted into a smile. "Didn't want him to deal with a race *and* a breakup."

Tough for him, Matt thought. He shifted onto his side and leaned on his elbow. "So. What brought it up?"

"Sex." Abby laughed as Matt's eyebrows shot up. "You asked."

Matt's hand tightened on hers. "Does he force the issue?"

"God, no," Abby scoffed. "Jason's a sweetie. And he's not hard on the eyes and pretty damned good at—"

Matt covered her mouth. "I don't want to hear this, do I?"

Abby pressed a kiss on his palm and then shifted his hand to rest on her collarbone. "Maybe not. Anyway…despite that, I just…" She thought for a minute. "It doesn't feel right, for two reasons. First, I was all about the summer fling with the younger guy because I've never done that. I'm boring, and whitebread, and…boring." A frown line appeared between her eyebrows. "But I guess there was a reason I haven't done it before. It's not me. When I'm with Jason, I have a great time, but sometimes I feel like I'm putting on an act." She sighed. "I will never get the appeal of chainsawing video game zombies and bobbing my head to hip-hop. Ever. And I have a confession: I don't think Tupac was the poet of our age."

"Of course not. That would be Kurt Cobain," Matt deadpanned, and they both laughed. "Okay, so you don't transmit on the same frequency. Sounds like a good enough reason to shut him down. What was your second reason?"

Abby's hand tightened. "I wouldn't be thinking about him," she whispered, "and that's not fair. He deserves better."

Matt leaned forward until his face hovered over Abby's. "You're right." He searched her eyes. "Who would you be thinking about, Pretty?"

Her breath came out in a rush, and she let go of his hand, sliding her fingers over his bicep and shoulder and onto his neck. Matt rested his hand on the blanket next to her head, bracing himself above her. "Your eyes are the exact color of the water," Abby murmured distractedly, looking from them to Matt's mouth. "This isn't fair either, because I said that I'd wait. But I can't. Kiss me."

He needed no further invitation. Closing the space between them, he dropped his mouth onto hers and tasted her lips with kiss after kiss, each one building in intensity until her tongue swept over his lips. Abby's hand plunged into his hair, fisting there. Matt felt a steady build of internal heat as her other hand tentatively rested on his lower back before she began tracing the long muscles with her fingertips. She flattened her hand over his shoulder blade, urging him closer. A tiny moan came from Abby's throat as Matt did just that, leaning his weight on his elbow so that he could caress the side of her face with his hand.

Lost in her touch and kiss and a deep desire to shift her on top of him so that his hands would be free, Matt was startled by a snicker coming from above them.

"Old people mackin' at the beach. Gross," said a low and decidedly youthful male voice.

There was a sound of hand against flesh, and the speaker yelped. "Would you shut up?" a girl's voice hissed. "I think it's cute."

Abby started to giggle as Matt rose back up to his hand and dropped his forehead onto her chest just below her shoulder. "Thanks, kid," he muttered.

Abby burst into full-fledged laughter. She came up on her elbows and kissed the side of Matt's neck. "C'mon, old guy."

"Don't think I can get up yet."

"Why?" Abby blushed when Matt looked at her sideways. "Oh." She darted a glance at his shorts and chuckled. "I thank God just about every day that I'm a girl."

"Not funny. And I'm pretty thankful you're a girl too."

They laughed together, and Abby extended a hand.

"Come into the water with me. It's pretty cold." Her eyes sparkled with mirth.

Matt grabbed her hand, standing gradually. "Yeaaahhh…not so much. Wet T-shirt won't help."

Abby looked down at herself in surprise. "Never thought of that." She smiled at Matt as he took her hand.

"So…is this happening?" he asked.

Abby looked out at the ocean. "I'd like to talk to Jason again. No more wait and see." Matt hesitated, sensing that there was more to her answer. "I've never done this before, Matt. Started a relationship with a deadline, I mean." She turned to look at him. "We live on opposite coasts. I'm going home in two months. I like you, and I want you…so much," she added in a whisper. His breathing roughened as he saw the heat in her eyes, and he embraced her. He could feel her breath on his neck.

"I just…I don't know," Abby admitted in a low voice.

"We'll play it by ear, okay?" Matt murmured into her hair, smelling salt and sunshine and a lingering note of her shampoo. Leaning back, he tilted her face up with one finger. "No pressure. I promise that." He smiled down at her. "Benefit of dating an older man. We can be patient. For a while."

Chapter Eight

Opening his front door, Matt was surprised to find a sheepish Chris sprawled on the couch, eating popcorn and watching *Kill Bill*. He sat up, brushing errant crumbs off his shirt and into his bowl. "Sorry about this, cuz. I couldn't find a flop tonight. I swear I'll sleep in the Jeep." His eyes darted behind Matt. "Where's the pretty lady?"

Matt tossed his keys toward the basket on the table and missed completely. "Crap," he mumbled, scooping them off the floor and dropping them safely inside the basket. "She's at home. I told you I don't bring women here. Best instruction I ever got from my dad." Matt didn't mention that he'd considered bringing someone home for the first time ever that night.

Chris looked down at the hands that were loosely clasped between his knees as his forearms rested on his thighs. "Dude. That's saying a lot—your dad is pretty badass—but you know he had his own reasons for keeping things simple."

Matt just shook his head, not feeling up to a discussion of his parents' relationship. Whether Ted Clarke had decided that his ex-wife was his one and only love or whether he just liked his peace had been fodder for speculation for years; either way, Matt thought keeping things simple made sense.

He dropped his bag on the floor and headed for the kitchen. "Well, it's worked for me for years, Chris. What did you have for dinner?"

Chris followed, bowl in hand. "That attitude, man…You're going to risk missing out on something that could be incredible because something bad *might* happen?" He shook his head. "Man, there's nothing like waking up with the woman you're digging on all warm and soft against you. If there's nakedness involved, it's even better."

Matt gave up on real food and grabbed a handful of popcorn. "Like that's news to me. Married once, remember?" He shoved a few kernels of corn into his mouth and crunched, wondering vaguely what Kate was up to these days. "Besides, what makes you think I'm digging on Abby? Why can't we just be friends?"

Chris yawned and returned to the couch. "Call it a hunch from the fortune-teller." He snickered. "Besides, you were a freakin' nervous mess this morning. Friends don't do that to you."

Matt shook his head, smiling, and Chris continued. "And Kate doesn't count. Too long ago. You were barely a zygote when that was on and over. I think I was in high school, maybe, when ya'll split up." He yawned again. "Try living with a crapload of men for way too long in the desert. Teaches you to appreciate a soft bed and a warm woman."

Matt had never pried, no matter how much Chris's mother asked him to, but for Chris to leave an opening to talk about his last couple of years in the military was rare. "There were women there, right?"

"Not where I was." Chris's eyes never left the screen, though his jaw tightened. He stopped on a channel and tossed the remote toward the coffee table. "How about a little *Matrix*?" The subject was clearly closed.

Matt settled back against the cushions and grabbed another handful of popcorn. "Only if you promise not to geek out on me again. Explanations of how this is possible just make my head ache."

"It was the tequila that made your head ache. My explanations were perfect. I know things." Chris tapped his temple and grinned.

As he got ready for bed after the movie, Matt pondered the day to come. Surprisingly, his meeting with Bambi and The Corpse occupied very little of his thoughts. Maybe it was because Claire would be there and Matt knew he could count on her to take care of all the real negotiations. What was occupying him were thoughts of Sarah and Pretty driving down an unfamiliar coast to a new town. She'd told him on the drive home that they planned on going to Monterey for the day, and that had him worried. He wished that he'd warned Abby about the panhandlers and the pickpockets that infested tourist towns, and he could have kicked himself for not recommending a few good places where they could get food at locals' prices.

The logical part of his mind reminded him that the panhandlers in Santa Cruz were usually far more persistent than those in more affluent Monterey. Besides, Pretty and her friend came from one of the most tourist-clogged cities in the US—they must have a dose of good sense about what areas and people to avoid—but Mr. Logic was being out-shouted by Mr. Worry. Matt even went so far as to consider whether Claire could handle the meeting herself; if it hadn't already been past midnight, he probably would have called her to ask.

Shaking his head at his own idiocy, he rinsed his mouth and wiped his face on the towel next to the sink. He made his way to bed and stripped down before climbing between the sheets. Plumping the pillow, he tried to relax on his back, throwing one arm over his head and listening to the sound of his heart. No good. He couldn't get comfortable, and the bed felt cold. He moved his hand restlessly against the sheet, remembering the relief of Abby's skin against his when their hands linked. His mind's eye traveled up Abby's arm and over the curve of her shoulder, lingering on the delicate structure of rib and clavicle at the top of her chest, the sweet dip between that bone and the muscle of her shoulder as it curved into her neck, and he could almost feel how silky and warm it would be under his tongue…

Damn it. Not where he wanted to go mentally, not when he had to be up in—Matt glanced at the clock and groaned—four hours if he wanted a run before the meeting. He flopped onto his side, hauled the other pillow over to him, and wrapped his arm around it. Unfortunately, that just reminded him of the way he'd wrapped his arm around Pretty, half-pulling her under his body and half-levering himself over her so he could kiss her the way he'd wanted to. And the way she'd asked him to. Matt could still feel her hands against his back, feel her shoulder move against his chest as her hand moved higher, her fingers curling around the muscles next to his spine and stroking the valley between them.

"Piss." Matt sat up and swung his legs over the side of the bed. It was clear that he wasn't going to sleep until he was exhausted. Sliding back into his shorts, he headed for the studio, knowing from long experience that work could calm his mind when nothing else stood a chance. As he passed his phone on the kitchen counter, he snagged it on impulse and carried it into the studio.

He was snapping on the overhead lights when its sudden chime made him jump. Looking at the display, he saw that it was after two in the morning. Who the hell would text at that hour?

Good luck w/ your meeting. I had a great time yesterday.

A smile crooked one side of his mouth upward. No need for any name.

I did too. Be careful today. Later. Whatever.

What are you doing up?

Matt approached the table with his Pretty statue, not even looking toward the finished Jason and almost completed Zoe mock-ups.

He replied, lifting the cloth off the clay so he could see his Pretty.

Can't sleep.

Me either.

Why not?

Gathering tools from their set places, Matt waited to see what she'd answer. When no response came for several moments, he gave up and tossed the phone onto an adjoining table. Just then, it chimed again.

You. Good night, Matt.

Matt grinned and tapped in a reply.

Good. 'Night, Pretty.

Putting the phone down again, he turned to his statue and envisioned the smooth movement of Abby's arms, the flexible strength of her body. Within minutes, he was absorbed in transferring everything he'd seen and experienced about her body into the clay before him. He shaped the roughed-in collarbones and shoulders into duplicates of the soft flesh and hard bone he'd had under his hands that afternoon. He'd intended to just work on the shoulders, but he found himself adjusting breasts and stomach muscles as well, shaping the curve of her waist and the swell of her hips. He became so absorbed in transcribing what he'd experienced, smoothing knife and wire marks with his fingers until all he could see was sleek clay, that he didn't even hear Chris enter the studio. Matt finally noticed him patiently sitting on a low table, watching his older cousin with interest.

"New statue?" Chris swung one leg back and forth at the knee and examined the clay. Matt nodded. "It's beautiful," Chris said with quiet seriousness. "Did she commission it? The pretty lady?"

Warmth rose up Matt's neck. He gently covered the statue, now more than half-finished. "No," he admitted, unable to meet Chris's eye, "and I'd appreciate it if you didn't say anything to her. It's just something to…de-stress, I guess. It's nothing."

"Right," Chris said. "Have you been to bed at all?"

"Briefly."

Chris held out the cup of coffee that had been sitting beside him. "Then you'll need this. Didn't you say that you have a breakfast meeting?"

"Yeah. I'm meeting Claire at the gallery at eight." Matt gathered his tools and carried them over to the sink, only to turn back toward Chris when he chuckled.

Chris was rubbing his head and smiling. "Dude, it's seven thirty right now. Don't you have to shower or something?"

Matt's eyes darted to the white clock face with stark black numbers and groaned. He'd spent five and a half hours on Abby's likeness and missed any chance at sleep. "Fuck me."

Chris strolled over to take the tools from Matt's hands. He nodded toward the now-covered sculpture. "No thanks, but if Abby sees you like you see her, I don't think lack of that will be a problem for long." He nudged Matt toward the door. "Go. I'll clean these. You've gotta get dressed up for The Man, right? Get that big paycheck."

Matt thanked him and rushed out of the studio. He hurried through a shower and slipped into a pair of slacks, a button-down, and jacket, choosing to forego the tie this time because he only owned two and didn't remember where either of them was.

He made it to Claire's gallery just as she was heading out the door. "Impeccable timing as always, Matt." Claire looked at him out of the corner of her eye as she locked the front door. "Of course, you were supposed to meet me here a half-hour ago, but at least you didn't stand the Bakers up." She walked toward her Lexus and nodded toward the passenger door.

"I'm so sorry, Claire." He slid into the indicated seat and snapped his seatbelt closed. "I lost track of time, and…" He shrugged.

"Please tell me you were working." Claire sounded amused. "Or have you gotten things straight with Abby? She impresses the hell out of me, you know. Smart girl." She patted Matt's knee. "Not enough of those over the years. Haven't I always told you that you'll never be satisfied with someone who doesn't challenge you? That's how I snagged Charles—I teased him cruelly and refused to let him sit on his piles of money and do nothing. Not unless he felt like being ridiculed."

"Food for thought." Matt rolled his eyes, and Claire slapped his leg. "Yes, I was working. And stop trying to play matchmaker. Abby… we're…" He waved his hand vaguely. "She goes back to Boston in two months."

"Mmm hmm. Try to play cool with someone else—someone who hasn't known you for almost two decades. You don't do 'summer things.' You do casual dates and hook-ups. None of which have ever made you smile like you do every time I talk about Abby." Matt shook his head. "Well, something or someone had you pretty damned preoccupied this morning. Look at your feet."

Glancing down, Matt was horrified. Instead of the dark loafers that he'd intended to wear, he'd slipped on his broken-down sandals. With socks. "Oh God…turn around."

"Too late," Claire said calmly. "Methuselah is known for his punctuality. Never early, never late. We just have time to get to the table—you can hide your feet under it. Pray you don't have to pee until breakfast is over." She reached into the back seat and grabbed a tie. "I brought one just in case." She looked at Matt's feet again and giggled. "Good Lord, Matt. I think you were wearing those when I met you in college. Don't you get rid of anything?"

"Maybe I should start by getting rid of funny friends," Matt grumbled, knotting the tie. "Thanks, by the way."

"Anytime. Does my favorite student and good friend deserve less?"

After the restaurant hostess led them to their reserved table, Claire and Matt went over their pitch. He showed her pictures of the finished mock-ups and emphasized how important it was that they push terracotta. Guaranteeing delivery of three finished sculptures in that clay within a couple of months was going to be hard enough; Matt didn't think the more traditional marble or granite would be possible at all.

Just as they were finishing, Claire looked up, and her professional smile covered her face. "Game time," she whispered.

Carefully keeping his feet under the table, Matt stood to shake hands with the oldest man in North America and his child bride. Mr. Baker scrutinized Matt's appearance and nodded approvingly. After they'd ordered and the meeting itself was in motion, Matt handed around the file of pictures he'd brought along. He had the feeling Baker had expected to see little progress; the old man seemed impressed that the two mock-ups were finished and the other sculptures already planned. Baker relaxed in his seat, lingering over the pictures of Zoe while his wife drooled over Jason, squealing that he was exactly what she'd had in mind.

Breakfast spilled over into lunchtime as Claire and Baker politely sparred over prices and materials. It became difficult for Matt to focus when his mind started to wander out the restaurant door. He hadn't realized the reservations were in Monterey. If he had, he might have suggested to Abby that they meet. He was longing for a look at her; the comparison between her lithe body and the plastic surgery wonder that sat next to him was not trending well for Mrs. Baker. He pasted on a smile at one of her more obvious innuendo-laden comments and took a deep swallow of his water to avoid having to reply. Then he cursed under his breath, because he really did have to pee now.

In the end, Claire got what she wanted. Matt was glad once again that he'd had her as a teaching assistant in one of the first art classes he'd taken at UC Berkeley, where he'd hit on her and ended up as her friend. After marrying Charles Eastman, she combined her love for the arts with the financial acumen of Warren Buffett and became the best friend any artist could have.

As they left the restaurant, Matt tried Abby's cell and found out that she and Sarah were in Carmel, celebrity-watching and having a great time. They talked for a few minutes, and then her table reservation for lunch was ready and she had to go.

Matt pocketed his phone as he and Claire drove back toward Santa Cruz. He looked over and caught Claire smirking at him.

"What?" he asked in exasperation.

"There's that smile," Claire sing-songed. "If I didn't have to be back in SC in a few minutes, I'd take you to Carmel right now." She shifted gears smoothly, roaring down the road at close to ninety miles per hour. "Of course, you could always get in your truck and—"

"Act like a crazy stalker? No thanks." Matt pulled the knot of the tie down until he could slip the silk from under his collar and toss it onto the backseat. Unbuttoning the top three buttons of his shirt, he yawned. "Besides, I have a lot of work to do. Some slave driver just committed me to six statues. And I need a nap."

"Six easy sculptures in a friendly medium. For an assload of money, don't forget. And you wouldn't need a nap if you didn't stay up all night thinking about your girlfriend." Matt's head whipped around, and Claire started to laugh. "I was right! Holy shit! How old did you say you were again?"

Matt slouched in his seat and pushed his hand through his hair. "Shut up," he muttered, and Claire giggled again.

When she dropped him at home, Matt found the house blessedly empty. Taking advantage of that fact, he exchanged his slacks and jacket for a pair of shorts and buckled down on his first sculpture, a solo of Jason. By the time he was ready to quit, arms and shoulders stiff from the big motions needed to rough in a large sculpture, it was late afternoon. Chris still wasn't home from what Matt supposed was another busy day tending to the tourists on the boardwalk, so Matt decided to go for a run and then maybe catch his cousin for dinner.

Slipping on shoes and a tee, he set off, trying to outrun the weariness of his body and his tension about Abby having dinner with Jason the next evening. He fought the little whisper of uncertainty in the back of his mind that kept asking what would happen if Jason convinced her to change her mind. No, that wasn't fair. A woman like Abby wouldn't let someone else make decisions for her. The real question: what if *she* changed her mind? Would Matt push the issue or walk away? For the first time, the answer to that question wasn't obvious, and it pissed him off.

Veering to run past Abby's house happened without conscious thought. Maybe that was his answer. Unfortunately, the chairs behind the beach cottage were empty and the windows dark, so it was with a sense of disappointment that Matt looped around and headed for the boardwalk. Even having dinner with Chris and listening to funny stories about the tourists he'd "read" weren't enough to bring Matt out of his funk. Abby's text, describing the "asinine idiots" who were behind her and Sarah in a movie theater in Monterey didn't help, either, because it was obvious to him that the idiots were trying to pick them up. It irritated the crap out of him that that irritated the crap out of him.

By the time he walked home, Matt was ready to shower and fall into bed. He dropped into restless dreams that he couldn't remember the next morning. He awoke feeling surly, and so he spent a quiet morning finishing the Zoe mock-up. Luckily, Jason seemed to feel just as crabby when he got to the studio that afternoon. They used minimal language to set up the shots Matt wanted, working through the different poses with alacrity.

As an artist, Matt had to admire the form Jason had accomplished—a nearly perfect development of all the muscle groups, proportional and quite beautiful. As a…what the hell was he? A rival? The word made Matt cringe, but…yes, as a rival, Matt wanted to force feed him Ho Hos and tie him in front of Sports Center for a month or two. Or jump back in time a decade and a half, and…never mind. Matt had never looked like that at twenty-three. Completely different build. He wondered what Abby had preferred at that age.

It startled him when Jason said goodbye. Matt followed him to the outer door of the studio, outlining the schedule he had in mind. Jason agreed absently, a frown marring his forehead.

"Big date?" Matt asked casually.

Jason shrugged. "Pretty sure I'm getting dumped." He sighed. "I knew it was coming, but Abby tried to be nice by waiting until after the race. I won."

Matt felt a little sorry for the guy, but not sorry enough to step back. "Congratulations on the race, anyway."

Jason laughed ruefully. "I suppose." He glanced at his watch. "I suppose it's bad form to be late to be kicked to the curb. Today is not my freaking day." He walked to his bike and climbed on. Pulling his helmet on, he waved Matt over.

"Listen, thanks," he said. "For the congrats. You're a good guy."

Matt felt like guilt should be written large across his face. He evidently hid it better than he thought, because Jason just flipped him a salute and rode away.

Then there was just the waiting.

Through cleaning up his sculpting tools.

Through the dinner he picked at.

Through a stretch of mindless comedies on TV, during which he laughed when Chris chuckled but didn't remember a word two minutes after each show ended.

Afterward, he scanned sculpting materials sites on the Net, pricing the clay that he'd need for the next few months. Matt tried to keep his head together for that one but didn't make the mistake of ordering when his mind wasn't fully engaged.

When his phone rang, hours after Jason had left, he snatched it from the table and stalked into the kitchen.

"Hey." Abby sounded weary.

"Hey." Matt tried to keep his voice pleasantly neutral as he opened the refrigerator and got a Coke. They were silent for a minute, and Matt sipped his soda, recognizing the ridiculousness of the situation. He'd barely known Abby for a month and had only spoken to her maybe a dozen times before spending the day with her. Oh, and he'd kissed her. But to be feeling this anxious about her was absurd. It would be better to avoid the potential drama and slide back into his easygoing life, right? The smartest thing to do would be to laugh the whole thing off and let the contact die.

"How did it go? Are you okay?" Apparently, Matt's mouth was not taking advice from his brain.

"Yeah." Abby paused, and Matt heard a door open before the susurration of surf started playing background to her words. "Jason didn't seem surprised, though he wasn't thrilled." Matt heard her swallowing, and envisioned the smooth motion of her throat. That led to memories of kissing her on the beach, the way she'd tilted her head back to allow him better access. After a moment, Matt realized that she had paused expectantly.

"I'm sorry. What were you saying?"

Abby chuckled. "Tired?"

"Yeah," he evaded.

"I said I'd like to stay low-key for a while, but I think we can get away with lunch. Can you take a few minutes tomorrow, maybe come over here?"

"Hey, for you, I can take a whole half-hour." Matt finished his soda and tossed the can into the recycle bin. "I'm glad that it went well, Abby. I'm sure it wasn't easy, but it had to be done."

"Oh…um…yeah." Abby sounded surprised, then wary. "I guess I'll see you tomorrow. Unless you find that you have other plans."

After awkward goodbyes, Matt dropped his phone on the counter and grabbed a beer out of the fridge, wondering where she got the idea that he'd cancel on her. He replayed the exchange in his head. Losing track of the conversation was probably the first strike. Sure, he'd been imagining Abby in his bed, but had he told her that?

Then the stupid, stiff congratulations on ending things with Jason…

He thumped the bottle on the counter. *No wonder I'm alone*, Matt thought. *I'm a moron.*

Striding into the living room, Matt grabbed his car keys out of the basket and headed for the door. Chris kept his eyes on the television screen, but a smile twitched across his lips. "Going somewhere, cuz?"

"Yep. Messed up already."

Chris tapped his temple. "I kind of thought you would. Bottle of Riesling and a couple of glasses in the cooler by the door."

"How—"

Chris let out a full-fledged laugh. "Never mind. Just try not to blow it again when I'm not around to save your ass. 'It had to be done.'" He shook his head.

Matt flushed. "Give me a break. Abby's not some random piece. She's…" Matt couldn't think of a word that adequately described what he thought of her. "Our time is just so damned limited."

"Then why are you wasting it? Enjoy the time you do have, and let the rest take care of itself."

Matt stared at him for a moment before scooping up the cooler and heading out the door. When he pulled up in front of Abby's house, the windows were dark, but he took a chance that she was still out back. He crept around the side of the house, hoping that neither of the women living there was trigger happy. In the faint glow of the moon off the water, he could make out the chairs that Sarah and Abby lounged in while scoping the ocean. An errant breeze lifted a hank of bright hair from the back of one of the chairs and waved it gently.

Walking down the beach, Matt didn't make any special effort to be quiet, so he was surprised when Abby didn't look around.

"I thought you were coming over tomorrow," she said, still looking toward the sea.

"I thought I wouldn't wait," Matt replied. He leaned over from behind her chair and cupped her face between his palms, gently tipping her head back so he could see her face. "How did you know it was me? It could have been anyone walking up behind you. You should be more careful."

Abby smiled. "I knew."

The warmth of her gaze stilled Matt's breath. He looked away long enough to pull the other chair close and eased into it as he reached over to twine his fingers with hers. Abby squeezed gently, looking out over the water again. Tracing her profile with his eyes and admiring the soft curves of her body under the dark, silky robe she wore, he visualized how her shoulders would glow in the moonlight if the material was pushed back and off of them. If they were bare. Which his mind insisted must be the case, probably because he wanted them that way.

Abby shifted her leg to the side and linked her foot around Matt's ankle. "So…" she began, and then let it hang in the air, a question implied but not asked.

"So."

Abby waited when he stopped speaking, her head resting against the back of her chair.

He cleared his throat and started again. "Abby, I don't know what I'm doing here. Not *here* here," he added hastily as her expression started to close up. "I'm *here* because I want to be with you." He chuckled nervously. "I feel like I'm fifteen again and at camp."

Abby's eyes crinkled at the corners. "Me, too! I'm the queen of over-thinking things. Boring, remember?"

Matt raised her hand to his lips and kissed it. "Boring is nowhere near how I think of you," he said, relaxing his head against the back of his chair.

Abby took an uneven breath and looked down at their joined hands. "This is new to me, too. New as an adult, anyway. But I want it. This." Her eyes flashed to Matt's face. "You. And I don't want to over-think."

"Enjoy the time you have, and let the rest take care of itself." Matt repeated Chris's advice, and Abby smiled.

"Exactly," she said, snuggling her head against Matt's shoulder. She inhaled deeply.

"Did you just smell me?" He laughed.

"Yep. I told you I was a sensual person. I'll be petting you next. Just a warning."

Matt tried to ignore the vision her words implanted in his brain. He snagged the cooler. Abby sat up, watching him uncork the wine and lift two glasses from the bag.

"Nice."

"You like that?" Matt smiled and handed her a glass after he'd half-filled it. "My in-home relationship advisor provided this." He poured himself some Riesling and settled back in his chair again.

"I think I need a Chris. Does he do house calls?" Abby laid her head on Matt's shoulder again and linked her hand through his arm. Her fingers began twisting through the hair on his forearm, and he smiled. Nothing like a woman who knew herself.

He stretched his legs out and rested his cheek on her hair. "Nope. I can't possibly spare him. How else am I going to impress you?"

"I can think of a thing or two."

Matt raised an eyebrow, and she smiled.

"So," she said.

"So."

Abby tipped her glass toward Matt's. "To beginnings?"

He clinked the edge of his glass on hers; the crystal chimed in promise.

"To beginnings."

Chapter Nine

Sarah's back was to Abby as she assembled a sandwich. She filled a cup with the caffeinated nectar of the gods and handed it to Abby. "Busy night."

Abby leaned one hip on the counter and blew on her coffee. "Mmm hmm."

Sarah took a large bite of her sandwich. She chewed for a minute, looking toward the door that opened to the beach. She swallowed. "Late night."

"Yep." Abby sipped.

"Want me to get another cup down?"

"Want some coffee?"

Sarah slammed her sandwich on the counter. "Fuck's sake, Abby! You're going to make me ask which guy is upstairs? Give me a hint. Will there be brownish hair or curls in the shower?"

Abby laughed and snagged a bit of Sarah's ponytail and a lock of her own hair. "Whatever you'd call these. Sarah, there's no one upstairs. Unless Tyler has figured out a way to shimmy up the side of the house, which I wouldn't put past him."

Sarah grabbed her sandwich and tore into it. She forced down a large bite, glaring at Abby. "I'm trying not to strangle you right now. Are you out of your mind? The boy toy appears and disappears—don't even think he's given up, by the way—and then Mr. Sexy-chuckle-that-tormented-Sarah-as-she-had-to-listen-to-it-in-her-lonely-spin-ster-bed shows up and stays until the ass crack of dawn…and no one is upstairs?" She kicked the cabinet next to Abby. Opening the refrigerator, she grabbed a bottle of beer and swallowed a quarter of it before slamming it down on the counter. "I hate you."

Abby slung her arm around Sarah's shoulders and squeezed. "What's the matter, baby? Things with Scotty not working out? I thought you'd be over the moon to have finally snagged him."

Sarah snorted. "Peachy, if you don't mind wrestling an octopus from hell who gazes adoringly at his own mug in every reflective surface. And the tongue? Please. Someone needs to teach this younger generation that a little goes a long way. I feel like I need a lobster bib when we go out." She held up a hand as Abby started to speak. "Don't even suggest it. I'm unwilling to train up a newbie. Even the pesty child was a better kisser. My God, that's something I never imagined saying. My mother would be so proud." She started to chuckle, and Abby gladly joined in.

Sarah slapped Abby's shoulder. "So, what's the deal? Jason didn't look happy when he left last night. Did Matt?" She took a swallow from her bottle.

Abby opened the door of the fridge and grabbed her own beer. "Yum. Great breakfast." Sarah's gaze was level. Abby started peeling the label from the bottle, watching her hands. "I think Jason and I are better as friends. He's a great guy. Funny, smart, no lobster bibs necessary, but…" She shrugged.

"And Matt?"

A smile tugged at Abby's lips. "All that, and then some." Snuggling in the beach chairs had turned into cuddling on the couch when it had gotten too cool for her to sit out by the water in just a thin robe, and cuddling on the couch had turned into…something more. Just thinking about the creamy texture of the skin on his neck, the rasp of scruff against her shoulder, the springy-soft feel of his chest hair against her palms…Abby gulped her beer, feeling heat race through her body.

Sarah watched her with narrowed eyes. "Tell me that you did not sex it up on my aunt's Ralph Lauren couch. Or that you had a towel under you if you did. That old bat has eyes like a hawk, and I can't afford to replace it."

Abby laughed and rolled her eyes. "No, we did not sex it up on your aunt's loveseat. Do I look seventeen? I'm a comfort girl." Sarah nodded. "Besides, it wasn't good timing last night. Jason had just left, and it would have been…weird." Abby remembered the sure way Matt's hands had moved over her skin, how he seemed to know just how and where to place a palm or trace a finger to make her gasp for air. She had an instant of real regret that she hadn't invited him upstairs. The summer wouldn't last forever…

"Abby, do you really have time for niceness?" Abby was startled when Sarah echoed her thoughts. "Jason's a big boy, and he'll have to suck it up and deal." She sighed. "Like the opinion of a man-repeller counts."

"What about Tyler?"

"That's not a man. That is a fetus."

Abby snickered. "Okay, then, how about David?"

Sarah looked startled. "David? My David?" She flushed. "I mean, my boss David? What about him?"

Abby kicked her in the ankle. "Come on. I overheard you talking to him the other night."

"We're just friends." Sarah stared into space. Abby had a feeling she was keeping something to herself. As much as Sarah craved real caring, she also feared it. Tyler might be her most embarrassing oops, but he wasn't the first.

"Call David and tell him about your man problem. I dare you. See what he thinks." Abby rummaged in the fridge and came up with a peach.

Sarah settled into a chair with one leg folded under her. "Oh, to have your problem. 'What's the right time to jump on the hot guy that wants me?' It's been so long, that if I got excited, dust would poof out."

Abby giggled and took a bite of peach.

"You think I'm kidding. Cougar, puma…who the hell cares? If you take kissing off the table, I'd do the grocery delivery boy right now."

"If such things existed outside *Leave It To Beaver*," Abby pointed out.

"Touché."

The shrill of Abby's phone made them both jump. They wrestled over it briefly until Sarah could be sure that it wasn't the museum calling again. When she saw that it was Matt, she handed the phone over, then flopped back in her chair and made lewd gestures until Abby hung up and sighed.

"Well, so much for lunch. Matt says that he overslept and has to work through. Do you want to go out? To the boardwalk?" Apparently, he'd had a hard time getting to sleep when he got home; Abby was glad that she'd had some effect on him, because Lord knew he affected her.

"Did you mention we might be at the boardwalk, maybe?" Sarah asked. Abby grinned. "Okay, you little floozy. Let's go make over-aged menaces of ourselves."

An hour later found them sprawled in the chairs of a boardwalk café while they watched tourists and locals mix in a wash of color and sound.

"He's doable," Sarah observed, staring at the back of a surfer who passed close by her chair.

"Nope. Men with thin lips leave me—" Abby grimaced to demonstrate her distaste. She took a bite of her delayed lunch. "So, let's get back to the subject at hand: what do you think I should do about the museum?"

"What do you want to do, Abby? You fought like hell to get that job, I get that, but if it leaves you—" she aped Abby's expression from moments before "—why do it?"

"Because I need to make a living!" Abby dropped her sandwich to the table, appetite gone, and pushed her sunglasses to the top of her head. "It's not like there's a knight in shining armor out there just waiting to sweep me off my feet and solve all my problems." She stretched her legs out into the sun, daring it to burn them. "All I can depend on having is a scheming intern and an incontinent cat." She thought for a minute. "Scratch the cat—when my mother called yesterday, she said Salvador Dali was thriving with her and 'Grandpa.'" She laid her head on the table. "It's sobering when you realize your parents are so sure that you'll never procreate that they're willing to change cat diapers. At least Eric was—"

She jumped when Sarah slammed her hand on the table.

"Do not start with that again, sister. Eric was a two-year-long mistake sundae with idiot sauce. Dali is cute but replaceable. And as for Clint… if he wants the damn job so much, let him have it. You've told me yourself that your boss is insufferable. Honey, you haven't even looked anywhere else—like here. You've made a connection with that gallery owner, right? Not to mention the connection with Wetsuit Wonder."

Abby slipped her sunglasses back over her eyes to hide her expression. "Be realistic, Sarah. This is an—an idyll. This isn't real life. Sexy men and beaches are summer things. Grown-ups realize that. And if we're going to visit la-la land, I wouldn't want Matt to take care of me." She held up a hand to stay Sarah's protest. "I worked too hard to get to where I am to give it up. Claire is a nice woman with a nice gallery, but she doesn't even have a full-time staff. Umpteen years of education and experience can't be tossed out for a summer hookup."

"Change."

"Work—" Abby's sharp reply was cut off by the shrilling of her cell phone. Sarah spun it around on the table so she could see the displayed name. She grimaced. Gretchen.

She pointed at Abby's face. "You touch that phone, and so help me God, I'll shank you."

"Do I need to stage an intervention, ladies?"

Abby tipped her head back and saw Jason standing behind her, his smile hopeful.

Her heart sank. Maybe Sarah had been right about him not giving up. She looked at her friend with mute pleading, willing her to restrain the smirk she knew had to be right below the surface.

Instead, Sarah gestured to an empty seat. "Nah. This is the way we've rolled for years—don't worry about it. What are you up to today?"

Jason balanced his frame on the bistro chair. "Wandering around with Scotty." He pointed at Sarah's latest conquest, who waved without coming over. Abby wondered if Sarah would be upset. To her amusement, she just looked relieved.

"He wants me to talk about bike racing to his touring group. It might be fun—aren't you in that?" Jason leaned his elbows on the table and focused on Sarah.

Abby let their conversation wash over her and settled into pleasant memories of the way Matt's arms had felt around her the night before. Less pleasant was the guilt she was feeling with Jason sitting across from her. She'd never actually verbally ended a relationship before—it always seemed easier to just withdraw and let them die a natural death. Now she knew why she'd chosen the easy road: the direct route sucked. Still, as Sarah had noted earlier, the summer wouldn't last forever, and for the first time, Abby felt an urgency to end a relationship sharply.

She realized that Jason was looking at her, a question in his eyes.

"I'm sorry—woolgathering. What was that?" she asked.

"I was wondering if you'd like to come on a ride with us today. As friends—" he held up his hands "—I promise, no expectations."

Abby considered different answers. "Yes" wasn't even a vague possibility, but she wasn't sure whether she had the guts to get into a detailed "no" in public. Cowardice won out. "I'm sorry. Sarah and I already have plans to go to the movies this afternoon." She named the latest chick flick, praying that it was playing in town. She also prayed that Sarah's disgust with all such movies wouldn't show on her face.

Jason shuddered. "Not my thing." He stood. "Let me tell Scotty where I'm going, and I'll walk you to your car." He caressed Abby's shoulder and strode off.

She grimaced. She'd thought that she was clear about being uninterested, but maybe she needed to be harsher. Had it been this difficult for Eric to end whatever it was they'd had? Had he been dropping hints forever, waiting for her to catch on?

"Well, that was gutless," Sarah observed, tossing a twenty on the table for payment and tip. "Was that your version of 'I am woman, hear me roar…oh look! Shiny things!'" She rose from her seat with a twisted grin.

"Smart ass." Abby laughed along with Sarah as they walked onto the boardwalk. Blinded by the angle of the sun, Abby stumbled over a tilted board and squawked.

She was startled when rough hands gripped her upper arms, though she could immediately identify their owner. Abby had felt those hands run over her shoulders and up her neck just the night before.

"Imagine meeting you here," Matt said with gentle humor, his hands clasping Abby's arms longer than was strictly necessary to keep her upright. He slid them toward her hands as Jason returned to stand next to Sarah.

"Imagine," Abby said dryly.

Matt smiled at Sarah and Jason. "Hello again, Jason. Thought you'd take advantage of this day off to get out of town."

"Sticking around." Jason's eyes locked with suspicion on Matt's hands as they lingered at Abby's wrists. "I thought I had a few things to clear up today. Maybe not."

Hoping to relieve the awkward pause, Abby said brightly, "Sarah and I were just on our way to see a chick flick. Not Jason's kind of movie, unfortunately." She smiled at the big man, hoping to get away without more hurt feelings.

"Nothing wrong with a little afternoon lovin'." Matt grinned and crossed his arms across his chest. Abby wondered why that reference made Jason's eyes snap.

He darted a look at her face. "I never said there was. I just—"

Sarah interrupted him with a snort of disgust. "—appreciate something with a little more balls and a little less shoe shopping? Me, too." She slid her hand around his arm. "Did you see that badass bike shop, Jason?" She started down the boardwalk after sending Abby a death glare. Soon they were ambling along, talking, with Matt and Abby trailing behind.

"So what happened to work?" Abby asked.

"Oh, it's still there," Matt answered wryly. "But it can wait for a bit." A smile lifted the corner of his mouth. "I hated being in Monterey at the same time as you were the other day and not being able to see you. I wanted to see you today, and I could. So I did."

"Charmer," Abby said. She resisted the urge to check if Jason was watching; maybe it would be best if he was.

"I try," Matt said. He entwined his fingers with hers, grimacing as they rasped against her skin. "Sorry. The clay—"

"Leeches the oils out of your skin. I know." Abby smiled up at him. "I like them." She folded one of his hands in both of hers before letting it rest, palm up, in one of her hands. Running her index finger of the opposite hand gently over his calluses and rough spots, Abby traced around his long fingers and narrow palm. "These are capable hands. Strong. Useful."

Comparisons to Eric's soft accountant hands forced themselves into her consciousness, making her wonder what she'd been thinking for the past two years. But after her catastrophe with a married man, she supposed Eric had felt safe…

Matt stepped around the side of the surf shop, tugging Abby with him. He gripped her hip with one hand and cradled her head with the other, pulling her flush against his body before dropping his mouth on hers. His kiss was urgent and insistent, a mixture of nibbles and long, slow pressure. Abby's jaw relaxed, and her lips opened as her head tilted so that they fit together seamlessly. Her hands found Matt's waist, sliding up his back and down over the tight curves of his ass. He rumbled deep in his throat before pulling back, breathing rough.

"That's more like it," he said huskily, his hands still moving over Abby's back. "That's the last time I want you thinking about someone else when you're with me." Abby's eyes darted up. "It's in the eyes," he said, pointing to his own. "You were gone for a minute, and then regret crept in. I'm vain enough to think that wasn't about me, so…" He grinned, lines around his eyes emphasizing his long lashes and high cheekbones. Gentle fingers came up to brush her cheek. "My schedule will make our time tight, so when you're with me I want you with me. Make sense?"

"Yeah." The reminder that this was a relationship with a time schedule was sobering. Abby slid her hand around the back of his neck and urged his head down for another, softer kiss.

Matt looped his arm around her and lifted her, backing her against the side of the building as his lips ran toward her ear. "I wish you'd invited me to stay last night," he said.

"I wish I would have too." Her hands twisted in his hair. "It's just…Jason…"

"Fuck Jason," Matt growled, nudging his leg between hers and pressing them even closer together. His kisses became more insistent, more passionate, until Abby seriously considered taking him home right then.

Sarah's cheerful voice rang out. "Hey, Abby! Where'd you go? We lost you."

The thought of what Jason would see if they came around the corner was horrifying. As much as Abby wanted the man whose chest was heaving against hers, she didn't want anyone hurt.

Matt watched the play of emotions on her face and sighed, lowering her feet to the ground and running a hand through his hair. He called out, "We're over here. I was showing Abby this mural." Abby turned and saw the large painting for the first time, noting its clean lines and bold colors right before Sarah and Jason stepped around the corner.

Jason looked suspicious, but his expression turned to interest when Matt launched into a tutorial on urban art. Working for a museum that appreciated more modern forms of art stood Abby in good stead, as she could add information on use of color and texture to complement what Matt offered.

"Wow." Jason looked dazed when Abby finished. "An hour ago, I would have seen this and felt sorry for the building owner for having his shop defaced."

Matt laughed. "This particular owner paid the taggers to do it. Challenged them to come up with something beautiful, and they did." He ran his hand over the bottom of the painting before turning to Sarah. "Listen, I need to get back to the studio, but if you're interested in art, I'm showing some of my sculptures in a couple of days." He looked from Sarah to Abby. "You should come."

Jason, still examining the mural, didn't seem to notice that he hadn't been included in the invitation. "Not really my thing, man. Not that art isn't interesting," he added, darting a look at Abby.

Abby was half-waiting for Matt's decided "fuck you" to Jason. He didn't give in to the temptation, though his eyes twinkled. "That's okay. The invitation is open."

"I suppose it will be dressy," Sarah said thoughtfully. Abby could see the wheels turning in her mind as she calculated the chances of meeting a wealthy, available, and age-appropriate Californian.

"Well, not ball gown dressy," Matt answered. "It's informal."

Sarah blew a hank of hair off of her forehead and grunted.

"No thanks, then. Unless I'm covering a show, it's not really my thing either. I suppose I can't get out of the chick flick as easy as that, can I?" She stretched up to kiss Matt on the cheek and waved to both men as she tugged Abby around the corner and onto the boardwalk.

"I'm sorry, I'm sorry!" Abby juddered out to Sarah, stumbling as her friend led the way with her longer stride.

Sarah's laugh was strained. "No problem. My freedom from girly films can take a backseat once in a while." She stopped at her car and waved at Matt. He'd come around the building and was watching them, arms crossed once again over his chest. He turned to head down the boardwalk, tossing a grin over his shoulder as he shook his behind at them.

"Cocky bastard." Abby grinned and waved to him before she slid into her seat.

"Okay, what's up, toots?" she asked as Sarah started the car.

Sarah glanced at her. "Nothing. Why?"

"Why? Maybe because you've been tense since you and Jason came around the corner. Did something happen? I'm sorry if he's pressing you about me—"

Sarah held up a hand. "He was a perfect gentleman. No worries." She sighed. "I need a change, Abby."

Abby laughed. "I thought this summer was all about change."

Sarah took a few minutes to answer, navigating the streets in silence until they reached theirs. "For you, maybe. I just packed up my personal crap and brought it along with me. Then I added a distillery worth of Jack Daniels to the sorry mix. This is not working out like I planned." She pulled into the driveway and shut off the engine.

"I'm sorry, honey," Abby said. "Maybe if—"

Sarah got out of the car. "I took your advice and called David while Jason was looking at bikes," she said as she headed for the porch.

"And?" Abby hurried to catch up.

"He told me to come home now and got quiet when I said that I planned on finishing my vacation. Then he said he had to go." She settled onto her wicker loveseat and put her arm over her eyes. "I can't believe I called my boss and blurted out all my personal crap."

Abby sat in one of the chairs. "C'mon. You know he's more than your boss. We've hung out with him a thousand times outside of work—he seeks you out." She searched her memories, praying she'd not fooled herself about David's interest in Sarah. She knew that he could be the perfect solution to her friend's man problem. And it was obvious that even if she'd never admit it, Sarah was beginning to see David as much more than a boss or a friend. "What did he say before he hung up?"

Sarah shrugged, eyes still covered. "That he'd talk to me in a couple of days."

She took a deep breath and sighed it out before standing and tugging Abby to her feet. "Not quite up to a happily ever after right now, though. Do you mind?"

"Of course not."

Sarah flung her arm around Abby's shoulders. "Then I believe we have a date with Christian Bale and a couple tubs of Cherry Garcia, don't you?"

Chapter Ten

Two nights later, Abby was putting in her earrings when Sarah bounced down the stairs, keys in hand. A couple evenings of violent movies had cheered her up enough that she was ready to assault Santa Cruz on her own again. She glanced at Abby and whistled. "You look yowza, babes. I thought this shindig wasn't dressy."

Looking down at the vintage sundress she'd found the day before, Abby smoothed the fitted bodice. "You think it's too much?"

"Nah." Sarah tweaked the flared skirt so that it swirled around Abby's hips. "Matt's going to love this look. With your hair up like that? Retro-hawt."

"I'd be happy with presentable, thanks. Hawt is beyond my powers." Abby grabbed her purse as they walked out the door.

"Whatever. Let your date decide."

Sarah drove to Matt's and beeped goodbye as Abby ran up to the door and rang the bell. Hearing him shout, "Come in," Abby stepped inside.

The living space was as neat as his studio, if much more cozy. A distressed leather couch and a comfortable chair grounded the small living room off the entryway. Both pieces of furniture were arranged around a stone fireplace that was flanked on one side by a floor-to-ceiling bookcase and on the other by a hickory armoire. Colored sketches of the local coast hung on the walls. Cushions and throws were piled in a basket next to the couch.

"Abby?" Matt's voice came from the back of the house.

She followed the sound, passing through a small kitchen and dining area before reaching his studio. She stopped to watch him gently lift a damp cloth over a sculpture in the corner. He moved to the sink, gingerly raised the cuffs of his white shirt, and washed his hands.

Abby whistled. "Looking pretty good, mister. I thought artists were supposed to be Bohemian. You look like you stepped off the cover of *GQ*."

Matt chuckled as he grabbed a towel. "According to Claire, only artists that want to remain starving or those that are already famous can get away with that, and she hasn't been wrong yet. I had my Bohemian moment last week." He told Abby about the sandals with his suit, and she laughed.

Tossing the towel aside, he crossed the room and circled Abby's waist with careful hands before leaning in for a slow kiss. When he pulled back, his eyes were dark. "You look amazing." He stroked the fabric that draped her hips and cursed as it stuck to his hands. "Just a minute," he said. He stepped over to retrieve a jar of thick cream and slather it on his hands. As he massaged it in, he looked her over again. "Beautiful," he murmured, his eyes straying to the canvas draped shape in the corner for a second before he focused on Abby again. "You're perfect. I don't want to mess you up. Yet." Matt laughed, finishing with the lotion and grabbing a jacket off the back of his desk chair.

Abby looked curiously at the canvas-draped shape. "I don't suppose you'd care to share your work?"

Matt glanced at her as he opened the door. "Eventually. Probably." He shook his head and chuckled, ushering Abby to his car.

Pulling up in front of Claire's gallery, she was stunned by the dollar value of the cars that were parked in the spaces around it. Abby examined her vintage-shop dress. "Maybe—"

Matt got out of the car and crossed to the passenger side to help Abby out of the open door. "Maybe, nothing. You look great. The perfect arm candy. These things are all about selling a product." He tucked Abby's hand in the crook of his arm. "As much as art feeds the soul and I wouldn't want to do anything else, it's also my job. I sell the sculptures by selling myself."

"That sounds really dirty, you know that?" Abby hip checked him as they approached the door, and Matt's somber mood broke with his smile.

Once inside, he headed for Claire. Abby breathed a sigh of relief: Claire's slacks and silk shirt were as casual as Matt had indicated. Wearing that, the gallery owner should have disappeared among the bright, bejeweled finery displayed on a succession of trophy wives with more money than taste, but instead, the perfect cut of her clothes and obviously real, heavy gold jewelry made her stand out. Charles stood grinning by her side, his hands carelessly pushed into his jeans pockets and his hair ruffled. Claire gazed up at him adoringly as he said something that had the crowd howling.

After greetings between the people who knew one another and introductions between those who didn't, the gathering fell into a pattern Abby recognized from cocktail parties she'd attended on behalf of her museum. She switched into her public persona, working the room and talking to those who Claire pointed out as especially able to help move Matt's career along. Claire also worked the room, leaving Matt available to charm potential buyers and discuss his displayed works. A couple of hours passed before Claire gathered her guests in the center of the gallery to talk about Matt and his sculptures.

After his impromptu lecture at the boardwalk mural, Abby should not have been surprised to learn that up until a few years earlier, he had taught fine arts classes at the university. She caught his eye, and he shrugged with one shoulder. He broke in on Claire's monologue and ordered her to just show the damned sculptures already. The crowd ate it up, tittering and watching raptly as Claire uncovered the draped figures.

Since his large statues were still in progress, it was the three completed mock-ups that were presented. A collective hum that presaged a good show went around the room. Abby couldn't blame them for being caught by the beauty and realism of Matt's work, down to a shaving knick on the Zoe sculpture's shin. Jason looked like he was about to step off the pedestal on which he stood, and the entwined bodies of the couple statue carried an eroticism that had wives nudging husbands.

The Bakers stood next to the sculptures, accepting congratulations as if they had created the works themselves. Mrs. Baker, whose name turned out to really be Bambi, announced that the completed statues would be at their house and only at their house. She slipped her arm around Matt and asked her friends to take her picture with the artist and "her" sculptures. Claire moved into the breach, reminding her that their contract was for the finished sculptures only; any other works surrounding them were still the property of the artist. Bambi protested, looking to her husband for help, and Claire led the couple into an office.

That seemed to signal the end of the reception. Charles started steering couples and singles toward the door, his easy smile and polished manners smoothing the way. Claire appeared a few minutes later, arm linked through Mr. Baker's. A quiet word with her husband was met with a smile, and within minutes, he was crating up one of his "finds" for the mollified couple.

Matt's arm went around Abby's waist. "Had about enough?"

Claire bustled by, dramatically covering her eyes. "Not looking. Lock up when you go." She waved over her shoulder and followed the Bakers and her husband out of the gallery.

"When we go?" Abby asked.

Matt smiled mysteriously and disappeared down a hall. He returned a minute later, carrying a basket, a bottle, and two glasses. He shook out a tablecloth on the floor and plopped down.

"Chris?"

He laughed. "Not this time." He unpacked sandwiches and a hoard of other small goodies. "Finger food isn't dinner, right?" He poured sparkling wine into a glass and held it out.

It was Abby's turn to laugh. She sat, curling her legs to the side, and waited for Matt to serve her. They discussed the reception, comparing notes on the attendees and their preferences. When they were finished eating, Matt packed away the leftovers and laid his head in Abby's lap.

"Better," he said in satisfaction. "So, did you get a good look at the…whatever it was…Charles boxed up for the Bakers?" He snorted laughter.

"Hush. Somebody somewhere loved that…whatever." She thought of the waving feathers that covered the piece and stifled a smile. "There was one couple, though, that did know art. They liked your mock-ups, but they're really interested in one of your others." She indicated a dimly lighted area.

Matt looked surprised. "How did they find that?"

"*Someone* must have pointed it out. I talked to them for a while and got a sense of what they'd like, goofy. They're nice people, and that piece is my favorite."

"Why?"

"Well," Abby said slowly, thinking, "the lines are very clean for a modernist piece. So many diverge into a half-assed cubism, all angles. That one has lovely curves, and the marble gives it a fluid feel." She smiled. "It reminds me of our surfing trip."

Matt rolled to his feet. He helped Abby up and walked her toward the piece in question. He stopped in front of it and pointed to the small brass plaque on the base. Though the letters were hard to make out in the dimness, Abby crouched down and read it: *Steamer Lane Swell.* She looked up in delight. "Where you swim with whales, right?"

Matt crouched beside her and cupped her jaw in one hand, leaning forward to press a kiss on her willing mouth. "Yes," he said. "Thanks for getting it. Chris insists that it looks like a fucked-up snail."

Abby laughed and slipped an arm around his waist as they surveyed the sculpture. She ran her finger over the plaque thoughtfully. "Swell…that's another word for a wave, right?"

"Sort of. More like a series of waves." Matt sat down on the floor and Abby sat beside him. "Swells happen when two storms collide. The best are when the storms come from opposite coasts. They can make for a hell of a season — unpredictable, but interesting."

"A swell." Abby stroked the lower curve of the statue. "I like that." She rested her head on Matt's shoulder. "This is what you really love to do, isn't it?" she asked. "Not the new statues?"

"The pool statues?"

"They're beautifully done."

Matt laughed. "They're silly and indulgent, but they'll pay the bills for a while." They stood, clasping hands. "I'm ready to leave. Beautiful, smart, and understands my work? Totally unfair." He swung their hands and looked at her in calculation. "Would it be forward to say that I need you naked, Pretty?" Though Matt's smile hadn't changed, his eyes were very serious.

Thoughts ran through Abby's mind in rapid succession, a roundabout of uncertainty with roads shooting off to yes and no and later. Each had their points. *No* was the sensible road. *Later* had weak appeal. It would give her more time to consider what she was doing, but then they would have even less time together. Matt waited patiently for her to decide.

"Take me home. And stay. I'm saying it this time."

Matt shut the door of the cottage and turned the deadbolt. "This will give us a little warning if Sarah comes home." He wrapped Abby in his arms and pressed gentle kisses over her face. Nimble fingers tweaked the pins that secured her hair and tossed them to the floor. Matt sighed when the last one was gone, burying his hands in the thickness of Abby's hair and exploring her mouth. "Are you sure about this, Pretty?" he asked, pulling away to take a breath. Their momentum carried them backward a step.

Abby's hip bumped a table, and she sniggered, reaching out to catch a teetering lamp. "Very sure. Let's take this upstairs." She tugged Matt toward the stairs. She was surprised when he tugged back, unbalancing her, and she caught herself with both hands against his chest.

A low sound rumbled from him as he used the hand that had come to rest on the small of her back to press her against him. "Touch me, Pretty." He started to unbutton his shirt. "I've been thinking about your hands all day, and I need to feel them on my skin." He grunted in frustration when Abby slid one hand between the plackets of his shirt and stroked his chest through his undershirt. "This shit has got to go." He moved back to shrug out of his jacket and yank off his tie, dropping them where he stood. With a wry smile, he ran his hand through his hair, which he had set on end by pulling the tie over it, and finished unbuttoning his shirt.

Abby curled her hands into the fabric as he started to shrug that off as well, kissing his neck, feeling his pulse race. "Let me help," she whispered, loosening her grip on his shirt as he relaxed, eyes closed and smiling. Making sure to slide her hands over every possible inch of his shoulders and arms, she pushed the shirt off, hindered only when he had to unbutton the cuffs so it could fall completely from his body. "Is this what you wanted, Matt?" she asked, trailing the tips of her fingers around the neck of his T-shirt before sliding them underneath to caress the skin that covered the tops of his shoulders.

"Mmm hmm…" he hummed, shivering as she touched the ball of his shoulder again. "More."

Tugging the hem of Matt's T-shirt from the waistband of his slacks, Abby trailed the backs of her fingers over the hair that covered his flat stomach. Breath hissed between his teeth, and then he yanked the shirt over his head and tossed it down with his tie and dress shirt. "Too slow," he laughed.

Matt unzipped her dress, and his hands found her skin, outlining her shoulder blades with sensitive fingertips. "I've wanted to do this all night," he said, sliding the straps over Abby's shoulders and down her arms. She let him go and shook the fabric off her hands, allowing the dress to float to the floor.

They started up the stairs, stopping frequently for kisses and touches. Abby's bra fell to the floor by mid-flight, and her panties joined it a couple steps later. By the time they reached the landing, she was tugging at Matt's belt and unbuttoning his slacks.

Matt drew a breath as Abby cupped him through his boxers. He covered her hand. "Remember when I said that I'm a patient man?" he asked in a low voice. She nodded. "That ends right now." He kicked his feet out of his slacks and dipped his knees to lift her off her feet. "Which room, woman?"

Abby shrieked, laughing, and pointed to her room. Matt dumped her on her bed. "Nice," she said. He sat on the side of the bed to flick off his socks.

"Well, I have caught you checking out the goods a few times…" He slid onto the bed beside Abby, half-covering her with his body and smiling against her lips. Hands and lips and bodies started to move, quiet moans and sighs of pleasure, little chuckles and the sound of skin against skin getting louder as the world narrowed to the two of them.

They froze when there was thumping on the stairs.

Sarah ran by the open door, holding her hand up to shield her eyes. "I'mnotlookingI'mnotlooking," she chanted as she dashed past. The bathroom door slammed, and loud sounds of retching began.

Matt flopped onto his back, throwing his arm over his eyes and breathing heavily. "Kind of a mood killer, isn't it?" he asked, starting to laugh. Each retch brought another spate of giggles from both of them. Matt kissed Abby on the forehead and sat up, reaching for his underwear.

She lifted up on her elbows, frowning. "I thought you said you'd stay."

Matt slid his slacks on and buttoned them. "Are you sure that's a good—"

"Aaabbyyy…" Sarah's wail from the bathroom cut him off.

"Damn." Abby slid her legs off the edge of the bed and looked for her robe.

Matt grabbed it from the hook on the door and extended it toward her, but he grasped on to Abby's outstretched hand instead of releasing the robe. "Pretty, will you let me look at you?"

Abby chuckled uneasily. "Haven't you been doing that already?"

"No. I've been touching you. For a minute, would you let me just look?"

It was funny how a simple request could rattle her so much. Somehow, his looking at her body unimpeded and with her permission seemed more intimate than touching.

"Please, Abby," he whispered, dropping the robe on the bed and taking another step back.

Abby's heart started to pound. She stood up, aware of every flaw and imperfection as he scanned her form from face to feet. Twenty had passed her by well over a decade earlier, and while Abby knew that she was in good shape, doubts about the firmness of her breasts and the tautness of her stomach assaulted her. Matt's eyes moved slowly over her torso, chased by her flush. He paused at her chest, and Abby was sure he could see the way her breathing had picked up—certainly the tightening of her nipples had to be visible. She fought the urge to harden her abdomen even as her stomach muscles clenched inside. She was acutely aware that her hips, while not large, had rounded with age, and even her feet came in for some quick mental criticism as Matt's gaze drifted toward them.

His eyes gradually returned to hers. The fire and softness in them took her breath away. "So fucking beautiful," he murmured, and Abby was in his arms again as his lips sought hers in a searching kiss. Though the passion hadn't changed, the urgency had; this kiss felt like a conversation, each of them giving and taking in equal measure.

"Now I really don't want you to leave," Abby whispered when Matt folded her robe around her shoulders.

A moan from the bathroom made him smile. "I think Pukerella needs you."

Abby slid her arms into the robe. They walked down the stairs, sniggering as they collected cast-off clothes. Matt tugged his T-shirt over his head and shrugged into his jacket, slipping his shoes on at the door.

"Stay inside, sweetheart. It gets cold after midnight." Tugging on the lapel of Abby's robe, he pecked her on the cheek.

"What's with the brother-kiss?" Abby teased.

"If I kiss you again, I'm going to say the hell with Sarah, so I'll just say good night." He touched Abby's cheekbone with the tips of his fingers and headed out the door.

She followed him across the porch and waited to wave goodbye. Matt turned around and walked backward after he stepped onto the walk. "Come over tomorrow? The Ancient Mariner and his plastic wife are visiting." One side of his mouth turned up. "Claire is desperate to get you and me together, so she'll let me hurry them along. Then we can spend the rest of the day together."

"What do you want to do?"

Matt raised his eyebrows and grinned, turning around to wave goodbye over his shoulder.

Abby felt a thrill of anticipation, only to have it quashed by Sarah's doleful moan from upstairs. Maybe it was time for a talk with her friend, as much as she dreaded that. No amount of vacation fun was worth the noise she was currently making. Abby heaved a sigh and started back up the stairs, dropping her gathered clothes on the couch as she passed.

A high-pitched giggle greeted Abby when she peeked around the door of Matt's studio the next day. Matt looked up and smiled before returning his attention to Mrs. Baker. Abby settled into his desk chair to enjoy the show.

Mr. Baker prowled the room, poking into cupboards and looking at tools, clearly bored. Only the black and white body shots of Zoe that were tacked on the board held his attention; he asked if he'd be meeting the model that day. When that was denied, Baker turned in a huff and walked away. His wife clutched at Matt's forearm and began a series of inane questions about his work. Claire distracted Bambi by complimenting her tiny outfit and big hair, and the girl ate it up.

"Now, this is more like it." Matt's head whipped around. Baker was standing in front of Matt's mystery sculpture, now uncovered. He admired it from every angle as he swiveled the pedestal on which it sat. "I'll give you five thousand for this right now."

The look of horror on Matt's face as he strode across his studio to return the cover to the sculpture might have been funny if Abby hadn't been so stunned. Though her brain tried to deny that the sculpture was of her, her eyes knew the truth.

Matt smiled tightly. "This one's not for sale." He turned back toward Claire and Booby Barbie. "Maybe you'd like—"

"Ten." Baker pulled a cell phone out of the inner pocket of his suit coat. "Ten thousand for an unfinished clay is more than generous. I can have it transferred right now. With whom do you bank?"

Matt's smile remained, but his eyes went cold. "It's not for sale."

Tension floated in the air between the men. Mrs. Baker looked from one of them to the other, confused.

The surprise on Claire's face resolved itself. Looping her arm through Baker's, she talked brightly about the statues that he'd purchased, stopping just short of promising him one of the smaller sculptures. She mollified his wounded pride by complimenting him on his taste in choosing Zoe as a model. Bambi trailed behind them, picking at her nails. Tossing out an invitation to a late lunch that she clearly didn't mean for Matt and Abby to accept, Claire led the Bakers out the door.

The silence in the studio was profound. Only the small sounds of Matt collecting the tools he'd been using that morning broke the quiet. He carried them to the sink and turned on the tap.

Abby raised her feet onto the chair's seat. She wrapped her arms around her legs and rested her chin on her knees.

"So," she said. "Do you have something you want to tell me?"

Chapter Eleven

Matt's shoulders slumped. He kept his back to Abby, as though he was still cleaning his tools, but his hands gripped the sides of the sink.

"I didn't mean for you to find out this way, Abby." It seemed safest to keep looking at the bottom of the sink.

"Did you mean for me to ever find out?"

The curiosity in her voice wasn't exactly friendly, but she wasn't tearing into him. "I'd like to say yes…the best part of me, the part I like, says that. But I'm just not sure."

"Hmm."

Matt waited for her to continue talking, but she was silent after her noncommittal grunt. A slither of cloth startled him, and he turned to find Abby stretched on tiptoe, removing the drape from his private work.

"Abby, I—"

"A minute, please." She cast the barest glance toward Matt before returning to her observations. She rotated the tabletop upon which the statue rested, occasionally stopping to look more closely at a singular spot before resuming the slow revolution.

Matt leaned against the table behind her. Watching. The longer her silence went on, the more convinced he was that he'd had his last chance to feel her skin underneath his fingertips; his stomach clenched at the thought.

"Well…it's pretty clear this wasn't done since last night." Abby's voice held rueful humor. She studied another section. "When did you start this?" She traced the curve of a shoulder that was identical to the one she washed each day. Matt desperately wished that she would look at him.

Lifting himself to sit on the high table, he thought for a moment. "That night at The Catalyst, you were holding your hair up like that. I saw you, and I wanted to touch the curve of your neck. It looked so strong and so very soft…"

Abby shrugged off her overshirt and tossed it on a stool, and he felt the same impulse to stroke her skin. He half-rose from his sitting position, and then thought better of it and sank back down.

"I had an image of you, of this statue, and I sketched it that night. After that…it sort of took over my brain. I've been working on it on and off since then." He studied her back, his gaze drifting down and over the curve of her bum, comparing what was before him with the sculpture's back; the clay form could use a tiny bit of adjustment.

Abby slid her hand along the sculpture's outstretched arm until she could touch the clay hand. "And this is the last part you worked on," she whispered.

Matt's head jerked up. "Pretty much. How—"

"'I've been thinking about your hands all day,'" Abby quoted his own words back at him, and Matt had a sudden and total recall of how it felt to finally have those hands on his skin after spending the day crafting their doubles in clay. Remembering how warm and gentle they were and the sound of Abby's laughter in the dark, how she'd felt to him…The words that might make her understand his need to sculpt her caught in his throat and left him speechless.

Rotating the table again, Abby broke the silence. "You've been doing this along with your other sculptures?" Her hand rose to her eyes. "This is…overwhelming."

Words came back to him in a rush. "Abby, I'm sorry. I swear I never meant for anyone to see the statue—I'd never show it, or sell it, or…" He slid off the table, reaching toward her shoulder before dropping his hand to his side. "You fascinate me, and I just…I never meant to hurt you. I…" This time he did touch her shoulder. "Christ, Abby, would you please look at me? I'm dying here."

Abby turned, a shimmer of tears in her eyes. "It's not perfect," she whispered. She looked back at the sculpture and chuckled, wiping at her eyes.

Matt turned her face back around with one gentle hand. "I can change it. I'll destroy it, if you'd like. Anything you want." He contemplated what it would feel like to destroy something that was so precious to him. The clutching in his chest distracted him so much that he had to close his eyes and breathe deeply, pillowing his cheek on Abby's hair. He was so preoccupied in readying himself to do whatever it took to stop Abby's tears that he almost missed her next words.

"I want you to finish it. That's what I want."

"What?" His head snapped up. "You said it wasn't perfect."

Abby smiled and shrugged. "Neither am I, Matt. Thank you."

Matt's head was spinning. "For what?"

"For seeing *me*. For not Barbie-ing up what you could have. For being honest, but kind." Abby brushed a tear off of her cheek. "For making me beautiful, but still me."

Matt wrapped his arm around Abby's waist and turned her toward the sculpture, then revolved the tabletop upon which her clay doppelganger stood. "This is how I see you, Abby. And you're beautiful. I didn't 'make you' anything." They stood quietly for a minute before Abby looked up into Matt's face, smiling at the tenderness written there.

"Thank you for that, too."

"Anytime," Matt murmured. He brushed a few stray tendrils of hair back from her face, searching her eyes for some sign of hurt and finding none. He leaned down, eyes asking for permission before he kissed the corner of her mouth.

Abby's hand cupped his cheek for an instant before creeping into his hair, fingers running between the strands before they traced the hint of a curl at his nape. He groaned, pulling her more tightly against him, but his kisses remained gentle, searching for response.

She turned in his arms and stroked from his throat to his stomach. He smiled against her lips. "Sure you want to go there?" he asked as he covered her hand.

"I thought you liked me to touch you." She caught Matt's lower lip between her teeth and teased the edge with her tongue before abandoning it to press slow kisses along his jaw.

Low laughter rumbled from Matt's chest. "I definitely like it." One hand sought the soft depths of her hair, smoothing the strands, as his other hand restlessly moved over her back. "You'll find out how much if your hand goes maybe an inch lower."

"What, here?" Abby whispered in his ear, letting her hand drift down that crucial bit. She chuckled at Matt's indrawn breath and the shiver that shook him, but it was cut off as he tightened his arms and dropped his mouth to hers in a hungry kiss. Despite Matt's efforts to distract her, Abby continued to explore until the sound of discrete throat-clearing finally stilled her hands at the waistband of his jeans.

Matt raised his head, but only far enough to rest his forehead against Abby's. He took a steadying breath before speaking. "This better be good."

Chris's voice was filled with laughing apology. "Sorry, cuz. Claire's on the phone. I told her this might not be the best time, but she answered in the 'don't fuck with me' voice. 'Scuse my language."

Abby chuckled. "Go," she murmured. "I'll still be here when you get back." Stepping back, she smiled at Chris. "How are you today?"

He leaned in the doorway and snickered as Matt discretely adjusted his clothes. "Can't complain." His eyes flicked between the still exposed statue and back to Abby. "Not doing as well as some I can mention." He caught the paperweight Matt hurled at him as he passed, and tossed it back and forth between his hands, grinning.

"Hello, Claire," Matt said, opening the fridge and reaching for the carton of juice. "Are you going to use the 'don't fuck with me' voice with me, too?" He swallowed the last two mouthfuls and lobbed the empty carton at the garbage can.

"I should, but I think I might have saved your ass." There was a pause, and Matt heard the tiny click of a lighter and the corresponding deep inhale.

"Charlie's gonna kill you when he smells that stink." Matt sank down on a kitchen chair and kicked off his shoes.

"Shut up," Claire said. "I've been good for a long time, and Charles is out of town until Friday. Besides, he'd understand in this case."

Matt rested his head against the wall and put his arm over his eyes. "What's the damage? Did I lose the sale?" He began to run through

the things he needed to do immediately, like stop the next ship-
ment of clay and get a firm commitment from the potential buyers
of *Steamer Lane Swell* before they had a chance to speak with Baker.

"It was a near thing," Claire grumbled. "You're just lucky that I
took lessons in charming the devil himself from my husband. Want
to hear the deal?"

"Shoot."

"Baker really wants that sculpture. Bottom line. He offered me
fifteen K on the spot, twelve for you and three for me, if I could
convince you to sell."

"Not gonna happen. Alternate offer?"

Claire laughed. "You know me too well." Matt heard her take
another quick drag on her cigarette. "I offered him the three statues
we showed last night. I know that together they're worth as much
as he offered, more if you have them cast in bronze like we talked
about. I just thought that giving up that sale was well worth the
small fortune I gouged out of him for the larger statues. Thoughts?"

Matt didn't even take a full minute to think about it. "Hell, he
can have all six of them as far as I'm concerned."

"We'll keep the other three back for now, thank you very much.
Considering the way you push Baker's buttons, we may need that
negotiating tool later."

Matt chuckled. "Probably a good idea." He paused. "So…what
do you really think about this? Hit me."

Claire sighed. "As your quasi-agent, I'd advise you to sell the
damned statue to him and keep the others to sell later. You're a fool
to throw away as much money as you're potentially trashing."

"And as my friend?"

"I'm thrilled for you, Matt, and I'll kill you if you ever consider
selling it." Claire's voice was warm. "The sculpture is striking, but it's
the sculptor who makes me smile. You really like this woman, and
it shows. It's about damned time."

Uneasiness gripped him. He glanced toward the studio to be sure
Abby couldn't hear. "Don't get your hopes up, Claire. I like Abby,
sure. But you and I both know—"

"—It's just a summer thing. Right. I've known you for too long.
Sell that to someone who's buying, because it ain't me." She took a

final deep inhale. "There. I've polluted my body enough for another six months or so, if you behave yourself. Now I'll call Baker and rave about the fabulous deal he just made and all the money he rooked you out of. Do I know how to play the man, or what?" After a wicked laugh and a brief goodbye, the line went dead.

Matt returned to the studio to find Abby and Chris in deep discussion. He watched with amusement as Chris pulled up his shirt to demonstrate a position he'd taken to represent a javelin thrower readying his throw. The tension in the lean muscles of his torso was obvious, each separate abdominal muscle in sharp relief.

"I couldn't hold this position for the days it took to get the abs done, right?" Chris explained. "So he takes a few pictures and, bada bing, I'm out of there and at Steamer Lane on a board while he does the hard work. I'm just saying; it's something to think about."

"'Bada bing'? You've been watching too many Scorsese movies." He mouthed *Get out* as soon as Chris looked at him.

"Right. So, I'm outta here. Don't worry about me for dinner." He headed for the public entrance of the studio, sliding sunglasses over his eyes. "You kids have fun." He laughed and dashed out the door as Matt lunged at him.

Matt locked the door behind his cousin. When he reentered the studio, Abby was studying the leg of her clay double. She had her pant leg tugged up and her calf exposed. The tiny frown between her eyebrows fascinated Matt, as he'd never seen it before.

"I'm still working on the legs, Pretty. I'll get them right, I promise."

"I don't doubt it." Abby wrapped an arm around her middle. "I wonder…" Her voice trailed off, reluctance mixed with excitement on her face.

"About what?"

Hectic color bloomed on Abby's cheeks when she turned toward him. "Would photographs help you in finishing this sculpture? I mean, you work on it at all kinds of odd hours, and I'm not here all the time, and…" Abby's voice trailed off as his expression went blank. "Never mind. Silly idea." She plucked her overshirt off the stool on which it rested.

Matt covered her hand with his. "Wait, Abby. I was just thinking. It's a good idea, if you're sure you want to do it."

Abby seemed to relax. "Okay, then. Where do you want me?"

"What—now?" Matt was startled, but the cool, clear eye of the artist within him started calculating shots and sizing up the areas of the sculpture with which he was still unsatisfied.

"Why not?" A thread of nervousness ran through her voice. "This summer is supposed to be all about change, and this is definitely something I've never done before." She dropped her shirt back on the stool. "So, how do you want me?" A twisted grin raised one corner of Matt's mouth, and his eyes twinkled with mirth. "Knock it off and take your damn pictures before I change my mind."

Directing Abby toward his photographic equipment, Matt got her settled on a stool. He wasn't sure if he wanted the sculpture's vague facial features to be in sharper detail, but it seemed like a good place to start.

He kept up a steady patter of questions and comments as he calculated his shots, capturing Abby's face in a range of emotions once she realized that he didn't expect her to remain motionless. Making her laugh netted Matt shots of the length of her neck and the sharp line of her jaw, while stories of a youth split between his surfer father in Santa Cruz and his banker mother in Philadelphia drew expressions of concentration and soft affection. The parallels between his parents' story and his own were disturbing, so he moved on quickly, choosing instead to dwell on the fluttering of the pulse in her neck and what it felt like against his lips.

Pulling a low stool in front of the backdrop, he had her rest one set of toes upon it to mimic the sculpture's stepping motion. He took several shots of the way her body naturally shaped itself in that position, noting small adjustments that would need to be made to his clay. He asked if she would raise her jeans legs to her knees so he could get clear shots of her calves.

"Wouldn't it be easier if I just took them off?" Her cheeks pinked, but she carried on in a steady voice. "You need full leg shots, right?" Without waiting for his answer, Abby lowered her foot to the floor and unbuttoned the worn denim, sliding it over her hips. Matt allowed her a measure of privacy and a minute to reconsider by checking his camera and dumping the pictures he'd already taken onto his computer. He kept his mind on his task, trying not to think of what was underneath her jeans.

When he turned back, she had already returned to her previous position, this time clothed in just her tank and underwear. She kept her eyes trained at the floor ahead of her raised foot. "Sorry. I wasn't expecting…" She giggled. "Well, at least I didn't expect there to be cameras involved."

Matt laughed as well. "No, not what I was imagining either. Ready?" Abby nodded, and he started moving around her, framing his shots to highlight areas he hadn't been able to closely observe previously. The gentle curve of calf muscle as it diminished into delicate anklebones. A sweep of long thigh as it curved inward. The secret darkness in the bend of a knee. Matt resolutely banished thoughts of strength and softness in her legs, trying to keep the same objectivity that he maintained with any other model even as the white lace that stretched across Abby's hips tantalized him with both what it revealed and what it covered.

Conversation died as the tension between them rose.

Crouching to get a close-up of her shin and the top of her foot, Matt glanced up to find Abby's gaze trained on his hands before it roamed up his arms and over his shoulders. Her intensity stopped him short, and he lowered his camera to stare at her face, frozen by the desire written there. Abby's eyes locked with his, and she whispered, "Am I doing this right?" Matt nodded once. "Then finish." Abby grasped the hem of her shirt in both hands and pulled it over her head. Dropping it to the floor, she unclasped her bra, and it joined the small pile of cloth near her feet. With shaking hands, she gathered her hair into an untidy pile on the top of her head, assuming the position of her sculpture.

"Abby…" Matt murmured, standing before her with his camera hanging at his side.

"Take the pictures," Abby said. Her mouth curved into a slight smile. "This might be your only chance, because I can't believe I'm doing this." She tilted her head to look at him as he raised the camera. "Your statue is beautiful, and it needs to be right." Her head returned to the correct position.

Matt moved around her, clicking the shutter or correcting positioning with a gentle touch on arm or leg. After just a few shots, he realized that he wasn't feeling the familiar itch to shape clay with tools or fingers, but an ache to caress the skin of the woman in front of him.

He began to pack away his camera.

"Are we done? Did you get all the shots you want?" Abby lowered her foot to the floor. She released her hair, and it tumbled down to caress her shoulders.

Matt turned his attention to the photographic lights. "I'm done. And not even close." He chuckled and shook his head. "I got the pictures I'll need. Want is a whole other thing. It's time to quit when I can't look at you as a professional anymore." With the last light extinguished, Matt was across the space in two swift steps, one hand clasped around Abby's hip to crush her against him and the other cradling her head as he kissed her with hungry intensity. The frustrated passion of the night before combined with the tension between them made his kisses rough and desperate.

Abby met his strength with softness, cradling Matt's face with gentle hands before trailing them over his neck and shoulders, stroking his chest and stomach and drawing a low, needy moan from deep in his throat. Rather than clash against his hard form, her body molded to his, offering softness where he had angles.

His restless hands skimmed her back before cupping the comparative roughness of the lace that covered her behind. Stumbling toward a low table, he set Abby onto her bottom and yanked his shirt over his head, tossing it to the side before leaning over her and caressing the gentle swell of her breast with his palm. His brain stalled, caught in the biological imperative to have, and to take, and to enter. Only Abby's softness and warmth mattered, and the aching need within his own body.

Abby's squeak as cool wood met heated flesh jerked Matt back to awareness of his surroundings. He rested his head against her shoulder, breathing heavily, listening to the clamor of his heart. "I'm sorry," he said. He turned his head so his ear rested on her chest, gratified to find that her heart was slamming along at a pace to match his.

"*I'm* not sorry. That was hot." She laughed, and Matt joined in.

He nibbled at the curve of her breast with his lips. "If you think that was good, you should see what I can do with a comfortable space and a little time."

"Show me."

"I plan on it." Pushing himself to his feet, he helped her upright. He cupped her face in his palms, lowering his head to hers in a slow, soft kiss. As much as he wanted her, and as difficult as it was to still hands that itched to stroke her body, Matt felt that he had to give her another chance to back out. "Are you sure about this? No pressure, remember."

Abby closed the gap that he had created between them, running her hands over his chest and shoulders and twining her fingers in his hair. "I'm very sure. I don't want to waste any more time." Matt felt her hands against his stomach as they worked at his waistband.

"Right," he said, and then his mouth was on Abby's as he backed her into the hallway. He pushed at the soft lace that covered her hips, tearing one side in his haste to feel all of her heat and softness, and when that slight barrier was gone, he cupped her behind and lifted, backing her against the wall as her calves twined around his thighs. Taking a hot, hard nipple between his teeth, Matt bit down. The sound of Abby's low moan called an answering sound from his own chest and made him not entirely sure that they were going to make it the few short feet into his bedroom.

Only the need to hold her up and his corresponding inability to rid himself of his jeans brought him back to hazy comprehension. He lowered Abby, relishing the feeling of her skin sliding against his, until her feet touched the floor. They were both breathing heavily, and Matt no longer tried to still his hands. He stroked Abby's shoulder and arm with one hand, cupping her breast as he braced his other arm against the wall next to her head. Abby's hands moved against him as well, fingering through the hair that lightly covered his chest.

"Damn, Abby," he joked breathlessly, "what are you doing to me? All my smooth moves went right out the window there." He glanced down at the scrap of lace at his feet. "Sorry about your panties."

Abby laughed, her breath stirring his chest hair. "Stop apologizing. I haven't had this much fun in years. Though I'm generally a comfort girl."

Matt pushed away from the wall and took her hands in his, raising them to brush his lips against her sensitive wrists. "Then it's about time this ended," he said.

"You can't seriously mean quit now. That's just cruel."

Matt grinned. "By 'this,' I meant wall sex, woman." He started backing her toward his room, dropping kisses wherever he could reach. "While that has its time and place, I want to take my time and enjoy, and that requires a bed." The backs of Abby's legs hit the edge of his bed, and she sat abruptly. "Like this one. Are you good with that?"

Abby scooted back until she could stretch out on the mattress, her arms above her head. She watched Matt shed the last of his clothes. "Very good with that," she said. "What's your plan?"

He paused for a minute, enjoying the view before him and wishing for an instant that he could take a picture of Pretty just like that, lying on his bed with her hair in a wild halo around her face. Instead, he used his artist's eye to impress every line deep within his brain. When he was sure it was indelibly set, he slid onto the bed. "Abby," he said, drawing his tongue along the tendon at the side of her neck and swirling it in the hollow under her ear as she arched against him. "My plan is to touch every inch of your body to begin with." His hand caressed her breast, traced the gentle curve of her waist as it flared into slim hips, and ended up between her legs.

"I plan to pay special attention here," he murmured.

"Smooth moves, huh?" she asked breathlessly, whimpering as he sucked her nipple into his mouth.

"Mmm hmm…" he hummed, smiling as the vibration against her hardened flesh drew another gasp. "I have years of practice to draw on."

"I love the sound of that," Abby said, fisting her hand in his hair and drawing his head up to kiss him fiercely.

Matt lost himself in her then, his senses overwhelmed by her tastes and smell and sounds, by the feeling of the curves and planes that he'd been thinking about for weeks. He rolled onto his back and eased Abby on top of him, freeing his hands to caress her even as his mouth explored. Her body responded to his touch like it had been made to do so.

Abby's hands against him were sure; she seemed to know where to touch him and when to move on, keeping him at the knife's edge of pleasure without sending him over the edge. Every kiss and lick and touch he gave her was returned with interest, their exploration aided by the knowledge of when and where to guide each other. Moving together slowly at first, kissing and touching hair-roughened skin and velvet softness, they learned each other's bodies.

Eventually the tight coil of need deep within Matt became too much, and he moved to the nightstand, plucking out a foil pouch. He watched Abby as she watched him roll the condom over his length. He took in her heavy-lidded eyes and swollen lips as she moved restlessly against the sheets, and he had to push down an urge to plunge into her right then. "How do you want me, Abby?" A flush covered her body, and her quick breaths raised and lowered her chest.

"I want to feel you all over me," she whispered, spreading her legs so he could rest between them. "I need you…"

Her tiny gasp turned into a moan as he held her hip and slid into her in one stroke, dropping his head to cover her mouth with his. Pulling her leg high, Matt felt her tighten around him. Her soft sighs and whimpers increased in volume and sharpness as the tension inside him built and he moved harder and faster. The feeling of Abby's body against his, the pleasure in her response, stilled Matt's mind, and he was want and need and fill; Abby's answering want and give and open made her his perfect match, and words gave way to sighs and groans and the sound of flesh against flesh.

When he could think again, Matt found himself curved around Abby, his head lying against her chest as he gasped for air. Gentle fingers smoothed through his hair as Abby's own rapid breaths began to slow. Matt stroked her stomach with a shaking hand, tracing the curve of her hipbone with a fingertip before settling it on her still-trembling thigh. "Abby, that was…" he began in a husky voice, and then trailed off.

"I know," she answered, a smile in her voice.

His eyes drifted closed. He settled his head more firmly against her chest and wrapped his arm around her hips. "Do you mind?"

Abby's soft laugh was cut off by her own yawn. "Not at all. You need your rest for later." She stroked his back with a languid hand before dropping a kiss on his head. "And there will be a later. I promise you that. I'm sure you still have a few smooth moves to demonstrate."

He chuckled. "More than a few," he mumbled as he drifted off.

Chapter Twelve

Juggling a glass of iced tea, a book, her iPod, and a blanket, Abby hooked the French door with her toes and pulled, closing it behind her. After a late night and a morning of fishing Play-Doh out of little mouths, she was ready for some solar therapy. Picking her way down the beach, she dropped her armload on a chair before shaking out the blanket and lying down in the shade of the umbrella. A smile crept across her face when she stretched and all the delicious aches from the night before settled into her limbs.

"Don't do that! Don't you *do* that!"

Abby tipped her head back and watched Sarah tiptoe across the hot sand with her own armload of goodies. "Do what?"

Dropping her things, Sarah plopped down onto the sunny side of the blanket and shook her finger in Abby's face. "That! That! You've been grinning and giggling all morning, and it's driving me crazy. Where's your stupid phone, Abby? Did Matt have to surgically remove it from your hand last night?"

Abby shot her the finger but realized that she hadn't thought of the museum in days. Sarah shoved a Styrofoam container forward. "Here — eat your lunch."

Balancing the container on her stomach, Abby propped herself up on one elbow and opened the box. She lifted out a piece of sushi, and after taking a bite, she closed her eyes and hummed in pleasure. "Good stuff."

"Yeah, well, it better be," Sarah said around a mouthful of rice and ahi. She chewed quickly and swallowed, grabbing Abby's iced tea to wash it all down. "I had to hide from Tyler and his band of flying freaks twice before I got back to the car. That guy in the surf shop thought I was insane when I ducked behind the sailboards. That's the second time this week. At least I didn't knock them over this time."

Abby laughed at the image, drawing another glare.

"Don't laugh! That kid's persistent as hell. Too bad I don't date tadpoles."

"Well, maybe not date…"

"I hate you. I really hate you," Sarah whined. "I didn't do that, either—thank you very much, by the way—unlike some people I could mention."

"Jealous?" Abby popped another piece of sushi into her mouth.

"Hell, yeah!" Sarah picked a piece of rice off her stomach. "Oh yeah…and I ran into Surfer Dude II—you know, the blond? He was picking up sushi too. He wanted me to pass a message."

Abby closed her empty container and reached for her glass of tea. "Chris? What did he have to say?"

Sarah nabbed the glass first and took a swig before passing it to Abby. "He said to tell you he's really sorry about this morning, and he should learn to keep his mouth shut, and he wasn't hinting at all, and…" She thought for a minute. "That's about all." She settled her sunglasses over her eyes and stretched out in the sun, adjusting her bikini. "He turned bright red—did he see your boobies?"

"Not even. I was fully dressed when I ran into his drunk butt outside the bathroom at about three o'clock this morning." Abby adjusted her own suit but stayed in the shade. "Secondhand tequila is a smelly thing."

"Assy jet fuel, I told you. So why the Walk of Shame? Seems a little silly when you've spent a whole Sunday in flagrante delicto. Did Matty-boy give you the cold shoulder? Make you sleep in the wet spot? Fail to live up to the promise so clearly defined in the wetsuit? Call you the wrong name? What?"

"If you'd shut up for a minute, I'd tell you. Your answers are: no, no, hell no, and he calls me the wrong name all the time—Pretty." They laughed. "No shame involved—it just felt like time to come home. I learned a lot about Matt yesterday, but not how he feels about sleepovers. Not from him, anyway."

Sarah lifted her head and raised her glasses to squint at Abby out of one eye. "The plot thickens. I take it this is where Chris comes in?" Abby nodded, a smile playing at the corner of her lips as she raised her head to take a sip of tea. "Well? Spill it, girl!" Sarah demanded, and then observed, "You have tea running down your arm."

Abby poked her tongue out to catch the errant drop, and the memory of Matt's tongue trailing along her skin made her shiver. "Chris congratulated me on being the first woman he knows of to breach the…what the hell did he call it? Inner sanctum? Cave of wonders?"

"Sounds deliciously dirty, whatever it was." Sarah lay back down. "Girl, you know what he meant. You're the Christina Columbus of that casa. You discovered a whole new world. And by invitation, too. Lucky bitch."

"Thank you." Abby grinned, popped in her earbuds, and grabbed her book. Before long, though, it was lying beside her. Her attention was too scattered to get anything out of the words. No matter how cool she'd sounded when relaying the basics of the conversation with Chris to Sarah, every time she thought about it, she felt a clutch of butterflies take wing in her stomach.

After Chris's slurred compliments, Abby had considered staying. Now she was grateful she'd called a cab. It would have been all too easy to forget that little issue of time. No matter how often her brain pointed out that this was the age of Skype and texting and unlimited cell minutes, her gut told a different story. Two months together was not substantial enough to give a long-distance relationship a hope of surviving between face-to-face visits; those would be few and far between if she was paying for travel. If Matt even wanted that. She'd rather have a perfect summer relationship—no strings attached—than wake up thinking it was more and find out she was wrong later.

"Can I make a suggestion, Abby?" Sarah's voice cut into Abby's ruminations.

"Sure. What?"

"Two things, actually." Sarah swiped sweat off of her brow. "First, finalize Jason. While you were off cavorting with Clayboy, Bikeboy showed up here, and I entertained him."

Abby leaned up on her elbows. "Jesus, Sare. I'm so sorry."

Sarah waved her hand dismissively. "No probs. Not like you wouldn't do the same for me. Just be clear, okay?" She sat up and swiped at her face. "I think we need an Independence Day party, babe. You can celebrate…whatever is going on with you and Matt, and I feel the need for many drinks and beach music." She leaped to her feet. "I'm melting here. An ice-cold beer and the AC sound good to me. You coming?"

"Not quite yet. I'm enjoying the sunshine that I'm not lying in." Abby laughed. "The water and the breeze are nice too."

"You're crazy, but I suppose that's why I love you." Sarah gathered up her things and the empty lunch containers and headed up the beach toward the house. "Have fun slow-roasting."

Abby rolled onto her stomach and opened her book. Hearing the door to the cottage open, she remembered that Sarah had mentioned two suggestions. "Hey! Sarah!" she called, waiting for her friend to turn. "What was the second suggestion?"

Sarah smiled. "Don't over-think this," she called back. "Enjoy the summer. Change, baby. Carpe-freaking diem." She leaped up the back steps and enclosed herself in the air-conditioned house.

Settling down after a sip of tea, Abby lost herself in her book. Eventually, though, the heat and her late night caught up to her, and she laid her head on her arms, letting her mind drift off with the music.

A whisper-light tickle on her stomach brought her swimming to murky half-consciousness. She brushed sleepily at the fly and encountered instead soft hair. She stiffened with a gasp but relaxed again as she glanced down. She popped out her earbuds. "Hey, you."

"Hey, you," Matt replied, tracing the curve of her waist with a finger as he crouched beside her. "I was running by and saw you sleeping in the sun. Not a great idea." His palm caressed her stomach before settling on her hip.

Abby shifted so the contact was firmer. Matt's lips quirked into a smile. "I was under the umbrella, I swear. The sun's shifted." She lifted her head and looked down. "Did I burn?" Sliding one hand down her stomach, she rolled the waistband of her bikini bottom down so she could check for a color difference.

Matt groaned. "That was just cruel."

"Speaking of ill-advised moments in the sun, what were you doing running at this time of day?" Abby asked.

"I had Zoe in this morning—bloodthirsty thoughts every time I had to reposition her. I decided to say bye-bye. I'll use educated guesses for whatever I didn't shoot." Matt grinned down at Abby. "It wasn't nearly as much fun as yesterday's photo session."

Abby felt a deep blush descend from her hairline.

Matt caught her downcast gaze. "Hey. Don't. Don't be embarrassed. Yesterday was…" He trailed off, searching for words. "It was pretty damned incredible."

Abby's lips began to turn up. "It was, wasn't it?" She stretched up to kiss him. "So, how does that relate to you killing yourself by running in the sun?"

"Needed to blow off some steam before my second favorite person shows up this afternoon."

Abby laughed. "What did Jason ever do to you?" One side of Matt's mouth crooked up into a smile. "Don't be such a guy," she admonished, squeezing his arm. "Do you have pictures of him too? You might need them…he showed up at the cottage last night. I'm going to talk to him later."

"I thought that was taken care of."

Abby slid her arm around his waist. "I haven't told him anything about you, Matt. I was thinking that it might be easier…and you're his boss…" She sighed. "It was the best I could do at the time. You might lose your model now."

"I'm sick of both of them anyway." Matt looked at his watch. "Playtime's over."

They got up, and when they reached the porch steps, he folded Abby into his arms, kissing her with slow intensity and thoroughness as his fingertips ran up and down her spine. He chuckled at the tap on the door and a muffled "Get a room."

"Is she always like that?" he asked.

"Sometimes she's worse." Abby aimed a kiss at his chin. "You'd better move it, mister. You'll be late."

Matt grumbled, but he nodded. His expression became serious. "About what Chris said this morning—he meant it as a compliment... a statement..." Matt brushed a hand through his hair. "He didn't mean for you to leave, Abby."

Abby smiled. "I didn't leave because of that, Matt. Please. I'm an adult."

"Then, why..."

"Because we hadn't discussed how to handle the morning. I know better than to assume. And because you already took an entire day away from work for me." Abby saw the protest rising to his lips and reached out to cover them. "Okay?" She kept her hand in place until he kissed her palm.

"Okay. Just, next time..." There was conflict in his eyes. "Wake me up and say goodbye."

Abby refused to let disappointment show on her face. "Next time? What makes you think there'll be a next time?"

Matt smiled. "Oh, there will. I predict a lot of next times. And you'll love every one." He kissed her again and murmured against her lips, "I like you, Abby Reynolds."

"I like you too. But you're a cocky bastard." She kissed him firmly. "Get going, mister."

Abby watched him run down the beach, slow at first, but then faster, until he settled into a ground-eating lope. She admired his form and grace until he passed beyond her view. Then she turned with a sigh to enter the cottage.

"That looked fun," Sarah observed.

Abby reached past her friend to grab the phone. "No, this is the fun part," she said ruefully. She only had to wait through a single ring before Jason answered.

A few days later, Abby toted another cooler out the back door. She surveyed Sarah's party preparations, including the improvised fire pit. "Sarah, are you sure you can have a fire on the beach?"

"Pretty sure I can't," Sarah answered cheerfully, plopping a case of beer on top of a cooler. "But we've invited all the neighbors, and we won't light it until full dark. By the time the beach patrol shows up, it'll be late. Then I'll argue whether the pit is on my property or on the public beach, which doesn't matter, but they'll be so worried about scaring off the tourists that they'll play nice and argue quietly. By the time they get pissed, I'll be ready to evict people anyway." She pushed her hair back from her forehead and grinned. "It's a win-win situation."

Abby shook her head. "You scare me. You really do." She looked around critically, noting the mostly empty food tables. "Are you sure everyone was okay with pot-luck? Doesn't seem like the neighbors' style."

Sarah draped red, white, and blue cloths on the tables. "Grab that cake, would you, Abby? Our oh-so-wealthy neighbors were…'tickled pink' is what I think Mrs. Bowman called it. Old lady Drake said it was 'delightfully Bohemian,' too. I figure if we play oldies for the first couple of hours after dinner, their Metamucil will have kicked in, and they'll all toddle off home, happy to have been asked to party with the youngsters."

"Youngsters?"

Sarah waved her hand dismissively. "Comparatively speaking." A frown creased her brow. "Now, if the fireworks show nicely over the water and the real youngsters stay away, my night will be perfect." She gave Abby a sideways glance and an evil grin. "Again, comparatively. Though not quite as nice as yours, I'd imagine. Tired today?"

"Shut it. I was home before dawn, and you came rolling in just a few minutes before I did. Don't lie—you had shoes on, and you never wear shoes inside for longer than five minutes." Ignoring her friend's whispered "Damn," Abby changed the subject. "Wow. Now that you mention it, I think this is the first time we'll have missed watching the fireworks over the Harbor since…forever. David won't know what to do with himself."

"He'll survive," Sarah muttered. She started to shift chairs around violently.

Abby sighed. Though she was initially glad Sarah and David had started to communicate with each other rather than through her, she was starting to worry that they'd never admit they cared about each other. "When are you guys going to stop texting and start talking?"

"Tried this morning. No answer." Sarah turned with a bright smile, a sign that the subject was definitely closed. "Good thing I told people to bring beach chairs if they had them, right? I'm going to check if we have all the s'more stuff." She swept up the stairs and into the house, leaving Abby to start the grills and greet the first guests as they came around the side of the cottage.

The next couple of hours passed in a blur of cooking, eating, and drinking, punctuated by greetings of newcomers. The gathering became more boisterous as the beer coolers and wine tubs emptied. Sarah had set dinnertime for seven, and by the time that rolled around, her normal good nature had returned. She circulated amongst her guests, greeting the faces that she'd known vaguely since adolescent visits to her aunt with the same bonhomie as she offered to those she'd met weeks earlier.

Abby moved around the group, greeting people and getting anxious about Matt. She'd awakened him to say goodbye before she left early that morning, and as soon as he'd opened his eyes a crack and smiled, she'd longed to crawl back between the sheets. As the evening sky darkened and Sarah started the beach fire, though, Matt had yet to make an appearance or to call.

She was hesitating, phone in hand, when Sarah hissed from behind her, "Lordy, lordy…look who showed up. If looks could freeze, you'd be Antarctica."

Abby caught Jason's eye as he came around the corner of the house, towing a hesitant Zoe. Claire and Charles were at his heels.

"Glad you could come, guys," Sarah said cheerfully.

Abby took in the younger woman's tense posture and suspected Zoe had guessed Jason was using her for spite. "Zoe, you put us all to shame. You're gorgeous. Thanks for coming."

Visibly relaxing, Zoe smiled. "Thanks. Is there anything we can do to help?"

Before Abby could answer, Jason broke in to the conversation. "Zoe wanted to come. That's the only reason I'm here." He looked around. "You wear out our ex-boss?" he asked belligerently, snapping his gum. Abby tried to think of an answer both cutting and clean enough for the elderly neighbors who were listening to the exchange with great interest. Jason tugged Zoe's hand. "Never mind. Let's dance." Zoe looked back with a mixture of apology and laughter in her eyes.

Claire kissed Abby's cheek. "Darling girl, tell Charles where he can put his load down before he has a hernia and I miss out on my little bit of somethin' somethin' tonight."

Charles grinned, face red and arms straining from the case of wine he held along with the mesh bags full of goodies that hung from his elbows. "God forbid the little woman go without when I'm home," he said breathlessly as he flicked his hair out of his eyes. "Nice to see you again, Abby. Welcome to my sex life." Abby laughed and pecked him on the cheek.

A general cheer went up when the local benefactor was recognized, and eager hands relieved Charles of his burdens while another contingent went back to his car for another load. He grabbed his wife's hand and a beer at the same time before heading toward a boisterous group near the fire. Sarah pumped her fist in the air. "Yes!" she hissed. "I was getting worried about the noise, but now that Santa Charles is here…" She laughed and walked down the beach, dropping her load of chairs before joining the dancers.

A pair of warm arms wrapped around Abby's middle, and she turned to see Matt. "I was getting worried about you. Thought maybe you'd changed your mind."

"Nah. I just got caught up in the clay again. I didn't even realize what time it was until I heard Claire shrieking that she was tired of waiting around for me."

Abby kissed his mouth hard. "What was so absorbing?"

"This curve right here." Matt traced the small of Abby's back and over the slight rise of her bum. She shivered, and he laughed. "But before that, I finished the first Jason statue." He nodded at his subject, dancing on the sand, and got a shrug and a frown from him in return.

"One down and two more to go before September."

Abby's stomach plummeted when she thought about the end of summer, but she kept her bright smile. "That's wonderful! I guess we know what you'll be doing for the rest of the summer, right? Can't lose the momentum now."

Matt smoothed Abby's hair with one hand. "Not the only thing I'll be doing." He paused for a minute. "Wow. I did not mean that how it came out." They chuckled together. "I plan on spending time with you, is what I meant. Fuck momentum. If I can't manage my time and efforts by my age, I'm screwed anyway." Not leaving any time for a response, he kissed her urgently. He didn't release her until a wild catcall from the beach drew their attention to Sarah, who was giving Abby a big thumbs-up.

"I don't care how much she drinks tonight; you are not taking care of Pukerella again." Matt smiled and waved at Sarah. He tucked Abby's hand in the crook of his arm. "What is there to drink around here?"

Grabbing a bottle of zinfandel and a couple of plastic cups, they walked toward the laughing group seated near the fire. Plopping into couple of chairs, they caught the end of Charles's story about dodging a particularly determined bar girl in the Philippines by jumping out the men's room window.

"Last time I act like a gentleman and buy a lady a drink," Charles said to general laughter.

"At least, the last time you forget to look for an Adam's apple." Claire nipped Charles's bottle from his hand and took a swallow before setting it down beside her chair. Charles laughed right along with the gathered partygoers.

As the time for fireworks neared, people started to drift away from the fire, spreading out along the beach to get the best view of the show. Matt nabbed a blanket off the sand. "Coming down to the water?" he asked Charles.

Charles snuggled down in his chair, pulling Claire onto his lap. "Nope. I plan on taking advantage of the lack of wild partiers up here to listen to Otis Redding and feel up my wife." He flapped his hand in a shooing motion as Claire laughed. "Carry on. Fireworks don't last long enough these days."

Matt draped the sandy blanket over his shoulder and took Abby's hand. They headed down the beach, away from the revelers who were busily setting up chairs and laying down blankets. They walked until the person furthest from the house disappeared into the darkness. Taking advantage of a sheltering clump of tough beach grass, Matt laid the blanket down and sat, spreading his feet on the blanket.

When Abby was settled between Matt's legs, her knees up and feet aligned with his, he wrapped his arms around her. She leaned her head against his shoulder as the first brilliant flash exploded over the water.

They watched the fireworks for a while, and Abby almost drifted off while counting the beats of his heart against her back. The boom of a particularly loud firework jerked her back to reality, and she sat upright, watching the huge explosion disintegrate into a million tiny stars. "Beautiful," she breathed.

Cool fingers brushed her hair off her neck an instant before warm lips descended. "Beautiful," Matt agreed.

Abby tilted her head to give him better access. "I thought we were watching fireworks." Humor balanced with need in her voice. Matt glanced at the brightly illuminated sky before returning to his explorations.

"Fireworks lost their appeal copared to girls by the time I was ten," he murmured. His right hand skated over her stomach and upward.

"Ten?" she asked. "Are you sure about that?"

"Early bloomer," he whispered. The combination of his warm breath and the soft hair that brushed her skin made her gasp.

Matt's fingers were no longer cool as he slid his hand under the waistband of Abby's gauzy pants. He traced her hipbone, swirling his fingertips in the hollow to the inside. "You know, I wanted to touch this exact spot that day you had the wreck." He stroked her freshly healed skin gently before finding the soft hollow once again. "I was supposed to be checking out your injury, and I was restraining myself from this. Is it wrong to be glad you're biking-challenged, for a variety of reasons?"

Abby laughed.

"I need to taste this spot," he murmured, pushing her tank-top strap down and kissing a path to her shoulder.

She whimpered and shifted around. The grit of sand beneath her hips made her realize where they were. She cupped Matt's cheek with one hand as she smoothed her shirt down with the other.

"This isn't a good place," she said.

"Why?" His voice was muffled against her skin. "It's dark. There's a blanket."

"And sand."

"There's a blanket," he repeated, chuckling into Abby's ear.

Abby caught his hands and tucked her chin down until he sighed and lay next to her. He rested his mussed head on one palm and raised his eyebrows. Abby smiled at his obvious impatience. "As much as I'm enjoying the whole *From Here to Eternity* vibe, sand in the naughty bits is not fun."

"It's just a little sand," Matt coaxed, sliding his hand over Abby's stomach again.

She slapped it. "One grain is too much. Voice of experience." She rolled to her feet and extended a hand to him. "Besides, fireworks are over."

Matt let himself be tugged to his feet. He pushed Abby's hair away from her ear and kissed the hollow beneath. "The fireworks are over *for now.*" He scooped up the blanket and Abby's sandals.

"See? There's that cocky thing again," Abby teased. They walked along the sand, their joined hands swinging between them. Sarah's wicked laugh rang out above the music as they approached the party. They exchanged smiles that turned to twin frowns when the laugh became an angry shout.

Abby could see Sarah in the light of the fading bonfire, surrounded by Tyler and his boys as the last party guests looked on in confusion. She dropped Matt's hand and took off down the beach, shouting, "Hey! Stop that!"

Before she got near enough for any of the jeering boys to grab her, Matt stopped her and pointed to the figure moving swiftly toward the loose group, closely followed by a uniformed officer.

Tyler grabbed Sarah's arm, and she shook his hand off roughly. "I said go home, Tyler. You're drunk, underage, and repulsive."

"That's not what you said before," he said. His friends laughed.

"The lady told you to go home, kid," a voice said. Tyler turned to sneer at the rumpled man behind him.

"Who are you?" Tyler asked belligerently. "This is none of your business, little man."

David slid between Tyler and Sarah and shook his head. "See, that's another reason not to like you. You speak like a comic book thug. Go home, kid."

"If you're the boyfriend, you've been had, man."

David rubbed the back of his neck. "Kid, I'm telling you right now. Get out of here."

"Why the hell do you keep calling me kid?" Tyler asked. "I'm old enough for *her* to mess around with." He jerked his head at Sarah. "I'm eighteen."

"Good. I'm not going to jail then," David said calmly, then in two compact moves drew his fist back and popped Tyler in the face.

Tyler looked at David in astonishment, bringing his hand up to touch his nose right before he plopped on the sand. The police officer moved forward, wearing a grin, his hand on the butt of his gun as he silently warned the other boys off. He crouched before Tyler and started to examine his gushing nostrils.

"David." Sarah threw herself into his arms. "I thought he was going to kill you."

David chuckled, rubbing her back. "Age and experience count in a fight." He thought for a minute. "It didn't hurt that he was surprised and drunk, either." He kissed her mouth passionately, then stepped back to look at her. "Why do you look so shocked? I said I'd talk to you again in a few days."

She took his hand and held it tightly. "But…"

David pushed his hair off his forehead. "I've wanted to come out here since the first time you called, but it took time to find someone to cover for me, and there was a mess with City Council that I had to track down, and a last-minute direct flight from Boston to San Francisco was impossible to find, and…" He sighed. "Life. Anyway, I don't want to talk about this tonight. I want to go back to my hotel and sleep for several hours. Then I want to talk about all this and about how I don't want you as a friend anymore." Sarah's eyes filled with tears, and David wrapped his arm around her waist. "Come with me."

Her smile was gigantic.

David noticed Abby then and walked over to hug her. "Good to see you. I'd love to talk, but I'm crashing. Tomorrow?" His eyes flicked to Matt, who was waiting nearby. David put his hand out and the men shook as Abby made the introductions. Soon the mouse roar of Sarah's Hyundai broke the stillness, and she and David were gone.

Abby and Matt walked toward the house, hand in hand, smiling at each other as they noticed Charles and Claire still curled together in one chair, watching the goings-on with interest.

The couples looked at each other in silence for a moment, and then Charles spoke. "You Yankees know how to throw a hell of a party. Drama, romance, jealousy, fights, sex…" He pointedly looked at Matt's open shirt and wind-tunnel hair.

Abby snorted, and within seconds, they were all laughing. "It was like a wreck…sort of horrifying, but you can't look away."

Claire heaved herself out of Charles's lap. "Next time I complain my life is boring, darling, refer me to this night." She hugged Abby and kissed her on the cheek before doing the same to Matt. "Come to dinner later this week, my loves. I can't promise a show like this one, but the dinner will be fabulous and the company even better."

After Charles had his turn at hugs, he swept Claire into his arms and strode around the corner of the house, her laughter trailing behind them.

Matt and Abby looked at each other in the sudden silence. "I suppose I should get going too…" Matt made a weak effort to pull his hand from Abby's.

She wrapped her fingers inside the front of his shirt. "I have plans for you."

"I suppose I can set an alarm or something, because you know I'm going to sleep afterward."

Abby's stomach tightened with need and anticipation, and she backed up the porch steps, towing Matt by his shirt. "No need for an alarm, unless you want one. I want you to stay."

Matt smiled before cradling her against his body, giving her a slow, soft kiss that left her breathless.

Chapter Thirteen

Matt left the bedroom cautiously, peering across the hall toward the bathroom and Sarah's open door. He didn't want to chance running into Sarah in just his boxers.

"Abby?" he called. Silence. "Sarah?"

"Well, shit," he muttered, grabbing his shirt and heading down the stairs after a quick stop in the vacant bathroom. He called for Abby twice more on his way to the living room, but it was apparent that she wasn't there. After a check out the back door, Matt faced the fact that Abby was nowhere to be found. A search of the cabinets and freezer revealed filters and coffee, and he settled down to making a pot.

As it brewed, he thought about his first reaction to finding her side of the bed cold: disappointment. He'd fallen asleep looking forward to the morning, to slow kisses and warmth and beginning one day the way he'd ended the last—with her curled up beside him. It didn't matter how many times he told himself that he was being idiotic for missing her; hell, waking up alone should make him feel free and unencumbered, the way he'd lived his life for a very long time.

He poured his coffee, trying to ignore the uncomfortable feeling that Abby might have been trying to send him a message—that she liked their "no sleepovers" arrangement and that he'd made an ass of himself by staying. It would be no more than he'd learned to expect since childhood: a boardhead shouldn't expect more than a businesswoman could give.

His reverie was interrupted when the French door opened and Abby entered the kitchen, carrying a box and a newspaper. His rush of relief was immediate.

"Hey, sleepyhead!" she said cheerfully. She toed off her walking shoes and shrugged out of her jacket as Matt took her burden and set it on the counter. Abby rested one hand in the open front of his shirt and reached up to kiss him. "Miss me?"

"You bet your sweet ass I did," Matt murmured, dropping his face down to nuzzle her neck. "I thought we were going to spend the day in bed."

Abby laughed. "I guess I'm getting used to slipping away in the dead of night." Matt felt a pang. "I woke up an hour or so ago. You were sleeping peacefully so I went for a walk." She reached for a cup.

Matt admired her shape in the shorts and tank she wore. As soon as she put the pot down, he was behind her, kissing her shoulder and running his hands over her hips. "Was that really necessary? I was looking forward to the morning." He tipped her chin back so he could see her face.

"Perv," Abby said, dipping her chin to nip at his hand. Matt jumped back, and she turned to lean against the counter. "And, yes, it was very necessary if I want this 'sweet ass' to stay smaller than South Dakota."

"I like you the way you are," Matt protested.

"And I wouldn't stay the way I am for long if I didn't move my arse. I rest my case." Abby set down her cup and lifted the box lid. "Besides, it makes it possible to have one of these beauties when I get the urge."

She revealed an assortment of pastries. Matt's eyes zoomed in on the prize but caught only air as Abby snatched it up.

"No way. The chocolate croissant is mine," Abby declared, holding it behind her back. She eyed the rest of his outfit. "Nice boxers. What if Sarah had come home?"

Matt feinted left and almost nabbed the pastry out of Abby's hand. "I would have been really, really careful about the flap. Besides, I couldn't find my jeans." He started towing her toward the stairs. "Bed. Now."

"Hang on, Speedy Gonzales." Abby grabbed the pastry box and one cup of coffee. "Grab your cup and the paper, will you?"

"Do we really need those?" Matt swooped in for a kiss, making a stealthy grab for the croissant.

"We do. We really do. Because you're going to need something to occupy yourself while I eat this delicious, chocolaty—" Abby dashed for the stairs with a screech when he lunged.

Taking the steps two at a time, Abby just had time to set the pastry and coffee down before Matt pushed her onto the bed, slid his hands under her tank top, and yanked it over her head. He dropped it beside him, kissing her shoulders and the tops of her breasts.

"Are you telling me you wouldn't give it to the man who does this to you?"

"Unfair. But, no, I'm eating it."

Matt grabbed the newspaper and settled against the headboard. He shook out the front page.

Laughing, Abby sat up and curled one leg beneath her. Grabbing her pastry, she took a bite, chewing slowly and moaning in delight before she swallowed. "You're really going to cut me off over a croissant?"

"Mmm hmm." He held the paper out a bit further, a smile teasing the corner of his lips.

Abby sighed and took another bite. "That's too bad. Really." A glop of filling spread at the corner of her mouth, and she swiped it with one finger as she chewed, popping it into her mouth when she finished. Dipping a finger in the melted chocolate at the center of the flaky pastry, she brought it toward her mouth again, only to find her wrist captured in gentle fingers.

"Although…" Matt dragged the word out as the paper fell to the floor. He brought her finger to his mouth and sucked the chocolate off. "I could be persuaded, if you share."

"Oh, that's how it's gonna be?" Abby murmured. "I have to give in?" She scooped up more of the chocolate, daubing it on Matt's lips.

"You *want* to give in," Matt whispered, smiling as he captured Abby's lips in a deep kiss. She moaned and clutched at his shoulders, unintentionally squeezing the rest of the filling onto Matt's chest. He grinned and wiped at it, taking the opportunity to transfer some of the richness to Abby's skin while leaving some on his own. "Darn. Whatever can we do about this mess?"

Muffled ringing sent them both scrambling for cell phones. Abby muttered invectives against her persistent intern, but it was Matt's phone under the edge of the bed that had interrupted them. He flipped it open and barked a greeting.

"Nice, Matt," Claire drawled. "Here I thought this would be a good time to call because you'd be all sexed-up and relaxed."

"The sexed-up part is right," he responded. Abby whapped him on the head and headed for the bathroom. Claire's over-bright giggle at his lame joke made him wary, though. "Why do you need me relaxed, Claire?"

"Hear me out."

Matt sat up straighter and closed his eyes. "Shoot."

"Well, you know Abby talked to the Peerys, right? *Steamer Lane Swell*?" Matt said nothing. Claire was incapable of dropping a topic unfinished. "They love your work. So much that they've been talking you up in their circle."

"The same circle as the Bakers, who no longer care for me much. So, no net gain."

"Not necessarily," Claire warned. "The smart ones perceive that the Bakers know nothing about fine art, and by extension, they realize that the Peerys know a lot. Anyway, they've been talking, and important people are taking notice. Most particularly Mrs. Peery's father, chairman of the board of directors for the de Young Museum. Guess who happened to find room on the calendar for a private show next weekend? Not the main gallery, of course, one of the private suites. Still…"

"I can't do it. Nothing is ready. I have two more statues to finish by the middle of September or Baker will have my nuts."

"Baker's grip on your nuts is exactly why you have to do this," Claire insisted. "What do you think the chances are that you won't piss him off again before you're finished? I say slim to none." She paused but pushed on when she got no response. "Matt, these people are big league. You impress enough of them this weekend, and it won't matter what Baker says. You have all the pieces in my gallery, which I will pay to have transported to the museum. You can't show the Bakers' statues, contractually, but you can show the models. I know you don't consider them your finest work, but they're damn good and far above the average for pool statues." She paused for a minute. "Even unfinished, you could show—"

"Not happening," Matt said flatly. His outright dismissal of showing Abby's statue didn't trouble him a bit, but the thought of having to make this decision on the fly did. "Can we wait—"

"Nope. They need to know within the hour so the arrangements can be made. Saying no to this would be the dumbest thing you could do. So?"

Matt's thoughts raced. A week wasn't long, but if he pushed, he could have another two models finished. "Yes. Okay. I'll do it."

"I thought so." Claire's grin could be heard in her voice. "I already took the liberty of telling Doug Peery that when I talked to him this morning. Glad you didn't make a liar of me."

"Claire…"

"You love me. Speaking of which, we'll have to push our dinner party back a week. I'll talk to Abby when she gets to the gallery. If you don't bring her along, you're a bonehead McSpazatron. *Ciao*." The phone went dead, and Matt snapped it closed.

Abby re-entered the room, wrapped in a towel, hair in disarray around her face. "Was that Claire?"

"Yup." Matt lounged across the bed and grabbed at her towel. "I love Naked Sunday. Let's do this every week, minus your going out. Screw exercise. I'll bring breakfast."

Abby laughed. "Aside from this being Monday and me having kiddie art school, that sounds like a very good way to spend the rest of the summer."

They both grew quiet, and Matt wondered if she was thinking about the end of her vacation with as much dismay as he was feeling right then. Abby let him tug the towel out of its tuck and toss it onto the floor. "By the way," he asked, "how do you feel about spending next Naked Sunday in San Francisco?"

Up early on Saturday, Matt had just started another long day of working on his last mock-up when Abby strolled into the studio. He watched her. There was something in the lines of her body that intrigued him, made him want to cover the statue he was working on and move to his Pretty statue. She came across the room, smiling, and Matt anticipated the first contact her hand would make with his body, expecting her to lean in to kiss him. Instead, she took the knife out of his hand and laid it on the table, careful not to brush it against her clothes.

"Ready to go?" she asked.

Exhaustion made Matt question whether he'd lost several hours somehow. "But—"

"But nothing. You've been a machine since Monday night. I know you planned on leaving late afternoon, but we're going right now." She started shutting down the big halogen lights that illuminated his workspace.

It had been a very long time since someone had made a decision for him, and it delighted him. As he looked at the organized chaos surrounding him, though, his smile began to fade. "Abby, I can't."

"What's the issue?"

Matt explained, and she listened in grave silence. When he was finished, he waited for her to say something. Abby studied the sculpture from all angles, turning it on the revolving table. "Screw it. You have a perfectly good set of ribs here, Matt. No one who's going to see this knows Jason, right? So, give it a rest and stop worrying."

Matt laughed. "Why didn't I think of that?"

"Because you are cursed with man-brain, which only travels along one track, while I am gifted with the multi-tasking marvel known as woman-brain. Chris threw your bag in the Jeep; Claire and Charles will meet us at the gallery. So, now you're mine." She stretched to brush a kiss on his jaw.

He rested a hand at the small of her back, curving her body toward him. "I like the sound of that." He gestured at the statue before him. "However, unless you have a magic genie in your pocket, you have to at least let me cover this."

"Got it, cuz." Chris brushed past Matt, nabbed the sculpting knife off the table and headed to the sink, flip-flops slapping the concrete floor. "Good idea, girl. Get this guy out of here."

Matt grinned, knowing that Chris would take care of his clay properly. Pulling Abby against him, he caught her mouth in a slow, hot kiss, which she returned enthusiastically.

"Get a room," Chris bellowed, covering his eyes.

"That's the idea." Matt's lips twisted into a wicked smile, and he led Abby out the door.

Driving down the coast, Matt kept the window open to help him stay alert as he pointed out the places he liked to surf and the things that made his heart sing.

"You really love it here, don't you?"

"Yeah." Matt looked out over the ocean. "Feels like forever since I've been out there." He shook himself and smiled. "What do you do at your ocean?"

"Well, not surfing. I swim, mainly. And I love sailing! I learned when I was a kid, and it's my favorite thing to do when I'm at my parents' place in Maine."

"Well, then, you'll have to take me sailing, Pretty. It's popular here too, but I've never tried it." Matt recognized that he was trying to find things to entice her to like his home, and he changed the subject before she caught onto him. "Anyway, what do you want to see in San Francisco?"

Abby's face lit up. "Ghirardelli Square! The pier—can't remember the number—and…Chinatown! The Golden Gate is a given. What?" she asked when Matt winced.

"Tourist stuff? Seriously?"

"I am a tourist, goofy. You have to indulge me. I take everyone to Boston Common and the Old North Church, even though I've seen them a thousand times. And that damned *Cheers* bar! It's not even real."

Matt laughed. "Okay, so we compromise. I'll take you to as many of the places you want to see as we have time for, but can I show you the things I think are worth seeing as well?"

"I'd like that."

They pulled up to the Hotel Vitale a while later. A bellman grabbed their bags out of the back while Matt handed the valet his keys. "What's the sense in having friends with influence if you never take advantage of it?" he joked as the obsequious desk clerk handed Abby the key cards. As they made their way to their room, he added, "Claire probably told them we're European millionaires or royalty in hiding."

"Or she flashed a stack of cash," Abby suggested with a slanted smile.

"Well, sure." Arriving at their door, Matt opened it. "But that alone is not devious enough for Claire. She likes to add a little glamour to everything." They stepped in, and he flipped on the light.

Abby looked around and whistled. "Like this room."

Matt grinned at her obvious delight. He dropped the bags and stretched out on the bed. Abby joined him and lay back too, her head resting on his shoulder. "So, what's first on the agenda, Pretty? Ghirardelli?"

Without answering, she brushed the hair near his temple. Matt closed his eyes, focusing on the sensation for a moment, and then he caught her hand and brushed his lips against the fine skin of her inner wrist. "We'd better go right now or the only sights you'll see in San Francisco will be inside this hotel room."

He lifted his lids and caught Abby's face in a moment of unguarded longing. They locked eyes and then smiled. Matt savored the delicious curl of tension in his lower stomach.

Rising to his feet, he held out his hand. "Come on, tourist. I'll give you the full treatment today, but tomorrow morning is mine. Deal?"

Abby took his hand. "Deal. I guess."

Chuckling, Matt led her toward the door. "Don't sound so excited."

They spent the afternoon drifting from attraction to attraction. Matt's initial reluctance was overcome by Abby's joy at each new place. Seeing the common sights through fresh eyes, he remembered his own excitement at seeing many of the same attractions as a child when he stayed with his father. Even though his mother never accompanied him on those visits, they had been good times.

In that spirit, he allowed himself to be dragged from cable car to cable car, one line into Chinatown for lunch and a wander through the twisty streets, sifting through flowers and trinkets, another line to Fisherman's Wharf. Abby rested her head against his shoulder as they collapsed onto a bench.

Matt curled his arm around her, comfortable and happy with their day so far. "So, Pretty…had enough yet?"

Abby chuckled. "You wish. I want to go to the aquarium and the Ripley's Believe it or Not Museum, and I want to see the boats, and maybe go out to Alcatraz, and—"

Her flow of words was stopped by Matt's lips. Abby curled her fingers in the front of his shirt, not caring about the stifled chuckles coming from their seatmates. When she relaxed, Matt lifted his head and brushed his nose against hers. "What were you saying about going back to the hotel?" he asked in a husky voice.

"Not a damned thing," Abby replied in the same tone. "We're at the Wharf; now I want to see everything it has to offer."

Admitting defeat, Matt got up and helped her off the bench. They went from one area to another, collecting a shopping bag full of souvenirs for Abby's friends and family at home. She grew quiet the longer they walked, and Matt found himself becoming rather sober as well. He was glad when Abby quit shopping and moved back onto the pier to watch a street artist draw a portrait of two children.

A frown drew her brow down, and Matt asked why. Abby gave a rundown of where she felt the artist's technique could use refinement. "Have you ever thought about getting back into painting?" Matt asked.

Abby's laugh was short and sharp. "Not likely. Those who can't do or teach curate, remember?" She shivered in the wind that had picked up over the water, and before Matt could even wrap a warming arm around her shoulders, a fierce cloudburst started dropping fat, cold drops. The artist squawked and grabbed up his supplies, and people dashed for cover.

Matt and Abby sheltered under the awning of a sweater shop. While they waited for the rain to lighten, she chuckled and wrapped her arms around his waist. "What kind of crazy city do you have here? In Boston, we swelter through July, we don't f-freeze."

"Hold on a sec," Matt said, darting into the shop. Within a few minutes, he was back out, carrying two Aran sweaters. Pulling a green one over his head, he grimaced and yanked it back off, handing it to Abby before putting on a cream sweater. "Sorry," he said as she rolled the sleeves of her sweater over her hands. "I just grabbed two. The cream one's bigger."

Abby grinned. "It's perfect. Smells like you now." She looked out into the rain, not noticing the smile that bloomed on Matt's face. "What's next?"

Matt curled his arms around her midriff and rested his chin on her shoulder. "You don't mind the rain?" Abby shook her head. Matt tipped his arm up so he could see his watch and sighed. "It's about time to go change for the show."

"Okay. Can I do one more touristy thing, though?"

"Anything."

She led him toward the brightly colored merry-go-round, giggling at his long-suffering expression. Matt handed over the fee and tugged her into a swan boat so he could hold her close.

Abby squeezed Matt's hand as they stood in the gallery doorway and watched the expensively dressed crowd mill around. She smoothed her hand over the heavy red silk of her dress, on loan from Claire. "Are you nervous?"

"Not at all. The pressure's off," he said in a low voice, touching the hair at her temple with one finger. The artist in him enjoyed the contrast she made to the many black gowns on display. "I know I'll never create anything as beautiful as you look tonight. I can just enjoy the show now."

Abby grinned. "Flattery will get you everywhere." She waved, and he turned to see Claire. "Into the breach, right?"

Matt tucked her hand into his arm, and they strolled into the room. The first couple of hours at the de Young passed in a blur of faces and names as they circulated, champagne flutes in hand. The attendees represented the crème of the local arts scene, and they discussed Matt's works knowledgeably. When Claire called Abby away to greet the Peerys, Matt couldn't keep his eyes off of her.

Apparently someone else was watching her too, because when Matt returned from a trip to the restroom, he found Abby cornered by Mr. Baker. She appeared to be calm and confident, but she stiffened when Baker took a casual sip of his champagne and reached out to snake his arm around her hips. Matt cut through the room as quickly as possible, but Claire got there first. She slid between Baker and Abby with a bright smile and clutched the older man's arm. "How are you enjoying the show, Mr. Baker? Can you feel how well your statues are going to go over in September? You made quite a find in our Matt."

Baker rolled his eyes and tossed back his wine. He looked at Matt with calculation. "About that. Since you're far enough ahead to take weekends off, I'll assume that you will be delivering four statues in September? I think that should be sufficient, as long as we can come to a satisfactory agreement on the last two."

Matt's temper strained at its leash. "I have a better idea. How about you—"

Claire placed a warning hand on his arm and her tone became frosty. "We have a contract for *three* statues by the end of September, Mr. Baker."

Baker grunted his acknowledgment. "Huh. Didn't hurt to try. Lovely evening you've arranged, Mrs. Eastman." He strolled through the room, greeting people in a hearty tone, as if the soiree was arranged for his personal enjoyment.

Claire collapsed against the wall, shaking her head. "Matt—"

"Save it. I'm not sorry. The man's an ass," he said, the strain of keeping his voice down made it rough. "We're going."

"Matt, we can't," Abby said reasonably. "There's a half-hour left yet, and you can*not* leave." She turned to Claire. "How many sales, Claire?"

Claire glanced at Matt, rubbing her temples. "All but two." She chuckled wearily. "I even have an offer on the new models, though I know you need those."

Abby stood in front of Matt, looking him steadily in the eye. "Then let's sell them and go home."

As the last people left, Claire waved them off, claiming that only the very last arrangements for deliveries of the purchased statues remained. Matt didn't fight her, tugging at the knot in his tie and loosening the top buttons on his shirt with one hand as he and Abby walked to the Jeep and drove toward the hotel.

Matt looked out the car window, gripped by an impulse to share something with Abby. "Hey…would you go somewhere with me?"

"What…now? Sure." She gestured at her dress. "Is this okay?"

"It'll do."

Matt refused to answer any of Abby's questions until they were at a lookout point at Twin Peaks. They got out of the Jeep and walked to the edge. Abby looked around at the expanse of the city laid out before them, lights twinkling far below. "So beautiful," she whispered.

Matt gathered her wind-whipped hair and draped it over one shoulder. He wrapped his arms around her from behind and rested his cheek on the top of her head. "Yes." He answered in a low voice, not completely sure whether he was talking about the woman or the view. "This is one of my favorite views of the city."

Abby snuggled into his arms, rubbing one hand up and down his bicep. "I can't believe that I might never see this again," she said wistfully, tightening her grip on Matt's arm.

"Yes, you will," Matt answered without thinking.

Abby twisted her head to look up at him, a smile spreading across her face. "Sure of that, are you?"

"Mmm hmm," he answered. "I don't do 'summer things.' Ask Claire."

He took her hand and started backing toward the Jeep, smiling. "Know what I want to do now? I want to work on my Pretty sculpture. That's how I get to sleep lately." He smiled wistfully. "I work the clay and think of you until I relax enough to go to bed. Weird?"

"Nice," Abby said softly, cupping his cheek. He closed his eyes. "Tell you what, since you lack clay, why don't you touch me instead?"

Chapter Fourteen

When Matt turned into the driveway of the cottage the next day, Abby laughed a little at her guilty disappointment in seeing Sarah's car there. She'd been half-hoping that Sarah and David would be out enjoying their last day together in Santa Cruz. Matt's twisted smile let her know that he'd been thinking along the same lines. As he carried Abby's bag to the front door, he suggested, "We could still go to my house."

Abby held a finger over his lips. "Rest. We agreed that we need rest tonight." She had to snatch her finger back when Matt nipped the tip.

She opened the door and called for Sarah. Matt followed her into the living room. Abby's laughter stopped abruptly when she saw Sarah's miserable expression. "Sweetie, what happened? Where's David?" She reached back blindly for Matt's hand.

Sarah expression became even more forlorn. "He got called back to Boston yesterday." She sighed. "Some strike thing. And he said I might as well stay here, because he'll just be living at the paper for a while, and…I'll be heading home next week…Abby, I'm sorry." She looked at Matt sadly. "I'm sorry to you, too. I'm not the only one going home."

"What?" Abby asked faintly. "But…I thought…"

Sarah took a drink from the bottle on the coffee table. "I thought, too. But Aunt Filiz called. She met someone at her retreat, and she's bringing him home with her next week. We've been not-so-politely evicted, doll." She took another swallow and grimaced. "I'm so fucking sorry, Abby. I didn't know what to say. It's her house."

Abby's first thought amounted to a wordless howl of dismay. She closed her eyes, struck anew by the thought that she'd stumbled into this relationship accidentally: a freak whim to travel to the opposite coast, a chance meeting. By all rights, she should be lounging at her apartment right now, watching television or reading, unaware that Matt was doing the same thing three thousand miles away. Two months earlier she hadn't even known this man into whose life she now felt inextricably linked. This was further from Boring Boston Abby than she'd ever imagined traveling that summer, but she couldn't bring herself to resent it.

She took a steadying breath before raising Matt's hand and kissing the back. She dropped it and crossed to Sarah, taking the rum and capping it tightly. "That's that, then. And this won't make it any better. Enough." She carried the bottle into the kitchen and slammed it into a cupboard, trying to get hold of her flying thoughts before she had to face Matt again. She rearranged her expression into a bland mask and returned to the living room. Walking over to Sarah, she cradled her friend's head. "Not your fault, so don't stress." The friends leaned against each other.

Matt caught Abby's arm as she headed for the stairs. "Abby?" he asked in a low voice, and she shook her head.

"Nothing's changed," she said, covering his hand with hers and looking up at him with pleading eyes. "Okay? I can't deal with this right now. Call me tomorrow?" She squeezed his hand and headed up the stairs. She heard Matt say an awkward goodbye to Sarah, and she closed her bedroom door with a quiet click. How was she supposed to face a reality where five weeks together had suddenly dropped to one?

Matt slammed the door of his Jeep and thrust it into gear. On his drive home, it took all of his concentration to avoid the natives and tourists; their nonchalance as they leisurely crossed the road was born of lazy days and the lure of the sea. Their dismay as they jumped out of his way meant nothing to him.

It was only when his ancient engine began to whine in protest that he slowed down. He whipped into his driveway and cut the motor. In the sudden silence, he could hear the tattoo of his heartbeat. He rested his head on the hands that clutched the steering wheel and closed his eyes.

What a fuckeroo of a way to end the weekend. He wished he'd obeyed his first impulse and passed Abby's cottage. All he'd really wanted was to listen to her humming from his kitchen as he got back to work, but did he listen to his own good advice? No.

He strained his ears to hear the whisper of the sea, his surest comfort for most of his life, but all he could hear was his neighbor's VW belching and farting down the street. Matt sighed and opened his door, keeping his mind a careful blank as he grabbed his bag out of the back of the Jeep and carried it into the house.

He called for his cousin, thinking that maybe Chris's patter could fill the yawning hole that seemed to have opened in his chest. Silence.

"Screw it," Matt muttered. He kicked his shoes into a corner and ripped off the silly Hawaiian shirt he'd slid on so playfully that morning. He'd hoped it would make Abby laugh, and it had. The ghost of her giggles rang in his ears. It was unbearable.

Striding into the studio, he cranked up his music and yanked the cover off of the statue he'd abandoned so gratefully the day before. There was Jason, nearly as big as life and just as handsome as he'd ever been. Envy shifted through Matt; he might have had more time with Abby if it hadn't been for those weeks she'd spent with Jason. And now she was leaving, and…

Matt deflated. It wasn't fair to blame Jason or Abby or even Sarah. Things just happened — that's what his dad had told him each time Matt had asked him why his parents couldn't live together. Asking whose fault it had been. Ted had never lost his temper, no matter how many times his young son asked. His solution was always for Matt to trust the sea to wash away his worries, and if that didn't work, to pound clay.

In that spirit, Matt opened the drawer that held his tools, faced his statue, and cleared his mind. Within minutes, he was lost in the battle of clay versus man. When he got tired of Jason, he uncovered

Zoe and started on her. Hours passed, and he didn't think of Abby any more than every few minutes.

Matt jumped as something slapped his calf and dropped to the floor behind him. He shook his head and kept washing his carving tools as Chris scooped up his flip-flop.

"I see we took our six-year-old pills today," Matt observed, smiling over his shoulder.

"Got a lifetime prescription I have to use up," Chris shot back, laughing as he plopped on a high table. "So…Abby coming over for dinner?" he asked, swinging his feet as he leaned back on his hands.

Matt turned back to the sink. Nabbing a lint-free towel from the stack on the counter, he started to dry his tools. "Not tonight."

"All-righty, then. Grab your board. Don't shake your head at me. It's been weeks since you were out there. The water misses you. The gulls miss you." He grinned slyly. "The old ladies that wait for us to come in miss you. They say hi, by the way."

Matt laughed, rubbing his eyes with one hand while setting the tools down with the other. "I can't. I just have to finish Zoe's feet, and this thing is done. Tools were just getting sticky; I wasn't quitting for the day."

Chris was relentless, sweeping the tools off of the table and whisking them over to the cabinet. "Now you are." He shut the cupboard door with a click. "There will always be another project, Matt. You'll choose that over and over, and then one day your choices will be gone, because the good things will get tired of waiting for you or you'll be out of practice at doing them."

Matt was taken aback by the shadow of age that settled into his cousin's eyes, and he answered gently. "All right. Lead on."

Chris's sunny smile broke from his momentary clouds. "Great. Meet you outside in ten minutes." He headed for the door, already slipping off his threadbare tee and kicking his flip-flops into the corner.

Matt located his wetsuit on his closet floor. Twisted around it was a ribbed tank clearly too small to be his. Matt balanced in his crouch, impulsively bringing it to his face and inhaling. It was faint, but he could still detect the blended scent of Abby's lotion, sunshine, and his cologne. He smiled and laid it on his pillow.

"Ready, cuz?" Chris's bright voice shook Matt from his fugue.

"Sure," Matt answered. He ignored the tiny smile on Chris's face when he spotted the tank top.

An easy walk took them to the beach. As he paddled out, Matt realized that he wasn't looking forward to his ride with any great enthusiasm. If he was being honest with himself, and he was trying very hard to be so, the pleasure he'd seen in Abby's eyes the first time she'd watched him walk out of the water had become the reason for his afternoon rides. At first, the knowledge that she found him attractive had been an ego thing, but it had quickly evolved into a simple happiness that he made her smile.

"Head in the game," Chris called in warning across the water. "Big one coming in."

Matt spotted the wave, grateful that Chris had given him time to scramble to his feet before it was upon them. The concentration needed to maneuver the surf to shore provided a welcome relief from the stress party Matt's life had become.

Ever since he was a child, Matt had found a peace in the forgetful Pacific that he'd never found anywhere else…until he was curled around Abby. He wondered if it had been the same for his dad with his mother. He'd never had the guts to ask, but he wondered if it had come down to location for his parents. Did Ted balance woman against water, with Janet the loser, or was his lifestyle just not enough for his wife? In the same position, which he found uncomfortably close to home, what would Matt do? He pushed the thought away, unwilling to consider a world in which he might have to choose one or the other and terrified that it wouldn't be up to him. He paddled out time and again, letting the water and the sunshine wash his mind free of worry.

By the time the surf had calmed for the day, Matt was feeling more relaxed than he had for days, and even more so after a shower, a quick dinner, and two scotches. He and Chris lounged on the floor of their living room, tossing popcorn into their mouths and watching movies until late that night.

Finally, Chris snapped off the TV. "I'm done being your distraction because you were dumb enough to send Abby off tonight — g'night." He ambled down the hall, and Matt heard his door snick closed.

Wham. All it took was that simple statement, and the worries Matt had been repressing all day resurfaced. *What the hell was I thinking?* battled with *Gotta be realistic — she's leaving* until he decided to let them duke it out in his subconscious while he handled stress in the best way he knew. Grabbing the bottle of scotch, he flipped off the television and lights on his way to his studio. Once there, he uncovered his Zoe sculpture again. After getting out his tools, he poured another drink and downed it before setting to work.

An hour later, he stepped back, smoothing the left toenail with his thumb. Done. Pouring another two fingers of scotch, he sipped it, thinking. Too late and too much drink to start the kiln or start on anything new. His eyes flicked to the covered sculpture in the corner. Probably not the best idea to uncover that, not when he was already fixated on sliding between Abby's sheets and nestling her against his chest, despite what he knew was the best course to follow. Still… sculpting Pretty's cold clay had helped him sleep before he'd fallen in… whatever…with the warm, human woman who was the inspiration.

He snapped off the lights and stood looking through the window at the moon. In five days, he'd have as much chance of touching Abby as he had of touching that silvery sphere.

A light tapping at the front door drew his attention. In his hurry to answer it before the sound awakened Chris, Matt bumped into a chair and then the doorway just before stubbing his toes on the bag he'd dropped in the living room earlier that day. Cursing and cradling his wounded foot, he yanked open the door.

Abby stood on the porch, hand upraised to tap again. She stepped back, startled, as the door flew open, and dropped her hand to her side. She leaned her head against the doorframe. "I'm sorry if I woke you."

Matt lowered his foot and searched her eyes. "I thought we were getting together tomorrow," he whispered. He glanced behind him and drew the front door closed as he stepped outside. "It's late."

"I know, but—" Abby's voice tightened, and she stopped. The unhappiness on her face tore at Matt's heart, and for one minute he wished he'd never ambled over to check on that bike accident so many weeks ago. Life had been so much easier when he didn't care. Then her eyes filled with tears, and he forgot about himself.

"Abby? Is everything all right?"

"I need you," she said bluntly. "This is probably stupid. But I can't think of anything worse right now than ending this day without you. So, would you take me to bed?"

Matt took her hand and drew her toward him. In five days, the small, strong hand he was now caressing would be on the other side of the country.

The thought put a knot in his stomach. Five days. It felt like a sentence.

He was torn. A large part of him was ready to step back, to keep the conversation light, the patter snappy, and the door open for a quick retreat. The better part of him, though, recognized that a line had been crossed.

It was the latter part of Matt that gently drew Abby into his arms, cradling her against him and bringing her into the house, into his bedroom. He could feel the slow thumping of his heart and hear Abby's heart beating in faster counterpoint when he buried his face in her shoulder.

"Matt?" Abby's fingers were soothing on the back of his neck.

"I just…" Matt stopped speaking as he pulled his face back and his eyes met hers. He traced the curve of her cheek with the back of a forefinger. Abby smiled, and he let his fingers drift to press against the back of her neck while his thumb caressed her cheek. He leaned in for a hesitant kiss.

Five days.

Matt kept his eyes locked on Abby's except for the brief instant when her sweater went over her head. He wanted to remember her exactly as she was at that moment, hair wild from his hands and her sweater, face flushed and lips parted.

Five days.

His gaze trailed down her body, followed by his hands. He laid her back on the bed, tracing her lower lip with his tongue before taking it into his own mouth and sucking gently. His hands caressed her skin, pebbled with gooseflesh in the cool room, and he tried to memorize each individual texture of her body. His breathing sped as he kissed her shoulders and her stomach and her thigh. "Abby," he whispered, his voice rough and almost unrecognizable as he tossed her jeans toward the chair.

Five days.

Abby whimpered when he left her to shed his own clothes, but he was soon back. He needed to feel her hands on him, tracing the muscles in his arms and chest, traveling lower to grasp his hips and pull him tight against her, stroking the insides of his thighs and the small of his back. He needed to feel the softness of her belly against his, the grip of her calf as she drew him deep inside her. He needed to hear her indrawn breath when he drew her leg higher, kissing the inside of her knee. To hear her whispered endearments, to call her his Pretty. To feel the tension ratcheting up in his body and hear her panting his name as her heart raced along with his.

Five.

Abby's cries of pleasure mixed with his own gasps when their mouths parted and Matt buried his face in her neck, seeking solace in her scent, the salt-taste of her skin, the feeling of the blood pumping just under the surface. He refused to lose himself this time, trying desperately to store up all the sensations against the day they'd be gone.

Days.

He failed miserably. Long before Abby's low moan of release, even longer before his own body froze in orgasm, he was lost again, feeling rather than thinking, knowing nothing but here and now and yes. Abby stroked his hair and murmured low words of comfort and care. He needed that, too.

But most of all, he needed to fall asleep with Abby curled up warm against him and to know he would wake up and she would still be there.

Deep inhale.

Slow exhale.

A vague outline of Matt's face appeared as the moon shone through his bedroom window. Abby traced his features, the same way she'd tried to catalog each sleeping breath and the warmth of his skin against hers since she'd awakened.

She barely restrained herself from reaching out and touching the curve of his lower lip, not willing to wake him before she had a chance to finish her study. Looking at his features objectively, Matt wasn't perfect. His eyebrows were thick and untamed, creating a visual sign of his determination that belied his laid-back façade. Nose slightly crooked, mouth wide, jaw strong…in pieces, he was ordinary. But when his mouth stretched into a slow smile, Abby couldn't breathe.

A tear pooled at the corner of her eye and spilled over the bridge of her nose. Moving gently, she adjusted her hand so it wetted her skin rather than Matt's. *What the hell have you gotten yourself into, Abby?* she thought. *You'd think twenty years of dating would have taught you to not get attached, especially to a vacation romance.* She opened her mouth, trying to breathe in and out evenly so she wouldn't sob. She'd been doing so well, too, enjoying each day as it came and not living in any moment but the present.

Then Matt had looked at her, those eyes that always twinkled were suddenly intense and not laughing at all. And he'd touched her, loved her, like there was no one else in the world. Now all her careful barriers lay in pieces around her feet.

Matt's hand came up to cover hers before she had a chance to covertly wipe it on the sheet. He raised her chin. "Abby?" he asked softly, his eyes troubled. He stroked the side of her face, pushing her hair behind her ear.

"Our time's almost over," she whispered, her voice wobbly. "Ready to run away from the crazy lady yet?" Her arm snaked around his chest, and she clung to him.

Matt lifted her arm, and Abby had a moment of panic that he'd ask her to leave. No man like Matt remained unattached unless it was by choice.

Instead of sliding out of the bed, he moved closer. "You're not crazy, Pretty. We'll just have to make this the best part and worry about after summer later. If you want."

The unsure tone of his voice caused a pang in Abby's chest. She touched his cheek and smiled. "I want."

Matt's eyes scanned her face, and then he kissed her, hard and deep and hungrily, moving onto his back and bringing Abby with him until her body lay over his. She settled against him and listened to his breathing become deep and even.

Chapter Fifteen

After nearly killing himself roughing in the new statue, Matt was grateful when Abby appeared in the doorway of his studio he next morning. Dropping his tools on the worktable, he was across the room in four steps. He stopped her laughter with a hard press of lips that morphed into a searching kiss. She relaxed in his arms, and Matt gathered her even closer.

"I'm getting you dirty," he murmured.

"I don't care," she said, smiling. "Sarah called. She got an invitation for a last bike trip, and Claire had an extra day scheduled off from art camp, so I'm yours today. I thought maybe we could surf a little?" She laughed self-consciously. "Play in the water, anyway. What do you think?"

"I can't think of anything better," Matt answered with a wide grin. "Let me clean up." With a last kiss, he led her out of the studio. He stopped in his bedroom to grab a swimsuit. "I'm glad you came over last night. I'd never have slept if you hadn't."

Abby laughed. "You would have just worked on your sculpture. I know your methods now."

Matt tugged a shirt over his head before he answered. "No good anymore. I tried that. I need you."

"Abby, the human sleeping pill." There was an undertone of sadness to her voice.

"No. I know you're thinking about that idiot in Boston, and just… no." He smoothed his hands up and down her arms. "I can't lie, Abby. I do like your body. But more than that, I like you."

"Okay," Abby said.

"No, not okay. Really. I don't want to miss one more minute."

Abby's arms locked fiercely around him. "Neither do I." They rested that way for a moment, with Matt's cheek pillowed on Abby's head as it lay against his shoulder.

"We good?" Matt asked. Abby nodded.

She stepped back and smirked. "Well, if that wasn't a trip back to junior high summer camp. All we need to do now is exchange notes with 'Do you like me? Check yes or no' written on them."

Matt snorted. "You are a wicked woman, Abby Reynolds. Maybe that's why I l…ike you."

His slight hesitance didn't seem to register with Abby. She ran her finger up his side, and he let go of her, laughing. "Come and give me another surfing lesson."

After a stop at Abby's house to grab her suit, they hit the beach. Taking Abby out into deeper water than they'd entered last time made it prudent to ride a single board. Matt smiled at her enthusiasm as she called out each wave, and he obediently got to his feet at her command, if only to have an excuse to stand close behind her.

Coming in after yet another ride, he was surprised to see Chris standing at the tide line, tossing a football from hand to hand and grinning. "Hey, cuz," Chris said. "Two days in a row? The old ladies will go into shock."

Abby laughed. "I'm in the mood for ice cream. There's usually a guy over that way. Anybody else want something?"

Matt shook his head, and Chris said, "I'll take one of whatever you're having." As Abby headed up the beach, the guys began tossing the football.

"I'm not really riding today, just playing with Abby." Matt watched her walk away. "Thanks for yesterday, by the way. I needed it."

Chris laughed. "No argument here. And you owe me another one. I cleaned up your tools and covered the new clay." He snorted. "I'm starting to feel like a maid. You mess it; I clean it."

"Holy shit." Matt hadn't thought for a minute about the sculpture he was working on in his haste to be with Abby. "Thanks again."

Chris nodded. "So…speaking of serious…" he said, raising an eyebrow at Matt.

"Guys, remember? We don't talk about these things." Matt threw the ball harder than he had before.

"I claim a relative exemption," Chris said placidly, tossing it back. "Are you just playing with Abby? She's a nice lady. I gotta say it."

"I know that, I promise." Matt caught the ball and exaggeratedly crossed his heart.

"Good to know. Have you talked about after? Will there be an after?"

His cousin's questions were hitting too close to home, probing sores that Matt wasn't ready to tend. "Chris…" he warned.

"I'm just saying. I know it's not my beeswax, but damn…you're looser than I've ever seen you. Happier. She lives a long way away, and neither of you is getting any younger. This isn't the time to be timid with the words."

That stung. "That's my business. And you're not the one to talk about hiding and being scared. Do something with your life, then come talk to me about being timid." He fired the ball hard, and Chris leaped up to catch it with a quiet "oof."

He lowered the ball to his side, and they stared at each other. "You may be right, cuz. Maybe I am hiding. But at least I'm not hurting anyone else by doing it."

A soft hand ran up Matt's back. Abby was looking between the obviously tense men, a wrinkle between her eyebrows. "The ice cream guy wasn't there, and it's time to get ready for Claire's. Everything all right?"

Chris smiled at her. "Peachy. I probably need to lay off the ice cream anyway." He rubbed his solid middle like he was stroking a fat roll. "Don't wait up for me, Dad. It's all good."

"Yeah?" Matt asked. He relaxed when Chris nodded.

"Yeah. Y'all better not be late for Claire. She'll kill ya." He waved and walked up the beach.

"What was that all about?" Abby asked, gathering up the cooler and folding the blanket as Matt slipped on his shirt. "And don't say *nothing,* 'cause I'm not buying it."

Matt sighed. "Just me being assy again. Seems to be a trend." He flipped the blanket over his shoulder and took her hand. "Sure you don't want to run away right now?"

"Very sure."

Abby declined Matt's invitation to join him in the shower, claiming that would definitely make them late. She handed him a towel when he opened the shower door, telling him about the way Tyler now avoided Sarah on the street, even when she said a pleasant hello.

Matt snorted, drying his chest and arms before toweling his head roughly. Dropping the towel to his waist, he saw Abby smiling at him in pleasure, appreciative but not coy, and he realized that he'd never been so comfortable in this position, not even during his brief marriage. Thinking back, he didn't remember ever having a conversation with a woman while he was in the shower without a pre- or post-coital undertone. He liked it. He grinned back and flipped the towel up teasingly before going to work on his legs and feet. Abby laughed and headed to the living room to wait while he dressed.

After another stop at the cottage so Abby could change, they pulled up in front of the Eastmans' house. "This place is huge." Abby got out of the Jeep, taking in the brilliant white front of the sprawling manor house, anachronistic in its beach setting.

Matt walked around the car to take her hand. "Just think, this is the summer house. Charles's family is horrified that he lives here year-round."

The front door flew open, and Claire strolled out, holding out two drinks and smiling. "C started about a half-hour ago, so his stories should reach the level of unbearable in the time it takes you to drink these and two more."

Abby smiled as she crested the three steps up to the sweeping, colonnaded porch. She took the proffered drink. "And what's different if we drink these?"

Claire laughed. "Why, then he'll just seem charming, dear." She looped her arm through Abby's and led her into the house.

Abby zoned in on a painting tucked in a niche in the wall. "Oh my…Claire…"

"Rather good, isn't it?"

"That's a Dali that I've never seen before! Ever." She walked over to the painting and almost touched it with trembling fingers. "Has this ever been cataloged?"

Claire took Abby's arm. "You'll see many things here that are priceless, Abby, but may I ask you for a favor? Treat them like something you'd have in your home. They're pretties, nothing more, a normal part of Charles's life." She snickered. "He thinks he's just an average guy. And that's part of why I love him."

She opened a pair of French doors and led the way onto a covered patio so vast that it probably had the same square footage as Sarah's aunt's entire cottage.

"Abby, watch!" Charles called. He flipped a burger high in the air and laughed when it landed beside the enormous stainless steel grill.

Claire handed Abby another drink. "See? Incorrigible. You'll need this." She led Abby and Matt to a set of comfortable chaise lounges near the grill.

The conversation flowed easily over dinner as they devoured an astonishing amount of food, washing it down with glasses of iced tea and Claire's drink concoctions. By the time Charles had a fire going to his satisfaction, they had eschewed the chairs in favor of sprawling on cushions around the fire pit. Eventually, conversation got around to the show. Matt exchanged a secret smile with Abby, wondering if her mind had jumped to later that night as quickly as his. He was startled when Claire tugged at his sleeve.

"I asked if you took Abby to that old café in Sausalito for lunch before the show. The one with the green tables and chairs? Remember the rhapsodies Kate went into over those tables?"

Abby raised an eyebrow in query, and Matt smiled at her. "Ex-wife. Very ex. Like," he counted in his head, "eighteen years ex. Wow, almost a lifetime for your boy toy."

Abby rolled her eyes and asked, "Artist?"

"Kate could talk about paintings for hours. She just never got around to creating one."

Claire laughed. "That poor girl. Follows Matt out here from Philly, thinking she was ready to live like a Bohemian student. It lasted, what—eighteen months?—before she was back on a plane to Philadelphia. She was always a banker at heart. Do you ever hear from her, Matt?"

He shook his head. "She was doing something for my mother's company and stationed in Paris the last time I heard anything, but that was probably ten years ago."

"As I remember, she claimed she was coming back out until she met that guy, right? Long-distance romance." Claire snorted disdainfully, then looked at Abby in the sudden silence.

"We were kids." Matt swallowed the last of his drink. "And it was kind of a relief when she left. Not much of a romance." He glared at Claire, and she had the good grace to look abashed.

Charles cleared his throat in the awkward silence and then asked how Claire was doing on the sales. She gave him a grateful smile.

"Well, I've had one back out. Baker's pocket-monkey-yes-man. To be honest, Matt, you are very lucky that Peery has pull in that crowd. It could have gone either way."

Matt grunted. "Did I make enough at the show to tell Baker to kiss my ass, give him his completed statues, and move on?"

Claire glared at him. "Weren't you listening just now? Sure, you made a nice bit of cash, but Baker has influence. Call this your cushion…escape fund…whatever. He holds the big money. Finish this, and, with the Peerys' help…well, you'll be set up for a good, long time. Like maybe forever." She got to her feet and extended her hand to Abby. "Let's go get the ice cream. Mary made it just this morning, to C's exact specifications."

Abby looked at Matt hesitantly and then took Claire's hand. The women headed toward the house, talking quietly.

After a few minutes of silence between the men, Charles spoke. "Pissed her off again."

"Yep."

"Why do you do these things?"

Matt sat up. "It's a curse, I'm beginning to suspect. I've been cursed with assyness."

"True enough," Charles agreed. Another moment passed before it was his turn to sigh. "Do you think you can go in there and tell her to put it out, since you started all this? Ashtray breath is…" He shuddered. "I have no desire to argue with my hot wife tonight, so it's up to you."

Matt laughed, heaving himself to his feet and walking through the open doorway. He wandered toward the kitchen, touching a couple of his sculptures fondly and smiling at a few of Charles's unfortunate mistakes, which were tucked into hidden niches. As he neared the kitchen doorway, he heard the telltale whir of the exhaust fan and knew Claire was using it to suck her cigarette smoke away before it could permeate the room. Hearing his own name, he paused, feeling like a creeper but unable to resist listening.

"…Worried about dealing with another of the walking wounded, boobing about how his family has screwed him up and left him unable to commit?" Claire laughed. "Nope. Not Matt at all. His dad's a lovely guy. Moved to France a couple of years ago, following the surf, but I think he might be in Australia now. His mom—he's told you about her, right?"

"A banker of some sort?"

Matt heard Claire hum her approval as she took a deep drag. "She's a nice lady, too. Came down here on vacay, fell for the hot surfer, and was amazed that the feeling was mutual. She tried, I think, but they were too different. Moved back to Philly when Matt was two or three, but she brought him out here for every vacation until he was old enough to travel alone. He came to Cali for college and stayed. No big drama. They both love Matt to distraction."

Hearing his family dynamics described so succinctly left Matt feeling conflicted. Every word Claire said was true…but was it right? It seemed to him that a lifetime of niceness, of avoiding drama, might not have been such a good thing after all, because it was leaving him paralyzed when it came deciding what to do about Abby. Not to mention in figuring out what part a surf jockey could play in her life.

He shifted to step out of the shadow, but he stopped when Claire continued. "You haven't asked, but Kate isn't an issue either. Like I said, she was here and gone quickly—I don't think he found her very interesting, and she had no idea how to reach him. The split was mutual, and they were pleasant while they stayed in touch." Matt heard her bracelet jingle tellingly against crystal. "There. Done. I swear, that man of yours is giving me lung cancer by millimeters." She paused, and Matt heard her set the ashtray down. "Now, are you going to tell me what's wrong with you two? Something's not right."

Matt could hear the thread of sadness underneath Abby's voice as she delivered Sarah's news. "Silly to ask this stuff now, right? I'm leaving in less than a week. It's just been on my mind…" Her voice trailed off.

"I'm sure something will work out. I know it." Claire's voice was muffled, and Matt peeked in to see the two women embracing.

He cleared his throat and walked into the kitchen. "Ready to go?" he asked Abby. "I think we'll pass on the ice cream tonight."

"I think Charles must have eaten it all anyway. Bastard," Claire said fondly. She shrieked when Charles's stealthy tiptoe across the kitchen ended with a wet kiss on the back of her neck. Matt and Abby laughed at his huge grin when his wife slapped at his shoulder.

Claire walked with Matt to his side of the car. "I know you were outside the door, creeper. Do something, or you'll regret it for the rest of your life," she murmured in his ear before returning to wrap her arm around Charles's waist and wave goodbye.

Abby curled up on Matt's sofa, not questioning his decision to bypass her cottage. She rested her hands on the arm of the sofa and laid her head on her hands, watching Matt build a small fire. "What a day," she said when he returned to her with a blanket.

Matt sat beside her and covered them both. "Aside from the obvious, have you had fun?" He settled back, letting Abby adjust her head in the hollow of his shoulder.

"It's been beyond wonderful," Abby whispered, tightening her arm around Matt's middle. They watched the flames for a while in silence, each lost in their own thoughts.

Matt felt his heart clutch and then speed up when Abby started to sit upright. "I guess you should take me home. I'm bound to be rotten company for what's left of tonight."

He held on to her arm. "Then we'll be rotten company together. I don't want to take you home."

"I don't want to call a cab again, Matt. The drivers are going to start talking."

"I don't want you to call a cab either. Stay here."

Abby stopped trying to sit up. She stared at Matt in mock shock. "An invitation to invade the Batcave again, or whatever the hell Chris called it? First woman ever?" Matt smiled. "Ever?" Abby demanded playfully, and he nodded. "Then I accept." She snuggled against him again and smiled. "If I went back to the cottage I'd probably start packing anyway." Her smile faded.

Matt hurt when he thought of Abby throwing the last suitcase into Sarah's little car and driving away. "No. Stay," he whispered into her hair.

"I said I would, goofus."

Matt shifted her around until their heads were both resting against the back of the couch, facing one another. He brushed her hair over her ear. "No, Abby. Stay. Here. With me. Don't leave with Sarah. Finish your vacation and give me time to work something out."

"Matt…" Abby's voice was shaky.

"Don't say no." He trailed a line of kisses from her mouth to her ear, where he whispered, "I'm not ready for you to go. Stay with me."

Abby pushed on his shoulders. "This is crazy. You're willing disturb your peace here for a relationship that's been going for less than a month?"

"This has been the best summer of my life, and I stopped saying that about twenty years ago. I don't want it to end yet." He swallowed hard, ready to keep arguing until morning if he had to.

Abby hesitated. Doubt warred with hope in her eyes. Then she smiled. "Yes."

Matt rose from the couch, drawing Abby with him, and they started moving toward his bedroom. "This is right; you know it," he said.

Abby chuckled wryly. "I'm not sure it's sensible, but it's what I *want*." She stopped him in the hall. "I don't operate on 'I want,' ever, but this time I don't care if I'm being stupid. I need one thing from you, though." She cupped his face. "I need you to promise me that you'll say something right away if you're sorry for asking, even if it's tomorrow, or a week from now. Promise me, Matt."

"I promise." He hesitated briefly before he leaned in to kiss her, moving slowly and gently. He groaned, hands tightening on Abby's hips as his gentle explorations became more intense, but he let Abby decide when to move closer.

When she did, it was with infinite slowness, tormenting him first with her distance, then her body heat, and then the lightest brush of her breasts against his chest. "Tell me we won't be sorry, Matt," she murmured against his cheek, feathering kisses along his jaw. "I'll believe you."

Matt heard the vulnerability in her voice and gently disengaged her hands from his shirt, stepping back enough that he could see her eyes. "I think it's going to hurt like hell when you have to go. I still want you to stay."

Abby sighed out a shaky breath. "Thank you."

A few minutes later, in his room, the moonlight coming through the open window limned Abby's skin with silver as her skirt floated to the floor. Matt sat on the foot of the bed, eyes traveling from face to shoulders to hips to feet as Abby waited, seemingly unworried this time about her flaws. She had proof in clay of what he saw when he looked at her, and he was glad she was no longer nervous under his gaze.

"Will you come here?" he requested.

Abby walked over and stood in front of him.

With one hand, he reached out and touched her stomach with the tips of his fingers. Abby shivered, and Matt smiled. He trailed the same fingertips down her side, barely brushing the outer curve of her breast before ghosting over her sensitive ribcage, continuing over her hip, and down her thigh. After the third time, Abby gasped, and Matt looked up from following his hand with his gaze. "Is this okay?"

Abby laughed shakily. "Very okay. Really, really okay."

Matt smiled and urged her onto the bed to lie next to him. "Then I'll do it right," he murmured, starting his explorations in earnest.

Chapter Sixteen

Sarah leaned back on her hands on Abby's bed, watching her friend pack the last few things from her dresser. "Are you sure about this, babes?" she asked again and shifted her weight to one hand to hold up the other in a wait motion. "I know, I'm driving you crazy, but… Abby, you just don't do stuff like this. You dated Eric for two years, and moving in together never even flew onto your radar, and you've known Matt for what, like…two months? I mean…" She stopped, her mouth opening and closing in several aborted attempts at speech. She gave up and scratched her head vigorously in frustration.

Abby looked around for any loose items she might have missed. "Will you relax? You've gone on vacation with a guy, right? Right. I seem to remember two weeks in Barbados with…what the hell was his name? Jared? What's the difference?"

Sarah flopped back on the bed with a groan. "I thought we agreed to never mention that vile name again. He's an animal, not a guy." Abby laughed, and Sarah rolled to her side and propped herself on her elbow with a serious look. She began ticking off points on her fingers. "And there are differences. First, it was half as long as this will be. B, I worked with him for almost a year before taking the highway to hell. Number three, I do—did—stupid shit like that all the time. Last…" Sarah stopped ticking off points and chewed her lip.

"Last?"

"I didn't really care about Jared at all," Sarah blurted out. "I liked his body, he made me laugh, and I saw a chance at an almost-free Caribbean vacation." She flopped back again. "I hate being honest with myself. It's exhausting. I'd rather live in 'Sarah is a Perfect Princess' land." She sighed. "Anyway, that is so obviously not the case here. I'm totally self-absorbed, and even I can see that you're in lo—"

"Sarah," Abby warned.

"Yeah, I know, we're not talking about it. And you don't even believe in it anymore…but, Ab, won't this make it harder when you come home? You are coming home, right?"

Abby sank down on the bed and laid her head on Sarah's stomach. "A few weeks ago you were all gung ho about me dropping everything and moving here."

Sarah grimaced. "That's when I thought you would never in a million years do it. It sounds romantic until I think about you never coming home. Then shit gets real."

Abby sighed. "Of course I'm coming home. I have a job and an apartment and a life in Boston." None of that sounded appealing to her at the moment. "And, yes, staying will make it harder when I have to leave. But I don't care. I…I have to do this." Abby looked at her friend pleadingly, hoping that she was making sense.

Sarah's face softened, and she stroked Abby's hair back from her forehead. "I know," she said. They were quiet for a moment, each lost in her thoughts.

"Well," Sarah said, moving Abby's head to the bed and sitting up with a groan, "thanks to David's magic Visa, I'm flying home." Her face lighted at the prospect. Abby wondered how long it would take until the late night calls between David and Sarah would become lean-across-the-pillow conversations. She'd lay odds on two days.

"At least you'll have my car if it gets to be just…too much. Or too little." Sarah gave her friend a slanted smile.

"Not much chance of that," Abby answered, and they both snickered.

Grabbing Abby's bags, Sarah headed for the door. "I'm done lecturing. I suck at it anyway." She turned with an uncharacteristically sober look on her face and grasped Abby's hand. "Just promise me, doll…promise me that you will leave if it hurts too bad. September is going to be a nightmare for you, you do realize that?"

"Yeah…" Abby answered. "Everything else around here finished?"

"She said, decisively changing the subject," Sarah shot back with a grin. "Yes. All perfect and pristine…except for the damn stain on her loveseat, but her new, improved door should make up for that. She doesn't have to know that Matt did the whole thing, right?"

"Not the loveseat."

"No, that was all me. Or David. And I worried about you and Matt on the stupid thing."

"Lalalalala, not listening." Abby plugged her ears. "Let's just get you to the airport before my ears start bleeding from all the details you've already offered."

The drive into the city was uneventful, aside from a massive amount of teasing on both sides, and Abby dropped Sarah off at San Francisco International Airport after a flurry of kisses, hugs, exchanges of keys, and last minute messages to friends on both coasts.

After leaving her friend, Abby drove to Golden Gate Park to see some of the things she hadn't had time to visit with Matt. Then she took the long way back to Santa Cruz, driving along the coast on Highway 1, pulling off at times to take in the magnificent views. Despite how calm she'd been in front of Sarah, the reality was that doing something so drastic as moving in with Matt, even if it was only for a month, was far out of her comfort zone, and she needed some time to herself. Finally pulling into the driveway at Matt's house, she felt a flutter of mixed anxiety and excitement.

As she got to the front door, it eased open and Chris appeared, duffle bag slung over his shoulder and a smile on his face. "Hey, girl! I thought I heard your car. Where you been?"

"I decided to sightsee a bit. Hey, you don't have to leave, Chris. I didn't mean to kick you out."

He set his bag down so he could use both hands to sweep his hair back into a rough ponytail. "Ain't no big thing. Matt's a good guy for letting me crash for as long as he has. And before you get that funny-ass stricken look on your face again, no, he didn't ask me to leave." Chris laughed. "Too late to stop the look. I'm staying at Jason's." He held up a hand. "I know, I know. But he turns out to be a pretty decent guy. He and his friend will be out of town a lot, so…" He shrugged and hefted his bag.

"If you're sure," Abby said uncertainly.

Chris grabbed the handles of both of her bags in his free hand and carried them into the living room, dropping them in the middle of the floor. "Hell, yes. No stress." He glanced back toward the kitchen and lowered his voice. "You might want to let him know you're back, though. He's been doing his own version of batshit-crazy since lunchtime. His sculpture would be almost finished if he'd carved as much as he paced." There was a beep from outside, and he smiled at Abby, ruffling her hair. "That would be Jason. Go set my cousin's mind at ease, woman. Be good to each other."

A half-minute later, he was gone, and Abby was left in the living room, looking down at her bags and chewing her lip. To take them right into Matt's bedroom seemed forward, so she decided to leave them where they lay and to go look for her artist.

She found him in his studio. The set of his shoulders was tense, far more so than his sweeping strokes at the waistline of the sculpture should have indicated, and Abby regretted not having called him. She slid her arms around his middle and rested her forehead against his back. "Hi," she said softly.

Matt stiffened; Abby had a moment's horror that he was going to pull away from her before he relaxed. "Hi," he answered in the same tone. He pressed her arms against his stomach before tossing the sculpting knife onto the revolving tabletop. "I thought maybe you got lost. Or decided not to come back."

Abby turned him around. "I'm sorry. I never meant to worry you. You were so absorbed when I left this morning that I thought you might appreciate uninterrupted work time. Plus, I'm not used to checking in with anyone, I guess. Boy, this is a good beginning, isn't it?"

Matt kissed her firmly. "Beginnings are usually awkward. I'm done here for tonight. Give me a few minutes to clean up, and then I want to hear about your day."

She smiled, turning her face up, eyes closed, for another kiss before retreating to the kitchen. After rifling through the cupboards and fridge, she set to work on a simple pasta dish. She turned when Matt hummed in pleasure as he entered the room a few minutes later. "You didn't have to do that, Abby. We could have gone out."

Abby laughed. "My not-so-secret: you've taken in a terrible bore. I'd rather stay in than go out most any night. Sorry now?"

Matt pushed himself away from the counter and reached over Abby's head to grab two plates from the cupboard. "Nope. I'm a homebody myself." They smiled at each other, delighted to find they had something so basic in common. "Wine?"

With no pressure to rush, dinner was a pleasure, and Abby found herself talking more than she thought she would. Matt's hands danced in the air as he described what he'd accomplished that day, and she smiled. Matt cleaned up after dinner, making short work of the few dishes. He grabbed a second bottle of wine and their glasses and headed for the living room when he was finished. He raised an eyebrow at Abby's bags, still sitting in the middle of the room.

"I didn't know what to do with them. I don't want to put you out for space for a month."

A shadow crossed Matt's face as he passed his burdens to Abby and picked up the bags. "You're not putting me out. I want you here. For however long, this is your home, okay?" He took her bags to his bedroom while Abby poured them both another glass of wine. When he returned, he asked, "So, what was your favorite thing during your sightseeing today?"

Abby curled up on the sofa. "The tea garden, I think. I was thinking how much my mom would like that." She laughed. "She's in a Japanese phase now. You should have seen the fit my dad had when she had her studio fitted out to fire raku pottery — expensive proposition."

Matt's eyes lighted with interest. He sat down beside Abby, pulling her feet onto his lap. "I didn't know your mom was a sculptor. What does your dad do?"

Abby shook her head. "Mom's more of a potter-slash-artist of all trades. Does a bit of everything. Dad's a wood carver and furniture maker. They're madly in love, when they're not driving each other crazy."

"Nice. So you come by this 'art thing' naturally."

"You could say that. Mom decided early on that I was born to be a painter, so I think I held a brush before I could use a fork." Her look turned pensive. "Funny thing was, I did love it, no matter what else I tried." Emotions flickered across her face. "Anyway," she said with forced brightness, "desire and talent don't necessarily go hand in hand, do they? Tell me about teaching."

Matt's struggle to not question her further was plain on his face. Abby squeezed his hand gratefully as he let the topic drop, but she recognized that it would probably be revisited in the future. They talked well into the night, switching to water when the wine was gone, and when Abby felt Matt curl around her after making love, pulling her back against his chest and tightening his arm around her, she knew her decision to stay was the only possible choice she could have lived with.

As it turned out, giving Matt space to work was easier than Abby had anticipated. Preparations for the children's art show ended up taking a lot more time than she had anticipated, though she had a suspicion that Claire was handing off more responsibility and making the event broader than it had been previously, partly because she had Abby's help and partly because she wanted to keep her artist focused.

Though Abby had been slow to warm to the challenge of working with children, she'd gradually come to enjoy her long days with them. Watching the determination with which they attacked each task, completely assured that everything they created was a masterpiece, reminded of her of the joy she'd felt as she had clutched a paint brush under her parents' loving eyes. She hadn't felt that confident since childhood.

Thinking of her mother gave her an idea for a pottery project. A simple oven couldn't be that difficult to construct. Maybe she could even convince Matt to let her borrow his kiln. Abby smiled, considering what type of payment she could offer.

"Matt!" She let the door slam behind her in her excitement. "Hey, I have an idea that needs your help."

"Back here," he answered, his voice already full of smiles.

Abby hurried through the house, dropping her bag on a kitchen chair. "I know you'll love this…"

Her smile became fixed when she spotted the addition of an easel to Matt's studio. Next to it was a low table covered with boxes, tubes, and brushes. Several blank canvases rested against the wall, and a large folder leaned against them.

Abby walked toward the table. She touched the items, lingering over the watercolors, a medium she'd not tried before. "Claire helped me pick that stuff out," Matt said, his tone anxious. "I wasn't sure which you preferred."

Abby tried to sort out her mixed emotions, not wanting to say the wrong thing and create tension during their last couple of weeks together. She reached out with a finger to stroke the feathery-light ends of the brushes.

"I thought it would be a way for us to be together during the day without you feeling like you're bothering me."

"It has nothing to do with your ex talking about painting but never doing it? Because, honestly, Matt, I could live forever without—"

"Oh, God, no!" Matt's expression was horrified. "Abby, just… no." He walked over to take her hand. "I told you, I don't even think about Kate at all. I just…" His expression was stormy. "I want you here with me, for as long as you can be."

Abby released a shaking breath. "I thought we were living for today, Matt." She leaned her head against him and listened to the thumping of his heart.

"I know, I know. I feel disgustingly clingy, but I have to prove to myself that you're still here, that you still want me. Yesterday afternoon…"

"Was incredible."

"Thank you," Matt said, grinning. "But I can't keep that up. I'll never finish this sculpture. And I might have a heart attack. I'm not as young as I once was."

"I have no complaints," Abby said, laughing as something loosened in her chest. Matt had no agenda other than being with her. "With age comes experience, and I'd choose that any day." She shooed Matt back toward his sculpture. "Go. Be a genius while I putter." Matt kissed her hard and headed toward his revolving table. He picked up his tools with renewed vigor and started to whistle along with the music that played on the stereo.

Abby considered the implements Matt had provided. Aside from quick sketches, she hadn't used real artists' tools since her junior year in college. Settling on a pad of paper and a pencil as the best way to ease into it, Abby began to sketch the first thing that came to mind: little Jeremy's broad smile that day as his fingers dripped paint. Before she knew it, the scene was sketched out and she was adding depth and shading with quick strokes of the pencil.

"Why did you quit, Abby?"

Matt's voice from behind her was gentle, and she answered without thinking. "My professor said I have mediocre talent." Her hand slowed to a stop as the scene replayed itself behind her eyes: the jeering tone in the professor's voice, sudden silence in the classroom. She'd dropped her brush right there and walked straight to her advisor to change her major to art history.

Matt evaluated her picture. "Your professor was an idiot."

"You're not exactly impartial."

"No, but I'm a professional and an academic." He pointed toward her sketch of Jeremy and the drop of paint that dangled from his elbow. "You've given that not only a sense of depth, but the illusion of liquid. Do you know how hard that is to do with pencils? You get gloss from oils or acrylics that help, but to make me thirsty with graphite or charcoal? That's talent." He looked very serious. "I wouldn't lie to you, Abby. This is very, very good."

Searching his eyes and finding no evidence of guile, Abby smiled brilliantly. "Thank you." She was surprised when she looked at her watch. "I can't believe it's three already! You want a late lunch?"

Matt smiled and took her hand. "How about an early dinner? I just talked to Chris; he wants to meet us at the Poet for burgers and drinks."

Abby was shocked that Matt had carried on a phone conversation and she'd not heard a word of it, lost in her own world for the first time in years. "I'd like that," she answered absently, picking up her pencil. She barely heard Matt asking about the great idea she'd mentioned when she'd come in the door. Lost in her sketch, she didn't recall answering that it was something about a kiln.

This time, it was Matt who chuckled at *her* distraction. He kissed her on the back of the neck and promised to ask again later. Then he headed back toward his own side of the room to pick up his wire clay loop.

Chapter Seventeen

"I can't believe I let you talk me into this. I know nothing about this boat, nothing about these waters…this has disaster written all over it." Abby chewed her nails and stared at the front of the Eastmans' house.

Matt smiled. "I trust your skills explicitly."

"See if you're singing the same tune when I crash us into a hidden reef, sharks eat your legs, and you're wheeling yourself down to the beach, Cap'n Dan."

"You wouldn't push me?"

"I went down with the ship. You're on your own."

Matt laughed and got out of the car, waiting until Abby had closed her door before he tugged her toward the house. "First, there are no hidden reefs around here. Second, there hasn't been a shark sighting in months—too many people during tourist season. The fish get scared off, and the sharks follow them."

"I was just kidding about the sharks! Now I have another thing to worry about."

Matt took her hand and kissed the back before ascending the porch steps. Claire opened the door at his knock. "Right on time. Charles is down at the boat getting everything shipshape. Ready?"

Abby exhaled a great breath. "Thank God you guys are coming with."

Claire looked at Abby quizzically as she gestured for them to enter the house. "Why wouldn't we? You don't know anything about the waters here. It would be dangerous to send you out alone."

"Oh, I agree," Abby said hastily, flushing. "It's just that Matt led me to think…"

Looping her arm through Abby's, Claire shook her head. "Matt is a tease. Or he's dumber than a bag of hammers, as my dad would have said." She looked at Matt in calculation. "I'd say the jury is still out on that one. Shall we go down to meet Charles?"

They walked out the back door and across the expanse of lawn. Claire talked animatedly, pointing out the sails as soon as they were in sight. Matt watched Abby's eyes light up. She giggled as they walked out onto the dock that jetted into a private cove. "That's a dinghy? I don't think so."

Charles grinned, his sky blue eyes crinkling at the corners. He leaped lithely to the dock, not seeming bothered by the brisk morning breeze across the water though he wore only a threadbare Rolling Stones T-shirt with shorts. "Well, technically, I think dinghy stops applying when the boat is more than eighteen feet long. This is a bit more than that, but it's the smallest boat we have, so…" He gestured with a flourish toward the side. "Care to come aboard?"

"Hell, yes!" Abby said.

After jumping back on the boat, Charles put out his hand to his smiling wife. As he was getting her settled, Abby wrapped her arm through Matt's. "A *bit* more than eighteen feet?" she murmured. "This is at least twice that. Makes our twenty-footer back home look like a toy." She reached up to take Charles's outstretched hand and leaped to the deck.

When Abby turned to Matt and held out her hand to him, her eyes shining, he decided that his sculpture wouldn't be enough; he had to capture this moment, this smile, as well. Claire must have read the distant look in Matt's eyes, because she rifled through the bag she'd carried on board and handed him a pad of paper and a pencil. He got immediately to work. Capturing motion in a static media was always a challenge, but he felt sure this subject wouldn't be a problem; he'd studied Abby so thoroughly that he'd see her clearly in his mind for the rest of his life.

He heard a groan from behind him. "This fantastic boat…this beautiful cove…and you're sketching me?"

Matt smiled down at the paper. "What boat? What cove?"

"Crazy man," Abby said. "Charles wants to show me around his baby and teach me a little about this coast. Do you mind?"

"Nope. Have fun."

Having sailed with Charles and Claire often, Matt knew enough to stay out of the way and just enjoy the sun. After finishing his sketch, he set it aside and stretched his legs out on the deck. He tipped his head back.

"Posing?" Claire teased.

"I thought you were a boat lackey."

"I've been supplanted by someone who actually cares."

Matt opened his eyes to slits and saw Claire holding two deck chairs as she clenched a book under her arm.

"Sit in one of these like a civilized being, for God's sake."

Matt rose with a groan and set up his chair. Flopping into it, he leaned his head back once more, enjoying the warmth now that the morning cool was dying off. He unzipped his jacket and closed his eyes, listening to the murmur of voices discussing rigging and water conditions and a thousand other sailing things that didn't interest him in the least. Claire settled into her chair with a sigh of contentment.

"So, we can pretend this is a working trip…" she began with a laugh. "Where are you on Baker's stuff?"

After a rundown on the latest sculpture, Claire hummed in satisfaction. "That far? I knew this was a good day to spend some time with your lovely girl. This is the fastest I've ever seen you work, Matt. You need a break before you burn out. Plus, time's—"

His smile faded. "We're not focusing on that."

Claire was quiet. "Fair enough."

Matt listened to the gulls and willed his shoulders to relax.

A throat clearing drew his attention. Claire was staring at the side of his head. "Yes?" he asked, eyes closing again.

"Deciding," Claire said thoughtfully.

"About?"

"That hammers thing."

Matt smiled. "Verdict?"

"It's still up in the air, depending on if you really let Abby go home without you."

"Claire…"

"I know," she said, "it's an off-limits topic. But screw that. We've known each other a long time, and I'm a nosy bitch. So, what are you thinking?"

"We're planning to get together at Christmastime." He heard her snort of disgust and looked at her. "What else can I do? We're not kids that can just walk away from real life whenever we want to. Abby has a job that she likes and has to go back to, and I have Baker's damned statues to finish, unless I want to be sued for breach of contract, and you know he'd love to have a reason. It's just…I'm screwed, you know?"

Claire's gaze softened and she relented. "Yeah. Ready for a sandwich?" She got up from her seat and extended a hand to Matt. "Hey, you two?" she called toward Charles and Abby as they conferred gravely over a maritime chart. "Can you take a break to eat, or will we crash and be shark lunch?"

"Sharks again," Matt heard Abby mutter, and he grinned.

"Dropping anchor right now, captain," Charles said with a grin. "I'm starving." After a few moments bustling about, the boat was still and lunch set out. "Courtesy of my favorite housekeeper," he said in satisfaction, taking a huge bite of sandwich as he lounged against the side of the boat. "She's a wonder."

"She's an enabler," Claire observed, taking the lobster salad on pillowy French bread from his hand and replacing it with a turkey on whole-grain. "You know the doctor told you to watch your cholesterol." She took a bite of his former sandwich.

Charles shook his head. "You are a cruel woman. I'd divorce you for that if I didn't love you so much." They ate in silence for a few minutes before he spoke again. "So, how do you like our coast, Abby? Enough to come out again and save my long-suffering wife from pretending to care about all this sailing business?"

"It's beautiful," Abby said. "I'd love to come out again, if I get a chance before I leave. I'm sure Claire cares more than you realize, though."

"About my husband," Claire said with a rueful grin. She wrapped her arm around Charles's waist. "I'm afraid he's right about the sailing, though I thought I hid it better." She brushed an errant lock of hair off of his forehead. "We only have each other, so whatever I can do to spend time with him is worth it."

Charles caught her hand and kissed its palm before resting it on his chest. "So…what are your plans for the next couple of weeks? I need to go to Thailand next week, and I'd love to make it a group trip, my treat. Great surfing, Matt, and you could probably catch up with your dad—he's in Australia, right? Easy side trip in the jet."

Abby laughed. "You don't do things by halves, do you? I'm afraid I don't have my passport with me."

"Yes, dear, don't tease," Claire scolded. "Besides, Matt has a ton of work to do, I have slave driving to do, and Abby has painting. How's that going, by the way?"

Matt admired the skillful subject change and used the opportunity to sing Abby's praises. Charles responded with a request for a sketch of his boat, on the spot. Abby complied, taking the pad that Matt had laid aside and setting to work as the others finished their lunch. She worked so quietly, her hand flying, that Claire and Charles seemed to forget what she was doing as they chatted.

Matt sat next to Abby, snatching occasional glances at her work. He restrained a smile. Charles wasn't going to get what he'd envisioned. Abby finished her sketch with a flourish and handed it to Claire.

Claire smiled delightedly. Though Charles's request was partially fulfilled, in that a significant portion of the side of his boat was shown in detail, the focus was clearly the man as he lounged against the edge of the boat, laughing, arms outstretched along the top rail.

"Abby, this is just…lovely!" Claire said after studying the picture.

Charles peeked at the paper and grimaced. "Are the lines on my face that deep? Maybe I should follow Grandmother's advice and have some work done."

"Hush," Claire ordered. "You're ruggedly handsome. I like that face, shameless fisher-for-compliments."

Charles smiled. "As long as you put it that way…" He tapped the page. "I don't claim to know much about art, but I'd like this if I wasn't the subject." He turned to Claire. "What do you think?"

"I want this in more permanent form. I *do* know a lot about art, and this is very good, Abby, especially for a spur of the moment thing."

Abby flushed and handed the pad back to Claire. "Here. It's yours." She looked surprised when Claire tore off the sheet and handed it back.

"Keep this. You'll need it for my painting. Oils or acrylics, whatever medium you prefer. I'm serious. Consider it a commission. You're talented, and this is wonderful." Claire looked at the drawing again. "In fact, lots of people should see this." She thought for a minute, and then she smiled.

Curling her hands around Charles's arm, she looked up at him. "I've had the best idea. Don't you think there's probably a lot of untapped talent in Santa Cruz, C? We already have a show planned for the children, so why don't we expand? I'll bet that if we, meaning you, put it out through the grapevine that we're looking for Cruz arts and crafts, we could pull something together in a couple of weeks."

"Not much time for advertising." Charles said.

Claire waved her hand dismissively. "We're not trying to compete with Sausalito. Just a little show for ourselves. Local artists… civic pride…"

Charles chuckled and slung his arm around his wife's shoulders. "You don't have to sell me, sweetheart. Make it happen. Just give a featured spot to the painting of the old man and the sea. We need to spotlight our local stars." He grinned at Abby.

"If it's for locals—"

"Do the old ladies that watch for surfers talk to you?" Charles asked sternly.

"Yes."

"Then you're local," Charles said firmly. "They wouldn't be caught dead paying attention to a tourist, unless it involved a monetary exchange. In fact—" He cursed as the phone in his pocket rang. He walked a few feet away before he answered.

Matt felt a tug at his heart. In just a few weeks, Abby had become a local, something not easy to achieve in a tourist-inundated town. He didn't think his mother had ever accomplished it, even with living there for a few years. Maybe she'd always had one foot out the door and his father's friends had sensed that. He edged closer to Abby, and she responded by resting her head against his shoulder. By the time of Claire's show, she'd be leaving.

His attention was drawn back to their company when Charles spoke. "I'm sorry, folks. I'm going to have to cut this short. Grandmother has apparently made an appearance, and my presence is desperately needed for serious business. Or just because she's bored.

Who the hell knows?" He grimaced and headed for the wheel. Abby asked if he'd like help and got his enthusiastic okay.

Matt felt Claire's calculating gaze.

"Don't say a word."

She smiled slyly. "I don't need to. It's written all over your face. And I'm back to that bag of hammers issue." She slipped her own jacket off and adjusted her sunglasses as she took a seat. "Don't bother arguing with me. I plan on enjoying these last few minutes of freedom before the old dragon sucks away my will to live."

The trip back to the Eastman dock was accomplished without issue, and soon Claire was repacking her bag and sliding on her shoes. Abby picked up her shirt and jacket, but Charles stopped her.

"No reason for you guys to cut your day short," he said. "Why don't you take the boat back out? We went over the area pretty thoroughly. Just stay around here, and you'll be fine."

Abby looked flustered. "I don't…"

Charles grinned at her. "I trust you. Just don't hit anything. We'll leave you the cooler." He leaped to the dock and helped his wife out. Slinging her ridiculously flowery bag over his shoulder, he wrapped the opposite arm around her waist, and they walked toward their house, heads close together as they laughed at some private joke.

Abby watched them go, a wistful smile on her face, until they disappeared over the crest of a small rise. "They're great, aren't they?"

Matt nodded and put his hand over hers as it rested on the rail.

"Well, shall we try to pilot this beast a bit?" she asked, smiling. "Nothing to lose but a boat worth more than I'll earn before I die."

Matt laughed. "Why not? Just tell me what to do."

Within half an hour, Abby had reached the limits of both the water she felt comfortable sailing and her courage. Dropping anchor, she accomplished a number of tasks that remained a mystery to Matt before she pronounced them safe.

"Wanna swim?" Matt asked, stripping off his shirt and toeing off his shoes.

"Oh! I don't think I should. I mean…shouldn't someone stay with the boat?" Abby stammered.

"Nope. We do it all the time." Matt tugged at the waistband of her shorts. "There are no sharks," he murmured in her ear. "Come on…it's hot out here, and the water's cool. We don't have to stay in long. Don't make me beg, Abby."

She snorted and stepped back, slipping her feet out of her shoes and sliding her shorts over her hips. "Far be it from me to deny you anything." With two large steps, she was at the rail and flying into the water.

Matt followed her a bare second later, cutting into the water cleanly and coming up behind her. A brief, fierce water fight followed. With a choked laugh, Abby capitulated after a sweeping armful of water had filled her open mouth. Matt held her as they treaded water. Relaxing, Abby closed her eyes and sighed in contentment.

Leaving her to her thoughts, Matt swam a slow lap around the boat. As always, time spent in his element wiped away any thoughts other than enjoyment of sea and sun. He rounded the front of the boat and paused to watch Abby float. Her hair drifted around her head while her hands moved lazily in the waves and the swells of her breasts rose above the water. He didn't think he'd ever wanted anyone as much as he wanted her right then.

Moving silently beneath the surface of the water, Matt watched for the smooth roundness of Abby's thighs before sliding his fingers over her skin.

What he didn't anticipate was her shriek and splash as she bolted upright in the water, submerging rapidly. Diving, he grasped her under the arms and kicked for the surface, holding her up as she choked out water.

Once she could breathe, she slapped at his chest, startling him into releasing her. She swam for the boat, grabbing the rungs of the ladder as soon as she could reach them. "That wasn't funny." Her foot slipped on a rung as she neared the top rail, and she scrabbled for purchase.

Matt restrained his laugh, perceiving it was no time to push her. "I wasn't trying to be funny," he protested, swimming for the ladder.

Abby leaned over the side and pointed at him. "Don't you dare! I'm pissed off, so you'd better stay there until I calm down. And don't try to tell me you weren't being funny. First you scare me about sharks, then you grab my leg…"

This time he did laugh. "Swear to God, I wasn't thinking about that, Abby." He held on to the lowest rung. "I wasn't playing shark."

Abby stared down at him for a moment. And then she grunted acknowledgment. "Stay down there anyway. Punishment for scaring the piss out of me, and I do mean literally. I hope sharks aren't attracted to pee." She disappeared from the railing.

Matt waited at the side of the boat, hoping that she'd relent and let him ascend. When she didn't reappear, he set out around the boat again. He chuckled to himself as he swam, seeing first her panicked jump and then the angry scowl as she glared down at him from the deck. As he rounded the back of the boat and neared the ladder again, he hoped that the twinkle he'd thought he'd seen in her eye as she'd stepped back from the rail hadn't been a figment of his hopeful imagination. He climbed quickly, trusting that innate kindness would keep her from ordering him back into the water once he made his goal.

Abby paid no attention to him as she rested in her deck chair, legs outstretched and eyes closed. Matt walked closer, relieved to see the tiny tilt to her lips that she tried to hide. He kneeled beside her and rested his cold, wet head on her chest.

"Am I forgiven?" he asked, scooting closer and wrapping an arm around her torso.

"I suppose," she sighed. Matt turned his head and kissed the swells of her breasts. "What is it with guys and boobs?" she asked, laughing as he tweaked the end of the string that tied around her neck.

"They're warm and soft, and we don't have 'em. What's not to like?" Pulling the bottom string, he felt the bow loosen and removed the cloth from her body before dropping it on the deck.

Matt sat back on his heels, tracing her shape with his eyes and his hands. "Beautiful," he said softly, leaning forward to nibble at her belly, inhaling the mixed scents of sea, sun, and skin. "I want you."

"You're a tease," she murmured, hands gripping the sides of her chair.

"Not at all." Matt stood and helped Abby to her feet, catching her hands as she moved to cover her chest. "Don't. There's no one around but me." He walked backward, holding her hands and her gaze until he had to locate the handle of a particular hatch. He twisted it open and extracted a light blanket, raising an eyebrow in question.

"No way."

Matt smiled and led her toward the spot he'd chosen, between the masts and hidden from view unless a boat came right alongside.

"Are you telling me you've never enjoyed outdoor sex? I find that hard to believe."

"Of course I have, but…" Abby hedged.

Matt shook out the blanket and stood in the middle of it. "The ocean, the sun, and you, all at once. Since you've nixed the idea of the beach, this is the next best thing."

Abby nodded hesitantly. With a tug, she loosened the ties that held the bottom of her suit together. She let it fall and sank down onto the blanket. "I'm going to get burned."

Matt squatted down, his eyes serious even as he watched his hand glide down her body. "No you're not. I never want you to hurt, Abby, in any way. Trust me."

She nodded and reached up to stroke his face with the backs of her fingers. "I trust you," she whispered when he was stretched out next to her. Matt shifted her over him, running his hands over her back and bottom, trying to save every bit of sensory input from this moment: the warmth of sun and skin against him, the smell of the sea and her body, the taste of salt on Abby's shoulder, the soft sound of her breathing.

The last vestiges of thought warned him that something wasn't right. He looked up and noticed that Abby's eyes were tightly closed, her body tense.

Matt kissed her eyelids. "Look at me, Abby. Please."

Wetness started to seep around her lashes, and she shook her head.

"Yes," he insisted. "Don't shut me out."

Abby opened her eyes slowly. Matt felt a sense of wonder at what he saw there. He'd never imagined he'd see love looking back at him.

"I'm sorry," Abby whispered. "I didn't mean for this to happen. I just…" She trailed off as Matt covered her mouth with his fingertips.

"Don't be sorry. Please. I'm not, even if you scare the hell out of me. Abby, I lov—"

Abby kissed him fiercely. "Can we not say it?" she asked, her voice trembling. She shifted the tiny bit needed to sink down onto and around him. "Please? Not yet."

Matt nodded, then concentrated on pleasing them both.

Please became *yes*, became *fuck*, became *God*, became laughter and sighs and gasps and *now*…and then their cries mingled with the sounds of the gulls that wheeled overhead, careless of the magic and mystery taking place far below them. And then it was quiet.

Abby's gentle hands on his face brought Matt out of his doze. "Hey, mister. You can't go to sleep now. You'll cook." Her fingers trailed over his bum. "Not all of you is brown."

Matt groaned and rolled to his side, grabbing the edge of the blanket and pulling it over both of them. "Your fault," he said, his yawn interrupted by a laugh as Abby nudged him in the stomach.

They lay listening to the sounds of the sea as it slapped against the side of the boat. Matt smoothed Abby's hair away from her ear. "Abby, why won't you let me say——"

She twisted around and covered his mouth with hers, effectively and pleasantly halting his words, but he refused to be entirely distracted.

"Why?" he murmured when she drew back.

Abby searched his face before lying back down, her face turned toward the side of the boat. "Because that makes it more real, Matt. Because I've never felt like this. Because I'm leaving in less than three weeks, and if this falls apart after that, those words will echo in my head forever, and I'll start to doubt this really happened, and that will kill me." She took a shuddering breath. "I know. You know. That will have to be good enough."

"You don't have to go," Matt murmured, curling himself even more closely around her.

"Yeah, I do. I have a life in Boston. Maybe I'll figure something out by Christmas, I don't know…" She trailed off, clutching Matt's hand to her chest.

They listened to the sounds of gulls and surf until Abby chuckled. "This would be so much easier if I just wanted your body." She turned in his arms and ran her hand up his back, tracing the muscles between his spine and his side. "It's a nice body."

Matt laughed. "The feeling's mutual." He drew back until he could look into her eyes. "I wish I could wish that I'd never met you. But I can't." His eyes softened and crinkled at the corners as he smiled. "You're my muse, pretty Abby." She smiled back, and then she snuggled against him, her head below his chin.

"Fair enough." Abby rose lithely to her feet, stretching before she reached for her bathing suit. Matt lounged unselfconsciously, hands behind his head and feet crossed at the ankles as he watched her dress; she nudged his thigh with her toes.

"Get dressed, goofy. It's getting late, and we need to get this beast back."

Matt smiled and stretched. "Tell the truth. You like me all nekkid."

"Too much. Charles probably thinks I wrecked his boat." Her gaze traveled over his form. And then she chuckled and turned to locate her shirt. "Besides, I can't imagine something more painful than a sunburned willie, and you're already turning pink."

Matt got to his feet and reluctantly pulled on his shorts after a quick and satisfactory check of the maligned part. "Lies. All white and all right. But we'll do this your way, cap'n. Are we returning under sail or engine power?"

"Sail, I think, unless I can't get us in that way." Abby smiled at him. "It will take longer."

"Sounds good to me."

Claire met them at the edge of the patio after their uneventful trip home, apologizing again for leaving them alone before pressing them to stay for dinner. Charles stepped out the door, drink in hand, and added his invitation.

They exchanged a glance before declining, citing the long day and a desire to get to sleep in order to get an early start the next day.

Claire smiled knowingly before kissing Abby on the cheek and handing her over to Charles for a quick boat debriefing. She drew Matt into a quick hug, whispering, "See? I got you time alone on the boat—and away from work—with your sailor girl."

Matt appraised Claire's twinkling eyes. "No grandmother?"

"Nope. It was Mary asking what Charles wanted for dinner."

"Crafty of him to improvise."

"Taught him everything I know," Claire said proudly, stepping away as Charles and Abby joined them.

Chapter Eighteen

"Well, that was relatively painless," Claire said in satisfaction, stepping into Matt's studio and heading for the canvases drying along one baseboard. "I expected at least a sulk, and a hissy fit wasn't out of the question."

Abby laughed, starting the process of putting Matt's clay away for the day. "Oh, he's not as bad as that."

Claire snorted. "You wish. He'd be going with me to this lunch no matter what, but you made it infinitely easier by backing me up." She stopped, putting a hand on Abby's sketchpad. "Do you mind?" She flipped through the pages. "I have to give you props. I think the hand on his forearm and the soft voice carried the day. 'It's just a couple of hours, right? I'll stay up with you late tonight to make up the time you lose,'" Claire repeated Abby's words in a whisper and then laughed. "What man's going to turn down an offer to make it worth his while?"

"I didn't even think of it that way. Of course, now I can't stop." They both chuckled. "Really, though, I do understand the magnitude of his good fortune. You can't predict the breaks that are falling into his lap right now. A lunch with the money boys won't kill either of us." Abby repressed the tiny voice that cried out at the unfairness of the timing of fortune. With less than two weeks left until she went home, every minute was starting to feel precious.

"Smart woman." Claire went back to the canvasses. "These are good, Abby. Clean lines…emotive…" She hummed to herself as she studied them.

Abby drew out some watercolor paper, hoping to catch the right light on the wild, sun-dappled wisteria that draped across the pergola outside the window. "Thanks."

Claire watched her for a minute. "Charles's grandmonster would like her own copy of my picture, by the way. She intends to come to our little street festival and offer you a mint to paint one for her—ask for double whatever she offers."

Abby kept her eyes on her brush. "We'll see how much time I have when I get home." She tried to drum up enthusiasm for the curating work she'd done for years. "The museum is crazy busy with school tours in the fall, and we have a new exhibit of cubists."

"Abby, what would you say if I offered you a job in my gallery?"

Trying to catch her heart's headlong leap into her throat while keeping a cool head wasn't easy. Abby had been working hard in her field for too damn long to devalue herself or her work. The knowledge that an unnecessary job was created for her to please her boyfriend would eat at her until she resented both Claire and Matt. But having the deepest wish—the absolute yearning—of her heart offered to her…it was hard to question.

She did any way.

Abby drew the brush down the paper. "I'd ask if the job existed before right this minute."

"Of course."

Abby leveled a look at Claire. "Really?"

"No." Claire blew out a breath and slumped against a table. "But it could. Look how much help you've been to me this summer. I could have never dealt with the freaks coming out of the woodwork lately by myself. You didn't even bat an eye when that woman brought in the stuffed woodchucks and called them art." Claire shuddered. "And now Charles has decided to add musical talent to the mix, and that all has to be organized. I need you, Abby. Someone has to deal with Tyler Oda and his band of weirdoes."

Abby let out a guffaw. "Tell you what. If you still find that you need me after this—and I mean it, you have to really need the help—I'll be happy to apply for the position in December."

"No kept woman, huh?"

"Nope."

"You take the fun out of being rich." Claire sighed. "I'm supposed to be able to get whatever I want with my magic checkbook."

"Tough." Abby stood. "Shall we see if that man of mine is ready to go hobnob?"

"If we must." Claire looked around the studio. "Where's Matt's Pretty?"

"He's having a bronze made. Horrible?"

"Smart. Best thing he's ever done. Now, about our homegrown talent or lack thereof…"

They walked out of the studio discussing stage placement and how to best display the variety of arts and crafts that had been submitted. At the doorway between the kitchen and the living room, Claire, who was in the lead, came up short and sighed, leaning to the side so Abby could look around her.

Matt stood at the ironing board in his boxers, long muscles in his back stretching and contracting as he ran an iron over the mostly smooth shirt.

"Some men should not be allowed to wear clothes," Claire whispered. "They should just walk around butt nekkid for my viewing pleasure."

"I heard that, and I'm telling Charles," Matt said, his shoulders shaking with laugher. He carefully set the iron on its butt and swung the shirt around to put it on.

"Go ahead. I wasn't stricken blind or stupid just because I got married." Claire grinned and tossed him the pants that lay across the chair nearest her. "Besides, Charles reaps all the benefits of my contemplating pretty surfers, so he's not complaining. You have five minutes to meet me in the car." She kissed Abby on the cheek, slid her large sunglasses over her eyes, and stepped out onto the porch.

Matt laid his slacks over the end of the ironing board and walked over to envelop Abby in his warm shirt, wrapping it around her to pull her against his warmer skin. "Are you sure you're okay with this, Abby? 'Cause I can stay right here. I'm not afraid of Claire."

"Three minutes, Clarke."

The sharp voice coming from the porch made him jump, and Abby laughed. "Liar."

"Maybe a little," he qualified, "but not too scared to say no to her if you ask me to stay."

Abby closed her eyes and rested her head against his chest, listening to the thrum of his heart and attempting to marshal her rebellious tongue. She'd been flippant with Claire earlier, but she respected the opportunities that Matt was being offered, opportunities for which some artists worked a lifetime. If what was between them had any chance of working, it couldn't start with his sacrifice of this chance.

So, she contented herself with wrapping her arms tightly around him before stepping back. "Shoo. I'm going to putter around here. I have to pretend to be a serious *artiste*, remember?"

He cupped her face and tipped it upward. "You *are* an artist."

Unwilling to look into his eyes for more than a few seconds, afraid that her desire for him to stay was too clear, Abby kissed him hard before lifting the pants he'd set aside. "Yeah, yeah…and you're over your five-minute limit."

Claire said from the doorway, "You two are ridiculous." The amusement in her voice belied her scathing words. "I *will* take you to this thing pantless, Matt. Who knows, that might appeal to a couple of these gentlemen."

"On that note…" Matt caught the slacks Abby handed him and slid them on. He yanked her against him and up, bending her back until his mouth was against the shell of her ear. "Think about me all day. I'll be home before you know it." He nuzzled under her ear, lips seeking the sensitive spot right below her earlobe and making her shiver. Abby was still frozen to the spot as the screen door slammed and she heard Matt's laugh drift back to her even as Claire criticized his lack of socks.

Home. Abby looked around, scratching a spot on her right calf with the opposite big toe as she scanned the rooms. Evidence of her life there, however brief it might have been, was everywhere. Her socks and shoes tumbled companionably with Matt's in the basket next to the door, her shirt dried on the back of a kitchen chair, her beloved copy of *The End of the Affair* lay open on the arm of the couch, a cheerful mug she'd spotted in the shop of a local potter sat on the kitchen table. The scents of her lavender soap and favorite coffee mixed with leather from Matt's furniture and the citrusy body wash he favored, all entwined with the scent of the ocean that curled through the perpetually open windows to create a potpourri that whispered home to her heart.

Abby sank to the floor, unable to still the tremors that shook her. She summoned a vision of the small apartment that she'd called home for over a decade. She'd been lucky to find anything near the city that she could afford, and she'd poured all of the art that lingered in her soul into making it bright and lovely, a comfortable haven in a busy world. It made her smile to recall all the hours it had taken her to find the furniture that filled her world, and she had a moment's wistfulness for the aged chintz-covered club chair that was her comfy spot. She imagined it next to Matt's bookcases; she should be ensconced there with a book and her grandmother's afghan, Matt smiling at her over his own book from his favorite corner of the couch. An insistent thought played over and over in her head: *What if I took Claire's offer?*

A cheerful Celtic tune from the kitchen counter startled Abby out of a pleasant daydream of pulling a sweater over her head and watching a November storm roll in off the ocean while she stayed safely snuggled against Matt's chest. The start of the second verse brought her to her feet. She glanced at the caller ID on her phone — she'd stopped taking calls from the museum the day she'd decided to stay with Matt, and she wasn't about to take one now — and smiled.

"Hello, Sarah," she said, settling into a kitchen chair and leaning against the wall, ready for a chat.

"How's my beach bunny?" Abby could hear sloshing and imagined her friend holed up in her darkroom.

"Is it safe to use your phone in the darkroom?"

"I covered the screen with duct tape. Duh. How's wetsuit man?"

"Perfect in all ways. You dream of that suit, and you know it."

"Lies. I lost all beach memory when my knight in shining…tie and leather shoes came to rescue me. That's my story, and I'm sticking with it. I never even think of swim trunks or wet thighs." They both snorted laughter. "So, what's up in the land of ease?"

That launched a rambling conversation about the Santa Cruz residents that Sarah knew, an update on the statues and the art camp, and settled on the upcoming Cruz art show. Sarah laughed as Abby regaled her with stories of the beautiful and bizarre things she was responsible for displaying and squealed at the mention of music being included, saying she knew for a fact that there was incredible talent based around Santa Cruz. Abby was about ready to tell her about Claire's job offer when Sarah interrupted.

"You'll never guess who I ran into outside Macy's yesterday. A2 — from your building? She asked if I'd let her in to have a look around your apartment! She wants your view — said the landlord would let her switch apartments as soon as you give notice. Can you believe the brass balls on her?" Sarah didn't wait for Abby's answer. "I told her hell no and that you'd be home in two weeks. That's right, isn't it?"

"I'm supposed to be home in a little less than that," Abby answered evasively.

"Exactly. Only a complete dumbass would throw away a place like that and a good job for a summer fling. Now that I'm home with David, that seems so clear." Sarah laughed, not seeming to notice Abby's silence. "Everyone knows that no matter how bright things look in summer, real life is a deal breaker. I mean, change is a great mantra, but can you imagine gambling your whole life on a fling? I must have been insane."

Abby sleepwalked through the rest of the conversation, laughing automatically when Sarah paused and asking the right questions about the friends they shared in Boston. She tried to feign interest in David's latest work turmoil, barely restraining herself from remarking that an editor at the *Boston Globe* would always be jumping from one fire to the next. Her mind drifted to Matt's quiet calm, even as he worked hard and fast to complete Baker's commission. No amount of tension stayed long in his home or his body. It seemed to float away on the wind and the water, and Abby could no more see him happy in David's bustling city position than she could imagine him swallowing broken glass. But he'd lived in Philadelphia — was he happy there? She realized that she didn't know the answer to that question any more than she knew if she could really give up the energy of Boston for a perpetual vacation. The bubble of happy "what ifs" burst, and a swell of sorrow begin to crest in her chest.

"Abby, are you listening to me?"

"Mmm hmm."

"I thought you'd wandered off there. Anyway, do you think Matt would want it? My aunt is going to throw it out. I guess real shabby isn't chic enough for her."

Abby rewound the conversation in her head to find the part where Sarah had asked if Matt wanted the wicker loveseat. "Um…I don't know. I can ask him when he gets hom — here later. Or I guess I can go pick it up, if she's antsy, and let him decide later."

"Excellent! I'll text her that you'll be over." Sarah paused for a second, and her voice was softer when she next spoke. "I'll be so glad to see you. I miss you. Will it be too hard to come home?"

Abby had to try a couple of times before words could get past the lump in her throat. "A bit. I'll probably survive." *But maybe not.*

After a few more minutes of planning and jokes, they said goodbye. The phone hung loosely in Abby's hand as she stared into space.

What was she thinking to even consider Claire's offer? She and Matt had a plan, a perfectly workable plan that would bring them back together in December. If they couldn't keep something together for three months apart, was there really anything there in the first place? Abby moaned, feeling torn inside at the thought that this…thing…this huge, wonderful, warm thing that filled her could be nothing more than a crush. The thought of the feelings they shared trickling away to die a quiet death horrified her. She'd heard too many awkward, post-relationship conversations to think they were rare.

She took a deep breath, putting away the fantasy of relocating her favorite things from home to these quiet rooms. If two weeks was all she had guaranteed…"Enjoy to the fullest and move on," Abby murmured, getting to her feet.

Getting the loveseat out of the cramped hatchback when she got back to Matt's wasn't easy. Abby leaned as far into the back of the car as she could and prayed that her shorts weren't crawling up her ass. Cursing, she tugged at it. "Come on, you stupid mother—" She ended on a shriek as a snagged nail popped free, and she toppled backward.

Visions of a cracked skull flashed through her mind an instant before strong hands caught her under the arms. Abby looked up and saw Jason's deep dimples. "If I'd had a camera, I might have let you fall. Hello, YouTube," he joked. Setting Abby on her feet, Jason easily extracted the loveseat and held it up with one hand. "Where do you want this?" Brushing off her declarations that she could handle it, he headed for the front porch. He set it at one end of the empty porch and sat down. "Got some iced tea for a hard-working man?"

After getting them both a glass and bringing a chair out from inside, Abby sat down. They chatted awkwardly about the weather, dancing around the elephant of what they'd been to each other at the beginning of the summer. Abby was a little sad that the camaraderie they'd shared since the first night in the bar seemed impossible.

Jason finished his glass of tea. "Anyway, Abby, I just came by to tell you goodbye. The gloss has sort of worn off of Santa Cruz for me."

A sense of creeping guilt filled her. "Jason —"

He held up his hand. "I'm not finished. I also wanted to apologize for acting like a dick right after…well, you know. What happens, happens, I guess, and sometimes we don't have a choice in what we want, right?" A slow smile spread across his face. "We did have fun for a while there, didn't we?"

Smiling back, Abby grasped his hand. "Yes, we did."

After squeezing her fingers, he stood. "I really did just stop to clear things up and say 'bye. I have a long way to go, and I'd like to get a start tonight."

Abby walked him to his bike, watching as he picked up his helmet.

"Be glad you have a level head, Abby. Experience counts, I guess." He pressed a kiss on her cheek and swung a leg over the seat. The roar of the engine would have drowned out any attempt at more goodbyes, so Abby just waved as she watched him speed away.

She put the cushion on the seat and sank down, thinking about what Jason had said. *Level head.* Abby barked a harsh laugh. Experience was breaking her heart. Leaning her head against the arm of the loveseat, she felt the first salty drop slide down her nose and drip onto the rough wicker.

"Abby? Sweetheart?"

A rough, warm hand gently brushed the hair back from her cheek. Raising her head from the thin cushion, Abby was grateful for the dimness of the deep porch and the setting sun. The fewer questions about the puffy eyes she was sure she was sporting, the better. "Time's it?" she rasped out, swinging her feet to the cool floor as she sat up.

"A lot later than I was supposed to be home." Matt sighed as he sat down beside her. He tugged his tie down wearily and took Abby's hand. "Lunch turned into drinks and drinks into dinner. Claire was wheeling and dealing, and I couldn't get her out of there." He leaned his head back on the seat after urging Abby's head onto his shoulder. "Swear to God, this is not what I imagined would come out of one deal for some stock statues. It's crazy."

"Nothing you do is stock, Matt."

"Whatever. They're certainly not inspired. It's a job." Tension rolled off Matt in waves. He glanced over at Abby and smiled. "Why am I wasting what's left of our day on this crap? How about you? How did you spend your day?"

Genuine interest and affection showed in his eyes, even in the dimness, and that was Abby's undoing. She hugged him tightly and tried to absorb this moment: the smell and feel and taste of him. "Nothing even remotely as good as right now. I'm so glad you're home."

"I like the sound of that," he murmured, drawing her face up for a lingering kiss.

Feeling a desperation born of her long day of running circles in her mind, Abby deepened the kiss, urging Matt to lie back on the seat as her fingers worked at his buttons.

Matt chuckled and complied, leaning his head back so Abby could reach under the shelf of his jaw. "I think I'll stay away all day again if this is the welcome home I get. I love you, Abby."

Tears rose in Abby's eyes again, from a well that she was surprised wasn't empty yet. She nodded and hiccupped back a sob as a hot tear trailed down her cheek.

"Hey, hey…" Matt said, shifting so he could hold her trembling form. "Not exactly the reaction I expected. I'm sorry, Pretty — I know you asked me not to — "

"Just shut up." Abby's voice trembled. "I love you too. I just — " She clung to him wordlessly. Matt waited, stroking her hair.

When her personal storm passed, he led her into the house and into bed. When they were settled, he curved around her, whether to reassure her or himself Abby wasn't sure.

"What happened today?"

Abby's first urge was to downplay her misery, but she resisted. If she couldn't share what was on her mind, how could she ever share her heart? "I missed you. I talked to Sarah, and it just…it hit me that it's almost time to go home."

Matt brushed her hair out of her face. "Three months isn't so long, right? We can do this." His eyes were serious, and his hands shook.

"Matt, does this ever work? For anyone?"

"We're not anyone. We're us. Kiss me, Pretty."

Abby complied, and then she stroked his stubble-roughened cheek. She felt him smile before he turned his head to kiss her palm. Resting their linked hands against his chest, he twined his feet with Abby's and snuggled her head under his chin. Abby drifted off with the music of his heart soothing her ache.

Chapter Nineteen

Matt sat up on his board and let his arms rest, watching the sun begin to sink. The water around him was peaceful, a marvel in summer when surfers of all shapes and abilities swarmed the beaches he loved. The season was ending for all but the serious surfers; the tourists were going home.

He jumped when something brushed against his leg, and then laughed at himself. Hadn't he told Abby that the local sea life would come right up to her if she was out far enough and quiet…in fact, hadn't he promised to bring her out to see them? Matt felt a sudden twist in his chest. It wasn't going to happen this summer. She hadn't had the time to gain the experience she'd need to come out this far.

Damn. *I came out here to forget that*, he thought. Restlessness had built as he'd watched Abby put away groceries and listened to her chatter about her day. She'd joked about dazzling him with the last dinner she'd cook in his kitchen, and it hit him: this domestic ballet was nearly over. The feeling of being trapped by circumstance was new to him, and he dealt with it like he did most other sorrows — retreated to his element.

Lying down again, Matt started paddling at a punishingly fast rhythm, pushing his body so hard that he couldn't think through the strain. He was so intent on getting as far out as he possibly could that he narrowly avoided a deceptively calm patch of water. He cursed himself for his inattention and thanked God that he saw it in enough time to avoid the riptide that lay beneath, waiting to whisk the unwary out to sea.

He caught the swell, letting movements that had become instinctive guide his board into but not on top of the wave. The water rose over him, creating a tube of jade green. He could hear nothing but the crash of the water and the thunder of his own heart. Time seemed suspended as he used all of his skill and strength, his years of finesse, to ride the water without letting it pull him down.

Good exhaustion and a peace that he'd been lacking lately settled on him as he walked up the beach afterward. Abby met him at the water's edge, quiet as she took his hand and walked with him to the blanket she'd laid out. She hadn't resisted when he'd asked if they could change dinner plans to come out here instead. He lowered himself and closed his eyes.

"That was beautiful," Abby said. Matt chuckled, watching the tiny crimson veins in his eyelids get less vivid as the sun lowered in the sky. After a few minutes of silence, he opened one eye and looked at Pretty. She was studying him with a wistful look.

"What?" he mumbled.

Abby shoved a bag at him. "Eat."

Matt watched the sea, content to feel the warmth of Pretty's thigh inches from his own, and he remembered how many times he'd done this same thing all by himself.

Nudging her thigh with his knee, he got her attention. "Sorry about dinner."

Abby licked peach juice off her fingers. "Dazzling in the kitchen was never my forte anyway."

"Your talents lie in other directions?" Matt slid his hand from her knee to a spot high on her inner thigh. She slapped it sharply, and he laughed. "Seriously, Abby, thanks for this. I started thinking about that 'last dinner' thing, and…" He looked toward the water and sifted sand through his fingers, trying to sort his tangled emotions. Before this summer, people had drifted in and out of his life like the tides that measured his days and left just about as much of a mark. A warm hand entwined with his. Abby rested her head against his shoulder, and he remembered watching the sun rise over the water, his arms wrapped around her as he told her he'd never regret any of this. He smiled grimly. Who needed ocean tides to yank a guy out to sea? He'd already hit his own personal riptide months ago.

"You could never leave this." Abby's voice broke into his rumination.

Disengaging his hand from hers, he leaned back on his elbows, trying to gauge the seriousness of her statement. "Of course I could. This is just a place." He thought about living in a city, as he had most of his youth, and his gaze returned to the sea.

"That was convincing." Abby nudged his shoulder. "You'd be miserable anywhere else. Admit it."

"'Miserable' is such a subjective term…" A smile twitched his lips. Lunging to the side, he grabbed her by the waist and wrestled her onto his body, regretting the wetsuit that separated them. No matter the emotional cost, he wouldn't give up this feeling for anything. "Don't make fun of me, missy," he ordered, tucking his head into the crook of her neck and rubbing his scratchy chin against her. She shrieked laughter.

Grateful for the lightened mood, he snuggled her against his chest and stroked her hair. "Pretty…I have an idea. Why don't we take tomorrow off and come back here?"

"Claire would kill us. Show, remember?"

"Fuck the show. I'd rather spend that time with you."

Abby stopped him with her mouth against his. She adjusted her position until she straddled him. Matt held her, enjoying the moment. "Mmm…nice. But you're not going to distract me."

Abby sat up. "Well, damn. Losing my touch." She grasped the zipper of his wetsuit and started pulling it down. "Sure I can't distract you?"

Matt grabbed her hand. "I'm sure you can. But what's up?"

She traced the shape of his cheek and the fan of lines around his eyes before she answered. "Changing our plans tomorrow…" She stared at him for a minute. "Can't we pretend it's a normal day, and that good night is just good night? December will feel closer."

Pretending went against Matt's grain, but he thought he understood what she was saying. Keeping things normal did feel more hopeful than the cocoon he craved.

"Okay," Matt allowed. "Give me today though? This Naked Sunday has to last me awhile."

Matt lost track of Abby almost as soon as they reached the show. Claire was waiting in the parking lot. Her huge glasses reflected the sun as she muttered into her phone. After a dismissive glance at Matt, she led Abby away to consult on issues that had already cropped up that morning.

With nothing else to do, Matt wandered the displays. Long before the show's official opening, the area was crowded with the people he'd known for most of his adult life, some showing their talent, some exploring, but all having a good time. Street performers vied with food vendors for the space remaining between the displays, creating a carnival atmosphere that was enhanced when the show opened and bands began playing half-hour sets. Matt eventually caught sight of Abby at the edge of the bandstand, camera pointed at musicians of many shapes and sizes as one group after another took the stage. She smiled at him and waved before turning back to her duties.

Sighing, Matt tried to find Claire. He located her at the center of the roughly concentric circle of displays. "Does Abby get a break today or are you going to work her to death?"

"Death, probably." She looked around at the happy crowd. "I wouldn't have been able to get it done without her."

Abby's voice came from behind him. "Hey, surferboy. Ready for a break?"

Matt smiled and arched back in an exaggerated stretch, lacing his fingers behind his head, and groaned as his back popped from neck to ass.

"Such a show off," Abby teased.

"The body's what got your attention, remember?"

"Maybe…but it was the ass shake that sealed the deal. I have a weakness for smart alecks."

"Good thing for me. I can keep smart-assyness and eat ice cream after every meal."

"Sickening." Matt had almost forgotten Claire was watching them until she spoke up, her voice amused. She addressed her husband as he sauntered up. "We were never like that, were we?"

He swept her into a passionate kiss, to the amusement of those watching. "Worse," Charles said. He set Claire back on her feet. "I distinctly remember groping you on the Golden Gate while singing 'I Melt With You' at the top of my lungs." He thought for a minute. "Was that the one that made the news? I think so. Grandmother still hasn't forgiven me." He turned to Abby. "If you're going for food, you'd better do it quick. Didn't you say you wanted to record Tyler's group? They're up next."

"This should be deliciously horrible," Abby said, moving away from Matt to check her camera before taking his hand. "Let's go."

"They're leading off with a little ditty called 'Riding the Cougar,'" Charles informed Abby mildly, though his eyes were shining with laughter. "Still want to record it?"

"Hell, yes," Abby crowed, pulling Matt toward the stage. "This will be good for a lifetime of torment. Sarah's, of course. Food can wait."

She was still giggling when the set ended. Claiming a need to change her SD card, Abby rose on tiptoe to kiss Matt before shooing him toward Claire, who was collapsed in a shady lawn chair.

"I do think we have a success." Claire swept her hand around her. "We should do this again next year, when you have some new things to show. I imagine we can leverage the Baker deal into big money by then. You're set for life, kid."

Wanting to stop her before she went any further, Matt crouched in front of her. "I want to talk to you about Baker. I want to hand over what I've already finished and be done."

Claire took off her glasses and dropped them in her lap. "Matt, you can't be serious."

"I am. I've been thinking about this. I don't want to have to wait until December to be with Abby."

"Oh, honey." Claire's eyes softened as she laid a hand on his arm. "Baker will sue you, you know."

"I know. I don't care. The third sculpture is almost done, and as soon as it's finished, I'm leaving. I can go and Abby can't stay, so that's how it has to be." He willed his friend to understand.

"Understood. If you think she's a woman worth giving up a bundle of money for, I support you."

Matt rose to his feet, his heart feeling lighter than it had for days, now that the decision was spoken aloud. "Thanks for not thinking I'm crazy, Claire."

She laughed. "Oh, I know you're crazy. But I also know you're not stupid."

"Some people might disagree." Matt smiled wryly. "Would you mind not saying anything to Abby? I want to talk to her about it first."

Claire waved her hand. "Of course. Speaking of your muse, she's over there with my husband."

Matt spotted Abby sitting on the grass by Charles and idly pulling up tufts by the roots. She smiled as he approached and rose gracefully to her feet.

Enfolding her hand in his, Matt was concerned by its coolness. The evening breeze off the water often had a bite that surprised people who expected balmy weather in summertime California. He wrapped his arms around her bare shoulders. "Charles, I think we're going to head out," he said, glancing down at Abby to see if she agreed. She nodded.

"No problem. I'm sure this will be raging until dawn." Charles took his hands out of his pockets to shake with Matt before holding his arms out to Abby. Matt saw him murmur something in her ear and was curious when she shook her head with a wry grin. He caught Charles's question, "You sure?" as Abby drew back, nodding as she squeezed Charles's hand. "I'll tell Claire you've gone if I ever catch up with her again. Me and my big ideas." With a final wave, he jammed his hands back in his pockets and wandered into the crowd.

Hands linked, Abby and Matt walked toward the parking lot. Matt tried to keep his curiosity in check, but he had to know. "What was that all about?"

Abby smiled and scuffed her toe in a pile of ever-present sand. "Charles has discovered a sudden need for a personal assistant."

Matt laughed. "Nice one." He let go of her hand only long enough to wrap his arm around her. "They love you, Pretty." He dipped his head until his mouth was against the shell of her ear. "So do I."

Abby shrugged, barely missing his chin. "Matt."

"What?" he teased. "You don't want to hear that I love—"

She covered his mouth with her hand. "Nope."

"I do. Not saying it doesn't make it go away."

"I know," she whispered. A veil of sadness fell into her eyes.

Wanting to get the teasing lightness back, Matt dropped her hand and started walking backward, grinning. "I love Abby Reynolds!"

"Matt!" She looked around in embarrassment and trotted toward him.

He backed up faster, shrugging and holding out his hands in a "what can you do?" gesture. "It's out there now. Can't take it back. At least ten people heard it. Wait, there's another bunch—I love Abby!"

Laughter came from the small group of older women. "Those are the surf birds. They'll tell anyone who isn't here. I'm officially off the market now." Matt grinned.

"You are such a dork." Abby lunged forward, her fingers skating over the fabric of his shirt as he jumped back.

Turning, he jogged toward home, intermittently shouting his feelings as he ran, ignoring Abby's pleas for him to be quiet and staying just out of her reach until she put on a burst of speed and caught him at the porch. Pulling her arms around his waist and holding them there with one hand, he laughed as he fumbled with the key and shoved the door open.

As he closed it behind him, he let Abby shake her arms loose and heard her plop on the couch with a huff. "Well, that was embarrassing," she grumbled.

"Why?" Matt crouched by her feet and slipped off one of her sandals. "It's the truth. I love you, Abby." He gently brushed sand off the top of her foot before pressing a kiss there. He trailed his mouth upward, cradling her calf in his hand as he brushed her ankle with his lips. "I love you," he murmured, looking up at her but not moving his mouth from her skin.

Abby closed her eyes. "Please don't…"

Matt shifted his weight to his knees and slid her skirt up her thigh. He kissed the inside of her knee and smiled at her indrawn breath. "Don't stop?" he said, choosing his own ending to her sentence as his lips traveled higher. "Okay. I love you, Abby."

Abby tugged at his shirt, pulling him over her so she could bury her hands in his hair and kiss him fiercely.

"Can I take that as an 'I love you too?'" he joked, pushing her hair off her forehead.

Abby's eyes filled with tears as she stroked his face. "So, so much."

"Then let's go upstairs," he said, untangling his legs from hers and standing. He twitched her skirt down and held out a hand to help her up. "Couches are for kids. I need more room to stretch out if I'm going to do this right."

"No, wait," Abby said, tugging him toward the back door. "I have a surprise for you."

"Outside?" he said doubtfully. "Can't it wait?"

"Can't you?"

Matt considered. "Nope. Can't wait."

"Tough." Abby backed toward the door.

He stopped on the deck and grinned. Abby dropped his hands to grab a lighter and go from table to table to light small candles that had been set about. The low tables usually flanked a padded bench underneath the pergola. It was one of his favorite places to relax with a book and catch the ocean breeze undisturbed because the greenery largely screened his haven from view. Tonight, though, the bench was gone, and his blanket-lined hammock was in its place. His down comforter was folded at the bottom.

"When did you do all this?"

Abby shrugged and started unzipping her dress.

Matt rested his hands on her shoulders for a second before pushing the straps aside, following his hands with his mouth. "You've succumbed to the lure of the beach?"

"Well, I'm still not willing to get sand all up in my business, but yes, I get the appeal now. I want you to be happy, Matt."

"I don't need this," he whispered. "You make me happy."

Her hands were against his skin, fingers light and cool against his belly as she unbuttoned his shorts. "Show me, Matt. Love me."

He did his best, letting his hands and mouth travel the curves that had absorbed him for months. Soft words and whispered laughter made a cocoon that wasn't carried far by a kind wind that seemed to die down just for them. Matt closed his eyes and relished the feeling of her hands moving against him, the motion of the gently swinging hammock bringing a new dimension to the rising and falling of their bodies. He could taste sea salt and sweat on her skin when he nestled his face on her neck. He fought to memorize each sound she made, and the smell of her, and the way her fingers curled into his lower back as she arched below him.

Shifting until she was above him, Abby rested her hands on his shoulders. She relaxed when he grasped her hips tightly and groaned out his pleasure. When he opened his eyes, Matt stared at her. With her face dappled with shadow from the wisteria, she looked insubstantial, like a dream that could pass away in the morning light. He didn't think he would ever forget that exact second.

"This rarely works out for anyone, you know," she whispered.

"We're not anyone, remember?" He draped the comforter over them. Curling around her, he held her against his body. The heaviness of sleep caught him, and he could barely keep his eyes open. "Pancakes for breakfast?" he mumbled, feeling her soft laugh as she held his hand against her chest.

"Matt? Honey, wake up."

Matt tried to roll over. His eyes flew open as the hammock swung, and he remembered where he was. The blue light of dawn lit the sky behind Abby as she crouched beside him, fully dressed.

"Wha…?" was all he could get out of his sleep-sodden brain.

Abby tried a tremulous smile. "I promised I'd wake you up before I left, remember?"

Matt blinked rapidly. He pushed himself up on one elbow and reached out for her.

Abby clasped his hand tightly. "I can't do this if you…I need to get going."

Matt tried to sit up. "No."

She stood and stumbled back. "I can't handle a sad, drawn-out goodbye. I want to do this right — no regrets."

"Abby, wait." He swung his legs over the edge of the hammock and scrubbed at his face. "Don't go."

Abby took a shaky breath. "I have to. December isn't so long, right?"

"I — I don't even know what to say," he rasped out, searching the sand around his feet for his shorts. "I talked to Claire last night, and I'm ready to tell Baker to go to hell — I don't care if he sues me. I was going to tell you over breakfast — I'm coming to Boston with you."

"No. Don't do that." She wrapped a hand around the back of his neck, kissing him with quick desperation as her façade crumbled and tears started to fall. Before he could do more than grasp at her shirt, she was backing away from him. "I love you, Matt. I don't want to be what holds you back. I'll call you from the road tomorrow morning, okay?"

"Doesn't this—don't we—matter?" Matt surged out of the hammock, but not before she disappeared around the corner of the house. He heard the Hyundai's tiny motor roar away before he could yank his shorts over his hips.

Matt stumbled into the house. He found a pot of coffee already brewed and a pastry on a plate beside the carafe. Ignoring the food, he poured a cup and sank down onto a chair, wondering what would happen next. He had an urge to call his dad and compare notes—how was he supposed to handle this morning? The sun continued in its arc as the coffee grew cold in his cup.

He ignored a tap at the French door, but Claire entered anyway. She slid into the chair opposite his and waited for him to acknowledge her. When he hadn't after several minutes, she reached out to touch his hand. "I'm sorry, Matt. Abby stopped to leave a note, and Charles talked to her. I came right over."

Matt clutched his cup, swallowing the cold, bitter liquid.

Claire flopped back in her chair. "What a crapfest this summer has turned out to be. If it makes you feel any better, three months isn't really that long."

"It doesn't," Matt said shortly. "And it won't be that long. I can't do this—I'm leaving today."

"Matt, be reasonable," Claire pleaded. "At least finish the sculpture that's almost done like we talked about last night. I might be able to reason with Baker…" Her voice trailed off, and she blew out a great gust of breath. "Fat chance of that. I really thought she might stay with the job offer."

"Please. She has some self-esteem. Charles's offer was kind, but…"

"Not Charles's," Claire said, playing with the salt shaker. "Mine."

Matt froze. Abby would have no reason to take a personal assistant job that was so far from her skill set and so much below her education, but an offer from Claire…that was a whole different thing. "You offered her a job?"

"Yeah. She didn't tell you? She didn't even seem to consider it, though I assured her it was genuine. She did say she'd apply in December if the position was still open." Claire chuckled in reluctant admiration. "Proud woman. Anyway, what's your decision? Going into the studio, or am I helping you pack?"

He thought for a minute, his mind a jumble of betrayal and suspicion about her desire to not be the one to hold him back. Maybe the business end of his art was more important to her than he'd realized. "Studio. I have to respect her decision, right?" He pushed himself away from the table.

Time to get to work.

And to pray that they weren't "anyone" after all.

Chapter Twenty

Looking back later, Abby would have liked to have been able to say that the Matt-less months passed easily, if slowly—at worst, to say that they left her numb. But then she'd be lying to herself, and if there was one lesson she learned that fall, it was that lies come back to bite you in the ass. The reality was that numb was nowhere near any of the shifting emotions she'd felt during the endless drive back to Boston.

After placing her last bag in the back of the car early that morning, Abby had walked around Matt's house, putting things back where they'd been the first time she'd seen them. She wasn't foolish enough to think that leaving would be easy on either of them; the least she could do was to leave Matt's life the way she'd found it. He wouldn't want reminders of her popping out at him when he tried to relax.

To hear Matt say he was willing to risk a lawsuit and a ruined career over Baker's statues was serious business. There was a singular thrill in knowing that she was that important to him. Closely following that, though, was a shiver of uneasiness. Abby had seen enough relationships founder under disappointment when one person felt they'd sacrificed too much. Despite Matt's seeming indifference to the importance of the connections he was making, Abby knew that personal lightning rarely struck twice in a lifetime.

Three months. She could do three months without him.

The miles passed quickly at first, fueled by Abby's determination that she was right, but eventually monotony and doubt set in. It started with the memory of Matt's expression as she fled around the corner of the house. The mixture of confusion and sleepiness was bad enough, but the pain she'd seen at the end was worse.

Abby turned up the radio, singing along to a song she hated just to distract herself. "He'll be fine, I'll be fine, end of story," she said, tossing back her fourth cup of coffee.

That was the first lie.

By the time she neared the Nevada state line, she was making deals with herself. *If he calls before I cross, I'll go back. Never mind that I've wasted a whole day and will have to start out again tomorrow. Maybe the next day. I'm sure they can get along without me for one more day.* But Nevada came and went, causing another storm of doubt and frustration and more than a little self-pity. *I guess this isn't as hard on him as it is on me*, she thought, slouching lower in her seat and trying to ignore the fact that she'd told Matt she would call him.

That was the second lie.

She gave up in Salt Lake City, pulling into a small motel and dragging herself through the door of her room to flop on the bed. She toyed with her phone for a minute, debating whether she was ready to talk to Matt, before she tossed it on the nightstand. Abby slid between the sheets and stared at her phone.

It stared accusingly back at her.

She snatched it up and switched on the lamp. *Just a text to let him know that I'm okay.*

Third lie.

She didn't even have time to drop the phone back on the nightstand when it rang in her hand. Abby glanced at the name and almost dropped the phone in her rush to answer.

"I said I'd call you in the morning." The words tumbled out of her mouth as she tried unsuccessfully to restrain a grin.

"I thought I wouldn't wait." Hearing Matt's voice, strong and warm, brought tears to the surface. "How are you doing, Pretty?"

Fine! This lie stuck in her throat. "I'm…" She took a shuddering breath. "I'm awful. I miss you."

"Good. You should feel awful. I know I do." The tinge of bitterness was softened by the concern in his voice.

"I know." A few words were enough to lay out her whole sorry thought process, and when she was finished, she waited anxiously for his reaction.

"Can we be in agreement that I'm capable of making my own decisions? I thought I mentioned once or twice that I'm not a kid, Abby. I know what has to be done to balance work and life."

"I'm sorry," Abby murmured, picking at the comforter.

"I am too." Abby heard the creak of wicker as he settled back, and she imagined the way the breeze would be drifting through the deep porch, bringing the scents of sea and sun to wrap around him. "Come home?" he asked.

Wiping her hand under her eyes as they welled again, Abby paused a minute before answering. "I can't. Not because I don't want to," she added when she heard his indrawn breath. "I just can't do this again in a day or two. And that's all I'd have, at most."

"Right," Matt sighed. "Don't cry anymore, Abby. You're breaking my heart, here. We'll survive. So, tell me about your trip so far."

They talked until Abby couldn't hold her eyes open any longer. The mood gradually lightened as they found places to laugh together at how tormented their individual days had been. Abby could even giggle at Matt's strangely intense description of how much he'd accomplished that day. Drifting off to sleep with his last good night still whispering through her head, Abby relaxed, convinced that nothing had changed.

As she dragged herself through the back door of the Fiona Grant Shaw gallery and stumbled to her office, Abby wasn't so sure that was true. Three days in the car had turned to four when she realized that one driver alone couldn't make the same time as a pair of drivers, and as a result, she'd only had one night to rest before returning to work. Maybe that was why the Boston traffic and crowds that used to make her feel vibrant and alive now drained her of patience and energy. The trundling delivery trucks that had awakened her at four thirty that morning had gotten a sound cussing out, too, before she'd sleepwalked into her shower and realized that the soap in the dish had turned into a brick in her absence and her shampoo had been left behind at Matt's house.

"Abby? Oh *my!* What happened to your *hair?*"

Abby dropped her purse on her desk and turned around to smile at her intern. "Nice to see you, too, Clint." Her smile turned into a grin when the intern's slight face flushed. "Don't worry about it. I just got back into town yesterday, and I haven't had time to get it cut." She pivoted to look into the ornate mirror that hung behind her desk.

Boston Abby was almost absent. Her trimmed and straightened bob now curled around her shoulders, while the porcelain-pale complexion she'd protected from the sun for fear of lines was light gold with a sprinkling of freckles. Just remembering the thorough way Matt had kissed each spot, how he examined every tiny line and declared that she was finally smiling enough, the feeling of his face nuzzled deep in her hair made her shiver.

"It's not *that* bad, Abby." Clint brushed his own fashionably shaggy hair to the side. "I can make you an appointment with George right away." His voice dropped as he sat on Abby's desk and made himself comfortable. "Just don't let Gretchen find out I did it. She's been a *total* dictator since you left. I think she wants me to be her own *Igor*, but I told her 'personal aide' isn't in my job description, and then *she* said…"

Abby sat down and shrugged into the same sweater that had hung on the back of her chair for the last few years, letting Clint's running commentary on office gossip and politics fuzz out. The one-upsmanship that she'd thrived on, that was an integral part of pulling oneself up and putting oneself forward in a tight and very specialized job market, a part that she'd been very good at playing, now just left her…tired. Her mind wandered back to her call with Matt the night before. They'd laughed at Claire's attempts to be diplomatic with a patron who'd donated what could most kindly be termed a mess of a statue. It was apparently going to end up as yard art at the Eastmans' house…very near the sea, in hopes that a tide might want it more than Claire did. As funny as it sounded, Abby could appreciate the lengths her friends would go to save someone's feelings.

Not much chance of that happening here, Abby thought, tuning into Clint's scathing appraisal of the gala a fellow curator had planned and hosted in Abby's absence.

"Can you *believe* that she brought in a trio and not a quartet? *Totally* unsuited for the period of the display. And the caterer…my *God*…" Clint snorted laughter, and Abby had had enough.

"Speaking of the display, how has attendance been? And what happened to…what's his name?" Abby felt bad for not remembering her second intern's name, but he was apparently gone anyway. She straightened her chair and looked at Clint with a perfect, plastic smile. Catching the hint, Clint gathered some data from his own desk before delving into the minutiae of what Abby had missed in her months away.

After a few minutes, her attention wandered, and she heard nothing but the sea. It was only Clint's bark of laughter that brought her attention back into the office.

"Hmm?" she asked.

"I've been reciting the names of all the states and their capitols for the last ten minutes." Clint laughed again. "Am I that boring?"

Abby scrubbed her hands over her face and shook her head. "I'm sorry. I got in late, and I guess I still have…road lag? Is there such a thing?"

"There is now." He rose from his perch on her desk and gestured to the door. "Let's get you on your feet and out on the floor. You missed the illuminated texts display, of course, but I could really use your help with the Ibo masks."

Following Clint out the office door, Abby listened closely this time, determined to get back on top of her game. After a snapshot check of all the different displays, including a rundown on upcoming events, she felt far more clearheaded and in control. This was what she did best, after all. Comparing the treasures that were under her care to her own few watercolors and oils was like comparing a symphony to a jug band.

Still, though…Abby paused in the middle of her favorite room and closed her eyes, allowing herself the satisfaction of sensory recall: the satisfying feeling of a brush between her fingers as colors blossomed on the canvas in front of her. For just a minute she could hear Matt's absent humming as he worked…and then she opened her eyes, sighed, and smiled at Clint. Abby was surprised that he was being so helpful. Maybe a few months alone with Gretchen had taught him a lesson about being careful what you wished for. Or maybe she was the one who'd changed.

"Shall we move on?" she asked.

"Are you even listening to me, Abby?"

The sound of a happy lunch crowd broke through Abby's mental fog, along with the smell of the lobster roll that lay untouched on her plate. She focused on Sarah and tried to remember her last few words. Lunch…Sarah's car…damn tourists…birthday…yeah, that was it. "What? Of course. You were telling me how David's birthday party went."

Sarah picked up her fork. "About five minutes ago. Did you catch the part where I thanked you for showing up?"

Abby groaned and laid her head on her arms. The scratchy tweed of her jacket sleeve was irritating. "I've apologized fifty times since Sunday. I was up late talking to Matt on Friday night and ended up sleeping all day Saturday." She peeked up with one eye to see Sarah gazing at her skeptically. "Give me a break. I just got back to town a couple of weeks ago. I did send you the SD card with Tyler's band for party entertainment."

"Another thing to thank you for. David…not so much. He choked on birthday cake when he caught the title of the song. Though the rest of the party guests didn't understand what was so funny."

Abby laughed loud and long.

Sarah held her exaggerated frown for a few seconds before leaning back and joining in. The deep tan that she'd sported in Santa Cruz was already fading, though her dark eyes were bright with more contentment than Abby had seen in them for a long while. Her city "uniform" of black-on-black clung to her lithe figure and served to highlight the glittering emerald on her ring finger. She kicked the leg of Abby's chair. "It's good to hear you laugh. I've missed you, kid. About time you got out of your house or the gallery." She studied Abby. "You look like hell, though."

Abby smoothed her newly styled hair. "What? George squeezed me in yesterday."

"You know I'm not talking about your hair, Abby. I kind of liked it wild anyway. I'm talking about your eyes." Abby dropped her hand to the table and twisted her napkin between her fingers. "I'd guess you aren't sleeping much?"

"Not much." No need to admit that her bed was too big, her house too quiet. "I'm sure it will get better—back to normal—when I get used to…you know…again."

"Mmm hmm…" Sarah murmured. "Normal. *Normally*, it wouldn't take me more than a week to get you out to lunch at McCormick's. *Normally*, you wouldn't miss David's birthday for anything—you've known him forever, for hell's sake. *Normally*, you would have given me all the gory details about what you did in California, and you know I'm not talking about surfing. And *normally*, you'd have come in talking about whatever horrors were wrought in the gallery while you were gone and dragged out some dusty book to show me where they went wrong." She covered Abby's hand with hers. "Maybe I don't have the right to say this, but, whatever: What are you doing back here? I look at you, and you're two thousand miles away."

"It's called a job," Abby said, lifting her glass to drink and not bothering to dispute any of her friend's observations. "I have one. Matt has one. Life rolls on, whether we want it to or not. It will get easier. Things will go back to normal."

Sarah's eyes were calculating. "Right." She straightened her silverware and smiled at the approaching waiter. "Then, let's get right back to normal." Abby smiled, thankful that Sarah seemed ready to drop the topic. "Come to the Sox game with David and me this weekend. You've missed so much of the season, girl!" She straightened her napkin and started recapping games Abby had missed. "So, this is where we are now…"

Despite her best effort to pay attention to Sarah's detailed recounting of the season thus far, Abby's eyes glazed over after five minutes. Even after the conversation had moved on to wedding plans, the holidays, and why David's family sucked, Abby only listened with half an ear. Her mind had started its two thousand mile trek to Santa Cruz once again.

Abby sighed as she looked at the detritus of the week, strewn around her living room. Newspapers covered tables and the cushion of her comfy chair. Shoes were landmines. Clothes covered the bright pillows on the couch, which were crushed anyway. She'd given up on sleeping in her bed days ago. Her parents had refused to return Salvador Dali, so she really was alone in her sty. Looking around, she sighed again. The things that made up her nest, her haven from the storm of the city, had lost their luster.

She picked up her bag when the doorbell rang downstairs, shouted out the window that she was on her way, and gave herself a quick pep talk. "This is fun, damn it. You love the Sox. Batter up." The smile she tried out felt unconvincing. Desperate to avoid another inquisition from sharp-eyed Sarah, Abby thought of her chat with Matt the night before and smiled. Baseball talk and frustration led to all kinds of corny-but-fun metaphors.

Sure enough, Sarah's examination once Abby was seated in the car was a close one. "Better," her friend concluded. "Have a Sam Adams or two, and you'll feel right at home."

"Sam Adams? Do I look like a tourist?"

Sarah laughed and relaxed back into her seat. "Smaaat-ass," she said in a broad Boston accent. Shifting gears, she peeked over at Abby again. "Maybe you still belong here. I'll reserve judgment until after you tell me what you think of the new bullpen lefty." She kept up her jibes at Abby and a running commentary on all things baseball, how much Narragansett beer she planned on inhaling, the comparative sluttiness of that day's baseball h00rs…everything except an explanation of why they were meeting David at the field instead of all riding together, which Abby didn't think about until they got to their ticketed seats and found David waiting, a nervous smile on his face.

Next to his face, or rather looming several inches above him, was the reason for the nervous smile.

Abby looked up at six-and-a-half feet of gangling limbs topped with an unruly shock of red hair and laughing blue eyes. She stomped on Sarah's foot before forcing a smile.

"Abby, this is Conor Grady. Conor, Abby Reynolds." David waited for Abby to shake Conor's hand before he rushed back into explanation. "Conor just moved back here a few weeks ago—been trolling California, right?" He elbowed his tall friend. "We've been getting him up to speed on 'The Nation.'"

Abby and Conor exchanged tight smiles, each enduring both David's ham-handed attempts to create a conversation between them and Sarah's encouraging smiles when they managed to exchange more than a couple of simple pleasantries. Even Abby's sharp pinch and whispered, "What were you thinking? I'm going to kill you!"—which was ground out when David and Conor started screaming at the umpire for a truly foul call—couldn't shake Sarah's beatific grin.

Eventually, though, David's attention lapsed as he got more engaged in the game, and when Sarah left to get more beer, Conor leaned close to Abby's ear. "I apologize for…yeah." He chuckled as her face warmed. "I had no idea."

"Me, either," Abby said, mentally completing a thousand murders of her friends. "This is…ugh." Her blush deepened as Conor laughed aloud. "Not you! You're lovely. Wait! No! I mean —" She stopped there and, after a fresh resolution to kill Sarah, Abby sighed. "Can we just start again?" She stuck out her hand. "I'm Abby Reynolds."

A large, warm hand enfolded hers, and bright eyes sparkled with mirth. "Conor Grady. It's very nice to meet you, Abby Reynolds." He raised her fingers to his lips and brushed a kiss across her knuckles.

"I have a —" she blurted, but she quit when she realized she was stymied by what word to use. "Boyfriend" sounded like she was sixteen…"significant other" was just silly…"lover"…*oh my God*…

"A headache? A question? A problem?" Conor teased, leaning back in his chair with a sly smile.

"I have a friend…" Abby finished weakly, realizing that there was just no good term for everything she felt for Matt.

"I do too. Lots of 'em. And a cat." Conor nudged Abby's shoulder with his own. "I get you — no biggie. But don't you think it's fun to watch them watch us?" Abby looked up, startled, to see both David and Sarah staring at her and Conor with identical astonishment before they looked away quickly. "Having a 'friend' doesn't mean we can't still enjoy this game, right?"

"Right," Abby answered, relieved to see nothing but kindness in her intended date's eyes.

She did enjoy the game — and the company. Conor was funny and genuine and nothing but a gentleman throughout the game and their late dinner afterward. Later, he offered to drop her at her apartment, sparing Sarah the slow torture Abby felt she so richly deserved.

As Abby dug through her bag for keys after waving goodbye to Conor, she was still smiling. Despite the awkward beginning, the evening had turned out to equal some of the best nights she'd ever spent with friends. It had felt normal and natural…and damned good.

"Abby, dear?"

She turned to see the elfin face of her landlady as she peeked around her door. Heavy night cream shone on her softly lined face and tiny pin curls of gray hair peeped from under a night scarf.

"I'm sorry, Mrs. Case," Abby whispered. "Was I too noisy coming in?"

"Oh, no, love. I was still catching up on my stories. Thank God for DVR." They both chuckled. "I just wanted to tell you to be careful as you get up to your door. A big package came for you earlier today, and I signed for it. I had Henry take it up a bit ago, but you know him…" She huffed out a breath. "I don't know what's wrong with that boy. It's like he doesn't have a brain in his head."

Recognizing the beginning of her landlady's favorite rant, Abby patted the older woman's hand. "Thank you, Mrs. Case. I'm sure I'll find it." She yawned. "I can't believe it's so late. Have fun watching your show." She started up the stairs.

Wondering idly what she'd received and who'd sent it, Abby walked toward her door. She thought of Mrs. Case's lumpy and browbeaten son and decided that wherever the package had ended up, she'd give his mother a good report in the morning.

She slowed when she spotted the box outside her door and mentally gave Henry props for dragging it up three flights of stairs. The container wasn't huge, but the sturdy way the box was constructed told the story of something quite heavy inside. *Thank God Henry left the hand truck next to the box,* Abby thought, generously choosing to believe that it was foresight rather than laziness on his part. She unlocked her door and pushed it open. Then she examined the crate.

Her heart skipped when she spotted the logo for Claire's gallery.

Sliding the plate under a bottom edge, she tipped the box against the back of the truck and rolled it to the center of her living room. A trip to her utility room yielded a short crowbar, and Abby levered off the top of the box. Taped to the underside was an envelope, which Abby set aside for a moment so she could lift aside packing material.

She gasped as the light caught the soft, pearly pinkish glow of marble. Abby yanked out packing, uncovering more of *Steamer Lane Swell.* When the sculpture was fully revealed, she sank down beside it and drew a tentative finger down the curve, remembering the first time she'd seen it in the gallery…the day Matt had confided that it was his favorite of all his sculptures.

He'd looked and seen *her*, and Abby realized that she had never once been uncomfortable or nervous around him, not even that first day. Hell, she'd even teased him a bit. She remembered the sharp pang of disappointment when she'd seen Zoe slide her arms around Matt as if she owned him…and the relief when Abby realized that he wasn't one of *those* men. She remembered the twist in her stomach when she'd first felt Matt's finger against her neck at The Catalyst and the first time she'd watched him sculpt. She ran her palm over the stone, and her eyes filled.

A hundred memories of days spent lounging on the sand, listening to gulls and children laughing, or on a board with Matt's hands, warm and rough, against her hips, the sound of his laughter across the water, the feeling of sunheated skin against hers, and cool, just-out-of-the-sea lips against hers…memories all contained in the curves and whorls of the sculpture Abby had thought long gone.

She drew a shuddering breath, reached out, and snagged the envelope that she'd laid aside, then she leaned against the cool marble to read. The first letter was from Claire:

> Abby –
>
> Matt's had me holding this for you since before his show. He said it's been yours since the first time you saw it. Don't you love my silly, romantic boy? Come home to us soon.
>
> Claire

Matt's letter was even shorter:

> Pretty –
>
> Remember.
>
> M

Did he think I could forget? Abby wondered. Normally, she and Matt would be settled down with a bottle of wine or a drink right about this time, listening to music or watching a movie. But was that "normal"? The habit of a month versus a decade? Hadn't she just been thinking cozily about how nice and normal a ballgame and a laugh with friends had been? Her head swam, her heart ached, and she realized that it was time to pull out the big guns.

Abby stumbled into her room and then into her closet. She pawed through the mess of clothes that had already accumulated on the floor until she found her overnight bag. Digging deep into the outside pocket, she tugged out a plastic bag and carried it with her to the sofa. Opening the bag, she pulled out Matt's navy blue T-shirt and held it to her face, inhaling deeply and letting the tears fall.

After all of the accumulated lies she'd told herself recently, it turned out that "normal" was the worst lie of all.

Chapter Twenty-One

"You're looking mighty pleased with yourself this morning, Matt."
"Don't you believe in knocking anymore, Pesty?" He grinned down
at the cup he he held, still basking in the glow of hearing Abby's voice.

Claire snorted and tossed her sunglasses onto the kitchen table
as she sank into a chair. "Since when have I had to knock?" She
narrowed her eyes at him. "Looks like your chat went well. Did you
apologize for the massive manipulation stunt—sending that statue
to Abby? And don't give me innocent eyes, mister." She pointed at
him. "You know and I know that you were using it to get a certain
reaction. Did it work?"

"That's a lot of knowing, Claire," Matt hedged. She crossed her
arms over her chest, and he gave up, dropping into his own chair with
a sigh. He leaned his elbows on the table and rubbed both hands over
his face. His voice was muffled when he responded. "Did what work?"

"Is she coming home?" Claire's voice was matter of fact.

Matt dropped his hands quickly. "Jesus, Claire! Is that what you
think of me? That's not what I was looking for." *Really?* his conscience
asked, and Matt had no answer to that. He did have an answer for
his friend, however. "I have to respect what she said she wanted.
Christmas. We re-evaluate then and make a decision."

Claire raised three fingers. She folded one down dramatically. "Okay, first: she made that decision based on what she thought was best for you. This stupid timetable is all dependent on how fast you finish Baker's inane statues. I refuse to call them sculptures." She folded down another finger enthusiastically, causing her charm bracelet to jingle. "Second: do you even give a damn about those anymore? You made it pretty clear at the art show that you don't. Far be it from me, as your agent, to encourage you to court a sure lawsuit for breach of contract." Her expression softened as she placed a hand gently on his cheek, "But further be it for me, as your friend, to watch you this way. You *care*, Matt. I've never, ever seen that from you, not even with Kate."

Matt covered her hand with his and closed his eyes. "Stupid, isn't it? Almost forty and I'm…" He stopped, at a loss for words. He'd never felt quite as alone as he had these last weeks, and no amount of work was completely filling the void left by Abby's quiet absence.

"I know," Claire murmured. "Wanna hear number three? I don't care, because here it is: I'd bet all Charles's money that Abby feels the same. Go to her."

"I can't. She's right. Baker will sue the shit out of me if he doesn't get the rest of his statues by New Years'. This is my job, you know?" He released Claire's hand as he looked out the window. "No matter how much I'd do it for love alone, I *like* being able to do what I love *and* make a living." His thoughts turned to Abby and her encouragement for him to finish and profit from his success. "I want to be good enough…"

Claire turned his face toward hers once again. "Matt, I hope you're not seriously thinking that Abby gives a damn about your money, what there is of it. Because if that's the case—"

"Whoa." He raised a hand, and she dropped hers to the table in relief. "Nothing like that. It's just…being successful, you know? Her equal." Matt paused, moving onto a different train of thought. "When I called, Abby was upset—crying—because of the sculpture, partly, and because she'd been out last night and had a great time. I think she felt guilty, which made me feel a little glad and a lot like a shit." He took a swallow of his coffee before he set it down again. "Believe it or not, Claire, I did feel bad about sending *Swell* then. It wasn't a completely nice thing to do."

"Why did you send it, then?"

Rubbing his hands on the tablecloth, Matt thought before he answered. "I wasn't trying to manipulate her into coming back, I swear." *Not consciously, anyway.* "We talk every night, right? And I hear about all the crazy times she's having, and all the work — really fascinating exhibits, Claire — and the hours she puts in are insane, but she's falling into the groove again, and…I just wanted to be in her life physically. A part of me, a really good part that she sees every day. So I can be right there in the front of her mind. *Me.*" He looked down at the table and then glanced out of the corner of his eye at his friend. "Sarah and David surprised her with a blind date. Not my favorite people right now."

Claire snapped her mouth shut. "All right. If being finished with Baker is what you need, let's do it. He wants to meet with you next week for a progress report and delivery of the first statues, so I'll set it up." She reached out to squeeze Matt's hands again. "If we have to feed you intravenously and run a catheter, I'll get you out of here before Christmas, and that's a promise."

Matt smiled as he rose to his feet. "Let's hope it doesn't take that." He shuddered. "Catheter? Good God."

Matt slammed his front door when he heard Claire's Lexus peel away from the curb. He loosened his strangling tie, tossed the jacket he'd so carefully steamed that morning in the corner, and poured himself three fingers of scotch. Tossing it back, he winced at the burn before pouring three more.

He toed off his shoes and sank down on the couch, feeling the leather cradle his body as he rolled his glass on his forehead. "Son of a bitch," he whispered.

The meeting with Baker had been a complete disaster. It started to go downhill when the first statue was uncrated and Baker found fault with the terra cotta medium, then segued into snide comments about the models' comparative endowments, and ended with Matt insinuating that Mrs. Baker would be the best judge of that. Slouching into his couch, shame at his outburst mixed with continued anger and a sense of wounded pride. Suddenly, the house he'd considered his haven was just too damned lonely.

No sound of humming from another room. No smell of paints or even the whisper of herbal scent. No firm hands on his shoulders or gentle fingers caressing his temples. No pale gold skin or laughing brown eyes to tempt and tease him.

No warmth.

Matt slumped forward, forehead resting on the heel of one hand as his elbow rested on his knee. Though he'd happily been alone for most of his adult life, it was just too hard now. He craved Abby's companionship like he craved the sea.

His mind roiled, and his emotions crashed, and he came to a decision:

Fuck this.

Fuck Baker.

Fuck the fucking statues.

Fuck waiting.

One weekend wouldn't make or break his ability to finish what remained of the stupid statues.

He paced his house, deep in thought. He was pretty sure Abby would be okay with having him for a weekend, and it might give him an opportunity to have a well-thought-out word or two with Sarah, who had continued to throw Abby together with that Conor guy. Maybe it was time for Pretty's Boston to see them together, to know that a real guy was waiting for her on another coast.

Or maybe that would come off as über creepy and possessive, a tiny voice in his head suggested. Matt stopped in front of his sculpture, now cast in bronze, and caressed the facsimile of Abby's shoulder with a gentle finger. *If it's creepy and possessive, so be it,* he thought wearily. *I miss her. I want to be with her. Even if it's just for one weekend.*

There was a certain relief in having a plan. Matt returned to the living room to call his mother for information on things to see in Boston. Although he'd never visited the city, his mother was a native and frequently traveled there on business. He wanted to impress Abby by showing her around the least-touristy spots of her own city.

Matt changed out of the monkey suit and plopped into his hammock before he dialed. He couldn't stop smiling as he waited for his mother to answer the phone. Though he was sure he could happily go through the weekend without ever leaving Abby's apartment or his hotel room, Abby deserved to be very sure that she was more than a body to him. She was everything. She'd come to his world and immersed herself, and he planned on doing the same for her.

"Is this my prodigal son? After months of silence? Be still my beating heart." Janet Clarke's voice was low and pleasant, her tone teasing.

Matt smiled and lay back, watching the restless movement of the tide as memories of all the times he'd heard that voice washed over him. "Ha ha, Mom. Ha ha. How's my favorite girl?"

"Old and getting older." Matt knew she'd be making herself comfortable, probably with her feet on her desk and hands folded at her waist in preparation for a long chat. Though she'd always been busy in her role as a financial consultant, she'd never stinted on time with him. "When is my only chick going to settle down with a good woman and put my mind at ease?"

Recognizing his mother's standard opening lines in their ongoing tussle over his domestic situation and knowing that she expected a breezy joke in response, Matt opted to answer by staying quiet.

"You're kidding!" Janet sounded astounded.

"You wound me." Matt dropped one foot onto the sand to set the hammock swinging. "Am I that hideous?"

"Yes. A perfect wretch since the day you were born. I hope this isn't a stupid girl."

"I haven't noticed any particular infirmity, aside from the fact that she can put up with me." He dropped the light tone. "You'd like her, Mom. Seriously. Smart, funny, beautiful. Her name is Abby."

"Close to your age?"

"Ouch. You really know how to hurt a guy. Yes, mother. Close to my age."

"Good." Matt could picture his mother running her long fingers through her short salt-and-cayenne hair. "Nothing worse than an old goat chasing after a young girl. Embarrassing. Do I get to meet her?"

"In time. She's back in Boston tying up some loose ends with her job." Bending the facts a little to avoid a drawn-out discussion had to be forgivable.

Janet whistled. "Long distance, huh? Tricky." She sighed, and Matt imagined that she was thinking about her own experience with his dad. He'd never asked either of them for any details, but right now he'd give anything to know exactly what had gone wrong between them. The suspicion that his dad wasn't enough for this woman who'd remained at the top of her field when lesser men and women were long retired had irritated him for years; now it felt vital that he know the truth. He struggled with the right way to ask, but in the end, he didn't have the guts to pry into something so personal.

"We'll evaluate the situation when we get together at Christmas," he said evenly. "In the meantime, I'm thinking of surprising her for a weekend in Beantown, and I thought I'd ask the native where I can take my girl."

"First, don't say Beantown." Matt could hear the shudder in his mother's voice. "Next, I'm proud of you for giving this a chance and not being afraid of a little space. Last…is she a professional woman?"

"Yep."

"Excellent. But forget the surprise. Schedules can be a bitch, Matt. We can't all be beachcombers-slash-brilliant artists."

Matt wondered if the hint of bitterness he thought he heard in her voice was real or the production of his oversensitivity. "We're not so bad, are we, Mom?"

Janet's voice was warm. "Of course not. You just sometimes need a hint to remember that life's not all playtime. Ready for some ideas?"

An hour later, Matt hung up and hurried into the house to jot down everything his mother had suggested before he forgot what she'd said. It hadn't taken her long to lay out a weekend itinerary of her favorite places. The rest of their conversation turned into a detailed debriefing about all things Abby. Matt suspected that was the real reason he'd had the impulse to call his mother.

Plans set in motion, he threw all his energy into his statue, determined to have a good start before he saw Abby again. Maybe Claire's idea of his finishing the damn contract with Baker and getting out of California before Christmas wasn't so far-fetched after all.

Matt dropped off to sleep almost as soon as his head hit the pillow. He'd gone to bed without working until his hands hurt for the first time since Pretty had left for Boston. His dreams were sweet.

In the end, though, he discovered he didn't have the balls to show up completely unannounced. His mother's warning kept drifting through his head at odd moments, and he gave in to the urge to check his plan with Abby's schedule.

Abby's phone rang only once before she answered. She sounded both pleased and rushed. "Matt! You must have been reading my mind. I was just thinking about you."

"Good thoughts, I hope? Full of nudity?"

Abby laughed. "Always. Perv."

"You know it. Listen, Pretty, I have a question for you: How would you feel about a guest? I miss you. I have a good start on the fifth statue, and I thought I'd take a break this weekend."

"Oh, Matt." Abby's tone was heavy. "I can't this weekend. That's why I was thinking about calling you. I'll be in New York. Our sister gallery is wrapping up a display of some artifacts that we show next. I'm escorting them here on Monday. I'd invite you to meet me in New York, but I'll be working the entire time. I'm sorry."

"So am I." Matt closed his eyes and concentrated on the breeze that was stirring his hair away from his forehead. "We can't seem to catch a break, can we?"

"Nope," Abby whispered. They were quiet for a minute. "I miss you."

"Yeah." *Doesn't change anything, though, does it?*

"I want—I really need time, even just a weekend, with you." Abby sighed. "Can we try this again in a couple of weeks? I swear to God, no more weekend work plans after this."

"Sure," Matt answered, vowing to pay more attention to his mother's advice in the future.

They talked for a few more minutes before Abby was called away by her intern. Matt was sad to hear her tone go from warm and relaxed as they chatted back to tight and harried right before she hung up.

"Well, fuck." He tossed his phone onto the desk and crumpled up the list of activities he'd been planning. Childish? Absolutely. But the dull thump of the paper as it hit the bottom of the empty trash can echoed the feeling in his heart, so it seemed right.

When Claire entered the studio on Monday morning, she found Matt working on his sculpture with absolute concentration. Pearl Jam crashed in the background. His hair lay lankly against his head, his eyes were ringed in shadow, and five days' growth of beard roughened his cheeks. Empty plates and glasses were stacked on his desk with one of the glasses covering his phone, and the whitish rouge of dried terra-cotta daubed his bare chest and lower legs. Evidence of a weekend spent almost solely in the company of clay. Crossing to the stereo, Claire snapped it off.

"Hey, Van Gogh! I've been trying to get hold of you since yesterday morning. Answer your damned phone."

Matt never took his eyes off the shoulder muscle he was detailing.

"Don't you mean…I don't know—Michelangelo? Van Gogh was a painter. I'd fail you in my class for not knowing the difference." He measured his progress with a glance at his photograph of Zoe and applied the wire loop again.

"Van Gogh was the crazy one, right? I think I made the correct comparison." She was rewarded for her weak joke when Matt chuckled. He wiped a bit of dried clay off the side of his nose with the edge of his hand, unintentionally depositing another, bigger, clump in his eyebrow.

He dropped the loop to the table and nodded toward the statue, which was now fully roughed in. Its upper portion was beautifully finished. "Progress, right?"

"Right. But at what a price. You need a shower, mister, and something to eat. Then I have something pretty to show you."

She refused to say another word until Matt reentered the studio a half-hour later in clean shorts and a tee, with his wet hair swept back from his forehead and a sandwich clutched in his hand.

"Much better." She threw open the windows of the studio to a brisk breeze. Matt stared toward his statue in concern. Claire laid a gentle hand on his arm. "Taken care of. I haven't forgotten how to cover a fresh clay."

She tugged him toward the desk and started his computer. "I have something you'll like to see." She typed in a web address. After clicking through a couple of windows, she pushed away from the desk with an air of triumph. "There you go."

Claire's explanation of how she'd spotted the picture during her daily perusal of art news passed in one ear and out the other. It was a picture of an Abby he'd only had a small glimpse of in Santa Cruz.

His eyes jumped from one detail in the picture to the next, from Abby's perfectly fitted dress, highlighted with tiny jet beads, to her shapely legs, lengthened by high heels. Her hair was no longer in the loose waves he'd enjoyed shaping around his index finger, nor was it in the loose chignon she'd worn both times they'd gone out together. Now it was a shoulder-skimming expanse of shiny, straightened hair, smoothed back into a clip that glittered with stones. One hand balanced a wine glass and a canapé while the other rested on the forearm of an impeccably dressed, dark haired man. She was laughing up at him, leaning into his side.

Matt sank down into the chair, reading the caption below the picture: *Fiona Grant Shaw curator, Abby Reynolds, celebrates her successful presentation of ancient Indian terra-cotta panels.*

"Isn't it wonderful, Matt?"

"I had no idea her position was so…" Matt's mind was blank.

Claire opened another window. "You should look at this, then." The site for the Fiona Grant Shaw museum popped onto the screen. "This is a fantastic museum, Matt. Didn't you guys talk about this stuff?"

Matt shook his head. Pages of exhibits of both ancient and cutting-edge art were listed, many of them curated by Dr. Abby Reynolds. Special note was made of her curation of a display of Etruscan terra-cottas the previous March, her research for which had earned the museum a special award.

Lost in the museum's website, Matt didn't even notice when Claire kissed the top of his head and left.

It was dinnertime before Matt was finished tracking Abby online. He was ashamed that he'd never thought to research where she worked and how important she was there, though he'd been fine shaping their relationship around *his* work.

He shut the computer down and sat in the waning light, thinking about Abby and the life she'd built in Boston. Nothing he could do or give her could compare to what she already had—and what was ahead for her. Abby was worried about what Matt would give up if he skipped out on Baker for her, but that was a joke. Boston Abby was gorgeous and smart, with more to lose than she would gain by coming back to Santa Cruz to hang out with a beachcomber-slash-artist.

To come back to him.

No matter how badly he needed her.

Chapter Twenty-Two

Abby jerked from sleep when she realized that the banging she heard was real and coming from the door across the room. She drew her hand from between her legs with a moue of disgust, and her building orgasm curdled to a sour pain in the pit of her stomach.

Another hard knock rattled the door in the frame, and Abby recognized Sarah's anxious voice. "Abby, damn it! Open the door!"

Stumbling over the afghan that had been tossed onto the floor during her dream, Abby yanked open the door. Sarah pushed past her, looking around the room with worried curiosity.

"No one here?"

Abby closed the door. "Who would be here?"

Sarah wandered from the living room to the kitchen, peeping down the hall on the way. "How do I know? It just took you forever to answer, and it was your idea to go for coffee this morning. And the noise you were making?" She returned to the living room to collapse onto the messy sofa. Her shoulders were relaxed, and she even laughed at Abby's horrified face. "I couldn't decide if you were being boinked or strangled. I was going to get Mrs. Case's passkey, but I was afraid what I'd find." She ruffled her own hair and puffed out a breath. "Neither other people's nudity nor death is any way to start the day."

Abby dropped into a chair, groaning.

Giving her friend a minute to collect herself, Sarah rose and began straightening the cluttered room, tossing papers into the recycling basket and clothes toward the bathroom hamper. She stopped at Matt's sculpture, and her eyes softened. "Good for you, Matt," she whispered, tracing the glowing pink marble with one hand.

She straightened and fussed around the room until she paused again next to a sheet-covered form. "What's this?" she asked, not waiting for Abby's response or permission before tugging the cloth off what turned out to be a canvas on a stand. The swirl of color and shadow was wild and uninhibited, passion and pain and anxiety plain in every stroke.

Sarah stepped back, drawing a slow breath. "Abby…this is —"

"Nothing." Abby dismissed Sarah's sentence with a wave of her hand.

"No. It's not." Sarah turned to face Abby, her mouth set in a firm line. "You know better, and so do I. When did you start painting again? Because I haven't seen you touch a brush in forever."

"Matt tricked me into starting again after you left Santa Cruz." She smiled at the memory. "Then the other day…well, you know what a bitch work has been. I had another 'discussion' with Gretchen, and I had to get out of there. I got on the T, and the next thing I knew, I was at Blick's with my arms full of painting supplies and my credit card out." She shook her head. "Impulse buys."

"A good impulse." Sarah perched on the arm of Abby's chair. Wrapping her arm around her friend's shoulders, she squeezed. "Regardless, you need coffee and food, and I need the full story on why you were making sex and death noises on your couch, all alone on a Sunday morning." She dodged Abby's elbow jab.

After a shower, Abby felt as ready as she ever would be for a trip out. Residue of her dream clung to her, making her feel dirty in a way that no shower could clean. She welcomed the dash to the car through icy October rain, hoping it would refresh her soul.

Within a short while, she and Sarah were ensconced at their favorite table at Red Barn Coffee Roasters in Faneuil Hall, warm mugs of coffee cradled between their freezing palms.

"So? Hit me with the gory details," Sarah said, pushing her wet hair back from her forehead and smirking at Abby's red face. "It can't have been that bad."

"You wanna bet?" Abby said.

Sarah sipped at her coffee and looked at Abby through narrowed eyes. "You know I'll get it out of you eventually, right? And here—" she looked around at the almost empty shop "—is far better than Macy's during a sale."

"Fine," Abby grumbled. She launched into her dream, finding that her embarrassment and horror mellowed into a wry humor and snorts of laughter as she talked.

"Good God," Sarah snickered. "You don't do these things by half, do you?" She broke into a belly laugh. "That was like a misguided mixture of a bodice ripper and a horror novel. What did you eat last night?"

Abby groaned. "My brain hates me." They chuffed laughter into their cups until the barista looked at them curiously. "Everything about that was just wrong. It wasn't Matt, for fuck's sake. Not the sudden appearance, not the hokey words, not the rush to sex…"

"Not the Hawaiian shirt," Sarah offered. "No, really. I've seen him in plain button-down shirts and plaid button-down shirts and T-shirts and, best of all, no shirt." She laughed again when Abby threw a napkin at her. "But never a Hawaiian shirt. That would be too cliché for him. That's the first thing that would have tipped me off that something was wrong." She drained her cup and looked at Abby out of the corner of her eye. "Of course, you were sort of occupied…"

"Ha ha. Very funny." Abby emptied her own cup and caught the barista's eye, indicating that they needed refills. After the girl warmed their cups and stepped back behind the counter, Abby sighed. "This situation is a mess."

"It sure is," Sarah said. "You dreamed about Conor, Abby. This disturbs me on so many levels."

Abby kicked Sarah's chair. "I don't see why it should. You've thrown us together at every chance. I'm not worried about him being in my dream at all—he was the anti-Matt for the most part. You've got to stop the matchmaking, Sarah. He's a nice guy, but nowhere near what I want."

Sarah threw her hands in the air and crowed, "She sees daylight!"

Abby grabbed her friend's arm, jerking it down. "Would you hold it down, jackass?" she hissed. "What are you talking about?"

"Jeez, you can be dense." Sarah lowered her voice for emphasis. "I haven't seen anything as pitiful as the way you looked when you got home from Santa Cruz, but you refused to acknowledge that you'd made a mistake. You said you wanted things to go back to normal, so I thought, 'Fine. If she wants normal, I'll give it to her.' Conor is *exactly* what was normal for you before we left for the summer: pleasant-looking, easy-going, and most of all, not interested in commitment." She waited for Abby's mouth to close before she continued. "I thought you'd see through me and hop the next plane to sunny California. It totally freaked me out when you let me keep throwing you together."

Abby slumped in her seat. "That was a dirty trick."

"Then why did you let me do it?" Sarah shot back. "You don't want Conor, Abby. You just said it yourself."

"Maybe I'm hedging my bets." Abby looked down at her hands. "I'm beginning to hate everything about the museum. I have to work later and later, and all I can think of is getting home to paint or going back to Matt. But lately, all he talks about is his work. So maybe it's a hint that I'm bothering him. I hate this."

"Here's a novel idea: talk to him. You'll never know until you ask." Sarah tweaked Abby's cheek. "Buck up, lusty wench. All is not a loss."

A laugh burst from Abby's unwilling throat. "You really are a shit, you know? You will never let me live down that dream, will you?"

"Never." Sarah rose from her seat and grabbed her coat. "And I'm *your* shit, and you love me." She paused a moment and processed her last sentence. "Good lord, that sounded awful." She stared at Abby expectantly. "Well? Don't you have a call to make?"

Abby's heart dropped when she heard the weariness in Matt's voice. After asking about Sarah and David, he questioned her about how she was weathering the increasing cold and wet and seemed truly pleased to hear that she was painting again. Inevitably, though, the statues dominated his conversation. He seemed anxious that she understand how hard he was working. Hearing about new potential commissions terrified her—though it was great for his career, if he followed through with half of them, he wouldn't have a free moment for over a year.

"Matt, are we okay?" Abby blurted. She expected him to ask what she'd meant, but when he didn't speak, her heart began to pound.

Nothing couldn't be good. Nothing could mean he was gearing up to let her down easy.

"You have a great position at your museum, Abby. We spent so much time worrying about whether I'd be able to finish some stupid pool statues, you never thought to tell me you'd be giving up a job that some people only dream of?"

"Because…it's no big thing?" His snort of disbelief strengthened her hesitant response. "I have a great title, yeah, but it's in a small museum. I make a nickel an hour in one of the most expensive cities in the US, and I work sixty hours a week on a good week. Now I'm in the middle of planning an exhibit, and coordinating the different factions is adding at least ten more to that. My bank account regularly hovers around empty, no matter how many degrees I have. Dream life, right?" She ran out of steam and curled into the corner of the couch. She pulled her talisman from beneath her pillow and buried her face in its folds, mourning the loss of Matt's scent. "Worst of all, I'm thousands of miles away from the one thing that feels real anymore." She leaned her head against the back of the couch. "I miss you so much, Matt. What brought this on?"

"Claire. Not that she expected me to go nuts," he added hastily. "She pointed out a picture of you on the Internet, at that party in New York." There was wistfulness in his voice that Abby hadn't heard before. "After I saw you in your element and your name all over the museum website, I guess I have to wonder what you'd want with a surf bum like me." He hesitated before continuing, and the pain in his voice had brought tears to Abby's eyes. "Maybe this isn't going to work, Pretty."

"No." Abby clutched the phone like a lifeline. "I refuse to hear this. That woman in the picture is me, except she's not. She's who I used to be." She thought of the sleek haircut and pallor she saw in the mirror each morning before she slipped into her city disguise and stalked out to cut the feet out from under her competitors and colleagues. "Who I am again, I guess. But she's not all of me — the best part is who I am with you."

"Abby —"

"All I want with you is love, Matt." She burst into tears. "Just that."

"Pretty…don't cry, Abby. I know you do. I know it." He made comforting noises until her sobs tapered off. When she finally drew a clear breath, he sounded more normal, like something within him had relaxed. "Abby, this is making me crazy. Christmas is too long to wait."

"Agreed. This stupid exhibit opens right before Thanksgiving…" She left her sentence dangle, hoping he'd bite.

He did. "Good, because I'm ahead on Baker's silliness. If I push, I can be done by the end of November. Just a little over a month, and then I'm getting on the first plane to Boston." Abby could imagine him in much the same position as she was now holding: slumped into his couch, exhausted, eyes closed. "I never want to have to hear you cry on the phone again. It kills me."

After a long while of sharing the sweet and silly thoughts that only lovers understand, Abby hung up her phone with a smile. Thanksgiving couldn't come soon enough.

Or maybe it wouldn't come at all.

Abby glared up from her notes, irritated at being interrupted by throat clearing just beyond her desk. She rearranged her expression for the museum's director. "Sorry, Gretchen." She tossed her glasses on the desk and rubbed her eyes. "Just going over the agreement with the French government again. They're damn picky about loaning their treasures, and I want to be sure everything is copasetic before Thanksgiving."

Gretchen Dahl smiled in commiseration. "Just what I wanted to talk to you about. Would you come into my office when you're finished here? I think you'll be glad you did." Her heels click-clacked as she marched back down the hall.

"I'll bet I won't," Abby muttered, a hard knot of anxiety forming in her stomach. She finished her task and posted her final notes via courier to her compatriot at the French embassy. Tidying her desk helped Abby clear her mind, as did a quick check of her makeup and hair in the mirror. When she couldn't put the visit off any longer, she pushed her chair under her desk, smiled at Clint, whose expression was sympathetic, and headed out the door.

By the time she reached Gretchen's office, her professional smile felt painted on. Gretchen nodded to the chair in front of her desk. "I have great news for you, Abby." Her smile matched Abby's in brightness and veracity. "We think we've found a way through the thorny issues we're having with Paris over these terra-cottas. The Louvre is very willing to discuss the security arrangements and whatnot, but they want to do it in person. Jean said something about not being able to decide if their things would be in good hands without meeting the person who will be tending to them. It might be a Gallic thing." She smirked. "Or it might be the fact that he spent the whole New York party staring at you." She sat back in her chair and folded her hands over her stomach. "Either way, Abby, you're going to be in Paris for Thanksgiving! City of Lights, no family obligations…it's a great opportunity."

Abby swallowed past the lump in her throat. "But…I have Thanksgiving scheduled off. I have plans."

Gretchen's smile became strained, but her voice remained even. "Yes, you do. In Paris. I don't have to tell you how important these pieces are to our exhibit. They are *essential*."

"Can't you send Vickie?" Abby asked weakly. "She'd love the chance to travel."

"Vickie will have her chance with the African masks." The smile dropped, and Abby saw the steel in Mrs. Gretchen Dahl that had kept her firmly seated in the desk she occupied and the museum profitable in a harsh economy. "Abby, I have to wonder how committed you are to your position. You've only seemed to be half-here since you came back from your sabbatical. Though you've been better just lately. Your job is one many people in our field would kill for; you do realize that, don't you? And right now your place is in Paris, dazzling that silly man and getting me my terra-cottas. Are we clear?"

"Yes, Gretchen. Crystal." Abby rose from her chair as Gretchen put on her professional smile again.

"Glad to hear it." Gretchen picked up her pen and a piece of paper in clear dismissal.

Unable to stomach resuming work on the contracts, Abby returned to her office only long enough to grab her coat and mutter something about lunch to her startled intern.

Treading angrily through the crunching fall leaves, she thought about the work of the last few weeks — hell, the last couple of months. Gretchen, as big of a bitch as she was being at that moment, had one thing right: Abby hadn't really been present in her work since she'd returned from Santa Cruz. Each day it became harder to get out the door of her apartment, harder to drag herself through another call or another grant session, harder to resist going home to paint out her frustrations.

Harder still to keep herself on the coast where she'd lived for her entire adult life.

She stopped to look in a storefront window, adjusting her collar and scarf with quick, angry twitches. Checking to see if she'd gotten the look right, she was startled to catch the expression in her eyes. Even in the ghostly reflection of the glass, she could see that they were empty.

"I'm not happy." She watched her window-self nod in acknowledgment.

Though it would have been easy to lay the credit or blame for her change of heart at Matt's door, it was bigger than just that. Her trip to California had changed something inside her. She didn't want to drag herself up the career ladder anymore, rung by painful rung, kicking at whoever happened to be beneath her. Massaging egos, racing from one place to another, fighting the clock to meet deadlines, critiquing and caring for the creations of others…it all made her tired. She wanted to be creating something herself, to feel the drag of paintbrush bristles against canvas and to see the colors and shapes in her mind bloom in front of her eyes.

Even more than that, she wanted to feel strong arms around her and to know she was at home.

And none of that started with her going to Paris.

Abby turned and walked briskly back toward the museum, determined to convince Gretchen that she was not going to France over Thanksgiving. She practiced what she was going to say, imagining herself speaking firmly about fairness and limits to authority.

She marched to Gretchen's office and opened the door after a perfunctory knock. Gretchen looked up, her mouth hardening into a thin line at Abby's expression. She waited expectantly as Abby took a deep breath and readied herself to speak. What she said startled them both:

"I quit."

Chapter Twenty-Three

Matt ignored the phone through three calls, but the steady knocking at his door made it too hard to concentrate. Cursing and dropping the carving knife at the foot of his sculpture, he grabbed his T-shirt and stalked toward the glass studio door.

He was still pulling the shirt over his head when he flipped the lock. By the time he was situated, Chris was marshaling his mischievous twinkle into an apologetic smile.

"Did I disturb you, cuz? I tried calling a couple of times but got the machine. Claire saw me downtown and told me to just bang until you opened up." He grinned as he watched irritation war with apology on Matt's face until he stepped back so Chris could enter.

"Hey." He grabbed Chris's duffle bag and hauled it onto his shoulder.

"Hey, no, I can get that," Chris said, making no move to take his bag from Matt. When he'd made the polite protest and was ignored, he laughed.

Matt walked into the studio, clearly expecting Chris to follow. "I expected you back when Abby left." He looked around for some safe place to drop the bag and realized that his haven was a mess. Besides the statues he was currently working on, there were various half-finished and abandoned projects. Clothes and discarded towels littered the floor. What little space was left hosted an array of dirty dishes and takeout containers. Only Abby's corner remained untouched and as neat as she'd left it. His eyes immediately shied away from her easel, and he dropped the heavy bag onto his desk.

Chris leaned against a counter. "Been in Philly, visiting my mom. My grad school application was accepted for UC Santa Cruz—you schooled me good—but they couldn't fit me into the program until the next cycle begins in January." His voice trailed off when Matt picked up his knife and began shaving clay from one of Zoe's ankles.

Chris started wandering around the studio, studying the sculptures on the various tables. A few showed promise, and a few were surprisingly wretched. All had been indifferently abandoned, and the drying clay was cracked and unworkable. He stopped near a half-bust modeled on Abby's painting of a laughing Charles. "This *was* a nice one, Matt. Has Claire seen it?"

Matt stared at the bust with a blank look. After a minute, he shrugged. "No idea. I can't remember the last time she was here." He returned to his carving.

"It was a week ago," Chris said. He waited but got no response. Shaking his head, he moved to a cloth-covered figure in the far corner of the room. He tugged at a corner of the fabric, and it slithered to the floor at his feet.

"Hey! Don't do that!" Matt protested.

Chris raised his eyebrow and let the cover stay where it lay. "Why not?" Revolving the table on which the bronzed sculpture of Abby sat, he whistled. "This is…wow." He traced the metal arm with a gentle finger.

Matt winced before sitting on the table behind his sculpture, thus blocking his view of Chris and his bronze. It didn't stop him from remembering the perfect curves of arm and leg, the delicate toes detailed with as much love as the mass of hair that was held on top of her head with one exquisite hand. "You think so?" Matt asked, his voice low.

"Hell yes! I know human figures aren't usually your preference, but…damn! It looks like she's going to step off the pedestal. This is the best thing you've done yet."

"Maybe. Toss that cover over, okay?" As soon as the cloth settled over Abby, Matt rose and picked up his wire loop.

"So I was wondering…" Chris started gathering up food containers and stuffing them into an already half-full garbage bag.

"Of course you can stay. Your room's just like you left it." Matt took a breath and let it out. "It'll be nice to have a voice in the house again."

"Woo-hoo-hoo! Listen to you, Mr. Fortress of Solitude! How the mighty have fallen, and how your tune has changed." Chris was rewarded with a genuine laugh and a relaxation of Matt's shoulders. With the containers disposed of, he began picking up dishes. "I knew you'd miss my sparkling wit. Not to mention my mad *Brady Bunch* maid skills. You need an Alice." He balanced a final cup on the top of his pile.

Matt dropped his tools beside Zoe's foot. He sat on the table behind him and scrubbed his hands over his face while Chris went into the kitchen to deposit the load of dishes. He returned and leaned next to Matt. "Rough fall?" he asked, gathering Matt's tools in one hand.

"You could say that," Matt sighed. He started picking clay out from under his nails.

"Plans?"

"Christmas, at first. Then we pushed it up to Thanksgiving." Matt shrugged. He stood again and held his hand out for his tools. "I need to finish this, I guess—this and the other one. Then maybe I'll take a few more commissions…" He trailed off, looking unenthused.

Chris ignored Matt's outstretched hand and padded over to the sink. He started the water running and plunged the tools under the warm stream before answering. "Not tonight, you don't. Tonight we're gonna grill slabs of meat, drink many beers, and try to figure out how these two beach bums ended up waiting for women instead of peeling them off of us." He snorted laughter and slapped Matt's taut belly with the back of his hand as he passed him, heading for the kitchen. "Still not bad for an old guy. At least your mopery hasn't led you directly to the fridge. Nothing sadder than a boardhead who needs a 'bro' for his moobs." He turned in the doorway and pointed at his duffle. "Get that, will you?"

It was Chris's third belly laugh in five minutes that drove Matt to drop his knife and go looking for his cousin. Memories of the whiskey-fueled heart-to-heart they'd shared the night before were blurry, but he'd had a slightly brighter outlook when he'd woken up.

He found his cousin sprawled on the sofa, eating a bowl of ice cream and talking on the phone. He raised a questioning eyebrow, and Chris waved him off.

"Swear to God! Jason in a bear suit. I wish I'd seen the dog bite him in the ass myself—" He laughed harder. "Yeah, the things semi-pro athletes will do for a little scratch on the off-season are horrifying. Makes what he did for Matt seem like child's play, though I don't know what was worse: the dog or Zoe." He glanced at Matt and sighed. "I'll have to let you go. Matt's here and looking pissy. Talk to you soon." He handed Matt the phone and heaved himself off the couch. A moment later his door closed.

Matt sank down on the same cushion Chris had just vacated. "Hello?" he said tentatively.

"It's me," Abby said. "I tried to call you last night, but you didn't answer."

"Chris showed up. We got to eating and talking…and drinking…a lot of drinking." He groaned and was pleased when Abby laughed. "I'm busting my ass to get these sculptures done by Thanksgiving, I promise, but any weekend would be good. Who says we have to aim for a holiday, right? I just want to be with you, Abby." He heard the rawness in his own voice.

"Matt." She cleared her throat; Matt hoped it was from an emotion other than laughter at his neediness. "You're right. I'd say forget holidays, too, but it's not necessary. I quit."

"Abby, I…I don't know what to say. Shit." Elation at not having to deal with Abby's work schedule warred with shame. He flopped against the back of the couch and rubbed his forehead with the heel of one hand. "Is this because of me?"

He didn't even know that he was hoping for a polite lie until she answered honestly. "Yes and no. If I'd never gone to Santa Cruz, I'd probably work at Shaw Museum until a better deal with a bigger museum came along. Repeat cycle until I ended up a director somewhere." Her tone became urgent. "But, Matt, that's not the best thing now. Listen to me: this is not your fault. There is no fault. You made me face a part of myself that I'd locked up for a long time, and I realized I like that Abby better."

"But how will you live? I mean—not long term, but for now? Will you be okay?"

"Well, I'll be persona non grata for a while, but I've got some money stashed away that will hold me until something comes along. I might have exaggerated a bit about the 'nickel an hour and a bank account at zero.' I'm not a kid, you know. If I learned anything from growing up with artists, it was that you sock some away in the good times because they always end…until the next wave of money rolls in. That's why I've been so focused on you taking advantage of the Baker deal, I guess. Silly." Her voice held a note of expectation.

Again with these damned statues, Matt thought, and the rubbing on his forehead changed to pounding. "Not silly. Smart." He willed his heart to agree with his head. "Speaking of which, I left my Zoe uncovered when I came out here to recapture my pirated call. I need to get back to work."

"Oh. Okay." Abby sounded startled. "I didn't mean to keep you. I just thought you'd like to know…" She trailed off, sounding disappointed.

"I'm glad for you, Abby, if that's what you really needed to happen." He searched for the right words that would show his support but not pressure her. He fought the urge to say, *Damn everything else. Come home to me.* Because, really…God knew where else she might have to go now that she'd be job hunting. He didn't think he could handle saying goodbye again if she got a job quickly.

He hung on to what he knew was solid. "We're still on for Thanksgiving, then? I swear, these will be done then, Abby, and I need more than a weekend." He waited anxiously for her reaction.

Abby's voice was flat. "Thanksgiving for sure. It can't come soon enough for me either. Do you want to come out here, or…"

"Whatever works for you," Matt said. "Abby, did I say something wrong? Because I'm getting a strange vibe here."

Abby sighed. "Nope. Just reminded me about being a grown up." She chuckled weakly. "Not my favorite state of mind right now. I'll let you get back to work. Call me tomorrow?"

Matt agreed and ended the call after their usual endearments. He'd meant to make things better, but he had a feeling he'd done the opposite.

And he had no idea why.

Thunking his mug down on the table, Matt tapped a tempo on the edge, his eyes roving over the faces in the pub. In the hour since since he'd slammed into his house, already ripping off his tie and kicking off his shoes, he hadn't been able to sit still. He'd insisted that Chris accompany him to grab a burger at the bar, but his dinner had turned out to be a basket of fries and three beers, so far.

"So," Chris said, pushing a fresh beer to the side to join the one that was warming near his elbow. "Didn't you tell me Claire was against setting you up for more commissions?"

"Claire doesn't know what she wants," Matt grumbled. "She spent the first half of the summer telling me I have a great future ahead of me, then does a one-eighty after…"

Chris's brow furrowed. "Did you get the job?"

Matt laughed roughly. "Of course I did. Are you kidding? Easiest sale ever." He swallowed a mouthful of beer. "I just played it like you always say: charm the hell out of the wife and suck up to Mr. Deep Pockets. Claire, bless her reluctant little heart, got me a five-figure deal before we even left the table. All I had to do was busts of their family in full Greek god or goddess style. Oh, and fix any flaws, like Deep Pockets' double chin." He laughed again and downed his drink.

"*Had* to do," Chris said thoughtfully. "Do I detect a past tense there?"

"That you do, my friend." Matt pointed at his cousin. "Very perceptive of you. I say 'had to' because, when it came right down to it, I couldn't do it. Claire had notes for the contracts all prepared, we shook on it, everyone left happy…and Claire had to stop halfway back here because I couldn't breathe. I called the buyer from the side of the road and quit." He stretched his arms out in mocking display. "You see before you the dumbest man ever."

"Not so sure about that." Chris drained his mug. "Have you called Abby?"

"Let's not bother her with this tonight." Matt's voice was brittle. "She told me last night that she's packing up to go to Maine — R-and-R at the family cabin while King Dipshit—" he pointed at himself "—gets his act together. Little does she know…" He jumped to his feet. "Want to go to The Catalyst? Play a little pool? It's too quiet here."

"Sure." Chris got up and dropped some bills on the table. "Whatever you say."

The Catalyst was jumping. Now that the University of Santa Cruz was back in action, it was crowded most nights and unbearable for anyone over twenty-two on the weekends. Their slog through the crowd and up the stairs only bought them an hour's wait for a pool table. Matt filled the time by people-watching and working his way through a steady stream of glasses and bottles, so many that he lost count. Faces began to blur together. Chris swam in and out of his vision, then a barmaid, and then he was stumbling off the back of a motorcycle and wondering how he ever got on it.

Zoe spread her feet and braced herself to take his weight. "Be careful, big boy. I may be tall, but I can't hold you up for long."

"How about I hold you up?" he slurred.

"Promises, promises." Zoe slung an arm around his waist and guided him toward the door. When they got there, she looked at him expectantly. "Keys?"

Matt thought hard. "Nope. Chris took 'em. Try above the door."

Stretching on tiptoe took Zoe's skirt to dangerous new heights. In fact, if it weren't for the hand she fanned over her bottom, hanging on to the very edge of the fabric, she would have been completely exposed. Matt caught himself staring and felt color creep up his cheeks. He lowered his eyes to stare at his shoes until the door squeaked open.

"Home, baby." Zoe gestured toward the open door. Matt reached out to steady himself on a porch column. "Oopsie. Let's get you inside." Slipping an arm around him again, Zoe guided him into the living room.

Matt stumbled against her as she steered him toward the couch, the softness of her body cushioning his angles, and he felt a surge of lust. The hand on her shoulder that he'd used to steady himself trailed down her back. He was tired of cold sheets, tired of waking up alone. What he wanted—needed—was to lose himself in the current of flesh on flesh and sink deeply into a woman's warmth…

He'd barely brushed his lips against hers when she pushed him toward the cushions and backed away.

"I can't believe I'm saying this, but you don't want to do this. You're not 'that guy.'" Zoe smiled sadly. "And I'm tired of being a 'that girl.' We both know there's something better out there." She dropped a swift kiss on his head. "I'll see you around."

"Probably better if you don't."

Matt looked around with bleary eyes, not surprised to see Chris in the doorway, expression grim.

Zoe laughed. "I guess I deserve that. 'Bye, Chris." She patted his arm and closed the door behind her.

Chris watched her go and then turned back to Matt, now slumped on the couch, drifting in and out of alertness. "What the hell were you doing? I left you in front of The Catalyst so I could bring the Jeep around, and when I got back, you were gone. What are we going to do with you?"

"Shoot me. It will kill me faster and hurt less." Matt was asleep before he heard Chris's response.

Matt's shirt and shorts were already smeared with drying clay by the time Chris had grabbed a cup of coffee and chucked a piece of driftwood at the morning's first screaming gull. His last statue of Zoe was nearly finished; only the upper torso and face weren't perfectly smooth. Working with the finest of his knives, Matt carved a paper-thin curl of clay from the left side of her nose before stepping back to examine his work. His eyes flitted between a photograph on his corkboard and the clay. He nodded almost imperceptibly and switched to a wire loop to shape the underside of her breast.

Chris leaned against a cabinet, blowing on his coffee. When Matt hadn't said anything for a quarter of an hour, he boosted himself onto the counter and started to whistle softly.

That ate up another five minutes before Matt grumbled impatiently and paused to clean his loop on his shirttail. Keeping his eyes on his sculpture, he said, "Yes?"

"Oh, nothing," Chris said nonchalantly, swinging his feet and cradling his cup between his hands. "Just wondering what you're up to today. I thought maybe we could get the boards out."

"At this time of year? Really?"

"That's why God created wetsuits. C'mon. It's a beautiful day and not killer cold. Could be some tasty waves, dude."

"Not even tempting. I want to finish this one up today, and then I have some calls to make." He examined his tools and shook his head. He carried them over to the sink and started the water running. "Maybe Claire can smooth things over with Dunham — Deep Pockets."

"Why would you do that? Calling him and begging off is the most honest thing you've done since I've been back."

Having cleared his tools, Matt stomped back over to the sculpture and started shaping the clay with tight, angry motions. "Easy for you to say. You seem okay with whatever money you get from wherever you get it, but I have to work for a living."

Chris set his cup down, rearranging his expression so quickly that Matt almost missed the anger that bloomed in his eyes. "Since you never asked, I get an Army pension, earned by seeing and doing things you don't ever want to know about." He smiled grimly when Matt straightened up, looking surprised. "What, you thought I lived off telling fortunes?"

"I just assumed…"

"Why, because I never asked you for money? Making the complacent uneasy and soothing the upset or worried is a lot of fun, and I make a little money, but it's not enough to live on. That was a hell of an assumption. But then you seem to be making quite a few of those lately."

Matt glared at Chris before getting back to work with a vengeance. "I assume we're not talking about you anymore."

"You'd be right."

"It's none of your business."

Chris crossed his arms over his chest. "No changing the rules now. You gave me permission to plunder your private life when I had a life of my own, so here goes: You need to talk to Abby. Especially after what happened last night."

Guilt whispered across Matt's expression before it hardened. "Nothing happened."

"Not for lack of trying."

"I don't want Zoe."

"Of course you don't. You never have. You want Abby, so call her."

Matt circled his statue until his back was to his cousin. "It's not working anymore…We're running out of things to say. I want to see her and figure out what went wrong." His movements become jerkier, until he dropped the loop and started smoothing the clay with his hands.

"Then get the hell out of here. It's as easy as that."

"Really?" Matt shook his head. "Even if I wanted to go, I have these to finish."

Chris's temper broke. "Then finish and go! You have maybe two or three days' work here. Don't complicate things by getting into another contract to do something you hate."

Matt had never seen his easygoing cousin look so upset. "I'm not doing this for me. You know I only take commissions when I have to." He spun the statue around on its revolving table. "Do you think I want to do this forever? I'm not a whore—doing it for the money has no appeal for me. But—" He stopped talking, and his jaw tightened as he looked out the window for a minute. When he was sure he was under control, he sank down on a nearby table and sighed.

Chris settled next to Matt. "But what?" he asked gently.

Matt studied his hands. "I don't have anything to offer Abby that she can't get for herself. So maybe she's better off in Boston. Maybe it was inevitable that she left. Wouldn't be the first time."

"Who says she wants anything from you but you, Matt? She's known who you are and what you do from the beginning. Whatever's happened in your past—" Chris spun the statue around to face them "—you can't stop thinking about her, either." He looked at the statue's torso significantly before he rose and clapped a hand on Matt's shoulder. "No one says it's easy, but you'd better decide what's important."

He squeezed his cousin's shoulder before heading for the kitchen. "God help you when Zoe sees that," he tossed over his shoulder before he disappeared.

Matt sat, stunned, his eyes roaming from one telltale point to another. He traced the curve of the sculpture's breast with one fingertip, seeing a perfect reflection of Abby's body. Now that his eyes were open, he spotted more similarities to Abby than to Zoe in hip and thigh and waist as well.

He stared at his creation for a minute, then walked to the table in the corner and lifted off the drop cloth that had covered the sculpture since he'd uncrated it. He'd told himself it was too distracting to remain uncovered, but now he forced himself to face the truth: It was painful to look at the replica and not touch the reality. He spun the table, remembering the days and nights of work that went into crafting his Pretty, and how gratifying it had been to find out that the real woman exceeded his imagination in every way. As he looked at the vague outlines of features, he had a keen wish that he'd defined the face, because what he needed more than anything was to see Abby.

He folded the cloth and laid it on a table. No more hiding from reality. Maybe if he was a different person, a long-distance relationship could work. But he wasn't, and it wasn't…and…

"Pretty, what do I do?" he whispered.

The cool bronze had no answer.

Chapter Twenty-Four

Abby swayed from side to side as she stared out the window at the third day of steadily falling snow, a freak for early November, even in Maine. She mouthed the words to the song coming from an old record player, sipping a cup of coffee between phrases and trying to keep her mind blank. She glanced to her left, at the new painting that she'd started that morning, and considered taking up the brush again. Anything to damp down the thread of misery that had laced her days since she'd left Boston.

The power flickered, and she sighed. She'd better go out to see that the air stack for the generator was clear. Again. She pulled on her boots and gloves and slipped into an ancient parka that had been buried at the back of her parents' closet. It was a quick trip out the back door, a swift swipe of her hand to brush the thick, white mass away from the metal pipe, and she was back inside, soaked once more.

"Perfect." She peeled off her snow-heavy jeans and tossed them in the corner before stalking to the bedroom and emerging in a pair of thermal underwear from her mother's dresser and yet another pair of wool socks. She remained in the forest green sweater that Matt had bought her what felt like forever ago, on that rainy day in San Francisco. She'd put it on the morning she'd left home and had kept it on during daylight hours as a kind of superstitious totem. As long as she had it on, there had to be a possibility that she would leave Maine, right?

The record ended with that particular scratch-thump that Abby remembered from summer childhood evenings, when her parents had laughed and drank wine, cuddling her and arguing politics and art until she'd dropped to sleep in their arms. She rose and flipped through the box of albums again. She placed another on the turntable and dropped the needle into the groove, briefly wondering if she should be using up the gas for the generator on something so frivolous…but never mind. It was something of a miracle that the gennie even worked after so many years of disuse, and another miracle that the propane tank was full. Thank God her dad had a passion, however brief, for hunting, or the camp might not have had a generator at all. It was a gift, and Abby remembered what Nana had said to her when she had once tried to put a gift aside for later: *Nonsense, Abby. A gift is meant to be enjoyed when you get it. You never know what might happen tomorrow.*

Where was Nana's wisdom three months ago? Abby thought wryly. She knew what might happen tomorrow, after all. You might be three thousand miles from your gift, realizing you'd tossed it aside like an idiot, and hurting.

Abby hadn't realized how much she'd been counting on Matt's joyful reaction to her sudden freedom, along with a quick invitation to return to California, until it didn't happen. Even when he restated his genuine desire to see her at Thanksgiving, she felt small and reprimanded. She'd left Santa Cruz for a reason: to give him time without distraction, and she felt foolish when reminded that nothing had changed.

She dashed tears from her eyes. It seemed like there was a well of salt water deep within her that she'd never known existed until she'd left Santa Cruz, and she didn't like it. "I did this to myself," she said aloud, and the sound of her own voice in the silence started her off again. She sank onto the sofa and wrapped her arms around her middle. No amount of being smart or careful or practical or realistic or self-sacrificing was worth losing what she felt when she was with Matt, not even for a minute.

Like an animal licking its wounds, she'd crawled into her den, this cabin, and waited for time to pass and wounds to heal. Leaving

Matt, though, had made a cut so deep that she feared it might never close. She relaxed into the sofa's cushions and pulled a quilt around her shoulders. The beginning of summer, when she'd truly believed her capacity for love was gone, seemed like a long-past joke. Every wall that twenty years of dating and disappointment had built around her heart was turned to rubble the first time Matt stepped out of the surf.

She heard Nana Reynolds clapping in the back of her head, heard her whisper, *Finally. That's my girl.* And she let the swell of emotion that had been building crash over her.

She didn't know how much later it was that a particularly loud growl from the generator brought her back to the surface. She sat up and listened closely, feeling a skip in her chest when she heard another, quieter engine snarl.

"Stupid thing," she said, wiping her palms roughly over her cheeks. She headed for the back door again. Her hand hovered over the parka hanging on the hook next to the door before she let it drop to the door handle. Screw it. She'd just change when she got back inside.

Abby ripped the door open and stopped dead, staring at an equally startled Matt as he stood on her porch, a heavy parka half-shrugged off his shoulders and his hand raised to knock on the door.

He had just enough time to steady himself and let the parka drop indifferently to the wooden floor before his arms were filled with woman. Abby flung herself at him, nearly knocking them both ass-over-teakettle into the snow that had drifted over the porch steps.

She clung to him, her arms wrapped around his neck, holding on for dear life. Her face was tucked under the shelf of his jaw, where she could inhale him, taste the salt on his skin against her lips, feel the warmth of him. Her eyes had slammed shut when she leaped, trusting him to catch her, and she kept them closed as a thousand wordless prayers of thanks ran through her mind.

When she could speak, it was in a ragged whisper. "I thought… Thanksgiving…"

Matt held her against him, his cheek resting against her temple. He rocked her back and forth gently. His hands moved against her back, rough skin catching on wool, and for once he didn't pull them away. Releasing her, he gently cupped her face, long fingers sliding into her hair. His thumbs caressed her cheeks, and his gaze held hers.

"I thought I couldn't wait."

Abby moved back into his arms more slowly this time. She rested her head against his chest and listened to the steady rhythm of his heart. "I love you, Matt," she said. His arms tightened around her.

They might have stood there for hours, thankful for the way their bodies felt together and the way their breath mingled in one tender kiss after another, if a sudden gust of wind hadn't blown a swirl of snow under the porch roof and dusted their hair and eyelashes with icy, diamond flakes.

Matt shivered, and Abby first recognized the cream-colored sweater that was a near match of her own. She smiled and ran her hand over the wool that covered his arm, trailing downward until she could entwine her fingers with his. She stepped back, drawing him toward the still-open doorway.

"C'mon in, surferboy."

"Are you sure? I gotta admit I'm freezing my ass off here." He followed her through the door, nudging it closed with his foot as soon as he was inside. They stood facing one another with huge, foolish grins on their faces.

Abby's eyes roved over his damp hair and studied the shadows around his eyes. The laugh lines she loved had deepened in the intervening months, and the bones of his cheeks and jaw seemed more defined, even under the hair that was more beard than stubble. She saw love and need and sorrow in his eyes and wondered if her eyes were sending the same message. Matt's lips opened in a quiet, hitching breath, and she had her answer.

She held out her hand. "Still pretty as ever," she said.

"Hey, that's my line." Matt took her proffered hand and followed her to the living room.

They settled on the couch with Abby unashamedly sitting as close as she could get without sitting on top of him. He swung his arm over her head and around her shoulders, and she rested against him, feeling more at home than she had since the end of August.

"How did you get here?"

"Walked." He laughed as she jabbed his stomach with her elbow. Next came a story of a flight to Bangor, followed by a horrendous Jeep drive that had taken him to a sporting goods store when he couldn't get any closer to her cabin than the road above her lane.

"I was crazy," Matt admitted. "I'd already looked up your parents, and it was nothing to convince your dad to give me directions—he was just about to head out to check on you himself. Getting that close and not being able to get to you…" He stopped and kissed her. "Anyway, the sales guy got an earful, and then he offered to get me through on his snowmobile. After selling me the coat that is now iced to your porch."

He refused to let Abby up when she made a sound of dismay and tried to rise, instead he snuggled her more tightly to his side. "Forget the coat. This is way, way more important."

Abby nodded, relaxing again. The fire crackled and popped, warming the room. "This shouldn't be so easy," she whispered, her fingers reflexively clutching the wool that covered his stomach.

"Yes, it should. This is exactly how easy it should be, Abby. We're *right*. We just make it difficult."

Abby took a deep breath. *Here we go,* she thought, wistful for the perfect quiet her heart had felt, even if it couldn't last. She gently moved from beneath Matt's arm, though she kept hold of his hand. She needed to see his face for this talk. "So," she said, "do we try to do this? Or are we too scared?"

"I finished Baker's statues," Matt blurted. "All six, even the one I screwed up—I'll tell you about that later. I've been working my ass off for a week, no breaks except when I had to collapse for an hour or two, since you said you were coming here. And they're good, Abby. Really good."

"I'm not surprised. You're an amazing sculptor," she said cautiously, trying to understand his change of topic.

"That's the thing. I'm a sculptor. Not a copy artist. I don't want to do that kind of work, or at least not any more than I have to do to live. I've never wanted it, and no amount of client meetings will change that. I should have said so before, but I was afraid that I'd disappoint you…and then you quit a great job because of me…" He stared into the fire. "I'm all I have to offer you. Just me."

Abby turned his face back toward her. "Matt, I was burned out. I'd seen something better, felt something better, and I was *ready* to quit. I'll have to get another job, of course, but nothing so life-consuming again." She gestured toward the painting in the corner. "That's what I want to do. I don't care if you ever sell a sculpture again—that's never been important to me. I just want you to be happy." She smoothed her hand down his face, stroking the hair-roughened line of his jaw with her thumb. "That's all I've ever wanted."

"I want to be with you, Abby," Matt said. "It just takes a little courage to reach out with no guarantees and no…" He searched for a word, "…no masks. Is that the right word?"

"It's like you teaching me to surf. We just hold on to each other."

"Ooh! Surfing metaphors. Glad I wasn't the one to get so cliché." They both laughed, but Matt's eyes were serious when he spoke again. "I can't steady you this time, though, Pretty. I don't know any more than you do about this."

"We'll have to steady each other, then."

"Give me your hand, Abby."

She smiled and shook their joined fingers. "You've got it."

He drew her closer. "You know what I mean," he murmured. "Do you trust me?"

"Yes."

Moving slowly, his eyes questioning and getting a positive answer before he even touched her, Matt brushed the lightest of kisses against Abby's mouth. When he felt her response, he cupped the back of her head and brought his mouth against hers more forcefully, easing her back against the cushions.

Abby slipped her hand under the edge of his sweater and stroked his stomach.

"Abby…" he murmured.

"Is this okay?" she asked, stilling her gentle exploration.

Matt laughed breathlessly. "Better than okay." His eyes opened, sea-green clouded with stormy gray. "I promised myself, though, that I wouldn't rush this part with you. You're not just a body to me."

A slow smile spread across Abby's face. "Then don't rush," she teased, enjoying the flush that colored his face. "We're apparently snowed in, with all the time in the world. I suggest we use it well."

He laughed and pulled her upright, tugging his sweater over his head with his free hand and dropping it carelessly to the floor. He edged his hands under her sweater and slid it upward and off. She guided Matt's hands back to her waist, and shivered as they began to move over her skin.

Despite his eagerness, Matt's touch was tender, practiced. Each brush of hand on shoulder, on neck, on chest, was followed by a brush of lips, of teeth, of tongue. Abby gasped, sighed, moving her own trembling hands across Matt's body, retracing trails of pleasure that she'd discovered months before.

"I love you, Matt," she said, breathing raggedly as the roughness of his beard and softness of his lips stimulated nerve endings along her neck, trailing to the curve of her shoulder.

Matt chuckled, his breath adding to Abby's pleasurable torture. "That's twice," he murmured.

"What's twice?"

Matt blew in her ear and laughed when she squealed. "Twice is how many times you've said you love me when you weren't crying. I was starting to get a complex."

Abby laughed, startled. "Good lord, you're right. I missed a lot of chances to say I love you. But I do."

Matt lifted Abby off her feet and kissed her soundly. He moved his lips to her ear and breathed, "I'm gonna go back to junior high and say, 'Prove it.'"

So she did.

So well and so often that the sun was rising before they even thought of sleeping.

Abby sat in front of the window, watching the snow gradually lighten until she could see the lake through the trees. She rested against Matt's chest, snuggling into the warmth of his arms and the softness of the blanket that he'd wrapped around them both.

"If this storm ever stops, you'll have to show me your coast," Matt murmured.

"It'll end eventually," Abby replied. She thought back over the summer and smiled. "Maybe it will cause a swell next summer."

Matt laughed. "Maybe so." He kissed the side of Abby's neck. "Last summer's has worked out for me so far."

"Corny." They grew silent, watching the flakes fall.

"I still don't know what I'm doing, Matt," Abby said wistfully.

He rested his cheek against her hair. "Neither do I."

"Are you still scared?"

"Terrified." He tightened his arms around her. "But not of loving you. I'm scared of screwing this up."

Abby slid her hand around his neck and into his hair, pulling his face down so she could see his eyes.

"We won't." She rested her forehead on his, breathing a quick prayer. "Where will we be when the next swell hits?"

Matt rose and extended his hand to Abby. "Plenty of time to worry about that," he said, drawing her to her feet. "Let's pretend it's Naked Sunday and go back to bed."

The End

Acknowledgments

The idea for this book grew out of a fantastic online discussion between readers of my last book and me. It was fascinating to hear how women and men from a cross section of ages feel and what they think about relationships, especially as we get older and past disappointments have built up walls around our hearts. So to them, I tip my hat: Mel, Shiv, Sandy, Shannies, Judy, Leisa, and especially our brave men, Phil and Benjamin.

No book is created in a vacuum. All thanks go out to my editors: Lisa O'Hara, who took the first chance on this book, C.J. Creel, who never lets me get away with being lazy, Beverly Nickelson, who gets me (and who told me Filene's Basement had closed between first draft and last. I'm crushed!). Thanks also to Omnific's fabulous art department, and the copyeditors who make me look smarter than I really am. Special thanks to Elizabeth Harper, who started this craziness and keeps it all together.

None of it would be possible without my family. They have endured sketchy meals, cluttered rooms, and a sometimes distracted mom, with grace and aplomb. Love always to my dearest, who makes me laugh and still surprises me after a quarter century. Always, for you.

About the Author

Autumn Markus traveled far and wide as a military brat, but her heart was always in the American west, where she was born. She hikes, reads and writes there still, along with snuggling her husband, four children, and a horsedog. She freelance edits for other authors, reviews Women's Fiction for the New York Journal of Books, and is the author of the contemporary romances *Cocktails & Dreams* and *A Christmas Wish*. She is currently at work on her next novel.

Young Adult

The Ember series: *Ember* & *Iridescent* by Carol Oates
Breaking Point by Jess Bowen
Life, Liberty, and Pursuit by Susan Kaye Quinn
The Embrace series: *Embrace* & *Hold Tight* by Cherie Colyer
Destiny's Fire by Trisha Wolfe
The Reaper series: *Reaping Me Softly* & *UnReap My Heart* by Kate
Evangelista

Erotic Romance

The Keyhole series: *Becoming sage (book one)* by Kasi Alexander
The Keyhole series: *Saving sunni (book two)* by Kasi & Reggie Alexander
The Winemaker's Dinner: *Appetizers* & *Entrée* by Dr. Ivan Rusilko &
Everly Drummond
The Winemaker's Dinner: *Dessert* by Dr. Ivan Rusilko

Paranormal Romance

The Light series: *Seers of Light, Whisper of Light,* & *Circle of Light*
by Jennifer DeLucy
The Hanaford Park series: *Eve of Samhain* & *Pleasures Untold* by Lisa
Sanchez
Immortal Awakening by KC Randall
The Seraphim series: *Crushed Seraphim* & *Bittersweet Seraphim*
by Debra Anastasia
The Guardian's Wild Child by Feather Stone
Grave Refrain by Sarah M. Glover
Divinity by Patricia Leever
Blood Vine series: *Blood Vine* & *Blood Entangled* by Amber Belldene
Divine Temptation by Nicki Elson
Love in the Time of the Dead by Tera Shanley

Historical Romance

Cat O' Nine Tails by Patricia Leever
Burning Embers by Hannah Fielding
Good Ground by Tracy Winegar